CW00553205

Games in Londinium

Games in Londinium

JOHN DRAKE

LUME BOOKS

LUME BOOKS

This edition published in 2022 by Lume Books

Copyright © John Drake 2018

The right of John Drake to be identified as the author of this work has been asserted by them in accordance with the Copyright, Design and Patents Act, 1988.

All rights reserved. No part of this publication may be reproduced, stored in a retrieval system, or transmitted in photocopying, recording or otherwise, without the prior permission of the copyright owner.

ISBN 978-1-83901-515-1

Typeset using Atomik ePublisher from Easypress Technologies

www.lumebooks.co.uk

For Grace and George.

Londinium

Roman cities are strange because unlike my own city of Apollonis—long since destroyed by Rome—they have no police force, no public prosecutor and no agents of inquiry to solve crime. They have none because Romans believe that crime is a private matter into which the state does not intrude except to provide law-courts to punish criminals, which indeed they do, though *only* if the victims themselves provide evidence for prosecution. But if Romans are dull in mind, they still recognize a gold piece when they find one by chance. So when I—a Greek slave—solved the murder of my master, the billionaire Scorteus, and did so by working with Morganus, senior centurion of the Twentieth Legion, the Romans saw that the combination of an intellectual Greek and the power of the army gave them what they had been lacking. Morganus and I were therefore conscripted and became the nearest thing to a detective police force that had ever existed in the province of Britannia, and its capital city Londinium: a city unlike any other in the Empire, because it was so dangerous, bizarre, rich and sinister.

I know, because I lived in Londinium during Emperor Trajan's time, in the early decades of Roman occupation of Britannia: an island whose native people, the Celts, had been tribal, independent and free within living memory. Thus Roman troops had landed on the southern beaches of Britannia just sixty years earlier, and the Roman province was still dangerous, since it was pacified only within its cities. Outside of them were tribes who thirsted for blood, who ground their teeth in hatred of Rome, and who, given the slightest chance, would rise in rebellion with the fixed intention of slaughtering every man, woman or child in Britannia who was loyal to Rome. Indeed, they had done precisely that within *recent* memory, when Londinium was burned and its people massacred with hideous atrocity by Boudicca's army.

As a consequence, the post-Boudicca, re-built Londinium was profoundly neurotic, heavily fortified, and permanently garrisoned by an entire Roman legion plus auxiliaries, while two other legions plus auxiliaries were based elsewhere in the province, attempting to keep the peace. This total of three legions plus auxiliaries was the biggest army stationed in any province of the Empire and its huge size precisely defines the perilous nature of Britannia.

And there was more. Londinium was bizarre because although it was the Roman capital of Britannia, its enormous population was mostly non-Roman and non-Britannic. Leaving aside the Roman administrators—who were few—and the legionaries in their fortress outside the city, Londinium was full of immigrants, and even those who were native Celts came from different tribes with different traditions, so there was no communal identity even among them. As for the educated elite—the entrepreneurs and traders—they were a mixture of Gauls, Spaniards, Britons and easterners, who were ready to take risk to gain profits, while actual Romans went somewhere safer.

This entangled racial mixture was stewing in Londinium because the city was so enticingly rich. It was the focus of trade in everything that flowed in and out of the province: tin, copper, lead, iron, corn, hides, oysters and slaves, together with Britannic-manufactured goods like decorative glass and munitions for the army. All of this made billionaires out of traders, and generated massive tax revenues for the Empire, so Rome would never let go of Londinium, despite the fact that there was yet another factor that made the city unique.

Londinium was unique because Britannia was unique. It was on the edge of the Roman world and in its deepest interior hid something even worse than tribal rebellion. It was something that cast dread over the world-conquering Roman legions because it could not be stabbed with a sword nor shot with an artillery bolt. It was the sinister, malign, magical power of the druids.

Chapter 1

The druids and their warriors came at sunset: usually an auspicious time for them, but not on this occasion, because as they stepped so warily down a sunken path through high ground they were greeted by thirty Silesian slingers from the Black Sea in Asia, who rose from hiding to the signal of their officer. I saw them stand, barefoot and bare-legged in dirty tunics sewn with ragged strips of green and brown cloth, plus shabby turbans of dangling rag that merged man with foliage and made a shape hard to recognise even against the skyline. It was tribal hunting dress: traditional, ancient and cunning.

Thus they stood, and slung their missiles with skills bred by mothers who drove their sons to practise every day and flogged them if they missed the mark. So the druids and their accomplices went down under a battering shower of aimed projectiles, in a fine display of the Roman skill in conscripting native talent to the service of the Empire.

This, because while the sling is cheap and simple, and throws any round stone from a river bed, it is vastly difficult to use effectively. By comparison, an artillery ballista is expensive and complex but any man with sound eyesight can be trained to aim one within days. All he has to do is take a sight and pull the trigger, and even the trembling of his hands cannot disturb his aim because the machine sits steady on its mountings. But a slinger must work by whole-body, instinctive judgement. He is athlete and dancer combined: graceful and beautiful to see. But he has achieved this deadly grace only by years and years of tedious practice.

So slingers cannot be made, not even by Rome. They must be conscripted in full flower: a phenomenon I recognised because the Empire had done exactly the same to me, once it spotted my own Greek talents as a fully-trained engineer, a half-trained surgeon and an intuitive mind-reader.

I must add, to be fair, that plodding Roman discipline had actually improved the efficiency of slingers. Thus in warfare, Roman slingers used moulded lead bullets: dense, deadly and accurate, which out-ranged the arrows of archers. But on this special occasion they were slinging moulded projectiles of baked clay designed to inflict a heavy blow, but not to kill: at least that was the intention.

So the druids and their men went down as the Silesians delivered five shot each, then stood fast and looked to their officer. He was a Roman: a young centurion in the same ragged costume as his men, without any badge of rank, and—incredibly for a Roman officer—he too was barefoot. But that was all part of the drill for this profoundly secret unit. The centurion yelled a command, and another volley of projectiles hit flesh with a *chunk-chunk-chunk*, just to make sure. I looked down at the road, twenty feet below our ambush position. Two horses were on their sides dying from smashed skulls, a cruel sight, and men were struggling on the ground, mostly hit in the arms or legs by uncanny marksmanship.

There were eight of them, all stunned and dizzy. The two who had been riders were the actual druids: old men in white robes. The rest were warriors in mail and helmets, with long swords and shields, while three others whom the slingers had missed, ran back the way they had come: heads down, arms pumping. Four of the warriors managed to get up. They stood over the druids with drawn swords, and raised a battle shout.

The centurion made swift judgement.

'Never mind them!' he said, pointing at the runners, 'Get the rest. *Now! With me!*' His men dropped slings, snatched up wooden clubs and followed him, leaping down to the road, where they comprehensively battered anyone who fought back. I was amazed to see Roman troops fight like this, without shields, armour or swords, just wooden staves swung two-handed by men who howled like savages and the centurion as wild as his men. But it was all part of the plan to capture not kill.

Very soon there was silence among the long shadows of the road. The warriors were knocked flat and disarmed, but still they glared in hatred and huddled round the druids, while the druids themselves began to whisper to their men in the Celtic tongue.

'None of that!' said the centurion. 'Stop 'em talking!' And the Silesians dragged warriors and druids by the feet until they were all well apart. 'Now fix 'em,' said the centurion, and five Silesians ran back up the slope to fetch boxes of medical equipment: dressings, oil, splints, and instruments, while another man ran off at steady speed on yet another duty.

Again I wondered at the freakish nature of this encounter, because having tracked this band of men for days, and laid in ambush and battered them flat, the Silesians were now busy staunching blood and setting fractures. So there was as much busy healing as in a legionary hospital, except that the Silesians bound the prisoners' hands behind their backs so they could not fight.

They saved all but one, whose jaw was smashed and hanging, and who throttled on his own blood. Meanwhile, as further proof of Roman logic, three of the Silesians who had been wounded in the fight, patiently stood aside and received no care until *after* the prisoners were dealt with. They were not gravely wounded, but I suspect they would have waited, even if they had been. All they got was a joke from the centurion, who mimed a sword-stroke, and they grinned at his words and bowed heads in respect.

Then the centurion looked at me and beckoned. I walked down the slope, dressed like the rest in rags and turban, though I wore army boots because I'd never have kept up without them. The Silesians went barefoot all year round, the better to move silently and leave few tracks. They moved like the savages that they were. They moved like panthers. So their feet were leather-hard. But mine were not; I'd have been blistered and useless in hours.

The centurion smiled. His name was Gallus: Julius Lucus Gallus. He was a small man, sinewy and active. He was a Roman from the city of Rome itself, but a rough-spoken plebeian, as indeed he had to be, because no upper-class Roman would have taken command of barefoot savages. But Gallus had joined up for adventure and loved his work. Then he spoke, and I felt the same sense of oddity that I often do when Romans address me—especially young Romans—because he was polite.

'How d'you like that, Your Worship?' he said, with a bow. 'Did you see what my lads can do?' he looked with pride at his Silesians, and the six surviving Celts, all with wounds neatly dressed, arms neatly bound, and each one sat neatly away from the rest with a couple of Silesians on guard beside him. He had called me *your worship*: a form of words standing just below *your honour* in Roman address. He had done so even though I was a slave, and Romans normally address male slaves as *boy*. But I am Greek, and all Romans are nervous of Greek learning, even if they seldom admit it. Also, I am a tall man, with the speech and bearing of a scholar, and I have the grey hair which young Romans respect. So they are often unsure how to behave in my company. Furthermore, they cannot classify me within the usual hierarchy of slaves, because in those days I was neither field-boy, nor house-boy, nor even a rich man's *exotic*, that most extravagantly expensive category of slaves which includes girls of exceptional beauty and Greek engineers. I was none of these, because I was the property of His Imperial Majesty the Emperor Trajan, now in the fourth year of his reign.

I was therefore an *imperial* slave, a Greek imperial slave, and even the most arrogant Romans know that it is Greek imperial slaves who staff the civil service of the Empire, and that without us, the Empire would not run. They know it and it makes them profoundly uneasy, because it is not the way they think their Empire ought to run. But I kept this piece of Greek arrogance to myself, and I too spoke politely.

'Your men did well, honoured Gallus,' I said, looking at the captives. 'These men couldn't have been taken any other way.'

'Right you are,' he said. 'You have to knock 'em down, see? We learned that years ago. Or they just scatter and the druids ride off, and we can't have our horses with us, 'cos you can't hide horses, and druids can actually *smell* horses, anyway.'

'So,' I said, 'what now? It's nearly night.'

He nodded. The sky was dim and the stars appearing.

'Don't worry, Your Worship,' he said. 'I've sent a runner for our horses and wagons and they'll soon be here.'

'Can they find us in the dark?' I asked, and he smiled because I already knew the answer to my question. The Silesians were formidable trackers and woodsman, and thought of this led my mind down the familiar path of contemplating my own place on the long list of creatures conscripted by Rome for their talents: Silesians for their hunting skills, elephants for their strength, monkeys for their tricks, and myself, Ikaros of Apollonis, once a senator and cavalry officer of my conquered city, and now famous for my supposedly magical ability to read minds.

In fact there was nothing in the least magical about it. I simply have a natural talent that is more highly developed in me than in others, and which I must endure. I say *endure*, since there is no pleasure in mind reading because it reveals all the flaws, great and small, of those whom we would chose to respect, or like, or even love. But still I do it, and I do it as any man does: by observing faces and gestures. Thus everyone can tell a frown from a smile, and everyone knows that if a man picks up broken glass, he thinks of cut fingers. So I study the little flicks and gasps of expression, and the gestures, gulps and swallows, and unfortunately I do it better than most. Then I interpret these observations with such cleverness as the gods have given me and I record here,since it is also truth, that everyone says that I am an exceptionally clever man. If so, then my intellect is entirely without merit because it was not earned, merely inherited, and the gods punish me for it by contriving that my intellect brings little enjoyment of things present, much sorrow of things past, and introspection that keeps me awake at night.

Meanwhile Gallus was speaking. He was urging me to action.

'Will you have a go at the bastards?' he said. 'The druids? Sooner the better, Your Worship.'

'Of course,' I replied, 'but what about the men who got away? Can they bring trouble?'

'Naah,' said Gallus, in contempt. 'They're only bog-apes from the local Belgae tribe: animals hired as guides. It's not like they was tribal elders, and even then the Belgae wouldn't turn out.' He pointed to the prisoners. 'See this lot? These is Demetae tribesmen from Wales. Very superior buggers!' he sneered. 'They got their own little client state haven't they? With a king and everything. And the Belgae don't like that and they ain't going to risk upsetting Rome: not for the soddin' Demetae!'

So he took my arm again and led me straight to the nearest druid, which was exceedingly interesting. Most Romans are highly nervous of druids, whom they believe capable of witchcraft. But Gallus seemed to have no fear, standing right next to the white-robed old man sat with hands tied behind him, and bandages on his arms and legs.

'You seem unconcerned,' I said.

'That's 'cos I am! ' he said, looking down at the druid. 'That's 'cos we got protection, me and the lads. We're brother worshipers of Paragh the Slinger, and we give daily sacrifice to him.' He raised hands piously as Romans do in prayer or invocation: arms forward, bent at the elbow with palms forward.

'Paragh!' said the Silesians in the dark, raising hands in respect of their homeland tribal god, which Gallus had obviously adopted as part of his command duties.

'Yeah,' said Gallus. 'So we don't give a shit for no soddin' druids!'

'Yes,' I said, but he protested too hard. I guessed that because it was dark and I could not read his face: not his face nor the druid's. 'Can we have light, please?'I asked. 'I need to see. Then leave me with him.'

'Leave you?' said Gallus. 'With him?' He shook his head. 'Don't know if I can, Your Worship,' he said. 'I really don't. It's dangerous.'

'Trust me,' I said, 'I've faced druids before.' It was true. I had done so in past adventures.

'What about their … er … magic?' he asked. And there it was, the Roman fear of druids.

'Trust me,' I repeated, and after a long pause, he did. I sat down beside the druid, with flaming torches stuck in the ground, illuminating every line and hair of his face. The torches crackled, there was a slight wind, it was fully dark, there were animal calls far off in the night. And the druid looked at me and said nothing. He was very old, his hair was long and white, and he had the broad nose and black eyes of the Demetae tribe. He had great dignity too, even at such disadvantage.

But it was time to begin.

'You are a druid,' I said in Latin. You and your faith are forbidden under Roman law, and you are under sentence of death.'

'Death?' he said, ignoring Latin and going straight to Greek, having instantly judged my native tongue. 'What is death?' he asked. 'For me it is the pathway to glory. But for you and all these others,' he looked around at the Silesians, 'it is damnation. You are damned to eternal torment in the life beyond.'

I thought on that, and it was a most unpleasant thought, deep in the night of the Britannic wilderness with unknown gods standing behind the druid. But I was on duty and could show no fear.

'I may be damned,' I said, 'but *you* are betrayed: betrayed by one of your own.'

'Never,' he said, 'there is no betrayal among the elect.'

'Then how did we know that you were coming here?'

His face twisted in anger, but then he nodded, conceding what could not be denied, and he stared hard at me, gave a little smile, and began to speak in his own language in a rhythmic, pleasing pattern as if reciting poetry. This was a most deadly and fearful moment, but I was patient and waited for the first frown to appear. It soon did, when I did not react as he had intended.

'Your magic does not work on me,' I said. 'You are attempting what we Greeks call hypnosis, and it does not work on a prepared mind.' He scowled and nodded again, conceding that I had scored again. But then he stabbed back, in return.

'So,' he said, 'you must be Ikaro the Apollonite. We know of you. We have heard of you. You are the engineer who sees into minds.'

I tried hard to conceal my shock at his knowledge, but some of the Roman fear of druids must have shown in my face, even though I knew such knowledge came from not from magic, but from the druidic network of spies—long established and efficient—that runs throughout Britannia. But he read my face and gave me back my own words. 'Your magic does not work on me,' he said. 'It does not work on a prepared mind.'

'No?' I asked. 'Then how do I know that you are cursing the name of the renegade druid who betrayed you? And that you are fighting to control the pain of your wounds and the tightness of the ropes on your hands?'

He actually gasped at that—the accurate guess hit hard. But it was not really so clever. It was obvious that he must be in fury over being betrayed, and obvious that he must be in pain. 'Shall I give the name of your betrayer?' I asked, pressing my advantage, 'because I know that, too.'

'Be damned for what you know!' he cried in fierce anger, which was exactly what I wanted because Celts are not Romans. Romans control their emotions, Celts rant and spout in their passion and say more than they intend. 'You are *all* damned,' he said. 'Your Roman governor is damned!'

'The Governor of Britannia?' I said. 'A Roman nobleman of the first rank? You have no power over *him*.' I paused, then laughed and sneered. 'You must be even more stupid than you look. You've got shit for brains.' I used this cheap vulgarity with deliberate purpose, because given the reverence in which druids are held by the Celtic peoples, it was just possible that this druid was receiving the first insult of rudeness ever thrown at him in his entire life. Perhaps it was, because it worked. The druid's rage was hysterical. He screamed and shrieked, jumping from one language to another, mostly in pure spite—but there was something that made sense.

'Your games are damned,' he cried. He said that twice in Greek, and then the other druid was yelling in Britannic, such that my druid nodded and fell silent. He did, and all the rest did too, and not one more word did I get out of any of them that night, no matter how hard I tried.

The horses and wagons arrived later, with a Silesian optio—a junior officer—in command, and we made camp for the night. Tents were raised, fires lit, food prepared and the prisoners watered and fed. Or at least they were offered food and drink which the two druids refused, but the warriors took what was offered.

We moved at dawn with mounts for everyone, and the prisoners in two of the wagons. Gallus rode up and down the line to check everything and his men cheered. The sun was bright for Britannia, and I was on a horse again which is one joy that the gods have left me, because I come of the clan Philhippos—the lovers of horses—and was raised on horseback. So off we went with myself riding beside Gallus, who was eager to talk.

'A good job well done!' he said. 'We got two of the sods and four warriors and you can have a proper go at 'em, back at the barracks. But we have to be careful. We've got to get 'em back first.'

'What do you mean?' I asked. Gallus turned in the saddle and looked back at the wagons.

'See how we put 'em?' he said. 'Druids in one wagon, the rest in the other?'

'Yes.'

'We learned that the hard way, because if you put 'em together and let the druids talk to the rest…' he paused as fear of the uncanny fell upon him, even in daylight. He let go the reins to raise hands. 'Father Paragh, deliver us!' he said, and I too raised hands in respect of his god. It is a habit I have picked up from the Romans, because it always wise to respect the gods. 'If you let the druids talk to the rest,' he said, 'then the druids do a magic, and you end with them all dead, because they kill one another.'

I nodded, but said nothing, because I knew what the magic was. It was the same hypnosis that had just been tried on me, and while it might not work on a Greek engineer, it would be powerfully effective against those who did not know what it was. Thus hypnosis has nothing to do with magic, but it would have been hopeless to attempt explanation to Gallus.

Later, as we crossed the vast plain that lies to the west of the river Avon, we passed the place that the druids and their men had been heading for. It was a very special place, and one which Romans avoid, though we Greeks knew of it from the writings of the explorer Pythaes of Massalia :the first civilised man to set foot in Britannia, over four hundred years ago.

'That's it, Your Worship,' said Gallus, halting the column.

'Gods of Olympus!' I said, because although I had read Pythaes' description, I had never imagined the majesty and size of the phenomenon before me.

'That's the Ti Carregmawr,' said Gallus. 'It means *the great stone house* in Britannic.'

'The Stone-Ring,' I said, giving the Roman name.

'Yeah,' he said, 'That's it and we don't go in it, or near it.'

I nodded, but I was consumed with curiosity.

'Have I got time to ride across? To see it?' I said, pointing at the great stones. Gallus fell silent. He started to speak, but then said nothing. He was afraid, this man who cared nothing for druids. So perhaps I was unkind in my curiosity to see the Ti Carregmawr. 'Surely you aren't … concerned?' I said.

So we left the horsemen and wagons and rode half a mile to the stones. Gallus rode with me, bringing five mounted men with spears. Steel could not prevail over sorcery, should sorcery be active in the Stone-Ring, but I suppose the feel of a spear shaft gave comfort to the Silesians, who were all deeply uneasy. Meanwhile, as a practical defence, Gallus ordered that the daily sacrifice of meat and wine to Paragh the Slinger should be delivered while we were away at the stones. The optio would perform the ceremony, reminding the god of his duty of protection over Troop Four, Regiment Three, of Silesian Slingers: a sensible precaution, because the gods are busy and do not always remember us.

By these means, I was privileged to see the greatest wonder in the Britannic Isles: the huge stones that so much disturb the Roman mind. They do so because they prove that somewhere in the Britannic wastes, beyond cities and military camps, there was a native power that was greater than the marching legions. I felt the power of the stones myself, because they represented such engineering works as even my own city would admire. I counted thirty huge, grey uprights in the ring, each one of enormous weight, and each one linked to the next with a ponderous stone lintel as if the Greek letter pi——was repeated endlessly, side by side, round and round, in a perfect circle.

Within the ring, there were five, even greater shapes of enormous size, but free-standing, not linked by shared lintels, and there were other stone structures besides. I was fascinated by the ominous majesty of the site and its spiritual power, so I rode inside it, entranced in wonder. But Gallus and his men hung back and began chanting a prayer. To them, it was obvious that these colossal structures were unthinkably beyond the making of the native Britons and must therefore have been raised by magic: druidic magic. And who could blame them for believing that? But I was selfish in my fascination, and persisted in examining these formidable and monstrous works. Thus, nemesis followed hubris and I was punished, because when we rode back to the camp we found shame and despair awaiting us.

As the Silesians saw us coming, they ran forward and fell to their knees before Gallus, and the optio touched brow to ground, then lifted his head, spread his arms in sorrow and wailed in his own Asian language. Gallus listened to his words, then leapt from his horse and caught the optio a full-arm swing of a clap round the face, and looked up at me.

'Stupid buggers!' he said, 'Stupid, silly sods! They left the soddin' prisoners alone while they did the sacrifice. They let the soddin' druids talk to them, and the sods had a knife hidden among 'em.'

So I rode over to the wagons. The prisoners were all dead. Their throats had been slit. All our effort had been for nothing. It was failure. Yet it had all started so well, just a month ago.

Chapter 2

A further word on slaves, especially imperial slaves like myself.

Under Roman law, imperial slaves are the property of the Emperor, even though the vast majority of them never so much as catch sight of him, and they are called *slaves* only because imperial slavery is something new, arising from the need to run an empire, which caught the Romans by surprise. Therefore, being intensely conservative, the Romans used an old word which they knew, to describe a new thing which they did not, thereby providing further proof that they cannot invent anything, and further insight into the reason why Greek science makes them so nervous.

Meanwhile, the reality of imperial slavery is that tens of thousands of the cleverest men in the Empire, mostly Greeks and Jews, are retained by the Empire, to discharge all those administrative functions which need brains. Typically, these men live nowhere near the Emperor or Rome, but in thousands of locations across the Empire, with high salaries, lavish houses, and slaves of their own to attend them.

My own situation was different, because I was different. Thus *The Case of The Games* began, for me, at the headquarters of the Twentieth Legion in its fortress outside Londinium, where I was attempting to improve the legion's ciphering methods, with a staff of clerks to assist. I was teaching them code-cracking when they all stood up and leapt to attention.

They did so because although they were excused-armour pen-pushers, they were soldiers too, and an officer had just entered the room. He was the legion's senior centurion: Leonius Morganus Fortis Victrix, and was followed by his four bodyguards. Morganus was a very big man with a grey, scarred face. His armour was covered with medals, his helmet bore a swan-feather crest running side-to-side, he wore his sword on the right and dirk on the left, centurion-style, carried the vine staff which is the badge of a centurion's rank, and his bodyguards were chosen for muscle. So the clerks stood rigid, because Morganus was a charismatic figure who bore the hard-won military titles of First Javelin, Father of the Legion, and Hero of the Roman Army.

In addition, he was my friend and comrade, and was my owner under Roman law, standing in loco Imperatoris—in place of the Emperor—regarding myself. Thus he was personally entrusted with me as imperial property, and that just was one of the ways in which I differed from other imperials. It was a strange relationship, which meant that I had to live in his quarters with him. In fact this meant I lived with both him and his family, because unlike ordinary legionaries, centurions were allowed to marry. An odd consequence of this was that I rarely needed to spend any of the considerable salary which I received as an imperial. Thus all my expenses, from the bread on my plate to the nails in my boots, were met by the legion, and the money simply accumulated in the legion's treasury in my name. So I was steadily becoming rich—at least in gold and silver—and in those days I tried to believe that it soothed the shame of slavery. I tried very hard, but still I knew it was shameful to be a slave. It was something else that kept me awake at night.

Meanwhile, Morganus smiled.

'Look!' he said, pointing proudly to his leg, and the bodyguards nodded behind him, because Morganus had broken his leg during our previous case. He was supposed to be under medical care but he was up and walking three weeks before the surgeons said that such a feat was possible for a man of his age. 'And look at this,' he said, 'straight from the Legate!' He handed me a wax tablet, signed and sealed by the Legate, who was commanding officer of the Twentieth Legion. I read it and looked back at him.

'That's very odd,' I said. 'And very serious. What does it mean?'

'Nobody knows,' he said. 'Which is why we have to go and find out!'

So I stopped work, found the thick, hooded cloak that I wear for Britannia's foul weather, and we left the records block and went out into the Via Principalis—the main street—of the fortress. It ran north to south, as in all Roman settlements: north to south and never in any other direction, because that is how the Roman mind works, in its limited, systematic thoroughness.

'Where are we going?' I asked.

'To Government House,' he said. 'To be briefed.'

'Ah,' I said, 'by Petros the Athenian.' In my vanity, I delivered this guess as a statement and Morganus laughed.

'You're doing it again!' he said. 'Reading my mind.' I sighed, because if the Legate was sending us to Government House it must be to see Petros, because Petros ran Government House. Whom else would it be: the cook?

We moved at the quick march, with troops saluting their first javelin, and we crossed the fortress, which was enormous and defended with earthworks, artillery and gateways. It was home to 10,000 heavy infantrymen and auxiliaries, and was never still. There were troops drilling, craftsmen hammering, bugles blowing, beasts plodding, food cooking and shouted commands and marching feet. All this, but no women, children or old folk, because it was a town of young men constantly preparing for war. It was like that, because Britannia was Britannia.

So, it was a brisk walk of half an hour to Government House: out of the fortress, with challenges and formal responses at the main gate, then across the huge expanse of the Field of Mars—the legionary parade ground—and into the mass of Londinium itself. We entered by the North Gate, which was guarded by auxiliaries who saluted Morganus, raising spears and stamping boots. But there were no challenges, because the troops were there only to keep order and they let through anyone who behaved. Londinium was a thriving city, the biggest in the western Empire with every race of mankind in its grid-pattern streets. Thus it was a marvel of Roman imperialism, because it had been swamp and marsh before the Romans came, and now there were temples and shops, baths and theatres, and apartment blocks and enormous public buildings.

One of the most splendid of these buildings, though far from the biggest, was Government House, official residence of His Grace the Governor: Marcus Ostorius Cerealis Teutonius, who greatly favoured me after previous adventures. But Government House was more than the Governor's home. It was the centre of the political bureaucracy that drilled Britannia to Rome's command, and while all the formal diplomacy was performed by Roman aristocrats in Teutonius' train, the real work was done by imperial slaves. The most senior of them all was Petros of Athens, who was therefore, though unofficially and with great discretion, the most powerful man in the province. This was especially so because of certain flaws in the character of the noble and heroic Teutonius.

'Oh, look!' said Morganus as we walked up the broad steps leading to the entrance. 'It's the Governor's pretty-boys.'

The bodyguards grinned, because Morganus was speaking of the Governor's Guard, a squad of whom stood before the massive, gold-leafed gates, with an officer to one side, in mirror-polish armour, long red cloak and a huge plume of red ostrich-feathers on his helmet. I smiled too, because the Guard tried so hard to project the gravitas of their Roman republican ancestors. 'Huh!' said Morganus. 'Old-fashioned shields, broad-blade spears and bronze breastplates. Two hundred years obsolete, and not one of them's ever seen action. What a load of pansies!'

Thus spoke Morganus, because the legions sneered at the Guard, and the Guard sneered right back at the legions. So there was an over-loud yelling between their officer and Morganus and due presentation of the tablet with the Legate's orders, which the officer made a great business of reading, before the Guard stood aside.

This achieved, we entered an enormous hall, floored in a chequer of black and white slabs, and lined with elegant columns and lifelike, painted statues. Great lamps hung on chains, suspended from rings held in the mouths of silver lions, and a fountain sprayed water from the lips of a bronze nymph in a central pool. There we waited, while a runner was sent to announce us. In fact the messenger was a guardsman who made a point of *not* running, and with his officer nodding approval as he sloped off in slow-march time—just to show the legionaries who was important here and who was not.

But he was soon back, with a Greek imperial slave bustling ahead of him. I recognised the Greek: he was a small, ugly man named Primus, one of six shaven-head personal assistants to Petros the Athenian. They followed Petros everywhere as his walking note-book, calculating engine, prompt and memory. They were a formidable team, each one in a uniform tunic bearing the emblem of His Grace the Governor.

'Honoured Morganus, Spear of the Legions!' said Primus, bowing low to Morganus. I was given a brief nod, which was entirely proper, since slaves—even imperials—were not formally greeted at Government House: not when they came with prestigious Romans, because that was Roman etiquette. 'Petros of Athens awaits you in his sanctum sanctorum,' said Primus, 'his holy of holies!' He pursed lips in a little smirk, because he thought himself a wit. But Morganus stared at him and Primus flinched. 'if you would follow me, Honoured Sir?' he said.

We were led through art-filled chambers into the offices behind, which were filled with desks and scribes and cabinets and files and ink and tablets. Finally, we reached a waiting room with benches against the walls and a table with fruit and wine in the middle. I looked at the wine flask and Morganus frowned. Meanwhile Primus knocked on a door, a voice said 'enter' and Primus opened the door and bowed. Morganus told the bodyguards to wait, and he and I went in, with Primus closing the door behind us.

'Honoured Morganus!' said the man who rose from his chair behind a desk covered with maps. 'I greet you with respect,' he said. He was Petros the Athenian and he bowed low, as did the five shaven-heads standing behind his chair, while Primus slid smoothly round to join them, genuflecting as he went. Morganus nodded to Petros in return, and I bowed and Petros smiled at me—because we knew each other very well indeed.

Petros was a man in his forties, with a small beard and neat moustache, and intensely black hair, receded to leave a peak over the brow. He had dark eyes, a Greek's brow and was a politician and administrator of the first rank. He had to be, because the governorship of Britannia, with its force of three legions, was given only to the foremost men in the Empire, and the present governor, Teutonius, was a nobleman of the senatorial class who was an ex-consul and celebrated as conqueror of the Germanic hordes.

'I welcome you to my humble place of work,' he said, and I looked around, because the humble place of work was the most elaborately-decorated office I had ever seen. It had glazed windows, golden ornaments, a painted ceiling, marble walls, a mosaic floor depicting a chariot race, and furniture from Athens. So I had the impertinence to laugh. Morganus frowned, but Petros smiled.

'Be seated, honoured and worshipful guests,' said Petros. 'Serve!' he said to his staff. Thus the six bald scholars became waiters, and Morganus, Petros and I were soon seated around a table bearing cakes, pastries, wine and goblets. Wine was poured, and Morganus was frowning at me as he does on such occasions, because I like wine. I like it very much, because it is medicine for my afflictions. Thus I suffer guilt over my condition as a slave when once I was a free man in the free city of Apollonis. But my city opposed Rome and Rome destroyed it, and enslaved its people. So I constantly examine the entrails of the past and find nothing that gives me joy, and I drink wine because it is the second best cure for these sorrows. Or perhaps I just drink it because I like it. Who knows? In any case, I defied Morganus, drained my cup and looked for more, which was duly provided. Morganus sighed, but I was concentrating on Petros. He waved a hand and his six attendants bowed and went out.

'Now,' said Petros, looking at me. 'I'm not a peasant who believes in magic, but I recognise your abilities, Ikaros of Apollonis. So, read my mind and tell my why you are here!'

He smiled, and I knew without looking that Morganus was smiling too, because he certainly did believe that I worked magic. So I looked at Petros.

'You have a secret and serious problem,' I said, 'that cannot be solved, except by myself and the honoured Morganus. The problem is urgent and its focus lies outside this city, in the Britannic wilderness, by the great stone ring of the Celts. And it involves,' I paused before uttering that word which so disturbs Romans, 'druids,' I said. Morganus made the bull sign of Mithras to drive off evil: forearm raised, fist clenched, index and little fingers extended like horns. I continued. 'And you expect me to read the minds of druids.'

'Huh,' said Petros, and raised a goblet to me. 'I assume you guessed the stone ring from seeing the maps on my desk?'

I nodded. The maps had clearly represented the great stones. 'But as to the rest?' He shook his head in admiration.

But I was not all that clever. The matter had to be deeply secret, because Petros had sent out his six attendants. Also, Morganus and I had recently solved a complex murder case such that Petros himself had identified the two of us as something special: detective agents in the Roman service. Beyond that, the legate's orders had said that a legionary lightning was reserved for our use: a high-speed, four horse carriage that was the fastest-known method of overload travel. Also, the orders had mentioned trouble with native religions. That could only mean druids, whom Rome detested for their human sacrifices and their capacity to incite Celtic rebellion. Thus druids were under sentence of death, and hunting-teams were forever chasing them.

This was secret information, but Morganus had the rank to know it, and he had told me.

However.

'Which kingdom is involved?' I asked. Petros shook his head in respect. 'Who mentioned a kingdom?'

'Nobody,' I said , and uncovered another secret. 'But I know that Rome tolerates druidic worship in the Celtic client kingdoms, so long as the kings honour the Emperor and don't raise armies. Those kingdoms are the only places left where druids are safe.'

'Very good,' said Petros. 'But can't you see which kingdom it is? Can't you see that inside my mind?'

'No,' I said 'because you don't know.' He laughed and I admit to the egotism of pride, because I read that information from his face.

'Enough!' said Petros. 'I'll give you the rest.' He leaned forward. 'First you should know that my master Teutonius...'

'Gods save His Grace!' said Morganus, the loyal Roman.

'Hmm,' said Petros, and continued. 'My master Teutonius is about to be promoted.'

'Oh?' said Morganus. 'I didn't know that.'

'Nobody knows it,' said Petros.

'Even Teutonius doesn't know it,' I said, studying Petros's face.

'Gods of Olympus!' said Petros. 'Can you not abate your gift? Rein it in?'

'No,' I said, 'that is my sorrow.'

'Then at least be silent.' I nodded, and he continued. 'The noble Teutonius is about to be become Governor of Italia.'

Morganus whistled in admiration. 'Gods bless His Grace!' he said.

'Quite,' said Petros. 'The Governor of Italia is second in honour only to the Emperor Himself.'

'Gods save His Majesty!' said Morganus, with feeling.

'Quite,' said Petros, with little respect.

'Quite,' I added with less, and Morganus frowned.

'In celebration,' said Petros, 'His Grace will pay for a festival of games: the greatest ever seen in Britannia. There will be famous actors in the theatres, famous gladiators in the arena, and famous racing drivers in a huge chariot-racing stadium to be built by the legions outside Londinium!' Petros spread hands expressively. 'His Grace will spend a fortune for the glory of the Empire,' he frowned, 'and to persuade these heathen savages ...*to Love Roman civilisation*!'

Those last words came in a bark of exasperation: a rare display of emotion from the man most burdened with the task of pacifying Britannia.

'Chariot racing?' asked Morganus, deeply impressed, and he smiled like sunshine because of all the spectacles beloved of Romans, chariot racing is supreme. Thus, in Rome, the theatres seat thousands and the arenas tens of thousands, but the Circus Maximus, home of chariot racing ,seats the brain-stunning, barely-believable number of 300,000 people.

'Therefore,' said Petros, it's vital that nothing shall disrupt these games.'

'Quite right too!' said Morganus.

'Yes,' said Petros, 'but at such a time as this, we have learned that a civil war is brewing between the Celtic kingdoms, and such a war would ruin His Grace's triumphal parting from Britannia.'

'How do you know this?' I asked. Petros lowered his voice.

'Listen,' he said, 'we have a druid, alive and under guard.' Morganus blinked. 'The man is gravely wounded and receiving medical care.' Petros stared at us. 'Do you understand?' he said. 'We have a druid held prisoner. His name is...'

'A *druid*?' I said. 'When their faith is forbidden, and the law says that any druid must be killed on sight? Where is he?' Petros turned away from me and stared at a blank wall.

'I am thinking of an olive tree,' he said.

'What?' I said.

'Why?' said Morganus.

'Because if I think of an olive tree, in the Greek sunlight, with its leaves and fruit, if that is in my mind then you can read nothing else.'

'Oh,' I said.

'*Oh*, indeed,' said Petros, 'Because some things are too secret even for you. So please let me continue.'

'Of course, I said. 'And I apologise.'

Petros sighed as a man does who is burdened down with heavy duties, and he turned back to face me.

'Yes,' he said, 'but in the name of all the gods, do try to keep out of my thoughts just this moment, if you please.'

'Of course.'

'Yes, yes, yes ... So! This druid's name is Dernfradour Bradowr, which means...'

'Venerable teacher of the long beard,' said Morganus, who spoke Britannic because he had lived in Britannia for much of his service life and had a great store of knowledge on its peoples and customs. Also, his wife was a Celt of the Artrebates tribe.

'I am grateful to the First Javelin,' said Petros. 'Bradowr is a rival to the most powerful druid in Britannia.'

'Maligoterix of the Regni Tribe!' I said. 'High Druid of all Britannia!'

That was not mind-reading, but memory of a previous case. On that occasion Morganus and I had met the High Druid.

'Yes,' said Petros, 'Maligoterix. He cursed Bradowr by all the Celtic gods and sent men to kill him. He sent fanatics: the cennad angau tribal assassins.' Petros looked at Morganus and me. 'You've met one of those, haven't you: a cennad angau?'

'Met him and killed him,' said Morganus, 'but I don't want to meet another one.'

'And neither did Bradowr!' said Petros. 'He knew they were coming, but he couldn't trust any of his own people because they were terrified of Maligoterix. So he turned to Rome. He sent a message to us, and we sent a force to rescue him.' Petros looked at me. 'And I'll save you the trouble of mind reading, by telling you that Bradowr was chief druid of the Catutuvallauni client kingdom.'

I frowned. I was losing track.

'How many of them are there?' I asked. 'Client kingdoms?'

'Seven,' said Morganus, 'and if it was up to me I'd flatten the lot of them.'

Petros sighed. 'We can't, honoured Morganus. We tolerate them because each one is an example to all Britannia, that Celts may live peaceably under Roman rule. So we allow them their druids *inside* the kingdoms, and occasionally we even receive information from traitors among them.'

'Isn't that against the law?' I said. 'Doesn't that mean you are in contact with druids?'

'Not as such,' said Petros, and he shrugged as if at some small matter of no importance. 'But the authorities in Rome are understanding, since it is their will that the client kingdoms exist, and so long as I—that is to say, His Grace—merely receive information from others, then my actions—that is to say *our* actions—are tolerated, because the information received enables us to keep track of their religious politics.'

'Religious politics?' I said, so fascinated by the concept that I neglected to ask how a cry for help could pass from Bradowr the druid to Petros the Roman administrator. Did they already know one another? Surely not, that would be high treason…

Meanwhile, Petros plunged into a discourse that entirely turned the subject.

'Religious politics,' he said. 'The druids are constantly quarrelling over dominance and doctrine.' He shook his head. 'Which druid is the holiest? Which god is the best? Which word to use in a ceremony? Which stroke to kill the sacrificial victim?' He shook his head. 'I could go on to the point of boredom, so just take note that Celts will fight over these matters. They will fight because the druids command that they must fight,' Petros hesitated, 'which the druids do, because they believe that these differences of dogma represent alternative roads leading to paradise… or to damnation and hell.'

Even in daylight, safe in the heart of Roman power, Morganus shuddered at this awesome spiritual concept. He stood and made the bull sign, while Petros and I raised hands in respect of the gods, for the gods are everywhere, even the Britannic gods. Then we sat quiet for a while and Petros poured wine, and I freely admit that I recited the Hymn to Apollo, though I did it in my mind, because no philosopher likes to admit fear of barbarian religion. Petros likewise invoked Athena, goddess of his home city, I read that in his silently moving lips. *Anyone* could have seen it, let alone a mind reader.

Morganus recovered first, because Romans are like that.

'They can't fight,' he said. 'They haven't got armies. We don't allow that.'

'Indeed,' said Petros. 'But they have cennad angau assassins, and they have holy maniacs, and they have daggers and poison.' He sighed in exasperation. 'It's worse than Nero's and Caligula's times put together! So each kingdom works mischief on all the others, and there's a big power struggle going on at the moment, one which could overturn kingdoms, or even cause tribal risings, and either of those would ruin His Grace's record and annihilate his promotion.' Morganus and I nodded. 'So here's what we are going to do—what *you* are going to do.' He looked at me. 'Bradowr was very weak when he came here, but he told us of a meeting of druids at a place near the Stone-Ring. That's all he told us, except that it's a very important meeting. So you, Ikaros, will go there with a special hunting team. You will intercept the druids and interrogate them.'

‘Which team?’ asked Morganus. ‘It’d better be a good one!’

‘It is,’ said Petros. ‘Troop Four Silesian.’

‘Ah,’ said Morganus, and nodded.

‘What’s that?’ I said. ‘Troop Four?’

‘They’re the best,’ said Morganus.

‘Quite,’ said Petros.

‘So,’ I said, ‘I suppose these Silesian are adept at tracking and hunting?’

‘Oh yes,’ said Morganus. ‘As you’ll find out, or rather *we’ll* find out, because I’m coming with you. Me and my four lads.’

‘No!’ said Petros. ‘You’d make too much noise. You know that, Morganus.’

Morganus said nothing, because he *did* know that. He knew it very well indeed. Petros looked at me. ‘Even you’ll make too much noise, but you have to go because it’s a chance to question druids when they’re attempting something big, but they’re shocked and weak because they’ve been trapped. So I want the questioning done by the best man in the Province—best in the Empire, probably—and that’s you, and we cannot simply put a druid to torture, because that does not work with them.’

‘If you say so,’ I said. ‘But can I start by questioning Bradowr? To see what I can get out of him?’

‘No,’ said Petros, ‘he’s unconscious.’

‘I see.’

‘So you leave tomorrow,’ said Petros. ‘And that’s an order.’

Chapter 3

So I had my adventure with Troop Four Silesian, and the adventure ended in failure. But nobody judged us harshly, for two reasons. The first reason was the fact that the secret hunting teams very seldom managed to take a druid alive, and other teams had suffered far worse disasters than ours. Gallus the centurion explained this on the ride back to the legionary fortress.

'I'm sorry my lads didn't take more care, Your Worship,' he said, 'but these jobs—these chases—more often go bad than good.' He jabbed a thumb back at the wagons full of dead Celts that rumbled along behind us. 'Sometimes it's our lot that come back dead, but usually, if it does go bad, we just never know.'

'What do you mean?'I asked.

'Well,' he said, 'A troop goes out on a chase, 'cos some bugger—some druid—has betrayed some other bugger, 'cos they're rotten sods even to each other.'

'Yes?' I said.

'So they know where to go: the troop, I mean.'

'Yes?'

'And they ride out, and they never come back.' He shrugged, and spread his hands in a resigned gesture. 'And we never hear of 'em, not ever again.'

I shook my head in surprise.

'How often does that happen,' I asked.

'About one in five jobs, maybe one in four.'

'Gods of Olympus!' I said , but Gallus laughed, as a young man does who thinks it cannot happen to him.

'It's all right,Your Worship ,' he said. 'That's why we get double pay, and my lads get Roman citizenship in half the usual time!'

And so to the second reason why we were excused, and so to another of my flaws, because Romans have so very many holy days, and so many gods to honour, that I can never remember which one comes next, nor what it will be about. Morganus says that this is because my inner mind refuses to accept Roman rule completely, and that I should therefore keep a written list. Perhaps he is right or perhaps not, but when we arrived back at the Twentieth Legion's fortress, every man was furiously busy preparing for the biggest event of the year, which would be celebrated by every soldier and every citizen of the Empire: the Emperor's birthday. On this occasion it would also be the day when the men of the First Squadron of the Third Pannonian Auxiliary Cavalry Regiment were to be given Roman citizenship at the end of their military service, which in their case meant the full twenty-five years. Consequently, with two such major public events to arrange, the army had no time to worry about a few dead Celts, even if two of them had been druids.

As for me, I had left the fortress decently dressed, and in a legionary lightning that took me to the camp of the Silesian hunters. But now I was back, dressed in rags, unwashed for weeks, and accompanied by Troop Four who looked more like beggars on horseback than Roman soldiers. But Gallus the centurion had passwords, that got us into the fortress and to an office at the end of one of the barrack blocks, which turned out to be the headquarters of the druid-hunting teams. There were no signs that the office was anything special, except that here in a legionary fortress, the man in charge was a civilian with a clever face and the broad purple stripe of the senatorial class on his tunic. He was someone from the Governor's staff, I supposed. But he gave no name, and sat in his rich clothes, with richly-dressed hair, and a small staff of clerks around him. These whispered to each other, stared steadily at me and Gallus, and took notes of everything that was said.

So Gallus gave his report and I gave mine, though the civilian was barely listening because—judging from his desk-load of papers, which I read upside-down—he too was consumed with preparations for the coming ceremonies, and we were dismissed with barely a question. Gallus grinned in relief, and took then me to my own headquarters—my home, in fact—which was the First Javelin's house, next to the Temple of the Standards. There I dismounted, and following the traditions of my clan, I gave thanks to the horse that had carried me. He was a nice little creature, with pretty feet and a white mane, so I put my arms around his neck and rested my brow against his, and stood in a moment of communion with him, taking care to beg his forgiveness for my part in the ambush that had killed two horses. Then the horse snorted and stamped to show that my thoughts were appreciated, and I waved goodbye to Gallus and his men.

I was flattered to find Morganus's wife and three daughters waiting for me outside his door. I suppose a runner had alerted them. Morganus's wife was a plump, pretty woman, far younger than him. She was a dark-haired Celt, but now entitled to wear the stola: the prestige garment of a citizen's wife. She had a full name in the Celtic tongue but had taken a short, Romanised version on marrying Morganus. Thus she was now The Lady Morgana Callandra. The daughters were younger versions of herself, girls in their teens. As unmarried women they wore female tunicas, not the stola.

'I greet you, O Ikaros of Apollonis,' said Morgana Callandra, in formal Latin. 'I greet you in the name of The-Lord-my-Husband, who is busy on the legion's business.'

'I greet you in return, O Lady-Wife-of-My-Lord-your-Husband: he who stands in the place of my master His Imperial Majesty.'

'Gods bless His Majesty!' said Morgana Callandra and her girls. But that that was enough formal speech, because Morgana Callandra turned up her nose and pointed into the house.

'Get inside,' she said to me, 'you stink! The bath house is fired up and waiting, with clean clothes laid out,' she sniffed and pointed at my green rag costume, 'and you will please throw *that* out of the back door for burning, together with anything that may be living in it!' The girls giggled. 'Go on, now,' said Morgana Callandra, 'You'll feel better when you're clean. And have you eaten? Do you need a drink? Do you need anything in the bath house?'

I asked for some of the rose petal soap that I make, because I use soap even if Romans do not, and she sent one of the girls for it and fussed over me as she always did. It was strange but exceedingly pleasant, especially as the girls followed their mother's example, acting as if I were a youngster in need of care. When first I entered Morganus's house I had been nervous of such attentions, in case Morganus might be jealous. But when I mentioned it, he just smiled.

'We have no son,' he said, 'and my wife always wanted one.'

'But I must be ten years older than her,' I said.

'She doesn't care about that,' he said, 'and someone has to look after you, because you're off in your thoughts so much of the time.'

Later, I did feel better in my clean clothes and Morgana Callandra sent me off with a pass-tablet left by Morganus, to get me inside the Principia, the legion's main office block and residence of its commanding officer.

'He's been there every day for the last two weeks,' she said as she gave me the tablet. 'The whole province is inside-out, getting ready for the big event, and he's been awarded a special honour.'

'Has he?' I said. 'What's that?'

'He'll tell you,' she said, reaching up to adjust my cloak-pin which she thought was not quite at the correct angle. Then one of the girls opened the front door and I was out, reflecting on the odd fact that there were no slaves in this richly-furnished, elaborate Roman home. There were no slaves because the army did not use them. Thus the heavy housework was done by army defaulters as atonement for their sins, and Morgana Callandra and her girls did the rest, right down to holding open a door, which no freeborn Roman would dream of doing if there were slaves in the house.

The Pprincipia was nearby. It was a neat, immaculate fort-within-a-fort. It even had a ditch and drawbridge, and it had guards drawn from the elite first century of the legion. The centurion of the gate guard knew me well, as did the shiny-gleaming legionaries standing with him, but he went through the full process of reading my pass-tablet, and consulting a list to check that it had been properly issued, which of course it had.

'Right you are, then, Ikaros the Greek,' he said, and even raised his right arm in salute to me, as acknowledged comrade of the First Javelin. 'His Honour's inside,' he added, and turned to one of his men. 'Take the Greek gentleman to His Honour Morganus. Look lively now!'

'Yes, sir!' said the legionary, and saluted and set off at the quick march with me following. There were stairs and corridors, and more guards, and the same air of frantic preparation that hung over the whole fortress, with men rushing here and there on their duties. I should not have been surprised at this, but I was. As I have said, I never did know one of their festivals from another, and this was going to be a big one.

Finally, I was in a long office on the first floor, lit by bright windows, with benches and tables and wooden crates, and small plates of shiny new bronze being taken out of the sawdust packing in the crates, and lined up on the tables. The plates were covered in incised writing, but with some blank spaces, and there were legionary clerks with notes and pens, and several senior officers sitting in a row. The row ended with Morganus, his four big bodyguards standing behind him like iron statues. Everyone was concentrating so hard that my arrival went unnoticed, and I stood and watched what they were doing.

First a clerk picked up a pair of plates, blew off the sawdust and wiped the plates with a cloth. Then he took them to an officer who consulted a list and read out an auxiliary soldier's name and unit. These details were carefully checked, then the plates went down onto the table and another clerk, with a hammer and a slim, pen-like chisel struck the name and unit details into the blank spaces on the plates. Finally yet another clerk wired the pair of plates together, closed them one on the other, and took them to the first of the seated officers who, one after another, dipped their signet rings into hot wax poured into a recess in one of the plates—Morganus last of all—such that each pair of plates was sealed shut by its load of seals. There was silence in the room, apart from the clunk of hammer on chisel, and the shuffle of clerkish feet as all present concentrated on their task. Then Morganus spoke, as he withdrew his ring from the latest seal.

'Another one!' he said. 'How many more?' Then he looked up and saw me. 'Ah,' he said, 'Ikaros! How did it go?' He stood, came towards me and offered his hand. This caused some eyebrow-raising, because Romans did not clasp hands with slaves. Not even imperial slaves. But he smiled and I smiled. Then I shook my head.

'Oh?' he said, then looked round. 'Tell me later,' he said, given the deep secrecy of my late mission. But then he smiled happily. 'Come and see,' he said, 'you'll like this. It's interesting.' He pointed to the growing row of sealed bronze plates. 'Do you know what these are?'

I had a good look. Each plate was about six inches high, five inches wide and a quarter of an inch thick. Each one was drilled with holes so that the plates could be wired together in pairs, like the pages of a book-tablet. They were designed so that the wiring ran through a trough containing the wax seals, such that each two-page bronze book could not be opened without breaking the seals. In fact this was routine because all major Roman documents, wills and contracts for instance, were sealed like this, with an informal transcript on the outside for ready access, and the solemn document sealed inside. This was Roman legal practice, but I had never seen it applied to bronze plates.

'No,' I said, in answer to Morganus' question, 'I don't know what they are.'

'Diplomas of honourable discharge for auxiliary troops,' said Morganus. 'They grant full Roman citizenship after twenty-five years service!'I nodded. I had heard of them but never seen them.Then Morganus spoke to me in Formal Latin.

'Come forward and be presented to His Knightly Honour, Tribune Gaius Valerius Celsus,' he said, 'He who was recently made commander of The Third Regiment of Pannonian Horse,' Morganus bowed and continued, 'The First Squadron of the Regiment shall receive its discharge tomorrow, by order of His Imperial Majesty, gods bless him!'

'Gods bless him!' said all present, as Celsus stood up from the table.

'Your Honour,' said Morganus to the Tribune, 'Here stands my colleague Ikaros of Apollonis, a senator and cavalry officer in his own city.' Fair words, but all present knew that I was now a slave. So Celsus looked at Morganus, then looked at me, and then looked at everyone else. I read the hero-worship in his eyes for Morganus, and his puzzlement over myself. He was a thin, self-conscious, very young man: new to the army, new to Britannia and well aware that the troopers who would be made citizens tomorrow had joined up long before he was born. So he was unsure of himself, and wondering how a Roman knight should greet a high-status imperial slave like me. Worse still, he was afflicted by the usual, young-Roman puzzlement over the fact that, to them, I looked like the schoolmaster who had thrashed them when they got their lessons wrong. So what might be the correct form in addressing me? What was the proper etiquette? Romans are obsessed with such matters. Finally he glanced at Morganus again, gave an ingratiating little smile, and offered me his hand.

'Ah,' said the audience softly, and nodded. What was good for Morganus was good for them, even though Tribune Celsus out-ranked Morganus, at least in theory. But rank is one thing and a veteran of forty years' service is quite another, especially when the veteran had joined as a lad but risen to First Javelin, and had served from one end of the Empire to the other, and had won every decoration known to the Roman army, and was a living legend to the troops. Meanwhile I made my bow to Celsus, and took his offered hand and waited for him to speak first, as protocol demanded. But he blinked and wondered what to say.

'You are honoured to serve under Morganus,' he said at last, and I bowed again.

'That is true, Knightly Sir, ' I said, 'Just as your own name will be honoured, when your men are made citizens.' He liked that, and he smiled and relaxed which is what I had intended, because a little kindness does no harm. It was encouragement to the lad, and it helped him find more words.

'If we speak of honour,' he said, 'Then think of Morganus, who will hand out the bronze diplomas to the men.' There was a growl of approval from all present, and led by the four bodyguards, men began to stamp feet in time,while those who were seated beat the table with their fists.

'Morganus! Morganus! Morganus!' they cried, and he actually blushed.

'What's this?' I asked. Morganus was too embarrassed to speak, but Celsus explained.

'Morganus will perform the ceremony,' he said, 'he will do the granting of citizenship, and when he does it, he'll invoke the spirit of the Empire itself. And that's an enormous honour.'

'Is it?' I asked, because so much of Roman thinking is so very strange to a Greek.

'Oh yes,' said Celsus. 'Normally when a unit gets its discharge, the Emperor Himself gives out the bronze if it happens in Rome, or the provincial governor does it if it's in the provinces. But my men are getting their discharge on the Emperor's birthday…'

'Gods save His Majesty!' cried all the room.

'So, as a special privilege, the men can choose who does it.' Celsus smiled and looked at Morganus. 'My men, every one of them, voted to take their bronze from the hands of Leonius Morganus…'

'Fortis Victrix!' cried everyone. Morganus was still embarrassed by such praise, and covered this by showing me a completed bronze document.

'Look,' he said, 'this one is for Troop Leader Reburrion, son of Lucon the Pannonian. See where we've put in his name.'

I looked and nodded. 'So they're not made with the names already entered,' I said.

'No,' he said. 'They're made in bulk in Rome with blank spaces for the names, and then shipped out to the provinces, from time to time, so that they can be used when needed, with the unit filling in the names. Then the unit sends full details back to Rome, and a copy is inscribed on a big master plate, with the name of the unit and all the men who have been made citizens, and then the plate is fixed to the wall outside the temple of the deified Augustus,' he smiled. 'I've been there and seen them! There's rows and rows of master plates, with all the names.'

'Of those who have become shining new Roman citizens,' I said, contemplating this mass cleansing of the great unwashed. Morganus saw my cynicism and frowned, and I guessed his thoughts.

'Do you have to act like that, and spoil the occasion? Can't you control yourself?'

* * *

But on the next day I was genuinely impressed by the granting of citizenship. I was standing on the ceremonial dais of the Field of Mars: the Army's huge parade-ground outside Londinium. I was with other imperial slaves, including Petros of Athens, in a fenced-off, flower-draped, bright-painted enclosure reserved for imperial slaves. In fact, as there were so few Roman civilian citizens in Londinium, we imperials were second in importance only to the governor's staff and the citizens, whose enclosure was immediately to our right, raised up three feet above ours, and fenced off with gold-painted posts and ropes, as against our silver. Everyone was in formal dress; officers in scarlet cloaks and plumes, citizens in togas, ladies in jewels, and we imperials in chitons if Greeks, or turbans and fringed cloaks if Jews. There was the most enormous crowd of people, the band played, and everyone cheered while the drill team of the Twentieth Legion marched up and down in a programme of fancy manoeuvres.

But mostly the ceremonies had been deathly dull to me, beginning as they did with the sun's arrival over the eastern horizon and a comprehensive blaring of trumpets and the sacrifice of seven bulls—one for each hill of Rome—in the name of the Emperor. Much similar followed, with universal raising of hands and chanting, and myself grateful for the help of Petros and his shaven-skull team, who had written out the various prayers and responses for the benefit of persons like myself. Also, during the more tedious moments, I questioned Petros on the citizenship ceremony which was to be the high point of the day.

There was one unbearably droning-voiced ceremony in which a dozen toga-clad Romans blessed rows of white milestones, by putting sheep and goats to the knife on portable altars. So I turned for respite to Petros.

'Honoured Petros,' I said, 'how many auxiliary troopers shall become citizens today?' I spoke in Athenian Greek, so much more elegant than Latin, and Petros replied in the cultured accent which makes every Athenian sound like a prince.

'First take note, honoured Ikaros, of the *expense* of these proceedings,' said Petros, nodding at the milestones. 'It is the convention in Britannia that each road shall receive a new set of freshly-painted milestones each year on the Emperor's birthday.'

'Such profligacy!' I said, as if I cared. 'But what of my question?'

'How many new citizens?'

'How many?' I said. Petros leaned his head slightly back and one of his shaven-skull aides consulted notes and whispered in Petros's ear. Then Petros nodded.

'Three hundred and twenty-six,' said Petros. 'The survivors of 600 who joined up...' He leaned back, the aide whispered, Petros nodded, '...in the Year of Vespasian and Firmus,' he said, 'twenty-five years ago.'

'I am grateful for your clarification, honoured Petros,' I said, and repeated, 'the year of Vespasian and Firmus,' thereby noting the perverse Roman habit of giving years names rather than numbers. They give each year the names of the two consuls who head their senate in that year: a bizarre custom which means that nobody can tell which year is which without going to a library to look up the records.

But then, by the grace of the gods, the milestone ceremony ended and the stones were whisked away by swift-running legionaries. The band blared and a different, and huge, team of legionaries doubled out carrying a large, timber rostrum. It came complete with a flight of steps, and a table on the rostrum bearing the 326 bronze diplomas. It was a heavy load, but Romans are good at heavy loads, and the rostrum was smartly set down before the governor's enclosure, such that the Governor, and his aides, together with Morganus and Tribune Celsus, could take their places on it, processing down another flight of steps linking the enclosure to the field.

Petros nodded at these proceedings. He was a great enthusiast for Roman drill: a true connoisseur.

'Watch on!' he said. 'A unique moment follows.'

So I watched as t to a huge fanfare and great cheering from the assembled masses—The First Squadron of the Third Pannonian Auxiliary Cavalry Regiment, marched forward from the far end of the field, and two armoured streams of regulars from the Twentieth Legion formed up on either side of the Pannonians, drew swords and clashed arms overhead, and roared out the homeland name:

'Pannonia! Pannonia! Pannonia!' This done, they sheathed arms and marched beside the Pannonians, carefully keeping one rank behind them as an honour guard, and dipping their standards in salute as they would never have done to mere auxiliaries under any other circumstances whatsoever. I admit that I was impressed. It was an awesome sight.

'Now gaze upon the Pannonians' women,' said Petros. He pointed, and I saw that Roman efficiency included provision for them, too. There was a roped-off enclosure at one side of the field, and they stood in ranks as smart as those of their menfolk on the Field of Mars. They were strangely dressed, in long, dark cloaks with hoods thrown over their heads. 'Look in front of them,' said Petros, 'look at the platform!' I saw a long, low wooden platform set up in front of the women. It was about six inches high, two feet wide on top, and it ran from side to side of the women's enclosure.

'What purpose does that structure serve?' I asked, but Petros merely smiled.

'I advise that you be patient,' he said.

I suppose I should have guessed. Citizenship brought such huge benefits that—aside from the pay—the chance of getting it was the main reason why barbarians became auxiliaries in the first place. Only a citizen could vote, or hold office, or make a contract under Roman law, or own a house in a Roman city, or even give evidence in court or leave a will. Also, citizens absolutely could not be tortured or beaten, and could not be banished or arrested without trial. And still there was a further privilege of citizenship: one that was inestimably valued by auxiliaries because although they could not marry while in service, all of them, being men in their forties, had liaisons with native women and had children who were illegitimate under Roman law. But the bronze diplomas to be handed out today turned all such liaisons into legal marriages, and gave the veterans' sons full rights of Roman citizenship.

'See,' said Petros. 'The ceremony commences!'

Now Morganus was on the rostrum in full battle dress, with the Governor and Tribune Celsus behind him, and one of the bodyguards was handing him a bronze diploma from the table. An auxiliary trooper of the First Squadron Pannonians was mounting the rostrum. He knelt before Morganus, who placed hands on the trooper's shoulders and gave blessing by the gods of Rome. Then Morganus raised up the man, gave him his bronze diploma, cried out his name, and added in a mighty voice: 'CIVIS ROMANUS ES!' You are a Roman citizen!

This brought a huge cheer from the spectators, and Petros tugged at my arm and pointed towards the Pannonian women. As Morganus proclaimed citizenship, a woman—presumably the trooper's woman—stepped up on to the long platform, threw off the cloak and hood and stood proudly before everyone she knew in the entire world. She was revealed in a gleaming white stola: no longer a soldier's tart, but a Roman matriarch, the wife of a citizen and the respected mother of his children! It was a magnificent gesture, and dismissive as I am of Roman ways, I was none the less moved to tears.

Thus it went on, with one after another trooper receiving his bronze diploma and his now-legal wife stepping up onto the platform beside her sisters, to thundering cheers, until finally the ceremony was ended and everyone marched off the field to the music of the band, and the womenfolk, families and children moved off to riotous feasting and celebration, to be joined later by their husbands.

'What will happen now?' I asked Petros. 'Shall the Pannonians receive pensions?'

'Indeed,' said Petros, 'each shall be granted a sum in gold, together with rights in perpetuity to rich farming land to the west of Londinium. They shall form a new and loyal colony in this benighted province,' he smiled, 'another brick in the Roman wall!'

Thus spoke Petros of Athens, and I sorrowed for the very soul of him: so completely had he become Roman, so absolute was his collaboration with our conquerors. Another brick in the Roman wall. A mournful thought for a Greek like me, whose city walls had been smashed by Roman siege engines.

After that I was further depressed, since Petros had arranged a reception for us imperial slaves in a big tent to one side of the Field of

Mars, and there was no possibility that I could avoid it. The event was supposedly informal, but there were prayers and speeches—it *was* the Emperor's birthday after all—and Petros, who liked and even admired me, insisted on introducing me to everyone of importance. He meant well but I had to make small talk for hours and the wine was served in tiny cups, which never got re-filled, or at least mine did not. I did wonder if perhaps there was a slave with a wine-flask and I had missed him. Who knows? But when there is such a slave, I usually find him.

I left as soon as I could. It was night, but Petros had a troop of auxiliaries standing by to provide each imperial with an escort home through the dark. So I walked back to Morganus' house with four of them behind me, and one in front with a flaming torch. I was full of dark thoughts, cheered only by the prospect of a proper drink from Morganus' wine cellar. But I was disappointed. Morganus was waiting for me, his bodyguards behind him, and all of them frowning.

'Ikaros!' he said, as I came through the front door. 'There's been a murder.'

'So what?' I said, in sour mood. 'Who got killed?'

'The Celsus,' he said. 'Gaius Valerius Celsus: commander of the Third Pannonians, who've just been made citizens. It's worse than murder, it's a stain on Roman honour!'

Chapter 4

It was no more than few steps to the scene of the crime. Tribune Gaius Valerius Celsus—late commander of the Third Regiment of Pannonian Horse—had been murdered in his rooms in the tribunes' block , which stood beside the legate's house no more than fifty paces from Morganus's house in the very heart of the Twentieth Legion's fortress.

It was dark when I arrived with Morganus and his bodyguards, but it was bright-lit night, full of marching feet, gleaming armour, torches, shouting and challenges. The tribunes' block and the legate's house were entirely ringed by legionaries in full battle kit, with swords drawn and distant scouts posted to warn of any attack—and this actually inside the fortifications! But someone had actually been murdered inside the fortifications, and the fortress was on full alert, even though it seemed that the murderer was already found. Morganus explained as we walked.

'It's his slave girl,' he said, 'she did it.'

'Slave?' I said. 'I thought you didn't have slaves? Not in the army.'

'We don't,' he said, 'Not in that sense.'

'What sense?'

'Common slaves. House boys. We don't have them and don't want them. There's thousands of men in a legion to do the work, and we don't want them standing idle, waited on by slaves. And slaves gossip. There are no secrets where there are slaves. If you've got slaves in the house then the world knows every time you break wind.'

'Then what was this one? What was she?'

'His exotic. His companion.'

'Oh!' I said, and understood. Some services had to come from outside the army, especially for a young man on his own. But then we were passing the door guards and into the atrium of the tribunes' block. The building was high and broad, with two levels above the ground floor, and every inch of it made by the men of the Twentieth, because a Roman legion has every trade from glazier to plumber within its ranks, and when a legion is not fighting or drilling it is busy building. It is all part of Rome's historic mission to civilise the barbarian world: whether or not that world wants to be civilised. So the atrium was clean and bright with a neat geometric pattern in the mosaic of the floor, and in the painting on the plastered wall which included the constantly repeated monograms 'TIMP' over 'LXX' because Romans love abbreviations. Thus LXX stood for the Twentieth Legion and TIMP for the Emperor, TRAIANUS IMPERATOR in formal Latin. Note that this appeared only on the walls, not the floor, because Romans thought it improper to tread on the Emperor's name. Being Roman, the atrium of course included a central pool and fountain, and a square hole in the roof two stories above, complete with water spouts to drain rainwater into the pool: a refreshingly cool plan in Greece or Italy, but nonsense in cold, damp Britannia, where it rains most of the time.

The atrium was full of men, including the Legate, the officer in command of the legion. He was waiting with his tribunes standing to one side of him. They were his staff officers: the highest ranking men in the legion after himself. They had been summoned urgently, and were in every stage of dress from armour and boots, to tunics and slippers. There was a mutter of conversation among them and every man looked suspicious and alarmed.

'Ah,' said the Legate as we entered, 'Morganus! This has to be settled fast because Celsus, gods rest his soul...'

'Gods rest his soul!' said Morganus and I together, and we raised hands in respect.

'Gods rest his soul!' said all present, likewise raising hands.

'Yes, yes,' said the Legate, and frowned. He was very old, reputedly over eighty, and he was tired and worried, but he was a senatorial patrician from the highest nobility of the Empire and he held himself stiffly upright in a cloak thrown hastily over his night gown. He was Nonius Julius Sabinus, better known by his nickname Africanus for his dark skin and tightly-curled hair. He was a formidable man, deep in Roman power politics, and effectively head of the army of Britannia, since he out-ranked the legates commanding the other two Britannic legions which were the Second and the Eighth. He was withered and scarred, he had lost the tip of his nose in some long-forgotten battle, and his sight was clouded by cataracts. But he was ice-clear in mind and he stared hard at Morganus through misted eyes.

Note that he stared at Morganus and not at me. He did so because Roman aristocrats so completely regard slaves as the property of their masters, that even when a slave displays extraordinary talent, the master is praised not the slave. It would have been the same if I had been a dog that did tricks, or a performing ape. But Romans are pragmatic as well as arrogant, so finally, Africanus spoke directly to me.

'You will use all your gifts in this matter,' he said. 'You are hereby and herewith conscripted into my service. You will report to me, and to no other. Do you understand?'

'Yes, Noble and Honoured Sir,' I replied.

'Good,' he said. 'Now listen to me. Celsus has been in Britannia only a year and a couple of months. He has—he *had*—a powerful family in Rome, and this killing has happened on my watch, so I need answers at your utmost speed.'

He looked at the cluster of tribunes standing whispering to one another and I read fear in his face. Not physical fear but political fear, because tribunes are not lifetime professionals like centurions, but young noblemen serving for a few years before going home to a career in Roman politics. Each legion has six tribunes: a senior one of senatorial rank, with five others of knightly rank, so it was not only Celsus who had a powerful family in Rome, but every single one of them, and they were all wondering what might be the political outcome of the death of Celsus.

But Africanus was still speaking.

'His family—the Valerii—are in the garum business.'

'Garum?' I said. 'Fish sauce?'

Africanus frowned at my interruption, but gave reply. 'Yes. They have factories in Spain and Africa, and their ships take it all over the Empire.' He frowned at my slowness to comprehend. 'You know the emblem GVSN?' he said. 'It's on every pot and jar from here to Jerusalem!'

'Ah,' I said, 'GVSN.' The initials were a trade mark. They stood for Garum Valeriis Nulli Secundus, meaning Valerius' garum, second to none! Romans are obsessed with fish sauce and consume it in a pantheon of flavours. Personally, I was not obsessed with fish sauce but even *I* had seen the mark GVSN.

'The family is awash with money,' said Africanus. 'They're floating in it! They got Celsus command of a cavalry unit because that's prestigious, more so even than regular infantry.' Africanus shook his head. 'And Celsus was also floating in money! His first act when he arrived in Londinium was to buy a top class exotic. He paid over a million sesterses for her, and look where that's got him!' He leaned closer. 'So I need proof that his death was nothing to do with me, or my legion, or my officers. Do you understand?'

'Yes, Noble and Honoured Sir,' we said: myself and Morganus together, and Africanus looked towards the staircase that led to the upper floors.

'The body's up there,' he said. 'I ordered the men to leave it alone and to keep the girl safe. She's up there too ...*so get on with it!*'

So we did. The block was built on a square plan such that the tribunes' apartments faced inwards towards the atrium, spreading out away from it. There was a run of timber galleries around the inside of the atrium giving access to the upper apartments, and there were five sets of apartments on each floor, making fifteen in all, providing accommodation not only for the Twentieth's six tribunes, but for others—like Celsus—who commanded auxiliary units.

So Morganus and I climbed the stairs and found two legionaries and an optio on guard outside one of the doors. These stamped to attention on sight of Morganus. They hauled open the door, and we went inside.

There was a big living room with glazed windows—now black dark—looking out on the fortress, with closed doors leading to other rooms: one door on each side. The room was richly equipped with furniture and ornaments brought out from Rome, and lit by multi-flame silver star-lamps on elaborate tripods. I looked around. The optio came in with us and stood respectfully at attention, and the four bodyguards followed.

'Stand easy,' said Morganus.

'Sir!' said the optio, and relaxed.

'Where is he?' I asked the optio. 'Celsus?' The optio pointed to one of the doors.

'He's in there, Your Worship. That's the honoured Celsus' bedroom ... and ... er ... he's in there. 'He was nervous, so I studied his face. He was an old soldier in his fifties, very neat, very well turned-out and rather fat. I judged that he was a man who had found himself a most comfortable niche in life.

'What is your name, optio?' I asked.

'Lucius Secundus, Your Worship,' he said, and stiffened to attention again.

'And what are your duties, Secundus?'

'I'm in charge of the block, Your Worship.'

'Which means?'

'All domestic duties Your Worship: cleaning, repairs, food and wine, and making beds. All that stuff.'

How very cosy for Optio Secundus, I thought, *with gulps of the wine, cuts of the meat, and no drilling, marching or fighting!* That is why he was nervous. He was in fear that some blame might fall upon himself, and heave him out of his precious post.

'So you know who comes and goes?' I said.

'Oh yes, Your Worship. Nobody gets in our out without my lads knowing. We're here all the time.'

'So who came in and out of these apartments, when Tribune Celsus was killed?'

'Nobody, Your Worship. Only her. The lady. Nobody else, Your Worship! Not before Jupiter Maximus himself!' He raised hands piously, and I copied him. You can never be too careful with the gods. Meanwhile, Secundus was obviously telling the truth.

'I see,' I said. 'Let's have a look at his honour the tribune.'

'Yes, Your Worship,' he said, and marched to the bedroom door and opened it. 'I'll bring a light, Your Worship,' he said and took a silver lamp from its tripod.

'Oh,' I said, 'just one thing.'

'Your Worship?'

'Who found him dead?'

Secundus blinked. 'Me, Your Worship. Him and her—the lady—they always have hot mulled wine in the evening, and I brought it. And he was dead. And she was sitting on the bed beside him like a little wood-nymph, a little flower. She never even looked at me. She just said some stuff I didn't understand.'

'Hmm,' I said, because I could already see Celsus in the light of the lamp, inside the dark bedroom. I went in, followed by Morganus, and looked at the body. Celsus was laid out in a night-gown as if asleep, but a large kitchen knife was stuck in his throat, precisely where it would cut the great vessels that pulse beneath a man's chin. There was some blood, but not much. He must mainly have bled within himself, having received just the one, perfect death stroke. The bed was hardly disturbed.

Morganus looked down at the corpse. He took off his helmet, stood to attention and bowed in respect because Celsus had been a soldier of Rome. The four bodyguards followed his example. Then everyone put their helmets back on again, with a rustle and a clunk, and Morganus stared at the dead man.

'No struggle,' he said. 'He didn't fight back.'

'No,' I said, and Morganus nodded.

'She took him by surprise, didn't she? He must have been lying there and she just stuck him.'

'Whoever did it was left handed,' I said. 'The blade is on the right side of his neck. A right-handed stroke would have put it in his left side.'

'Yes,' said Morganus, and looked at Secundus. 'Could it have been anyone other than the girl—what's her name anyway?'

'Violacta Kalina, Your Worship, but everyone calls her Lady Viola.'

'*Lady* Viola?' I said, 'a slave girl?'

'Yes,' said Secundus, 'wait till you see her, Your Worship.'

'But could it have been anyone else than her?'said Morganus, and Secundus shook his head. 'So it was her that killed him,' said Morganus. I nodded, looked at the corpse, concluded that there was nothing more to do, and would have moved on—except that the philosopher within me guided the detective agent.

I was struck with the thought that perhaps the knife had not killed Celsus. What if some other wound had been inflicted, secretly? What if Celsus had been murdered in some other place, and the corpse brought here and the knife plunged into his throat to mislead investigation? What if the killer were even now hiding in the room?

Thus I realised that there was very much more to do.

First I drew out the knife, noted that there was blood on the handle, and set it aside and made a careful inspection of the body. I had the bodyguards bring in more light, and then take off the night-gown, and turn over the corpse so that I could look for other wounds or anything suspicious. I searched in his mouth, ears, anus, genitals, nostrils and armpits, and examined his skin for any bruising or signs that it might have been dragged. Then we checked the room, looking under the bed and in the storage chests, and feeling the walls for hidden doors or anything strange. I personally opened the window, and looked down on a smooth wall with a thirty-foot drop, and looked up to a smooth wall above with no means of entry to the room.

I have followed this procedure ever after, in all my investigations, and found it to be productive of evidence on most occasions. But this first time it revealed nothing: or rather it did, because the negative result—together with the other evidence—convincingly proved that the girl Viola had killed Celsus.

When finally I was done, Morganus, who had not at all approved of my intrusive examinations of the body, reminded us of the decent proprieties.

'Celsus was an officer and a Roman knight,' he said. 'He must be prepared for burial in a fit and proper manner.'

'Of course,' I said, although the thought had not even entered my mind.

'I'll speak to the Llegate,' said Morganus. 'He'll know what to do.'

'Quite,' I said. 'And I'll need to wash my hands.'

'There's a basin and jug in the big room, Your Worship,' said Secundus, 'and towels.'

'Good,' I said, and questioned him further as I washed.

'What do you know about the girl?'

'The Lady Viola?' said Secundus, and he shook his head in regret. 'I can't hardly believe she did it. Lovely little thing she is. All the lads think so. They'd do anything for her. They kiss the ground she walks on.'

'Oh,' I said.

'Yes, Your Worship.'

'And where is she now?'

'In the other room, Your Worship. His office and store-room.' He raised hands again. 'I mean, his late honour Celsus' office.'

So we went to the office.

Since truth is invincible and cannot be denied, I record here a great perversity of my character. I record that as we approached the office/store room, I smiled because I was happy, and I was happy because while the wine flask takes the edge off my melancholy, the only real cure is work, which to me means solving puzzles such as code-cracking, engineering problems, chemical investigations, and most all the solving of crime. It is a drug that I take with joy, and relish each future dose. It is indeed perversity within me, but I can no more be blamed for this fault than I can be praised for my talents, because both are the gift of the gods.

'Shall we go in, then?' said Morganus as I reflected on these matters.

'Yes,' I said, then, '*oh!*'

'*Oh!*' said Morganus and the four bodyguards, all in an awestruck whisper, because as Secundus opened the door into the well-lit office, we all saw the slave-girl Violacta Kalina, and understood why she was known as Lady Viola.

She was an exotic, just as I once had been, and like me she had been sold for an enormous price, though I was sold as a Greek engineer while she was sold for beauty, which of course comes in many forms. Sometimes a woman's beauty is voluptuous and sensual, sometimes it is elegant and patrician, and sometimes it is a sparkling charm that makes a man laugh and prickles the hairs of the back of his neck. But the Lady Viola was something different.

She did indeed resemble a wood-nymph. She was small and pale, and her hair was cut short so that it curled around her head, revealing a slender neck. She had small, perfect features, with a pointed chin, red lips and a most fetching habit of reaching up one small hand to brush the hair from her eyes, and then shaking her head to swirl everything into its proper place in a movement that was delightful to watch. Her figure was slim but shapely, and small as she was, she was a full woman in every way. These gifts were beautiful—but the real magic was in her eyes, which were enormous under dark, curving eyebrows and swept with lashes such that they flashed and gleamed and were truly lovely.

But that is what you get if you spend over a million on an exotic. Why else would anyone pay that sort of money?

When we first saw her she was sat in a chair, rocking forward and back, dressed in a silk gown, that left her arms and neck bare, and she seemed so small, so helpless and so appealing that even I wanted to put my arms around her in protection, and if some wicked person had shot an arrow at her, then any man born would willingly have stood between her and the shaft. Those were my emotions on sight of the girl, and I read exactly the same in Morganus, Secundus and the bodyguards. But such emotions must be set aside by a detective agent. Or at least, he must do his best in that respect, though sometimes it is very hard.

Meanwhile she was chattering something to herself. It was the same words over and over again. She never even looked at us as we entered the room. I briefly looked round. There was a desk with papers and pens, there were some cupboards and Celsus's armour and weapons on stands: two full sets, both parade armour and battle dress. Then there were some boxes of book-rolls, a storage chest, and more of the big silver lamps. Celsus had obviously liked plenty of light in the dark nights.

'Lady Viola?' I said, but she ignored me. I stood forward and put a hand on her shoulder. She felt cold. She ignored me and kept up her chant.

'She was like that with me, your worship,' said Secundus, 'and she knows me real well. She always has a smile for me, and a little word.'

I nodded and took her hands. I turned them over and looked into the palms. There was a smear of blood on her left hand.

I looked at her face but could read nothing. So I listened to her chanting. She was using a Celtic Britannic dialect. I speak Latin, Greek, Hebrew and other languages but I am weak on Celtic Britannic because it is an alien tongue, violently different from the civilised languages of the Mediterranean. Thus I stumble in Britannic, and struggle to be understood. But Morganus was fluent.

'What's she saying?' I asked him. Morganus leaned forward and concentrated.

'It's a prayer,' he said. 'A rhyming prayer. It goes something like,' he said, *Blessed be the gods of Catuvellaunia. Blessed be their glory. Blessed be Artos, and Barant and Silunii.* She's reciting a list of gods. The Catuvellauni tribal gods. She's Catuvellauni herself, I think. They're pale-skinned like her, and their women are small.' He frowned. 'But I can't follow her very well. She's mumbling and not speaking clearly.'

I nodded and did my best to get the girl to speak to me, or even acknowledge me. I addressed her in Latin, then Greek and I got Morganus to speak to her in Britannic, and it was all useless. I tried shaking her, patting her cheek, and even considered slapping her—but I could not bring myself to do that, and in any case, she just ignored us. She was deep in some sort of hypnotic trance, and my imagination screamed *druids*.

So we all went back into the big room, and I spoke to Secundus.

'Don't leave her alone,' I said, 'not for an instant, and don't let her near any sort of blade or weapon.'

'Yes, Your Worship,' he said, and frowned. 'Of course, Your Worship! Right you are, Your Worship! Wouldn't do anything else, Your Worship!' He was actually angry. He was chastising me for suggesting he would *not* take good care of her. Then there was a brief silence, and we all listened to the muffled sound of the girl's voice coming from the office.

'Now what?' said Morganus.

'Give me a moment,' I replied, and thought a while, and then pursued the only line of inquiry that seemed open.

'How did the Lady Viola get on with Celsus? I asked Secundus, and I saw the flash of alarm in his face. It told me that all was not perfect between Celsus and his girl. But Secundus licked his lips in anxiety.

'It's more than me rank's worth,' he said. 'More than me job's worth to talk about the honoured gentlemen. You have to keep your mouth shut in my job.'

'Optio,' I said, 'I see that there was trouble between Lady Viola and Tribune Celsus. So why not tell me the rest?' He gasped, and joined the long list of those who believe I work magic. He blinked and searched for words.

'It wasn't that bad,' he said. 'I mean it's just that he—His Honour—he was… well… he was…'

'Go on,' I said.

'He was a selfish little sod—oh gods of Rome, I never said that, I never said it—it's just that he never made no fuss of her, and he was selfish with her. Him—the tribune—he was always threatening to sell her if she didn't behave. But that's all there was to it. He didn't knock her about or anything. He just didn't care for her very much, and she didn't like him.'

I got no more from him than that, and Morganus and I left soon after, having warned Secundus once more not to leave the Lady Viola alone. We spoke briefly on the timber gallery before going downstairs.

'So what did we learn?' said Morganus.

'She did it, all right,' I said, and I don't think this has anything to do with the Legate or the legion, and I don't think it's really got anything to do with Celsus or the lady. There wasn't enough cause there for any woman—let alone a slave—to do murder.'

'No,' said Morganus. 'Slaves are bred up to expect bad treatment and make no fuss. It's flogged into them.'

'Indeed,' I said, 'and as for threatening to sell her, she'd go for a fortune to a master who valued her because of it.'

'Of course,' said Morganus, 'Celsus was stupid not to appreciate her. Who wouldn't want a girl like that?'

'Who wouldn't?' said one of the bodyguards.

'Yeah!' said the rest, and Morganus nodded rather than blasting their ears for so great an insubordination as speaking without permission.

'And yet she stuck a knife in his throat like a professional assassin,' I said. 'How did she know how to do that? Exotic girls are taught dancing, music, elocution and sexual technique. They're not instructed in the martial arts!'

'So?' said Morganus.

'So I think the Llegate will be pleased, because this is nothing to do with him, and we can go down and tell him that, right now.' I waved a hand as if to brush away the Legate's worries. 'He can tell the world that Celsus bought a slave-girl who went mad, and there's nothing more to be said. It's like buying a dog that goes mad and bites.'

'But…' said Morganus. 'You're going to say *but.*'

'But,' I said, 'I think this is bad in other ways.'

'What ways?'

'You said this was worse than murder, didn't you?'

'It is!'

'A stain on Roman honour? That's what you said, didn't you?'

'Yes!'

'Then we've got to go to Petros. I want to speak to that druid he's got hidden away.'

Chapter 5

We had to wait to see Petros. As the senior administrator of Britannia he was always loaded with work and was losing the intense black of his hair even then, and going grey with worry. Thus I wrote to him the night we came back from the tribunes' block. In fact, I wrote several times, with legionary runners going to and fro at top speed. I received replies pleading a packed timetable, then after two days, one of Petros's six attendants came personally to the fortress. He was Primus, the senior of the six.

Primus was brought to the Pprincipia, where Morganus was working. Then I was summoned from pacing up and down with nothing to do, and taken to a room in the Pprincipia that was emptied of clerks so that we could speak in private. The room contained a model of the chariot racing stadium that the legion would build for the governor's games. Romans like models. They are good at them and the models do indeed assist understanding of great construction projects. This one was complete with little chariots, horses and outriders and even the packed masses of spectators. It was beautifully made. Morganus was there when I arrived and his bodyguards were behind him, gazing entranced at the stadium model, already hearing the roar of chariots in their imaginations. Meanwhile Morganus handed me a wax tablet that he had just received from Primus.

'This is from Petros,' he said, 'An invitation to Government House.' He looked at Primus, who bowed politely. 'At least that's what *he* says.' Morganus sniffed as if at a bad smell. 'It's in Greek,' he added. Morganus did not speak or read Greek. Primus bowed again.

'It is a formal occasion, Honoured Sir.' Morganus sighed.
'It means I have to take a full-dress century and the Eagle.'
'Does it?' I said.
'Oh yes!' said Primus.
'Formal meetings, by Hercules,' said Morganus. 'When an officer's been killed and we should be finding out who did it and why.'
Primus bowed yet again.
'With utmost respect, Honoured Sir,' he said, 'Petros, my learned master has done his best in this regard, but cannot circumvent protocol.'
Morganus sighed, and I felt uneasy because Roman protocol was another mystery to me. So I looked at the tablet. The message was in neat, round letters, in Petros's own hand. Even his writing was beautiful. It was Athenian cursive, as clear as any scribe's best work. I read it.

From Petros of Athens, Secretary to His Grace the Governor of Britannia,

To Morganus and Ikaros, greeting!

The vicissitudes of duty, at this time of preparation for extensive games and entertainments, regrettably prevent my being able to allocate time to a personal meeting with Your Honoured and Worshipful selves. But by the beneficence of His Grace my Master—the Noble Marcus Ostorius Cerealis Teutonius, Chief Priest and Governor of Britannia, you are summoned to attend a provincial senatorial levee at the fourth hour of tomorrow during which levee I firmly promise some time for conversation with your selves.

So we attended Government House at the fourth hour of the next day. I wore my best cloak and tunic, Morganus was turned out in gilded armour, and his bodyguards and a full century of the Twentieth's first cohort came behind, in perfect step with bugles blowing. We quick-marched to Government House, and found a great business and clamour at the foot of the steps. Important men were arriving in litters bourn by teams of slaves, with other slaves fussing about, and there was a mighty chatter of voices and much pompous bowing of one vastly-rich man to another, and a display of togas by those few who were citizens, and of costly robes by the majority who were not.

It was comical. It was a piece of theatre. But it was deadly serious too, because here were the great and the rich of the province, all wanting to be first up the steps, and waving their arms and stamping their feet and shouting, because for any man who wants to get on in the Roman Empire—citizens and non-citizens alike—there is nothing that exercises more passion than *precedence*: who goes first on formal occasions.

'Look at the guard commander,' said Morganus as we marched forward. 'You could almost feel sorry for him!' He sneered as he said it, but with a miniscule drop of sympathy. the Governor's Guard were in ranks on the steps of Government House, in their antique armour and plumes and spears, and it was the duty of the commander—always a nobleman of senatorial rank—to make the fearful decisions on precedence, such as who goes first: an impoverished Roman citizen or a Celtic millionaire? A Greek shipping magnate or a Jewish banker? Some lucky few were already ascending the steps, noses in air, attended by body slaves, and waving condescendingly to those below.

But everyone gave way to Morganus and his men, because we were led by the legion's sacred and holy Eagle, carried by a standard-bearer with a lion-skin over his armour. In the Roman world, any officer on parade behind a legionary eagle directly represents the Emperor Himself, and takes precedence over every living thing that breathes. That is the Romans. That is how their minds work.

Seeing the Eagle, even the traditional hostility between the guards and the legion had to be suspended. The guard commander pushed aside the millionaires and citizens, bawled out an order and he and his men gave full, formal salute to the Twentieth Legion's eagle as Morganus and his troops came to a halt.

'Hail Caesar! Hail Caesar! Hail Caesar!' roared the commander and his men.

'Hail Caesar! Hail Caesar! Hail Caesar!' roared Morganus and his men in reply. It was all very proper and smart. Even I joined in at the third 'Hail Caesar' having, by then, learned the words: it seemed the proper thing to do. Then Morganus presented his formal summons, the guard commander read it, and made a business of bowing to the Eagle, then left his deputy in charge of the steps and *personally* led us into Government House and to the formal reception hall.

Crunch, crunch, crunch! went the nailed boots on the steps, and all the bugles gave fanfare.

The formal reception room was everything that might be expected. It was huge, high, echoing, marble-clad, lit by elaborate windows, and lined with sculpture: mainly Roman imitation of Greek originals. But the mosaic floor was intricate and well done, because Romans are good at that, and the fine white plaster of the walls was totally covered in elaborate paintings of scenes from classical mythology. The paintings were obviously done by Greeks and were excellent.

His Grace the Governor—Teutonius—sat on a throne at the far end of the hall, surrounded by his personal staff and slaves, which included Petros and his six shaven-heads. They were all on a marble platform raised three feet from the floor, with steps in the centre for access. The Governor wore a senatorial toga with its broad purple stripe, and he had covered his head with a fold of the draped cloth, as Romans do on formal or holy occasions. Others in his staff who were also citizens wore their togas likewise, as did a small group of the great and good who were already in the hall when we entered. These men turned towards us as we marched in, then stood aside, and bowed to the eagle. I noted that they bowed not merely out of protocol but with obvious reverence for this symbol of Roman military power. They seemed genuinely pleased to see us.

So we tramped in, over 160 strong, the first cohort having double-sized centuries. Then we lined up in front of the platform, marked time with knees going up and down, and finally stamped into stillness to a command from Morganus. Att least, the troops lined up and marked time. I was always embarrassed on these occasions, not knowing whether I should drill with the rest, or stand aside, so I shuffled my feet somewhat and was relieved when it all stopped.

As it did, Teutonius rose from his throne and extended a hand to Morganus, who climbed the few steps and clasped Teutonius' hand, the pair of them maintaining formal, Roman faces—stern and unsmiling—as they gave formal greeting. Teutonius spoke first.

'Hail, Leonius Morganus Fortis Victrix! First javelin! Father of the Twentieth Legion, Hero of the Roman army, whose feats of valour…'

I turn aside from recording the full boredom of this life-sapping, soul-draining conversation, save to say that each man gave a full and proper list of the other's many titles and achievements, while everybody else gave polite applause: civilians clapping their hands, and soldiers stamping feet. Inevitably my mind wandered, and I fell into a contemplation of Governor Teutonius.

He was a man in his forties, handsome, serious and patrician. He was the very image of everything that a Roman should be, with manly bearing and easy in the powers that he wielded as governor of an imperial province. He bore the nickname Teutonius in honour of his spectacular military victories against the German hordes beyond the Rhine. He came of noble blood and was extraordinarily trusted by the Empire, because the governor of Britannia commanded the biggest army in the Roman world and might therefore, should he become ambitions, constitute a threat to the Emperor Himself. Rome dealt with this by appointing other noblemen to the powerful posts of Lord Chief Justice of Britannia, and Procurator Fiscal of Britannia, such that the three great men would constantly be rivals—each one against two others—leaving them no time to act against the Emperor.

This very Roman solution to a very Roman problem would have worked well enough by itself. But in Teutonius' case there was another check on ambition, and that was Petros of Athens, who now stood where he always stood on such occasions: just behind Teutonius' right elbow, occasionally leaning forward to whisper into his master's ear, occasionally leaning backwards for briefing from his six attendants. This, because just as Teutonius' military victories had really been won by the legions under his command—which means the centurions who ran those legions—Teutonius' political victories had really been won by Petros of Athens, who advised Teutonius in all things. He did so because the handsome, noble and splendid Teutonius was distinguished by a spectacularly dull mind and a formidable inability to understand anything difficult. But no matter. Not when Petros stood at his elbow, where he had stood since the two of them were children.

But finally the formalities ended, and I realised that Teutonius was talking to me, and that I had not been listening. He spoke on, in the Athenian Greek he had learned as a boy when learning comes easy.

'...therefore, Ikaros of Apollonis, we express our gratitude for your inestimably valuable assistance in past times,' he said, 'which assistance reflected such credit upon your late master.' Fright stabbed. I had offended against Romans protocol! I had ignored the Governorin his own palace! But I saw Petros lean forward.

'May it please Your Grace,' he said to Teutonius in Greek, 'I fear that the unfortunate Ikaros of Apollonis is entirely overcome with reticent modesty regarding his past services to your noble self.' He smiled, gave a little nod of encouragement to Teutonius, and such was the control of slave over master that Teutonius—drilled by a lifetime of acting on Petros's advice—likewise smiled.

'Ha ha,' said Petros: a gentle laugh, then a small nod to Teutonius.

'Ha ha!' said Teutonius, and beamed upon me, and then laughed loudly, and all the chamber laughed, and I was thereby blessed as a good servant, standing in awe of his betters, and not cursed as a smart-arsed Greek away in his daydreams when the Governor was talking to him.

'I am forever at Your Grace's service,' I said and bowed low.

'Ahhhhh,' said all the room, in approval of a dog that knows its master.

Then Petros whispered to Teutonius and Teutonius smiled and gave a hand-gesture of approval. Petros bowed and stepped back, and Primus the shaven-head stepped into his place, and the five others closed ranks behind him as Petros slipped through the assembly like an eel through the reeds, and arrived at my side as Teutonius exchanged more formal words with Morganus. Around me the bodyguards and troops stood to attention, and the civilians in their togas smiled constantly towards Teutonius, awaiting their turn at the foot of the throne.

The two leaders of these civilians were mature men, grey-haired and bearded. I read them as consummate politicians representing some common interest, since they exchanged confidences in whispers and were attended by a considerable staff of followers, all of them citizens in togas. I also noticed an oddity: none of them looked like men bred up in Italia. They had a slightly eastern look, like Jews or Syrians.

'Follow me,' said Petros. We bowed to the throne and I followed. We went to a side room, laid out for a feast: tables laden with food, slaves ready with wine. 'Over here,' he said and we went to the far end by a line of long windows, too far from the slaves to be heard. 'We can talk here,' said Petros, switching to Athenian Greek. 'This is the optimum that I am able to contrive.' He shook his head. 'The mind cannot conceive of greater complexity than the bringing together—here on the edge of the universe—of some of the Empire's best-loved, precious darlings: actors, racing drivers and gladiators. Half of them hate the other half as rivals, all of them are terrified of the ocean crossing, and their agents are doubling their fees with every letter.' He gave a theatrical groan. 'Compared with this,' he said, 'the military conquest of Britannia was nothing!'

I smiled, and he nodded and raised arms, though somewhat in jest. 'But praised be the gods of Greece and Rome,' he said.

'Praised be!' I said and raised arms.

'I give praise because I have just discovered powerful allies in my task of organising the games!'

'Allies?' I said,

'Allies indeed! Did you notice the group of citizens standing before His Grace when you entered?' I nodded, he continued. 'They were the decurions of the city council of the veterans' colony of Flavensum, led by their two duovirs: Bethsidus and Solis.'

I nodded. A city council was a senate in miniature, except that the members were called decurions, not senators, and the two chairmen were duovirs, not consuls. There were always two duovirs, just as there were always two consuls, so that no man ever had too much power. That was standard Roman practice throughout the Empire.

'Flavensum is a city, is it not?' I said. 'On the Welsh borders?'

'Yes. It is a colony and a city, and an opulent colony at that. They have mines and foundries for copper and tin, and good farming lad. They are rich and they are loyal and they have vowed to put a huge sum of money into the games. And there is still more! It is politically vital that each of the committees and sub-committees running the games shall be led by a Roman citizen.'

'Is that indeed the case?' I asked. 'Irrespective of that citizen's merit and aptitude?'

He smiled at my innocence and explained.

'Merit and aptitude can be supplied by talented slaves,' he said. 'What resonates melodiously is that citizens should be *seen* to be in charge. But unfortunately—in Britannia—citizens are in limited supply, except in the veterans' colony of Flavensum. Thus, the colony will supply large numbers of young men for this duty.'

'Ah!' I said. 'So that explains why the Flavensum officials were given precedence over everyone else at today's levee.'

'You are correct,' he said.

'I see,' I said, 'But where do they come from? They don't look entirely Roman.'

'Oh but they are,' he said, 'they are the sons and grandsons of an auxiliary unit given citizenship, years ago. They were given citizenship and formed a colony.' He smiled. 'If my assistants were here they would tell you precisely when the colony was founded, and the original homeland of the veterans.' He nodded. 'So, yes, their fathers came from somewhere out east but now they are true Romans and they will pay for the games, and will run games.'

'So shall the Games proceed?' I asked. 'The governor's games?'

'And why not?' he said.

'Did you not read my letters?' I asked.

'Yes,' he said.

'So: we know that there is trouble in the Celtic kingdoms,' I said, 'and we know that at least one druid has cursed the Governor and his games.'

'The druid that killed himself?' asked Petros.

'Yes.' I said. 'He that we caught.'

'Go on.'

'And now that poor, unfortunate girl has been caused to kill Celsus.'

'*Poor* girl? *Unfortunate* girl? Were you that much entranced with her?' I ignored that.

'She was—is—in a hypnotic trance,' I said, 'and I believe that to be the work of druids because I am not aware of any others in Britannia who are masters of hypnosis.' I stared hard at him. 'Do you know better?' He shook his head.

'But why should they do that?' he said. 'Make her kill Celsus?'

'To dishonour the Empire. Morganus says it is an insult to kill the commander of men who've just been made citizens.'

Petros frowned.

'Yes. I suppose it is. So what would you have me do?'

'First, there is a small thing,' I said.

'Oh?' said Petros. 'I become suspicious when you say that.'

'If Celsus' family prosecute the girl...' I said.

'Which undoubtedly they will!'

'Yes, yes. If so, then the law says that, as a slave, she must be interrogated under torture.'

'Of course,' he said, 'that is perfectly normal and proper. It is the only way to get the truth out of slaves. They are cunning and devious.'

'Perhaps,' I said. 'But I ask you as a favour—as one Greek to another—to spare her that.'

He spread hands in a pretended gesture of surprise, and raised his eyebrows.

'How wonderful,' he said, 'to see so great a philosopher, so enslaved by a pretty face.' He was probably correct, but I protested.

'That is not the point,' I said. 'The point is that she is insane—or something close to it—and the law makes exception for the insane.'

'Yes,' he said. 'Under Roman law we do not torture lunatics.'

He thought about that. 'But what if she emerges from this hypnotic trance? I am no expert in the matter, but I believe that such trances are not permanent. And then,' he shrugged, 'Celsus' family would insist on torture, as indeed is their right.' He looked closely at me and I saw a mixture of pity and amusement in his eyes. 'Pah!' he said. 'I cannot bear the sorrowful look on your face.' He paused and thought, and came to a decision. 'I cannot bear it. So this is what I shall do… as a favour from one Greek to another.'

'Yes?' I said.

'Torture is a legal process. It must be supervised by a magistrate who is supposed to be present to record evidence.' I nodded. 'But a magistrate will usually avoid so unpleasant an experience and will leave everything to the professional torturers.' I nodded again, 'So I shall chose the torturer and contrive that the torture be a pretence. The girl will have to be taken to his workshop, but she will not be touched. In fact,' he added, 'you might be surprised how often this happens. Often a slave is in such terror that he blurts out everything and the torturers cannot be bothered to work on him, because they are as work-shy as any other craftsman, given the chance.'

'Ah!' I said. 'Then can she be warned in advance? So that she will not be in fear?'

'Gods of Greece!' he said. 'Shall we give her a sack of gold and a free pardon?'

'No,' I said, 'and I truly thank you.'

He laughed. 'You said that this was the small thing. What else do you advise?'

'I would respectfully suggest,' I said, 'that you take particular care of these celebrated and famous persons who are being brought into Britannia for the games.'

'My dear Apollonite,' he said, 'Do you imagine—even in your dreams—that I am not already doing precisely that? I have armed guards everywhere because if I lose even one of these precious darlings, then I am damned across the Styx and beyond.'

I smiled. 'Is it truly that bad?'

'Have you ever dealt with famous actors, or racing drivers? Or even gladiators?'

'No,' I said.

'Then be thankful!'

'And there's something else,' I said.

'What?'

I lowered my voice. 'I need to speak to a druid. The one you have hidden. I need to know how they turned that girl's mind.'

Petros fell silent. He looked away. He turned his back on me.

'Grant me a courtesy,' he said.

'Yes?'

'Allow me to form my thoughts before you read them.' He reflected a while, then turned and faced me.

'Listen to me, Apollonite!'

'I am listening.'

'This is a matter so secret that only three men know the truth apart from myself, and you will be the fourth. Even Morganus must not know what I am about to tell you.'

'No!' I said. 'He must know. He is my brother in arms. I trust him absolutely and ask you to trust him. He is the most loyal Roman in the Empire.'

'So is Teutonius,' said Petros, 'yet *he* does not know.'

I sighed. 'I imagine that there is much that Teutonius does not know,' I said. 'But that is entirely different. If Morganus gives his word you can trust him unto death.'

'Death?' said Petros. 'All druids are sentenced to death, and not only druids but those who commune with them. And this is not tribal law, or provincial law, but an imperial edict, because druids are damned and cursed by the Empire. Even His Grace could be put to death for contact with a druid, if his rivals in Rome found out.'

'Ahhh,' I said, reading the sub-text. 'So it is *political.* Druids are allowed in the client kingdoms, and a druid can be kept as a guest, and all this is accepted… unless the wrong people find out.' He said nothing, but bowed. 'So where is he?' I said. 'Where have you put your druid?'

'You will not believe me when I tell you,' he replied.

Chapter 6

Morganus and I walked through the Twentieth Legion's fortress, heading towards the hospital, with the four bodyguards behind us. They would not—could not—be with us throughout the whole of this particular expedition, but to leave them behind entirely would only have drawn unwanted attention to what we were doing, since they were as much a sign of Morganus' rank as the swan-feather crest on his helmet. Otherwise, everything was normal, and men stood to attention as we passed, and Morganus acknowledged them with a wave of his vine staff.

'It makes sense that it's here,' I said, 'in the fortress.' But my words were overcome by the swift *tramp-tramp-tramp* of a century of young soldiers doubling past, under training. They were in full marching kit, with pack-sticks on shoulders and leather covers on their armour and shields.

'Leff-two-three-four! Leff-two-three-four!' cried their centurion, then 'Right... *face!*' and ten ranks, eight abreast, went past, sweating and loaded, each man turning his head towards their first javelin.

'Legionis ...*Pater!*' they yelled in formal Latin, saluting Morganus as Father of the Legion, and Morganus stood to attention, and raised right arm in salute, until they had gone past.

'You were saying?' he said, and we walked on.

'It makes sense. It has to be here because a legionary fortress is the only place in Britannia where there are no natives: no Celts, no Gauls, no slaves. Only Romans, or auxiliaries.'

'I wouldn't be too sure of the auxiliaries,' said Morganus, 'they have some funny gods.'

'I know,' I said, 'so even they are kept out.'

'Ah,' said Morganus, 'here we are.'

The Legion's hospital was on the west side of the fortress, upwind of any smoke or smells, where it could get the fresh air and such sunshine as Britannia allows. It was a long, low, single-story building: an assortment of buildings, really. It was timber-built, plastered over, and had wings for the separate wards. It was enclosed by a white-painted fence, and planted all around with flower beds, that were half herb garden for medicines and half bright colours to cheer up the sick and wounded.

The Surgeon General, obviously a Greek, was waiting at the gate. His name was Agamades of Cos, and he was a small, swarthy man who looked intelligent. He stood with his staff lined up behind him: all two dozen of them, because any visit from the First Javelin was an important event. So the medics, orderlies and dressers were lined up in rows. The soldiers among them stood to attention, while the civilians bowed.

'Honoured Sir, be welcome!' said the Surgeon General.

'Honoured Sir, be welcome!' said the rest.

'I likewise welcome this visit of inspection, Honoured Morganus' said the Surgeon General, 'and my staff would be grateful if you would first accept our hospitality.' He bowed gracefully and awaited our response.

'We accept with cheerful gratitude,' said Morganus because the prepared story—which would conceal our real purpose—was that he and I would inspect the hospital, to consider a request for repairs. So we left the bodyguards outside—where they stayed—and Morganus and I had to cram into the Surgeon General's office, since the hospital had no reception rooms, and then we had to sit with him for an appropriate time while we were offered dishes of olives, cheese and pickles, followed by cakes. There was also a rather good wine, served in such large and cheerful cups that Morganus—who took only sips—stared as I finished my first and looked for a second. After that we toured the hospital, which was interesting: wards, beds, pharmacy, bath house, operating room and a surgical instrument store. I had myself studied medicine for three years, before I gave it up for engineering, so the tour stirred old memories. The hospital was a typical legionary institution:

well designed, well run and immaculately clean, so the only problem was finding anything wrong, but Agamades managed to discover flaws in the plumbing and damp patches in the lower walls of one ward.

Most of the hospital staff were dismissed to their duties before the tour, but one orderly-clerk, another Greek named Sotirios, followed Agamades throughout, taking notes of the agreed repair work. Once we were done, and back in Agamades' office, the notes were handed to Agamades for himself and Morganus to sign. Then Agamades gave back the notes, and told Sotirios the clerk to sit with us. Morganus looked surprised, but Agamades, the Surgeon General, explained.

'Honoured Sir,' he said to Morganus, pointing to the clerk, 'Sotirios of Cos is our accountant and treasurer, and also chief priest of the hospital, serving the god Mercury whose serpent-twined staff is the emblem of healing.'

Sotirios gave a small bow and raised hands. 'Praised be the staff of Mercury!' he said.

He was a broad-framed, young man with dark hair on his arms. He was strong in the limbs and looked like a typical peasant from the island of Cos, but he was obviously an educated man.

'Praised be the staff of Mercury!' we all said, and raised hands.

So an accountant was chief priest? That seemed odd to me, though I was well aware that Roman priests are not holy men, but public officials doing a job no more special to Romans than running the baths or libraries. That is why the Emperor is always chief priest of the Empire, and a governor always chief priest of a province. To Romans, worship of the gods is a bureaucratic process, whereby the gods grant good fortune in exchange for ceremony and worship. It is a business arrangement.

'Can we talk now?' said Morganus. 'We've wasted half the morning already!'

'We can talk, Honoured Sir,' said Agamades, 'though I must insist that the deception was entirely necessary.'

Morganus looked at Sotirios. 'Does he know everything?' he said.

'Yes,' said Agamades, 'because this is how we manage the problem.'

'Go on,' said Morganus.

'Nobody can approach this… er… man,'

'The druid?' I said. Agamades frowned.

'We never use that word,' he said, 'What if someone were to hear?'

'I apologise,' I said, 'Please continue.' He nodded.

'No Celt may approach the man,' he said. 'No Celt, nor any person who is superstitious, or simple minded, or lacking in education.' He looked at me. 'I assume you know why?'

'Yes,' I said. 'For fear of hypnosis.'

'Correct!' he said. 'Only men of education can resist his power, and even they can resist only if warned in advance. So it is best that only Greeks should go near him.'

'Huh!' said Morganus.

'I mean no offence, most Honoured Sir,' said Agamades, 'but problems of the mind are best solved by Greeks.'

'Very likely,' said Morganus. 'But I assume that *this* Roman is allowed in?' He tapped his chest. But Agamades dithered.

'I am responsible for your safety,' he said. 'Responsible to Petros.'

'Agamades,' I said, 'the honoured Morganus and I have faced worse than this.'

'Right!' said Morganus. 'So can we get on?' Agamades shrugged his shoulders and stood up, bowed, and went to a door on the opposite side of the office to the one we came in by.

'This door leads to the private garden of the previous surgeon general,' said Agamades. 'There's a summer house that we've converted into a bedroom.' He took a key from his pouch and put it into a heavy lock in the door. 'The lock is to keep out anyone who might wander in by mistake,' he said. 'The man himself knows that this is his only safe refuge, and he couldn't escape even if he wanted to, as you will soon see.' He turned the lock and held open the door. 'Sotirios will go with you,' he said. 'He knows everything, and I have important duties.'

I looked at Agamades. He was not telling the truth. His face said that he was afraid of the druid.

Morganus, Sotirios and I went out into the garden and Agamades closed the door behind us. The garden was very pretty, planted with flowering shrubs, and with multi-colour paving slabs for footpaths. There was also the inevitable fountain in the middle, since Romans build them everywhere, even in cold Britannia. There was indeed a summer house in one corner, large and overgrown with greenery, and there was a high fence all around, rising to more than the height of a man to give total privacy.

But I hardly noticed any of this because I was staring at a grotesque figure that dominated this quiet, restful place.

He was Dernfradour Bradowr, who had been chief druid of the Catuvallauni tribe until he fell out with Maligoterix of the Regni. I stared at Bradowr. He had been blinded with hot irons that had been plunged into his eyes, searing his face. His nose and ears had been sliced off, and he had been scalped, such that the crown of his head was brown-stained bone without flesh, and he had no legs beneath the knees. It was hard to believe that he was still alive.

He was seated in a Roman, basket-work chair fitted with wheels, and he held a stick in each hand to push against the ground and thereby move himself about, or turn around. I shuddered at his mutilations. The worst of it was the loss of his nose, leaving a ghastly hole, divided by a septum of bone.

Sotirios saw my expression.

'Maligoterix's men got to him before our rescue team,' he said. 'Maligoterix sent tribal assassins: cennad angau. They kill fast or slow according to instruction, and this time it was slow, *very* slow, and they save the blinding till last so the victim can see what's being done to him. Our men arrived before they'd quite finished, and chopped the lot of them. But they'd had him for hours.' He looked at me with a helpless expression on his face. 'We did what we could, when we got him here.'

'What happened to his legs?' I asked.

'They skinned him from the feet up, but they stopped at the knees so as not to kill him too fast. So we amputated what we couldn't save, and healed the rest.'

We looked at the ruined creature, and my first impulse was to wonder why we had been so afraid of him. He sat in the weak Britannic sunshine, and did not move. He was in the centre of the garden near the fountain, about thirty feet off, and from the look of him I thought we were wasting our time here.

'Is he sane?' said Morganus. 'Can any man suffer like that and not go mad?'

'I hear your every word,' said Bradowr in good Latin. 'We of the elect are strong in mind.' His voice was clear, despite all his afflictions. 'You may approach and declare your business.'

He spoke as if he were a monarch among courtiers, and I recalled Petross warning that torture does not work on druids. I learned in later years that they are trained up from childhood to control pain. They recite prayers, invoke the gods, and send the mind elsewhere. It is uncanny, yet they can do it. By this means Bradowr had kept his mind intact despite all that was done to him.

'Be careful,' said Sotirios, 'you don't know him as I do.' So we walked forward, and Bradowr grew more hideous at every pace.

'Sotirios?' he said. 'I hear your footsteps, my donkey: you who must put me on the chamber pot, and carry me to bed. Who do you bring before me?'

'I bring Morganus, spear of the Twentieth, and Ikaros of Apollonis,' said Sotirios, and the mutilated head nodded.

'A Roman and a Greek?' said Bradowr. 'Can a Roman do nothing without a Greek? Can he not even piss without a Greek to hold his dick? Can he…' and he rambled and cursed for some while until I began to think that his mind was ruined after all. But then I detected a rhythmic pattern in his ramblings, and Sotirios gave warning.

'Ikaros!' he said. 'Don't listen!' He spoke just an instant after I detected the danger for myself, but I was given sharp understanding of why even Agamades the Surgeon General was afraid of Bradowr, and I was horrified to see that Morganus' eyes had closed and his jaw hung slack. I shook him hard and he staggered, awoke, and made the bull sign.

'Mithras!' he cried, calling on his patron god, while the druid laughed and laughed.

'Greeks and Romans,' he said. 'We were here before you, and will be here when you are gone. You know so very little.'

'Perhaps,' I said, 'but Maligoterix himself failed to put me into a trance, whereas he did what he pleased with you!'

It was a cheap and cruel thing to say—there is no honour in taking advantage of a cripple in a chair. But what I said was true. Maligoterix had indeed tried—and failed—to hypnotise me, and in any case I share the Roman detestation of druids. So I was cheap and cruel and Bradowr threw a druidic temper tantrum as Celts do. It is a weakness they have, that—by the grace of the gods—may they never understand and correct. When he calmed down, I began my questioning, which proved surprisingly easy, because Bradowr took opportunity to put me—and Rome—in our place as lesser beings than himself. He did so because of another fault in the druidic mind: they are fearfully vain and especially love to show a Greek how clever they are. I think this is because Greeks are supreme in intellect, and the druids know it. But perhaps that is my own vanity, as a Greek.

Thus, first I told him about the murder of Tribune Celsus and about the girl Viola. I told him everything I knew, because there was no reason not to, and I needed his advice. I even got Morganus to repeat the Britannic chant that the Lady Viola had uttered. Bradowr nodded at all this, as if he already knew. Perhaps he did, or perhaps he pretended to, in order to belittle me. I suspect the latter. But then, when I asked about the druidic hypnotic method, he told me everything without the least sign of reluctance. I think he was boasting.

'So how might a druid have turned the mind of the girl Viola?' I asked.

'By casting her into a trance and implanting those ideas which we wish to implant.'

'How would you do this?'

'In private conversation.'

'Just one conversation?'

He sneered at that. 'You are so ignorant!' he said. 'You Greeks, with your engineering and machines. What do you know of the real powers? The Earth magic? No, my little Greek, there would be many conversations, repeated conversations.' He nodded to himself and I wondered how many minds he had personally twisted. 'All subjects offer some resistance,' he said, 'according to their strength of will, and it is especially hard to implant an idea which is against the nature of the subject. Thus a slave girl cannot easily become a warrior, let alone an assassin! That would take months, many months.'

'Can you tell me more?' I said. 'How would this implanting be done?'

He thought about that.

'We would make use of things already present in the deep of the mind: those sacred items of faith that are passed on from mother to child.' He swivelled his head towards Morganus. 'You! iron man! You say the girl called on Artos, Barant and Siluni?'

'Yes,' said Morganus. 'She repeated those names over and over.'

'Artos the Hammer, Barant the Anvil, Siluni the Fire,' said Bradowr. 'These gods are the holy trinity of the Catuvellauni tribe, so the girl was indeed Catuvellauni.' The deformed head swivelled back towards me, searching for me. 'Where are you, little Greek?'

'Here,' I said.

'These are the gods who howl in the darkness. Every Catuvellauni child knows this, and they know why. But do *you* know why?'

'No,' I said.

'Then listen!' he said. 'The gods howl for the great fortress which stood for a thousand years as the pride of the Catuvellauni people. It was the home of the gods. It was the centre of faith. It was invincible to all the armies of men. It was the Catuvellauni soul.' He paused. 'Then the Romans came and built their temples on the holy places, and the gods were driven out into the darkness.' Bradowr fell silent, profoundly moved by his own words. Morganus beckoned and we walked away.

'I know what he's talking about,' he said. 'The Catuvellauni had an enormous hill fort at Camulodenum, up to the north east of Londinium. It was the main target of our invasion—Claudius's invasion—sixty years ago. So we bridged the Thames and went straight for it in two-and-a-half days' march. It was huge: rows of massive earth embankments with palisades and gateways and tens of thousands of men.'

'And?'

'We took it! The artillery kept their heads down, the engineers filled the ditches and the assault teams went in over the top.' He shrugged. 'Straight out of the drill book. Nothing special.'

'It was to them,' I said. 'The Catuvellauni and their gods.'

'If you say so,' he said. But Bradowr was talking again.

'Such an apocalypse is a wound in the subject's mind,' he said, 'and we would tell the subject that the wound can only be healed in a certain way, which in this case would be a knife in a Roman neck.' He turned his dead eyes towards me. 'There you have it, little Greek. Those are the principles and I leave it to your clever Greek mind, to work out the details.'

'So who did it?' I said. 'Was it you?'

He laughed aloud.

'No,' he said, 'it was Maligoterix. Who else could it have been? He is High Druid of all Britannia, and he curses your governor and his games and the curse was acted out first in the killing of Tribune Celsus, to throw shame on his command.'

I continued my questioning but we learned nothing more: nothing of importance. Soon after, Morganus and I left the hospital, thanking Sotirios and Agamades for their help. We walked back to Morganus' house, with the bodyguards behind us once more. We spoke in whispers so the bodyguards should not hear too much.

'So,' said Morganus, 'was it Maligoterix that turned Viola's mind?'

'I don't know,' I said. 'Bradowr hates Maligoterix and might want to put the blame on him.'

'Indeed!' said Morganus. 'Then do you think Bradowr did it himself?'

I shook my head. 'No! Bradowr said: we *would have* done this, we *would have* done that, and he didn't give us the details because he's never had to work them out. If he knew the details he'd have told us, just to show how clever he is. So it wasn't him.'

'So who did it? Who turned that girl into an assassin?'

'I don't know. But now we definitely know that there is a druidic plot to ruin the governor's games, and that Maligoterix may just possibly be the source of it.'

'So what do we do now?'

'We need to find out what the Lady Viola did over the past year, where she went and who she met, *especially* who she met.' I paused and turned over certain troubles that lay deep in my own mind. 'And I know who can help us find out.'

Chapter 7

It had been my intention immediately to investigate the Lady Viola's behaviour during the year after she was purchased by the tribune, Celsus. But something intervened which at first I thought a distraction. When Morganus and I returned to his house, we found a message waiting for me.

'This is for you,' said his wife, Morgana Callandra, as we entered the atrium, 'A runner brought it this morning: a slave boy. He said that no reply was needed.' She gave a small bow and handed me a wooden letter-tablet, something very neat and practical that might—just possibly—be a rare example of a Roman invention because it is something that we did *not* have in Apollonis. The tablets are very thin strips of wood about eight inches long, by three inches wide. They are made with a heavy plane, which shaves off strips of wood from blocks ready cut to size and shape. The strips are then soaked in water and pressed flat under weights. Finally they are scored down the middle so that they can be folded with the writing inside, then sealed for privacy, and an address written on the outside. The writing is usually in ink, and this tablet had my name on the outside. It read:

IKAROS OF APOLLONIS
At the house of Leonius Morganus, Fortis Victrix
LXX

I broke the seal, opened the tablet and read the letter.

'Interesting,' I said.

'What is it?' said Morganus.

It's from someone I met at Petros's reception on the day of His imperial Majesty's birthday.

'Gods bless His Majesty!' said Morganus.

'Indeed,' I said, looking down at the letter. 'It's from Gershom Bar Meshulam. He's an imperial slave. He's head of imports and revenue in the Procurator Fiscal's office.'

'Bar Meshulam? Sounds like a Jewish name,' said Morganus.

'It is,' I said. 'He's a Jew. They're clever people. Clever as Greeks.'

'Gods be praised for a miracle!' said Morganus. ' I never thought to hear you say such a thing.'

I smiled. 'So what does he want?' said Morganus, and I showed him the letter.

'It's an invitation,' I said, 'Gershom runs a dining club for other men with wide interests. They have a meal, then discussions on technical and scientific matters and they exchange letters with clubs in other provinces.'

'Aha!' said Morganus. 'Sounds like just the thing for you.' He studied the letter, 'so long as it's not political!'

'It isn't,' I said, 'Their patron is Petros of Athens.'

'Good,' said Morganus, 'So when's the next meeting?'

'Today at the sixth hour,' I said, 'It's at Gershom's home near Government House. He apologises for the short notice and absence of a proper invitation, but says I would be welcome to attend; and he says my name was proposed as a member by Petros himself.'

'Petros,' said Morganus, 'aren't you the favourite one!'

'Yes,' I said, 'and it wouldn't do to snub Petros, so I'd better attend.'

Morganus laughed. 'So you'll force yourself, will you? Just to be polite?'

I smiled.

So I attended, accompanied by the usual guard of auxiliaries, provided by Petros. I found a whole troop of them formed up outside Gershom's house, having safely delivered the imperials attending the meeting. These senior beings were in lively discussion at the entrance, which was large and formal, with a pediment over a pair of columns and steps leading up. I was amused to see a profoundly-worried auxiliary centurion facing the precedence problem, since the club members displayed every bit as much anxiety as any citizen or millionaire, over who should go first. Then Petros arrived, accompanied by legionaries not auxiliaries, to make clear his superior status. Everyone bowed, and I feared I might make envious enemies as he greeted me with a smile and led me forward, first up the stairs.

'My dear Ikaros!' he said, 'I give you good day and am pleased to welcome you into our club.' But the members gave a united purr of approval, and bowed and followed. Then I suppose the soldiers marched off to their barracks; I never asked. But they were there again, at the end of the evening, with torches lit to take us home.

Meanwhile, Gershom was waiting in the atrium with a retinue of house boys behind him. He was a tall man with dark eyes, an eagle-beak nose, and a large, bobbing larynx. He had a vigorous, physical presence even though he had the reputation of being a human abacus: capable of advanced calculations whereby he made ferocious appraisal of tax returns. He wore expensive robes and jewellery and—as an act of faith—his head was covered with a skull-cap, even indoors.

'Honoured Petros!' he said. 'I bid you welcome!' Then he turned to me. 'Ikaros of Apollonis: the famous engineer and mind-reader!' He took a step back, and raised a hand in pretended fear, but in the most friendly and cheerful manner. 'We must all take care what we think,' he said, 'in case you should look inside our heads!' and everybody laughed. It was a welcome kindness, because my strange gift is well known and it afflicts people with nervousness, causing them to avoid my company. This especially true of men, because men are competitive and perceive mind-reading as an unfair advantage: like a dagger in a wrestling match. This is the reason why I was so very lonely until I entered the house of Morganus. But Gershom, with his joke, had made the company easy with my presence—or at least that was his aim—and I was grateful.

After that, Gershom greeted everyone by name, and I recognised one of the company as a man I had already met, or rather seen. His name was Bethsidus: the grey-bearded leading man of the delegation from

Flavensum at the governor's levee. He greeted me politely as did all the rest, and we were led inside to a formal Roman dining room with places laid for nine guests. Or rather, to reflect Roman protocol, the room was *not* laid out for formal dining, with couches for reclining, since we were a mixture of free men and imperial slaves, and no slave—however high his status—may attend a formal dinner with a citizen. So we sat in chairs around a table, even if there were nine chairs, just as there would have been nine couches, on three sides of a square table, leaving a space in front for entertainment and speeches.

Petros had the place of honour next to Gershom and I sat between the man who ran the city's water supply, and the man who certified apartment blocks as fit for habitation. But the two men were more lively than their work suggested, and it was an entertaining evening, especially as the food—cooked according to Jewish practice—was excellent and the wine was superb.

After dinner, house boys swiftly cleared away the food and Gershom introduced the first speaker, who turned out to be the certifier of apartment blocks.

'Brothers and members,' he said, 'please give attention to Potamon of Corinth, who will compare the inflexions of the subjunctive mood in Greek and in Latin.'

When I mentioned this later to Morganus, he said he would prefer crucifixion to the discourse which followed, but I found it fascinating. Potamon was followed by talks on a variety of topics, including a new-drawn map of Britannia, a letter from Rome on a novel design for an aqueduct, and best of all a display of a wine dispenser that delivered a cup of wine when a coin was inserted into a slot. The owner and maker of the device was a Syrian named Dothan, son of Nathan. He was severely practical man: short in speech, with hands like a labourer, and his slaves brought in the device to his command. It was a pair of iron cylinders, bound together on a tripod base with a small furnace at the bottom, a spout to one side and a filling port at the top for wine.

Dothan explained the device. 'A boiler here,' he tapped the bottom of the large cylinder, 'raises steam by boiling water over a charcoal fire.'

'Ahh,' we all said.

'The steam goes in here,' Dothan tapped the smaller cylinder, 'which it fills, until a coin goes into the slot here,' he tapped the slot, which was shaped perfectly to admit a one-denarius coin. 'The coin drops into a mechanism that sends a jet of cold water into the steam cylinder, which condenses the steam, and the vacuum so caused, sucks a piston down, which acts on another mechanism to pump a cup full of wine out of the spout here,' he tapped the spout and smiled. 'The purchaser, of course must provide his own cup,' he added.

There was much technical discussion of this ingenious device, and I expressed the opinion that, if made larger, the device could drive mills, olive presses and other heavy machinery. But Dothan shook his head.

'It does a fine job just as it is,' he said, 'making money for me!' And everybody laughed. So I fell silent, thinking it impolite for a newcomer to press his opinions on the company, and I regretted ever after that I never argued more fiercely nor found time myself to investigate steam-powered machinery. But a man cannot do everything in one life.

Finally, when the evening ended and everyone else went home, I was detained by Petros and Gershom, who led me into another room with slaves bowing and opening doors.

'I hope you enjoyed the evening?' Petros asked me.

'Indeed I did!' I said. 'I don't often get the chance to talk to scholars.'

'Good, good,' said Petros, and slipped out of relaxation and into duty, as quick as changing a shoe.

'Honoured Gershom' he said, 'Please show us your library,' and we entered a large room floored with actual Persian carpets. Their colours were deep and gorgeous, they must have cost a fortune and I could barely bring myself to walk on them. Gershom bowed, smiled at me, and waved a hand.

'See,' he said, 'my pride and obsession.' I saw row upon row of wooden shelves, which ran entirely around three sides of the room. The shelves were beautifully polished, and were divided up with vertical partitions, forming a great number of pigeon-holes, each containing a book-scroll.

'Bring more light!' said Gershom to his boys, and they swiftly obeyed. 'Alas,' said Gershom, 'I'm nearly out of room!' He smiled and pointed out the very few empty spaces. 'I shall have to get a bigger apartment, or knock down some walls!' He laughed and I looked around. There were hundreds and hundreds of books. I would have asked about them, but Petros spoke first, impatient to get to the point: *his* point.

'Gershom is a specialist,' he said,. 'He is a historian,' Gershom smiled and spread hands in a modest, dismissive gesture. 'In this library,' said Petros, 'you will find every author from Pliny to Vitruvius, and all of them describing historical fact.'

Gershom nodded. 'Mine is not a library of the arts or philosophy,' he said. 'I've travelled the Empire, I've been collecting books all my life, and I concentrate on historical fact. I'm not interested in art or literature but actual events, historical events.' He paused and made a slight correction. 'That and current affairs,' he said, 'so long as they describe things that actually happen. So long as they report facts.'

'So,' said Petros to me, 'I bring you here, my inquisitorial agent, because events today, are usually the consequences of events in the past.' I nodded, because it was an obvious truth: had not druids turned the mind of the Lady Viola by playing upon the events of sixty years ago?'And therefore,' continued Petros, 'the honoured Gershom has most generously offered you free use of this invaluable library, whenever it might assist your inquiries.'

I thought of this as I walked back to Morganus' house with my escort. The city was dark asleep, there was a thin Britannic drizzle and I shivered in my cloak after so warm a dinner in a warm apartment. I thought of the new resource of inquiry that Petros—in his wisdom—had given me, and I stress that it was entirely the foresight of Petros and none of my own. The thought of Gershom's library made me think of another resource of inquiry that was now closed to me. I thought of slave gossip, that vast stream of knowledge that flows beneath Roman civilisation or any other civilisation that has slaves. It flows because slaves are everywhere and see everything, and the more the slaves, the more they see.

Thus slaves know things both high and low. They know in advance how the master will vote in an election and which charity the mistress will support next year. These matters are at least dignified, but slaves—sniggering, and listening behind doors—also know when the master wets the bed, and when the mistress gives her lover fellatio.

Then, once the household slaves know these things, they cannot wait to pass them on to every other slave of every other household in the city, because they meet other slaves in the streets, fountains, markets, theatres, wine-shops, temples and brothels. In all these places they gossip and chatter, exchanging the intimacies of their own households, for those of others, and they do it with relish, because it is highly entertaining and a good way to get back at their masters.

Such a waterfall of information had been invaluable to my past investigations, but it was now beyond my reach because I was living within the Roman army that had no slaves. It had none because the army had thousands of hands to do all the work, and because it specifically wanted to isolate itself from slave gossip in order to preserve its military secrets.

And so my mind turned to the life I led before Morganus and the army. I was once a prized exotic, property of a Celtic billionaire, now dead, who owned an enormous house—a whole city block—in Londinium. The details are in earlier volumes of my memoirs, but I mention here a certain person within that house who was very dear to me, and who was the centre of slave gossip, because everybody liked her and confided in her. In past times she had been of enormous help to me, but we parted badly and it would be a poor attempt at reconciliation if I were to approach her now, not for herself, but out of a wish to use her as a source of information.

She was a slave in the house of Fabius Gentilius Fortunus, son and heir of my late master, and her name was Allicanda.

Chapter 8

Some days later, Morgana Callandra was acting as my mother again. We stood in the atrium of Morganus's house. Morganus was there with his bodyguards and she was there with her daughters. It was a typical Roman moment, an instant in time displaying the ever-present truth that no man or woman does anything alone in the Roman world. There is no privacy. There are always others present: family, slaves, officials, neighbours. Even the men in the public latrines sit side-by-side discussing the weather and sport and politics.

'No!' said, Morgana Callandra. 'You can't go like that. Your boots are scuffed, you're wearing an old tunic, and your hair is half way down your back. You look like a barbarian, not a Greek!'

Morganus nodded solemnly and the bodyguards tried not to grin.

'He's in your care, Lady-my-Wife,' he said. 'I leave it to your judgement to dress him, but will you cut his hair yourself or shall I send one of the legion's barbers?'

'Leave it to me, Lord-my-Husband,' she said, with a grim expression, which all the daughters copied, nodding in emphasis. I suppose that is how daughters learn to be mothers.

'Ooof!' said Morganus, and stepped back as if in alarm at so fierce a woman. Then he became serious. 'Ikaros,' he said, 'I have to go. Work on the racing stadium begins today, and we have a strict schedule to meet. Two thousand regulars are on that job, and five hundred auxiliaries will be on duty to secure Petros's precious darlings: the racing drivers, actors and gladiators. We're expecting a shoal of them to arrive by Road from

Dubris soon, several dozen of them. The troops will have to be turned out knowing who they're supposed to be guarding, and where to take them. It's all got to be arranged, and it's down to me.'

'Yes,' I said, 'I understand.'

'Good,' he said. 'The bulldogs have to come with me,' he jabbed a thumb at his bodyguards, 'but I've arranged for men to escort you there and back tonight.'

'I don't need that,' I said. 'It's only a walk through the town.'

'Perhaps,' he said, 'but it will be at night, and even at the best of times there are men in this town who'd cut your throat for your cloak, never mind your purse, and now it's filling up with savages, come in for the games.'

'I don't need guards,' I said, 'I was a soldier once.'

'I know you were,' he said, 'but then you could go armed, and now you can't.' Everyone nodded because no slave wears a sword under Rome, not even an imperial slave. Of course I could have taken a heavy stick, since military training in my city had included both cudgel and quarterstaff drill, and I was adept at both. I had even won prizes with the quarterstaff. But the truth was, that for this particular appointment, I wanted to arrive quietly and not with clumping boots to mark me out as special.

'Look,' said Morganus, ' you'll have an escort and like it. Right! I'm off now and will be back very late.' He bowed to his wife, the bodyguards bowed to his wife, and Morgana Callandra and the daughters bowed in return. It was a military household after all, and Romans are innately formal. Then Morganus and his men left, and Morgana Callandra turned on me.

'You will give me your boots now,' she said, 'and you will go to your room, and put on the clothes that I have already laid out on your bed, and then you will present yourself back here as soon as possible.' All the daughters nodded, and then she smiled, and took the tablets I was holding, for setting down my thoughts on druidic hypnotism. 'Give me those,' she said, 'You work too much and you don't take care of yourself. You'll want to look your best, won't you?'

'Yes,' I said.

Later I sat in a chair, wearing the clothes Morgana Callandra had chosen, and the boots that one of the daughters had cleaned. We were in the kitchen, which was large, warm, and well-equipped, and for once the daughters were not in attendance on their mother, but working on something: baking cakes I think, because the smell was delicious. Meanwhile a cloth was spread over my shoulders and Morgana Callandra was dressing my hair with a comb and a pair of shears. The feeling was inexpressibly pleasant as the comb slid across my head, the daughters were laughing and talking and I was very relaxed. I felt as if I was among my own people and my own family. Perhaps I was, and did not realise it.

'So how did you make contact with her?' asked Morgana Callandra.

'I didn't,' I said, 'your husband did it. He got fed up with my dithering and he sent a runner to the house of Fortunus with a message for the Major Domos.'

'That's Agidox, isn't it? You've mentioned him before.'

'Yes,' I said, 'He's a friend from my time in that house.'

'He's more than that,' she said, 'He owes you his life! All the slaves in that house owe you their lives. If you'd not found out who killed your old master, they'd all have been executed for the crime.'

'I suppose so,' I said.

'It's the truth!' she said.

'Yes,' I said, 'ao Morganus asked Agidox if Allicanda was still in the house, and would she meet me, as a favour to himself and the Twentieth, on His Grace the Governor's business.'

'Yes,' she said, 'he would do that, my husband. He is very direct.' She thought about what I'd said and the shears clicked and the comb moved and I was enwrapped in contentment. But she brought me back into the real world. 'You're going to meet her at a cook shop, aren't you?'

'Yes,' I said, 'a very respectable place.'

'Not full of tarts and sailors?' she said.

'Indeed not!' I replied, with emphasis, but all the daughters giggled and I realised she was teasing. They giggled even more at her next words.

'Just take care you don't end up in court on a charge of Stuprum!' she said, and I laughed too, because the word—a legal term for adultery—had connotations of illicit sexuality which Celts found very funny. But the philosopher in me was stirred.

'No,' I said, 'Stuprum doesn't apply. Slaves can't commit adultery. We're property, not people. Under Roman law, only citizens' wives can commit adultery.'

'Oh?' she said. 'Quite the lawyer aren't you? Then what does apply?'

'Either inuria or the Lex Aquilia,' I said, giving the Roman legal terms. The girls stopped giggling.

'And what do those mean?' asked Morgana Callandra.

'Well,' I said. 'Inuria literally means outrage. In this case it would be outrage against a master, inflicted by corrupting his slave, whereas the Lex Aquilia covers damage to property, and slaves are property, so...' I stopped. There was now complete silence in the room. The shears did not click, the comb did not move. 'Oh,' I said.

'You've studied this,' said Morgana Callandra, 'haven't you? You've been to the legion's library.'

I think that I blushed.

'So how do you expect to get round all that,' she said, 'in your Greek cleverness?'

'Your husband has already done it for me,' I said, 'by writing to Agidox rather than the master of the house—Fortunus—who actually *owns* Allicanda. Fortunus is nearly fifteen, and already a full Roman citizen, and I believe he's got his father's talent for business. But the house is actually run by Agidox the Major Domos, and Agidox owes me and Morganus a lot of favours.'

'But isn't he a slave,' she said, 'Agidox?'

'Yes,' I said, 'but he's an exotic. He's a tremendous businessman and he runs that house the way Petros runs...' I stopped, fearing indiscretion.

'The way Petros runs this province,' said Morgana Callandra. 'Everyone knows that!'

'Do they?'

'Yes!' She came round to face me and shook her head. 'You may be very clever with your books and your mind reading, but sometimes you don't know what ordinary people think!'

The words were harsh and her expression serious, but I looked at her and my gift stabbed me hard. It stabbed me with sadness, because I saw the depth of affection in her eyes: kindly affection, the affection that a mother has for a son. But I could not accept this affection, because I was burdened with memories of the time when my city, Apollonis, fell to the Romans, and my wife and children were lost in a manner too painful to recall, except to state that they died with honour. All this is in an earlier volume of my memoirs, giving explanation of why I was bound in my affections to the family I had lost and was unable—as yet -to be part of any other.

Thus I truly declare that if I had the power to throw away the gift that confronts me with such sorrows, then I would. But I cannot throw it away and must bear it as best I can, because I do try to be a stoic. I try very hard, especially at night when I am still awake.

'So tell us,' said Morgana Callandra, 'how is your slave girl allowed out so you can meet her? How can you even meet her without breaking the law?'

I concentrated on detail. There was no sadness in that.

'Today is some sort of holy day,' I said.

'Yes,' she said. She raised arms and the daughters copied her. 'It is the festival of Esidos, beloved guardian of the homely threshold.'

I nodded and tried to be polite because the gods are always listening, even those you have never heard of. 'Of course,' I said, 'Though with utmost respect to the divine and honoured Esidos, I regrettably know so little of him.'

'*Her!*' said Morgana Callandra, frowning.

'Blessed be the name of Esidos, mother of gateways!' said the daughters.

'Yes, yes, yes!' I said. 'And the senior slaves in the house of Fortunus, are allowed—that's to say allowed by Agidox—to hold a night-time formal dinner to celebrate this... er... beloved festival, which dinner is held at the cook-shop of Constantinos the Cypriot, on the east side of the forum. They walk there and back in a body, singing hymns, and with music playing.'

'They would do,' said Morgana Callandra, 'it's a night-time festival and it's popular with slaves because the blessed Esidos was herself a slave. So the city will be full of slaves out celebrating,' she said, 'and full of thugs looking out for anyone on their own.'

'But Fortunus' slaves will have the household litter-bearers to protect them,' I said. 'Eight of them. Huge Africans.'

'Good!' she said, 'then the Africans can talk to your escort outside, while you're talking to Allicanda inside.'

So at sunset I was sent forth by Morgana Callandra looking as elegant as a nobleman, and with an escort of the Twentieth marching all around me. It was a large escort because Morganus does nothing which is small, so in that respect I was now level in status with Petros. Or at least, that is how I would be perceived as I went through the streets.

In fact I soon became grateful for their presence because those neat, grid-pattern Roman streets were heaving with people, and deafening to the clanging and banging of cymbals, the blowing of horns, and the raucous singing and chanting of the many bands of slaves that were out that night, freed of their normal discipline.

Thus it was chaos, with torches flaring, feet staggering, mouths yelling, and here and there the snoring bodies of those who had drunk too much, too early. It was a relief to have army shields all round and a strong-voiced optio to bellow threats to the common herd, warning what they would get if they did not make way for the army. He meant every word of it too, because my escort had come equipped with wooden practice swords as well as the real thing, so that they could strike out without fear of prosecution for damaging slaves. This they did with enthusiasm and I suspect they were enjoying themselves. Then, when we stopped outside the cook-shop of Constantinos the Cypriot, the optio saluted me with a merry smile.

'Here we are then, your worship,' he said. 'I'll leave a man here who knows where we are, and he'll come and get us when you want to go home.'

'Where will you be?' I asked. He grinned again.

'A little place round the corner, your worship,' he said, and I nodded, knowing that the *little place* would have wine on sale. So I stared at him in the manner of the officer I had been, long ago in my own city.

'Don't let your men get too drunk, optio,' I said, 'it wouldn't be good for your rank.' It was an act, but it worked. The merry smile vanished and the optio blinked in fright.

'Of course not, Your Worship! Trust me, Your Worship!'

'Carry on, optio,' I said, 'I'll see you later.'

'Yes, Honoured Sir!' he said, and he led his men off at the quick march, knocking slaves aside as they went, and leaving one miserable soldier behind, stood stiffly to attention. He had his back to a wall and his shield in front of him, so he shouldn't be jostled and he tried to keep his eyes front, while sliding envious glances at his mates marching away. I wondered why he was the unlucky one. Was he a defaulter? Had they drawn lots? Did the optio simply dislike him?

'I'll be inside,' I said to him.

'Yes, Your Worship.'

'Stand at ease!'

'Yes, Your Worship'

So I went in.

The cook-shop, which was in a street just off the forum, was like a thousand others across the Empire. It was a solid, brick-built structure, in a continuous line of buildings that rose two levels above the ground floor. It was open wide at the front, with sliding panels drawn back. It dazzled with light from torches set in sockets over the entrance and there were three young slaves, one girl and two boys, all chosen for good looks, and all dressed in tunics embroidered with the house emblem, which was Venus riding a dolphin. The three laughed and smiled and grabbed at the arms of passers-by, and they kept up a chorus of sound.

'Fresh bread! Meat pies! Fish sauce! Gaulish wine!' they yelled, and 'Room for more at the back!' and 'Private rooms on the top floor!' Dressed as I was, and having arrived with a large military escort, they bowed low before me, leering and gurning, and calling for the proprietor to come out to greet me. Seeing this, even some of the people on the pavement began bowing in my direction. But I ignored them and looked over their heads into the cook-shop. It was easy because I was tall and they were not, and I was totally distracted with concern for what might happen next.

Like all cook-shops there was a long counter running across the shop, just inside the entrance, leaving a way through on one side. The counter bore a line of charcoal hearths, sunk into the stone of the bench, and over these was a mouth-watering display of food: porridge pots bubbling sweet, salt or sour, sliced rabbit frying on grills, chickens roasting on spits, and a whole hog turning slowly, basted continuously with drippings, while fresh bread, straight out of the oven was piled in decorative pyramids, and a huge menu and wine list, hung on cords over the counter, displayed the cost of everything on offer. I looked past that into the sweltering, food-scented interior, which was heaving with life and bulging with customers gorging and yelling and drinking, in long rows at tables. The noise was intense and everyone was shouting to be heard. I looked hard but could not see what I was looking for.

'Gods bless Your Honour!' cried a plump little man who had just rushed out from the depths of the shop. He looked like a Cypriot Greek. 'I recognised you at once, your honour,' he said, 'and the best table in the house is yours for the taking, and the best wine, which is reserved only for ...' I raised a hand to stop him. He bowed.

'Are you Constantinos of Cyprus?' I said.

'Yes, Your Honour, and I know well who Your Honour is, and...'

'The slaves of the House of Fortunus should be here.' I said, Where are they?'

'Yes, yes, Your Honour, they've got the first floor dining room, and...'

'Take me there, at once!' I said, and threw the trail of my cloak across my left shoulder in what I hoped was a stylish manner. I did my best to display aristocratic panache, but it is hard to do that when your heart is pounding and your knees are trembling. Perhaps Constantinos of Cyprus never noticed these weaknesses, but in any case he led me up a flight of stairs, into a room like the one below, except that it was even more noisy, with even more food on the tables. I glanced swiftly round the room and—Apollo support me—I instantly found the person I was seeking and my heart nearly stopped stone dead.

Allicanda was seated at table no more than five paces away.

She was looking straight at me.

Chapter 9

Allicanda was a Hibernian, captured in childhood by slave-raiders who had dared to risk the ocean that separates Britannia from its mysterious western neighbour. She was a small and very shapely women with fresh, white skin, red hair and green eyes. She was greatly admired by men, and confided in by everyone for her sympathy towards those with troubles. In my days as an exotic in the house of Fortunus' father, I had often gone to see her in her small office in the fish kitchen at the back of the enormous, luxury building. She had an office because she was head fish cook to the household: one of many expert cooks in service there.

For those who do not know Rome as well as I do, I stress that a fish cook in a Roman household did not deal only with fish, but with the sun-moon-and-stars of Roman cuisine, because the fish cook was keeper of the fish sauce, garum, which Romans adore. It comes in a universe of flavours, styles and consistencies, and is served with every meal, and its mastery is achieved only by persons of the most extraordinarily sophisticated palate. Allicanda was such a person, and was valued for it.

Thus Allicanda was a respected senior slave of the household. But that was not why everyone wanted to talk to her. They did that because they liked her and came to her with their troubles and were comforted, and in return they gave Allicanda every drop of slave gossip in the city of Londinium. In those days, I too went to her for comfort in my troubles, but unlike everyone else I needed Allicanda's special insight, in order to pursue my investigations.

As for myself I state—as simple truth—that women seem to like me.

They find me attractive and this overcomes their fear of my mind-reading. At least, it does at first. So in that great house, I did not lack offers of physical comfort. But I needed more. I needed the warm sympathy of a woman's company, and so I turned to Allicanda, and she received me with patience, and listened to my stories until I was so moved by her kindness, and so captivated with her beauty, that in time she should have replaced my lost wife—or rather, stood firmly beside her—in the deep of my heart.

With regret I have to repeat that this is merely what *should* have happened. It should have happened but it did not, and the fault was entirely mine through clumsiness of words, and through inept boasting of the new powers I had won, in working directly with Morganus under the command of the Governor of the province. On one occasion I foolishly implied that I could make Allicanda mine by command, or by purchase, since I had risen so high and had such influence in the world. I remember the cold stare in her eyes, and the small, white hand sliding away from mine as she sat across the table—and the warmth between us fading away.

Then I came out of my thoughts, and back to the first floor of the cook-shop of Constantinos of Cyprus. I realised that someone was trying to catch my attention. All I had seen or noticed was Allicanda, but Constantinos was fairly bouncing up and down in front of me, shouting over the din. I looked down at him.

'… a private room or even a suite, and with personal service?' he said. 'Your honour has only to ask, because such a room as this,' he waved a dismissive hand and the room and the company, 'is fit only for slaves, and Your Honour would be better…'

'Shut up!' I said. 'Go away!' I was so rude that his mouth fell open in surprise. In guilty regret I took a coin from my purse and gave it to him, not even looking to see if it were gold, silver or copper. From the look on his face it was gold, because he bowed almost to the floor, beamed in delight and managed the commendable feat of backing away down the stairs without falling over.

As he did so, the room fell silent. I saw men and women nudging one another, and looking at Allicanda and at me. They sat with bread in one hand, wine in the other, grease on their chins and chewing steadily, while the eight big Africans looked over all the rest. Almost everyone in the room remembered me, just as I remembered them. So there was whispering, and an uneasy reluctance to meet my gaze which did not surprise me, since in that household, the simpler minds believed that I had the evil eye. But Allicanda was still looking right at me, and there was a united gasp as she said a few words to the women sitting on either side of her, then she stood, looked round, saw an empty table at the back end of the room, and beckoned to me. She led, I followed and we sat down facing each other in a dark corner far away from the lamps that lit the rest of the room.

'Ooooooh,' said the room united, as heads went together, tongues wagged, and for a while nobody looked at anything other than Allicanda and myself. But it was a feast day, there was food and wine waiting, and soon the noise was as great as ever and everyone found other things to talk about. At least I think so, because my attention was a thousand miles from them.

I had forgotten how special Allicanda was to me. Even the Lady Viola, lovely as she was, had not affected me like Allicanda. Her green eyes were wonderful. I remember that before all else, even if they did not smile. Then she spoke.

'We are safe if we sit here,' she said.

'Safe?' I said..

'Safe. We are in public view and nobody here will give a bad report of our conduct.'

'I see,' I said.

'But we must stay physically apart. Do you understand?'

'Yes,' I said, and realised that on all such previous occasions, I had stretched out my hand to touch hers, just as I wanted to now.

'So what is it?' she said. 'What's this favour to the legion and the Governor?'

'Can't we greet one another first?' I said. 'As friends in the past even if not now?'

Her expression showed nothing.

'I wish you good evening and good fortune, Ikaros of Apollonis,' she said.

'I wish you good evening and good fortune Allicanda the Hibernian,' I said, and I smiled at the solemn words and by all the gods- just for once—I blessed my gift because I saw her expression and read that all was not lost between us, and I thanked Apollo in his mercy that such a thing should come to pass.

'So,' she said, 'I suppose you will want to know what the slaves are saying in the street?'

I saw the light dying as she said that. She was not pleased that I had sought her out for such a purpose.

'No!' said, 'I wanted to see you. That most of all. That before everything. I just wanted to see you.'

She smiled, and the light shone again, and we became easier in each other's company. I wanted very much to reach out and take her hand, but I knew that I could not.

'You poor, sad man,' she said, 'you're still burdened by your clever thoughts. You've got no friends but your Roman soldier, and you have to live in his house. Do they make you welcome, or are you just a slave?'

'No,' I said, 'they are kind.'

'Good,' she said. 'So now that you have seen me, what do you want to ask me? I know that you will want to know what the slaves are saying in the street.'

I did want to know. So I told her everything about the murder of Tribune Celsus, and the girl Viola, noting Allicanda's displeasure when I described Viola's beauty. But I forgave her that, because the vanities of women are different from those of men. It was much more difficult when I mentioned the druids.

'Allicanda,' I said, and despite all the noise in the room, I whispered when I first said the word. 'We have to talk about druids.'

Instantly, a fortress gate was closed in my face: slowly closed, smoothly closed, almost closed with a smile. But closed it was, and I was denied entry. Allicanda sat back on her bench, and her personality sank deep behind her eyes. She looked at me, gave a tiny shake of the head and rested one hand upon another. She uttered no words, but her entire body said *No! We're not going to talk about that.*

So I faced a dilemma. It was obvious that she had much to say if she chose to, and it was my duty to persuade her to say it. It was also my fascination and compulsion to persuade her. But how to do this without turning her against me? So I fumbled for the key that would open the door.

'For old times' sake?' I said. 'For days gone by?' I tried to smile but she did not, and she said nothing. I tried again. 'A woman's life could depend on this,' I said. 'Viola's life. She's a slave like you and me, and the Romans may put her to death.'

Something flickered inside her mind. She blinked but then shook her head. I had said something that impressed her. Was it Viola's fate? 'Will you help me,' I said, 'for her sake?'

But Allicanda said nothing. So what had resonated? I tried other approaches and she did begin to smile as she shook her head, so I could tell that she wanted to help me, if only she could. But that was all. Then just as I was giving up, I tried what must be my least persuasive argument, at least with her. I tried it because I had nothing else left.

'The druids are trying to ruin the governor's games,' I said, 'this is deadly serious to the Romans because…'

'*Romans!*' she said, and said it with such contempt that I found the key.

'I'm not Roman,' I said, 'I'm Greek. I am not a Roman!'

'But you're one of them now,' she said, 'Or are you?'

'I'm Greek,' I said. 'Rome destroyed my city and caused the death of my family.'

'Yes,' she said and stared at me. She was making her decision. I saw the doubt and the judgement. She frowned and spoke. 'You must swear that no Celt will suffer for what I tell you. You must accept my curse if you break your word, and know that I will despise you forever and never speak to you again.'

I nodded. I sat up straight and spoke the most sacred oath that I knew.

'I swear by The-Lady-my-Wife-Departed, and by the beloved faces of my children.'

I could never break such an oath, and I could see that Allicanda knew it.

'Listen to me,' she said. 'I know things because I am a Celt. But can tell them to you only because I am a Hibernian, not a Briton. Do you understand?'

'Go on,' I said, and she smiled, though the smile was sad.

'I any case, I'm going to tell you because you will otherwise look into my mind and see for yourself.'

'Never!' I said, 'never without your permission.'

She shook her head. 'You can't control your magic. You told me that long ago.'

'It isn't magic.'

'You still can't control it.'

I said nothing. She sighed. 'People trust me,' she said.

'I know!"

'So they talk to me. But no Briton would ever talk to you, or a Roman, about the druids. They wouldn't because the Britons are a conquered people, and the druids are the soul of the Celtic nations. While the druids live, the Britons think they may rise again one day, and they are bred up to revere the druids and fear them, and they're forbidden, at risk of hell and damnation, ever to speak of them to the Romans. Do you understand? The Britons are bred up like that, but we Hibernians are not. We're still free.'

I nodded. 'So,' she said, 'The druids are everywhere. They stand behind every Celt of every tribe. They're everywhere!'

She said much more, confirming what I already suspected: that every Celt knew someone, who knew someone, who knew a druid. She confirmed that all the efforts of the Romans to get rid of the druids had failed. Indeed, it was even worse.

'With druids,' she said, 'what one knows, all know because they send messages across the land by pigeons. Their words fly faster than a horse can gallop.'

'But they fight among themselves,' I said. 'Doesn't that worry the Britons?'

'No!' she said. 'They think the druids have their reasons, and the Britons don't ask questions. They just do what they're told.'

'What about the girl Viola?' I asked. 'What do you know about her?

'Viola,' she said, 'that Celsus bought from Helgax the Slaver? The girl you say is so special?'

'Well,' I said, reading her expression, 'What I meant was...'

'Never mind!' she said, and waved the matter aside. 'The boy Celsus was robbed. Did you know that?'

'No,' I said.

'He could have got her for half a million, because Helgax was desperate for ready money. He'd taken out loans and couldn't pay the interest. Everyone knew that.'

'Really?'

'Really! Celsus paid over one and a half million sesterses. He was robbed.'

I smiled to encourage her. She was more comfortable on this topic.

'How do you know all that?' I said.

'People talk,' she said.

'Go on,' I said, 'how did the druids get to her?' Her nervousness came right back as I spoke the words. I had to be careful. She was blinking fast. 'When was Viola away from Celsus?' I asked. 'Away from the army?'

'That's easy,' she said. 'The boy Celsus bought himself a villa outside Londinium. Everyone talks about it.' She looked at me. 'Didn't you ask that optio about the villa? The optio in charge of the tribunes' block?'

'No,' I said, 'I couldn't discuss any contact with... with *them*.'

'Well,' she said, 'Celsus bought himself a monster luxury villa—you *do* know his family owns GVSN, don't you?'

'Yes,' I said.

'Money's nothing to them, or to him. He bought a huge villa complete with slaves, livestock, gardens, everything. He went there whenever he could, at least once a month. He's like a lot of these young tribunes: only in your Roman army for a couple of years before they go back home to mummy and daddy. So, he took her with him to the villa, and sometimes left her there because she liked it, and she *didn't* like him. Not very much.'

'I know,' I said, 'so did the villa slaves talk to slaves in Londinium? Is that how you know this?'

'Of course!' she said, 'they come into town on a wagon, to buy everything they can't get in the country.'

'Thank you,' I said.

'Be careful with what I've told you,' she said, and I nodded. I now had most of the story. Left in the villa, Viola was surrounded by slaves, mostly Celts who would obey druids as she would herself. So the druids could order the slaves to let one of them into the villa to work on her, and that would be all the easier because the villa was away from Londinium and the Roman army.

That is as far as I pursued the matter with Allicanda, because there were some things I could not mention: Bradowr, for instance. I could not talk of keeping a druid alive inside an army fortress.

After that the evening was anti-climax.

'Are we done?' she said, when I asked no more questions.

'Yes,' I said. 'For the moment . though I hope we may meet again.'

'If it can be arranged,' she said, 'I would like that.' Then she looked at the room full of slaves. She was wondering what they thought of her being with me, for so long a time. But none of them were paying us any attention. At least I thought so.

'We'd better join them,' she said, 'go back to my table. Go back together so that there is no possibility we went upstairs to a private room like the others.'

'Which others?' I asked. She smiled.

'Those who take the opportunity for private entertainment upstairs, together.'

'Oh,' I said.

'Oh!' she said. 'But they're all slaves of the house, and that's all right because any offspring only increase the master's wealth.'

I nodded. Intimacy between myself and Allicanda would be impossible without her master's permission. As I had tried to explain to Morgana and her daughters, I would be committing theft at least, and might even be charged with rape. It was a field in which lawyers frolicked and played.

'So we must join the others,' she said, 'Best that we do it now.'

So we did, and after that there was indeed no intimacy between us, not even intimacy of words. I sat with Allicanda among her friends, who received me with much awkwardness and with the fear that I would look inside their heads. So the conversations were stilted; I was the water that puts out the fire, and I left after taking enough food for good manners. For once I took hardly any wine, and soon I stood, and bowed to them all, and they bowed to me, and with a polite nod to Allicanda I left. It was just a nod, just a glance, not even a word. What I wanted to do was take her up in my arms and carry her away, and never let her go. But that would have been unadvisable, to say the least.

So I went downstairs, found my legionary still standing by the entrance, and sent him to fetch the escort, who arrived sober enough to march in step. Before I left, I said good night to Constantinos and his slaves, who were still grovelling all around me, and I thought of the gold piece I'd given him. It was amusing, because by taking a coin from my purse, I had spent money with my own hand for the first time since I became an imperial slave. Living with Morganus under the army's protection everything, from my food to my boots—including the fine clothes I wore that very night—had been issued to me without need or thought of money. Either that or Morganus had paid. It was very strange, and all the while my un-used salary was paid into the legion's bank and my account steadily grew.

And so back to Morganus' house, and in the morning I discussed everything with him.

Chapter 10

We talked as we rode, and even a grey Britannic sky could not destroy my happiness which for once—after my meeting with Allicanda—was not entirely due to my love of horses and riding. But that would have been enough by itself, as we trotted out of the fortress: Morganus and myself, with the four bodyguards behind, bumping heavily in their saddles. We were on our way to inspect the works on the chariot-racing stadium, and a full company of legionary cavalrymen, twenty troopers and their centurion, came with us in escort. They were supposedly present because we were heading out into wild Britannia. But the tribes of the region had been peaceful for decades, even if others were not, and the real reason for the cavalry escort was status.

With Romans it is always status, status, status—and a first javelin did not ride unaccompanied when he was on his way to review major legionary works. But the centurion in command of the escort had been warned that confidential matters would be discussed by Morganus and his Greek colleague, so he and his men rode discretely far behind us. Even the bodyguards had been told to keep back. So it was exhilarating to hear the clatter of hooves, the jingle of harness and the snorting of horses, because all such sounds are music to an Apollonite of the Horse Clan, and if you add to that the gleam of armour, the cavalry standards, and the tight formation of a mounted military unit, you have a perfect mixture to exalt the spirits.

'You look pleased with yourself,' said Morganus, riding beside me:

beside and slightly ahead as protocol demanded. 'Is it your fish girl? How did it go last night?'

'Allicanda,' I said, 'her name is Allicanda, as you well know.'

He smiled. 'So what did you learn?'

I told him everything, and I told him my conclusions. We had been unable to speak earlier, because anything connected with druids was so secret that it could not be mentioned in front of Morganus's wife and daughters, nor even other soldiers like the cavalrymen. But riding down a Roman road, with the undergrowth cleared a hundred yards on either side, there was no possibility of being overheard, not with the rumble of hoof beats to cover our voices.

'I see,' said Morganus when I was done. 'And is that the full story?'

I thought that over.

I thought carefully, seeking anything I had missed.

'Yes,' I said, finally 'that's all of it, and I'll send a report to Africanus, who will be pleased to know that he's cleared of blame. Him and the legion,'

'Good!' said Morganus. 'So Viola was turned by druids, and made to kill Celsus to disgrace his men who'd just been made citizens, and through them to dishonour the governor's games. It's just the latest way for them to attack Rome and get away with it.'

'I suppose so,' I said, and glanced at him for reassurance because, to me, it seemed a very odd and indirect way to threaten the games. But I am Greek and it was Roman opinions that mattered, so I read Morganus' face and saw that he really did think that the dishonour was serious.

'It's a dirty business,' he said. 'It's nasty! There's no greater duty than granting citizenship to veterans who've served their time. This an insult to the Empire and it leaves a bad smell, and we can't have any more like that.'

'Ah,' I said, 'Then here's the problem.'

Morganus frowned. 'What problem?'

'Remember what Bradowr said? He said that it would take many months to turn Viola into an assassin. So, why did the druids start work on that girl so long ago? Was it months ago? A year ago? We have to ask that question.'

'Why?' said Morganus.

'Because if the object of killing Celsus was to dishonour the governor's games, then how did the druids know—many months ago and before the games were even thought of—that they should start working on that girl's mind?'

Morganus did not like that. He frowned and looked away, and I guessed what he might say next. I guessed and I was right, because he made the bull sign, and muttered a prayer. A prayer to Mithras, no doubt. Then he looked at me.

'They knew because they can see into the future,' he said. 'That's obvious! How else could they know?'

I breathed deep and kept calm, because I will not accept magic as an explanation of anything.

'I don't know,' I said, 'but I shall certainly seek other explanations.'

'Didn't you ask Allicanda?' he said.

'No' I said, 'I didn't want her to think—as you just did—that the druids could see into the future, because if that gets out it might start just the sort of panic and rumours that would do the druids' work for them.'

'What do you mean *gets out*?' he said, Don't you trust her?'

I was stung hard by that and I must have spoken with some passion.

'Of course I do!' I said, 'She is a most remarkable woman. She is wise and kind, and I trust her absolutely, and I believe that she … that she … returns my esteem.'

Morganus smiled. 'Oh,' he said, 'I see. She *returns your esteem* does she?'

'Of course!' I said, 'It is just that by some accident, some slip of mind…'

'She might tell half of Londinium everything you told her?'

I think that I lost my temper, at that. I think that I ranted somewhat. But Morganus was patient. When I had finished, he reined in his horse to come close alongside mine.

'Listen, you fool-before-the-gods. Why don't you just buy her?'

'What?' I said.

'You've got money in the legionary bank. It's just sitting there. You never spend it.'

'Yes I do,' I said, and I told him about Constantinos and his gold piece. But Morganus just laughed at that. He laughed, quite loudly.

'You've got plenty of money,' he said, 'and she's only a slave, so you could buy her. And then she's all yours! Why don't you? You obviously want her. You talk about her all the time.'

'I don't!' I said.

'You *do*,' he said, 'I know, because it's me you talk to.'

I fell silent after that. The temptation was enormous. I dreamed of being able, literally, to lift Allicanda off her feet and take her away. I dreamed of how I would explain that the purchase was only a formality, and I dreamed how easily I would get round her disgust, so clearly expressed on that past occasion when I had hinted at this very plan. So I dreamed and dreamed, until I crashed against truth like a war galley rowing into a rock.

Allicanda would never accept.

Or *would* she? I looked at Morganus, thinking of discussing that with him.

'Back again, are you?' he said. 'Feeling better?' He waved a hand at the scenery all around us. It was not Greece under the Greek sunshine, but the wind was fresh and at least the hillsides were green. 'This is supposed to be an outing,' he said, 'This is supposed to take you out of yourself for the day. That's why you came along. You've got nothing to do other than look at the works and you'll like that. Look over there!'

I looked, and I smiled.

The Twentieth Legion was cutting a chariot racing stadium out of the countryside, and the works were enormous, because a racing stadium is enormous. So the green earth was turned brown in a huge scar down a valley, where turf had been removed, and soil thrown up by the non-stop efforts of two thousand men.

The din of their toil was tremendous. It was a great roaring, resounding noise: the mixed thumping of pick-axe, spade, hammer and axe, and the buzz of saws, and the yelling of commands, and the tramping of boots, and the squealing of pulleys as loads were raised with block and tackle. I shook my head in wonderment, though also in sorrow and in envy. My own people were sophisticated builders who could surpass anything the Romans ever achieved in terms of technical design, but no race ever born could surpass Rome for organisation and energy. Indeed, it is a great and enduring truth that the Roman army won the Empire not just by victory in battle, but by massive building works.

And these particular works—being Roman—were formidably neat and tidy. Planked ramps were neat-spaced down the length of the excavations, so that wheelbarrow loads of soil could be hauled out of the diggings with cables, and the men who hauled the cables, actually hauled in step, chanting *heave-ho* to keep time! Even the dumped soil was being neatly formed into a boundary wall around the stadium, while a hundred yards from the works, the encampment for the men was a Roman grid pattern of lines, with the latrines all marked with flags, the cook-tents busy with the next meal, and the commander's tent on an actual pavement of stone slabs in the geometric centre of the camp, with guards posted at the four corners.

All of this was impressive even to a Greek engineer, but there were two further reminders that Romans were different from other men. The first was the determined sense of purpose in the way the troops went at their work. There was no holding back, no delay, just every man knowing his place in the team and instantly throwing his weight into the task. There was absolutely no idle chatter, no leaning on spades, and when each team was relieved by the next after its spell of duty, the departing team saluted the incoming team with a cheer, and moved off singing a marching song. The second reminder was the fact that every single man engaged in these works, wore full body armour: the lorica segmentata of steel strips, even as he cut with a saw or dug with a spade.

I mentioned this to Morganus as we rode forward.

'I see they wear armour,' I said.

'Of course!' he replied and waved his vine staff at the works. 'This is all peacetime work, but it's good drill for the real thing: fortifications in the face of the enemy when there might be a surprise attack.' I nodded. That made sense. 'So the men work in armour,' he said, 'because it's slow to put on.' He pointed to a team working close to us. 'See there,' he said, 'they're in armour, but their shields, helmets and weapons are stacked to one side.'

'Yes,' I said.

'That's because you can put a helmet on fast,' he said, 'and a shield and sword you can grab with each hand. That's easy, but it takes time to put on your armour.' Then he smiled. 'Anyway, we wouldn't want them getting soft, now would we? It's good for them to work in armour. Keeps them fit!'

Then the cavalry centurion rode up and saluted Morganus.

'Permission to go forward and announce you, Honoured Ssir?' he said.

'Go ahead!' said Morganus, and the centurion rode forward at the canter followed by his bugler and standard bearer. They headed for the tented encampment and the bugler blew a call which was answered by buglers in the camp, and we saw men emerge from the command tent, and orders given and the guard turned out to receive Morganus.

The usual protocol followed, with stamping and saluting and bows. I pass over the details, which are boring to a philosopher, but beloved of Romans. The camp commander was the legion's senior tribune. His name was Secundus Albinus Terentius, son of a senatorial noble family and doubtless destined for high politics in due course. But he was a serious young man who took his army career seriously, and he greeted Morganus with the respect I had seen so often before. In theory a tribune outranked any centurion, even a first javelin, but this young tribune was suckling at his mother's breast when Morganus was already a centurion, leading men forward in the face of the enemy. So the young tribune smiled and gave respect.

'Honoured sir,' he said, with a bow to Morganus as we dismounted, and our horses were led away.

'Honoured Terentius,' said Morganus and saluted, and Terentius presented his staff—even though Morganus knew them all already—and Morganus had to inspect the guard, and we had to accept hospitality, and Morganus stared at me when the wine went round. But then we were taken into the command tent, where I was surprised to see the detailed model of the stadium that I had previously seen at the legionary headquarters.

The tent was crammed full with men: Terentius and his staff, Morganus, myself and the bodyguards, and our cavalry centurion. Everyone other than me was entranced with delight at the model. Looking at their faces and reading their thoughts, I began to understand for the first time, the total degree to which Romans are in love with racing, racing drivers, racing horses, gambling, track-records and the whole world of wonder which—to them—it represents.

To his credit, Terentius gave a thorough account of the works in progress and explained the features of the model with considerable expertise. My respect for him grew as I saw that not all tribunes were gilded flowers, only briefly in the army vase. Thus, even I was interested in what he said, but I repeat that the main impression I had at that meeting was the delight on the faces of all present, and their united gasps of pleasure at what Terentius said, and the features he pointed out using a white-painted stick.

'The model is to scale,' said Terentius.

'Hmmmm!' said everyone.

'The completed stadium will be 450 yards long and 150 yards wide, including seating. It will allow a maximum of twelve chariots to race.' The white stick tapped one end of the stadium. 'The starting gates are here. Each chariot, with driver and horses, will be in a separate timber box, with a sprung-gate blocking access to the track. When the signal is given the gates shoot up simultaneously, and the race begins.'

'Ahhhh!' said everyone, and the stick moved towards a long structure that ran down the centre of the race-track, dividing it in two. It was thin and long and elaborate, with little temples and shrines and decoration and—judging from the scale—it rose up about thirty feet from the track itself. Tiny human figures were represented, here and there, waving and staring at the passing chariots.

'This is the spina,' said Terentius.

'Hmmmm!'

'The spina is precisely three hundred Apollonite yards long.' Morganus nudged me, and the company looked at me. They all knew me, after all. 'We chose Apollonite measure as being the most respected,' said

Terentius, and thereby made at least one friend in the audience. 'When the gates open,' he said, 'the drivers race for the bottom end of the spina, here.' The white stick tapped the end of the spina closest to the starting gates. 'They must not bump or jostle until they reach the right-hand side of the spina.' He paused, then he smiled and the company grinned in delight. 'And then, it's hell for leather, 300 yards to the top end turn, here!' The white stick indicated the upper end of the spina, where the chariots must turn. 'And round they go,' Terentius smiled, 'all those that aren't smashed in the shipwreck as they hit one another!'

The company laughed. Even I knew that the most popular seats in a racing stadium were those at the turns, where the collisions occurred. The white stick moved again. 'Then it's back down the left-hand side of the spina, to the bottom end turn, and that's one lap completed.' The white stick tapped on a key feature of the spina: a line of seven wooden dolphins, each one bright painted, supported at its balance point on a transverse rod, and each one huge in real life, and big enough for all to see in the stadium. The stick pushed one of the dolphins and it moved, nose down, tail up. 'One dolphin ...?' Terentius paused, awaiting a response.

'One lap!' said the company, and they laughed. It was obviously a racing phrase, known to racing folk.

After that we really did inspect the site. The horses were brought back, we mounted up, and Morganus—being Roman and diligent—insisted that we saw everything, so we rode from one end of the works to the other. He even sent word ahead that he was not to be saluted, because that would interrupt work, and the schedules had to be met. Later, we had an indifferent meal. It was heavy in bread and porridge as fuel for men engaged in heavy work, and there was nothing to drink but native beer. But that too was part of the inspection, so we had to eat and drink.

Much later, we rode back to the fortress where, even in darkness, I wrote a full report for Legate Africanus, of the murder of Celsus the tribune. I might have done this earlier, but in such matters it is best to wait a day or so to allow reflection and a matured opinion. I sent the report to Africanus by runner, before I went to bed, and found that his reply was awaiting me early the next morning. I showed it to Morganus at breakfast.

'He wants to see you, then,' said Morganus. 'Just you!' He looked at me, wondering what this might mean. Then he understood, and nodded. 'He'll want to put out his own version of your report. He's got politics in Rome to consider.'

Morganus was right. Later on I stood in an empty room in the Principia: empty of everyone but me and Africanus. It seemed that there were, in fact, some things that Romans did without witnesses. Africanus was in full military dress: muscled cuirass, decorations, scarlet cloak and a helmet under his arm, as he had field duties that day. He made swift summary of what he wanted from me.

'I congratulate you on the speed and efficiency of your investigation,' he said. I bowed and he made a small gesture to wave away my response. 'Such efficiency brings great credit to your acting master, the honoured Leonius Morganus Fortis Victrix,' he said. 'Now listen to me, Ikaros the Greek,' he lowered his voice and stepped closer. 'This is what happened... the tribune, Celsus, stupidly bought himself a mad slave-girl and got stabbed, which is exactly the same as stupidly buying a mad horse and getting kicked in the head. That is the explanation that will be given to his family. Do you understand?'

I gave no nod of agreement, so he stepped even closer. 'Listen to me, *boy*,' he said, using the lowest of all words for a slave. 'You will dig no further in this matter. I want no mention of druids, and you are forbidden absolutely to approach the creature we have hidden in the hospital!' I must have shown surprise at that. 'Oh,' he said, 'did you think that Petros confides only in a Greek slave?'

So I did not question Bradowr again—not then—and I did not ask him why the druids had worked on Viola long before the games were planned. It was an omission that I came to regret.

Meanwhile, events drove these matters out of mind, because there was another murder.

Chapter 11

Some days later I was woken in the night. Morganus beat hard on my door, then came into my bedroom with a lamp.

'Get up, Greek!' he said. 'We're on duty. Gershom's been murdered. The Jew. The one who runs that club you went to.'

I was barely awake. My mind was slow.

'Gershom?' I said. 'Gershom with the library?'

'Yes, him. A runner's come from Government House. You—we—have got to investigate: the Governor's personal orders! Even me, so I'm off all work on the games. It looks like he was one of the big ones. One of the important ones, in the tax office.'

'You mean Gershom was?' I said, my head still dizzy with sleep.

'Yes!' said Morganus, 'he knew all sorts of secrets, and had enemies everywhere because he was so good at finding out fiddles. You know, where the millionaires hide their money so they don't pay tax?'

'I see,' I said, and indeed I *did* see, because there is nothing the state loves more than taxation. The state hungers and thirsts after taxation, it adores taxation, it worships taxation, and the tender soul of the state howls in torment if any man avoids taxation. Consequently, those employees of the state who are charged with *preventing* tax avoidance are the most beloved of all the state's creatures. This universal law applies to every state in human history, and although Petros would have dictated the orders to myself and Morganus, even the dim-wit Governor Teutonius would have understood and heartily approved.

'Look!' said Morganus, and handed me a scroll-letter. I tried to read it as I pulled on my clothes. The light was bad and it was hard. It was an impressive, formal document bearing the governor's provincial seal. It was a commission from the Governor, directing and empowering myself and Morganus to use all resources of the province in pursuing justice in the name of His Grace. It was even signed by him: presumably with Petros guiding his hand.

Soon, we were tramping through the dark streets of Londinium, past locked and shuttered houses in the dead of the night, with boots crunching on pavements and torches burning. Morganus and I led, with the bodyguards behind, and a full century of legionaries in case of any danger. We found more light and soldiers waiting outside Gershom's large house. the Governor's Guardhad been turned out from its usual ceremonial duties and was lined up outside the doors—front, back and side—attempting to keep everything secure.

Their centurion spoke to Morganus, as our men stamped to a halt in an armoured body. The centurion was much stressed and was fraught with worry, being entirely unused to such duties as this. Like all the guardsmen he was a parade-ground soldier, who never got his feet wet or his armour dirty.

'There's been a murder,' he said, with horror.

'We know!' said Morganus. 'Gershom.'

'Yes, and some of his slaves.'

'Do we know who did it?'

'No,' said the centurion. 'Except that it was a body of men, all acting together.'

'Who gave the alarm?' said Morganus.

'One of the slaves. As soon as the killers left, one of the slaves ran to Government House, and we were ordered out.'

Morganus looked at the guardsmen in their gaudy, antique dress. Even their boots were gilded.

'You can stand down, now,' he said to the centurion. 'We'll take over.'

'Yes, Honoured S ir!' said the centurion, with utter relief, and he marched off with his men, in quick time.

'Useless buggers,' said Morganus, who never normally swore, and he placed guards on all the doors, and went up the steps and into the house with the bodyguards behind him. 'Draw!' he said, and swords hissed from scabbards. He looked at me. 'Here,' he said, handing me his dirk, 'keep close!'

I took the blade. It was a sensible precaution because I doubt the Governor's Guard had searched the house, there were only dim pools of lamp-light inside, and there might have been armed men around every corner.

But there was no danger within. There was only a large group of slaves huddled together with their arms around each other, and a small body curled up on the floor in its own blood. Morganus and his men sheathed arms and I gave back the dirk, while Morganus brought in more men and sent them running through the house, to make entirely sure that it was safe. Then I questioned one of the slaves: a big man who stood forward and bowed as Morganus and I approached.

'Honoured Ssir! Your Worship!' he said. 'I am Katarix, major domos to my late master Gershom Bar Meshulam.'

I raised hands. 'Gods keep the souls of the departed,' I said.

'Gods keep the souls of the departed,' said all present, voices mumbling in the dark.

'What happened here, Katarix?' I asked.

He replied at length. He was a highly intelligent man who reminded me of Agidox, Major Domos to my old master, and that is not surprising. The major domos of a big house must be a businessman, a manager, a leader and an accountant, because he is responsible for very large sums of money and many slaves. Also, like Agidox, Katarix was an import: a high-priced slave from Gaul, a province respected for its discrimination in food, and wine and the household arts. He spoke with a strong Gaulish accent, and chose words with careful correctness, as a senior household slave always does, for his dignity.

'We were deceived, Honoured Sirs,' he said in profound apology. 'In my homeland it is a known trick of burglars, and we should have been aware. But I was not on the doorway and the boy who was, knew no better.'

'So what did they do?'

'A man came to the door, begging for help. He said that he was a stranger in the city, that he was out late, and that wife had fallen and twisted her foot, and would we please send slaves to carry her to their lodgings.' Katarix sighed in misery. 'He was very plausible, he offered money, and the gate-boy opened up to let him into the atrium. And then… and then… the rest of them charged in with drawn swords.'

'Swords?' said Morganus, 'Do you mean actual swords? Not just knives?'

'No, Your Honour,' said Katarix, 'military swords like yours.'

Morganus frowned. 'That's serious,' he said, 'very serious.'

'How many of these men were there?' I asked Katarix.

'I don't know,' said Katarix, 'several of them.' He turned to the other slaves. 'How many were there?'

'Five?' said a voice.

'Ten?' said another.

'A dozen?'

They did not know.

'What did they look like?' I asked. Katarix nodded. He was more certain of that.

'They were wrapped in dark clothes and they all had hoods over their heads, formed into cloth masks, with holes cut out for the eyes but allowing nobody to see their faces.'

'Did they speak?' I asked. 'What could you tell from their voices?'

'They spoke Latin, Your Worship. They spoke like Romans and they had the manner and bearing of free men.'

'Romans?' said Morganus. 'Romans, by all the gods!'

'So what did they do, once they were inside?' I asked, and Katarix stood with head bowed, saying nothing. He was horribly burdened with guilt. I stepped forward and placed a hand on his arm. 'None of this is your fault, Katarix,' I said, 'a great wickedness has been done here, but it's not your fault. None of it! So just tell me what happened.'

'I heard them come in,' he said. 'I was awake quickly and came to the atrium, as did others of the house. The intruders were asking—*demanding*—to be brought into the master's presence. I took command

and told the others to protect the master.' He covered his face with his hands.

'Go on,' I said, and shook his arm gently.

'When we wouldn't tell them where the master was …'

'Yes?' I said.

'They seized the gate-boy: one held his right arm, one held his left and a third ran him through with a sword and killed him.' The other slaves moaned and wept in the darkness around us. 'And then the leader of the men said… he said… if you do not take us to your master, right now, we shall kill all of you just like him.' Katarix looked at me. 'He said that, Your Worship. He said it in good Latin, in the speech of an educated man.' Katarix turned away, and stared at the body on the marble flooring. 'There he lies,' he said, 'Ortos the gate-boy. He was only fifteen years old.'

'Then what happened?' I said, and Katarix bowed his head in shame.

'Two of the kitchen boys told them. They were new to the house and not loyal. I blame myself for that! These boys took some of the men upstairs while the other men stayed with drawn swords, so we could do nothing.'

'Go on!'

'We heard fighting. The master sleeps with a sword by his bed and he must have been ready for them.'

'And?'

'They fought and they killed him.'

'Why did your master have a sword by the bed?' said Morganus. 'What was he afraid of?'

'His enemies, Honoured Sir,' said Katarix. 'All those whose deceits he has revealed in the course of his work.'

'If he was afraid of that, why didn't he get a military guard?' said Morganus. 'He was an important man. The Governor would have allowed him a few auxiliaries.'

'Yes, Your Worship, but my master wished to live as normal a life as possible, and The-Lady-our-Mistress wanted no soldiers in the house, and the master still follows her wishes in the matter.'

'Where is she?' I said. 'The mistress?'

'Our beloved and honoured mistress died, Your Worship. She died last year, giving birth to the master's first-born son. Both died.'

'Gods rest her soul,' I said and raised hands.

'Gods rest her soul,' echoed Katarix. 'After her untimely and tragic death, the master occupied himself in his work, and in his library in the attempt to heal the wound of her loss.' I nodded. I knew how deep such a wound could be.

'Now then,' I said, 'Let's go upstairs. Take us to your master's room. I want to see everything.'

Morganus and I followed Katarix, with the bodyguards close behind. The upper floor had already been searched, but the bodyguards drew steel again as we moved up the dark stairs. Their duty was to protect Morganus and they took that duty very seriously, taking station with two in front of Morganus and me, and two behind us. The house was large, and we went past various rooms including the library. I noticed that the door was open, and that there was a strong smell of burning, though no embers shone in the dark. But I could not see into the dark interior. Then we entered the master bedroom, and found two more bodies. One was Gershom himself, and the other was a young man in a grubby slave tunic. Both bodies were hacked about the arms, and there was much blood on the floor.

'Who's that?' I said, pointing to the dead slave.

'He'll be one of the kitchen boys,' said Morganus, 'and it looks like he got loyal at the last moment. He put up a fight! Look at his arms. You get cuts like that trying to ward off a sword!'

I did look. I looked with extreme care, following the drill that I have already explained, examining every aspect of the two bodies and the room where they lay. The sun was rising by the time I was done, and there was soon no need for lamps. The room had large glazed windows and the sunlight helped.

'What did you find?' said Morganus as I stood, and he anticipated my next words. 'Get the Greek gentleman a bowl of water and some towels!' he said to Katarix.

'Yes, Honoured Sir,' said Katarix and moved out at a fast trot.

'They fought back,' I said, 'Gershom and his slave. But both men were finally killed by thrusts into the body: under the ribs and into the heart. I think Gershom cut one, or some, of his attackers. There's a sword over there, and it's got blood on it.' I pointed at a sword lying near the place where Gershom had fallen. 'Is that your master's sword?' I said to Katarix as he came back with water and towels.

'Yes,' he said. 'It is his.'

'Good,' I said and washed my hands while Katarix held the bowl.

'So,' I said, 'whoever they were, they came here to kill Gershom, and they did that but they touched nothing else. Look round this room, it's full of precious ornaments!'

Everyone looked. Hanging over the bed there was a six-point Jewish star, in heavy and solid gold, and there was much else, all undisturbed. I continued. 'The kitchen boy tried to defend his master. Or maybe tried to defend himself? I don't know. So they killed him. But the men who did this were after Gershom. They were here to do murder.'

Morganus frowned heavily. 'This sounds very bad,' he said. 'If it was done by a team of Romans with military swords, this isn't ordinary crime.'

'No,' I said, 'I don't think it is. It's something else.' I turned to Katarix. 'What did they do after the fight, after they'd killed your master?'

Katarix gasped. 'I forgot to say, Your Worship. There was noise in the library. Much noise and much disturbance, and one of them came down asking for the master's librarian: him or anyone who knew the library. They made the same threats as before, and the librarian stood forward. He was very brave. Then they took him upstairs.'

'Let's go and see,' I said.

There was plenty of light now, and the library instantly told its story. It had been comprehensively despoiled. Books were everywhere, having been snatched from their shelves then thrown on the floor, and then piled in a heap and an attempt made to burn them, but the fire had been put out with water. Among the books lay two more bodies, one still breathing, one quite dead. The live man was propped against a wall, holding his hand hard against a blood-spreading wound in his chest. He gasped and his mouth frothed in blood. I guessed he was the second kitchen boy, because his tunic was grubby and cheap. But the dead man wore expensive robes. He was obviously the librarian.

'Katarix!' I said, or rather I shouted.

'Your Worship?'

'Get me some bandages! Get them quick! And someone get me some pillows.'

The bodyguards did so, and we got them under the kitchen boy, and Katarix was soon back with an armful of linen bandages from somewhere. So I did what I could. I cut off the tunic and examined the wound, and found it to be mortal: two stab wounds into the ribs, sucking air as the boy breathed. The lungs were punctured and there must have been severe bleeding inside the chest. But I put a pad on the wound and bound it round, more to comfort the victim than in any hope of saving him.

Then I knelt beside the kitchen boy and tried to question him. It was very hard, because he was dying, and because he was a simple-minded peasant: a Celt from the rural interior, and not comfortable in Latin. But I persevered, and we talked a while, then finally he abandoned my questions, and began a native death-chant to ease his passage into the next world. So I stood, and raised hands in respect for his gods. Then I looked round the library for some time, looking for I-know-not-what, then I questioned the house slaves some more, but learned nothing. Then I turned to Morganus.

'I'm done here,' I said. He nodded. He knew me very well.

'It's early,' he said, 'but do you want a wine-shop? To think?'

'No,' I said, 'they won't be open. Can we go to your house?'

So we left the house of Gershom under guard, and sent for an army surgeon at the double in case anything could done for the kitchen boy. In fact, he died anyway but we had to try: he was a witness and a human creature besides. Then went back to Morganus's house, with the bodyguards behind as always.

Morgana Callandra was ready with breakfast: honey porridge, milk, bread and cheese, and hot spiced wine. Morganus and I sat down and talked, with the bodyguards at table in the garden outside, since it was a bright day.

'So what did we learn?' said Morganus. 'What did you get from the one who was dying?'

'They were there to kill Gershom,' I said, 'but for something else too. Something in the library. They were after a book, and I don't think they found it.'

'What happened in the library?'

'The boy said that they made him show them the library, and they went through it looking for a book, and when they didn't find it, one of them went downstairs and got the librarian.'

'Go on,' said Morganus.

'They told him to find the book they wanted.'

'What book?' said Morganus.

'The boy didn't know. He doesn't speak good Latin and the name of the book was too complicated for him to follow. He didn't even understand the words. But the librarian knew it all right. He knew it and wouldn't tell them where it was. So they did what they'd done downstairs. They grabbed the boy and stabbed him and told the librarian he'd be next if he didn't find the book. That frightened the librarian, and he tried to find the book—the boy saw him doing it—but the room was in such a mess he couldn't find it, and in the end they killed him, too.'

'In anger?' said Morganus.

'I don't know,' I said. 'It could be that, but let's think what they were trying to do. If they were searching for a book, then they either wanted it themselves, or possibly they wanted to keep it from someone else.'

'So?' said Morganus.

'So,' I said, 'if they didn't want someone else to have it, they might try to burn the whole library, and they certainly lit a fire in there, though the major domos doused it with water later on—that poor boy saw that too—and it never caught properly in the first place.'

'Yes,' said Morganus. 'You need a good draft under a fire, not books flat on the floor.'

'And then,' I said, speculating and guessing, 'if you can't find the book, or destroy it, and you think it's still there somewhere under the mess, then it would make sense to stop the librarian telling everyone what book you were after, because that would make everyone look for it, and that would be the worst possible outcome.'

'So they prevented that by killing the librarian?' said Morganus.

'Yes,' I said. 'Whatever that book is, it's important.'

'But why did they want to kill Gershom in the first place?'

'Well,' I said, 'in my city the philosophers taught that there are only five reasons for murder: greed, lust, fear, envy and revenge.'

'Very philosophical,' said Morganus, 'but your philosophers weren't Romans, were they?' He tapped off points on his fingers. 'Romans with swords? Acting in a team? All with masks? This isn't crime. It's politics!'

'Yes,' I said, 'it might be politics. We'd better talk to Petros. We'd better talk to him at once.' He nodded. 'And we can't leave these books here,' I said, 'whoever came here looking for a book, might come after it again.'

'Not with the house under guard!' he said,

'No,' I said, 'but we need those books where they're completely safe and I can get at them. Can we arrange for some men and some wagons to get them back to the legionary fortress?'

Morganus frowned, thinking of the legalities. 'Doesn't someone own them now?' he said. 'We can't just take them. They must be worth a fortune.'

'That's not a problem,' I said, 'Gershom was an imperial slave. That means he doesn't own anything, because slaves don't own property. He was just looking after those books for his master. And that's the Emperor. So if we take the books to the fortress, we're just acting for the Emperor.'

'Are you *sure* about that?'

I laughed.

'No. But I'm sure Petros will agree.'

He did, and the books were moved next day. But there was much more to discuss with Petros.

Chapter 12

Petros saw us at once, because Morganus had sent a runner ahead, bearing a white staff capped with a small golden eagle: the sign of an urgent despatch from a first javelin. So Petros received us even though he'd been working since before dawn and was almost drowned in the administration of the coming games.

We were taken straight to a huge office within Government House. It must have been twenty yards in each direction, it was high and bright, and lit with many windows, and was neat, white-plastered and it hummed like a bee-hive with busy work. Rows of desks bore piles of documents. Clerks and slaves went to and fro. Dozens of men were bent over their documents, writing and checking and holding urgent conversations. Each of Petros's six shaven-headed attendants was present at the head of a marked-out section delegated to a particular task. It was all very Roman and Petros was proud of it. He could not help but point to each section in turn.

'Construction, accommodation, defence, instruction, supply and regulation,' he said, 'each with defined responsibilities, and each ordered to be flexible and to report to me instantly in case of conflict or overlapping duties.' Then he saw the looks on our faces and sighed. 'So what is it?' he said. 'And don't tell me it's bad news.'

'Can we talk here?' I said.

'Not here,' said Petros. 'His Grace will join us within the hour, to make his daily inspection.'

'Daily inspection?' I said. 'How greatly you must tremble as he enters the room!'

Petros said nothing, but Morganus frowned. 'His Grace is a nobleman of ancient family!' he said.

'Of course!' said Petros.

'Of course!' I said.

'Come with me,' said Petros, and waved a hand to catch the attention of Primus, the most senior of his attendants. Petros shouted over the din, 'Call me at once if need be!' Primus bowed. 'And remember, the priority is racing-drivers first, then actors, and then gladiators last.' Primus bowed again, at which Petros walked off briskly and we went with him.

'Are they all here yet,' I asked, 'your *precious darlings*?'

'No,' said Petros. 'Most of the actors arrived yesterday, and we're expecting the drivers and gladiators in the next few days.' He shook his head, 'You wouldn't believe the trouble of keeping them apart!'

'What, drivers, actors and gladiators?' I asked.

'No, no, no,' said Petros, 'it's not like that. You can mix actors. They get along together. But the gladiators are all owned by different schools and you can't mix the schools because it's a point of honour with each school to hate all the others, and the drivers are even worse!'

Morganus nodded. 'You can't mix the different teams, he said by way of clarification, 'greens, whites, reds and blues?'

'Not in Holy Athena's name!' said Petros, and he looked at Morganus. 'Which team do *you* support?'

He asked with real interest, and a discussion followed which I found painfully tedious, but the bodyguards grinned and followed every word. It was a great relief when Petros led us into a side office which was empty, and where we could talk. The bodyguards checked that there was no other way out, then closed the door on us for privacy, and stood outside.

Morganus and Petros were still talking chariot racing when the door closed, and it was an astonishment to me that men of such serious minds, and at such a time as this, should be so enwrapped in the subject.

'My favourite was Adrimonides of Nicea, who raced for the whites,' said Morganus, 'one of the all time great drivers. He took the reins at only sixteen years old, and won a thousand races before he was twenty-five, and over thirty million in prize money.'

'A phenomenon, ' said Petros. 'And didn't he always use the same blood line?'

'Oh, yes!' said Morganus. 'Only Hellenic horses from the stables of Corinth.'

Eventually I had to interrupt.

'Honoured Sirs,' I said, 'forgive me. But can we proceed? Can I give my report on what happened to Gershom?'

Petros turned to look at me and switched from pleasure to duty in an instant.

'Proceed,' he said, so we left the world of chariot racing and I told him everything of our investigations so far. Then, having made clear that Gershom had been killed by a disciplined team of Romans armed with military swords, I asked if Gershom was, or could have been, involved in politics, and I was surprised at the firmness of Petros's response.

'No,' he said, 'definitely not.'

'Why not?' I asked.

'Because I knew him very well,' said Petros, 'and I can assure you that he took no interest in Roman politics. He loved his work, and his library—and his club of course—and he loved his wife... oh... did you know about her?'

'Yes,' I said.

'Very sad,' he said entirely without feeling.

'Yes,' I said, and Petros thought on. I could see that he was puzzled by a contradiction.

'It's odd really,' he said, 'because some of the material in his library bore heavily on political matters: the lives of the caesars, rebellions, wars, and subjects of that kind. But Gershom never used the library in that way. He was a pure collector. He loved the books for themselves. I think he was looking for complete accounts of events, in the same way as he looked for complete accounts in finance. He liked everything neat and tidy.'

'So how do we proceed, honoured Petros?' I asked, and he put his head to his temples and rubbed to ease the pain that my question had caused.

'If this murder were political,' he said, 'we would have to shut down the city. Close the gates. Fill the streets with soldiers. Question every inn, shop and house, and search everywhere that strangers could hide. We would have to declare military law and arrest anyone we think might be involved,' he looked at me and Morganus, 'and if we do that, then from the instant I give the orders—that is to say, His Grace gives the orders—the games would be ruined and all chance gone of His Grace ever becoming Governor of Italia!'

Petros looked straight at me, and I saw the question even before he asked it. 'So what would you do, Ikaros of Apollonis?'

In fact, I read the answer in his face, but I had to explain it, because a man does not always know what is in his own mind.

'I would first ask,' I said, 'what do we mean by politics? As I understand it, what Romans mean by politics is the conflict between the great families of Rome,' Petros and Morganus nodded at this obvious truth, 'and you, honoured Petros, have already declared that Gershom was not involved in any such conflict.' Petros nodded again, 'So,' I said, 'I think this is something different. I don't know *what* it is, but it's different.' I tried another approach. 'Could this somehow—by whatever devious route—have been contrived by the druids as another insult to the Empire? To damage the Games? Like the murder of Celsus?'

'No!' Petros and Morganus spoke together—and instantly.

'After you, First Javelin,' said Petros, with a small bow.

'No,' said Morganus, 'Celsus was an officer and a Roman knight, and his men had just been made citizens. Whereas Gershom was just a tax official, and he was a slave, and killing a slave doesn't count in honour: not even an imperial slave.' Petros and I, both imperial slaves,looked at each other and there was a small silence of embarrassment.

'What?' said Morganus looking from one to another of us in puzzlement. But Petros's face told me that whether or not he liked it, he agreed with what Morganus had said about slaves.

'Never mind,' I said, and accepted that line as similarly closed. 'Then who might have wanted him dead?'

Petros thought about that.

'I think you should look into his records,' he said, 'to find out which of our Celtic billionaires he's upset. In particular look at his dealings with the professional tax-gatherers. They are devious creatures who wouldn't like it if he stopped them putting their hands into the strong box.' I understood at once, because of the odd way that Roman taxation works in the provinces: it works by contract. That is to say that the Romans themselves do not collect tax, but contract out the work to local entrepreneurs who are supposed to keep a small, agreed proportion of the money and pass the rest to the Roman treasury. The system saves the cost of setting up a tax collection department, and benefits from the local knowledge of the tax collectors, but it is notorious for corruption.

'Then do we have your permission …'

Petros corrected me instantly.

'His Grace's permission!' he said, and I bowed.

'Do we have *His Grace's* permission,' I said, 'to enter Gershom's office in the revenue department, and question his staff?'

'Of course,' said Petros, 'your commission document already covers that.'

'And may we inspect his library and take away books if need be?'

'Of course!' He leaned forward and spoke with emphasis. 'You must understand that even with the generous support of the veterans colony of Flavensum, the cost of these games will be so appalling that we must impose utmost fiscal discipline on this province and its barbarous people. We cannot allow any suspicion that the provincial government would allow, or excuse, any attempt to avoid taxation, especially in so murderous a manner as this! So you must give this inquiry your uttermost efforts, and I—that is, His Grace—will support you in every way.

Given that imperative, the days that followed were some of the busiest in my life, because there was very much to do.

First with Gershom's library now safe in the legionary fortress we mustered a team of legionary clerks to sort through the books. There were five men, under a clerk optio named Silvius, who had worked for Morganus and myself on previous occasions. He and his men were excused armour specialists, from the large team who ran the Twentieth

Legion's considerable bureaucracy. They were literate, intelligent men and as far removed from the boot-slogging rankers as an eagle is from a duck.

I gave them their orders in one of the offices in the legion's records block: a big square room, with window shutters thrown open for the light. The books were now stacked on a series of long tables, in random order as they had come off the wagons that brought them here. They were mostly the usual scroll-books of classic scholarship, but there were a few wax-tablet books too, piled in disorderly heaps. I stood with Morganus and the bodyguards, looking at the dismal remains of Gershom's library with Silvius in front of us and his four subordinates behind him.

'Silvius,' I said, looking at the books, 'you have to bring order out of chaos. The books were once organised but now they're a mess. So go through the books, listing them by whatever system you think best. Just put them into some sort of order. Do you understand?'

I looked closely at Silvius because I was asking him to display considerable initiative. So I read his face and was pleased to see that he was ready for the task.

'With respect, Your Worship…' he said.

'Go on,' I said.

'Was there no written catalogue of the books?'

'The house slaves say there was one, but it's gone. Either burned or the killers took it with them.'

'Yes, Your Worship,' said Silvius, 'and are the books Latin or Greek? We'll have trouble with any other languages.'

'They are mostly Latin or Greek,' I said, 'but I believe some are in Hebrew or Aramaic.' Silvius frowned.

'Can we set those aside for you, Your Worship?' He looked at his team. 'We can't any of us read Hebrew, or anything else.'

'I understand,' I said, 'set those aside for me. Set aside any you can't read.'

'Yes, Your Worship.'

'Silvius,' I said, 'the most important thing to remember is that we don't know why Gershom was killed, but we know that his killers wanted a book from this library.' Silvius nodded. 'Either they wanted it for themselves, or they wanted to stop someone else—we don't know who—from reading it. We think that book is still in there somewhere.' I pointed at the piles of books. 'So, as you go through those books, look for anything that might be political, or dangerous, or treasonable. Anything like that.'

'Yes, YourWorship. I'll tell the men and we'll look out for anything that might be worth killing a man for.'

That same day we followed the only other line of inquiry. We went to the offices of taxation and revenue, at the residence of the Procurator Fiscal. This was a monster building, five stories high, at the upper end of the Via Principalis, between the temple of Jupiter Maximus and the temple of Heracles. The Procurator was one of the triad of great ones, the others being the Governor and the Lord Chief Justice that Rome appoints to govern a province, so that no one man has too much power. Among other duties, the Procurator dealt with all matters of finance within the province, and was third-ranking among the great ones, being only a knight, while The Governor and Chief Justice were always senatorial noblemen.

None the less, the Procurator's residence was as much a palace as an office block, and was highly decorated with statues, columns, pediments, and—on that day—the front of the building was covered with wooden scaffolding, for workers to re-plaster and paint the façade in time for the governor's games.

We marched with the inevitable escort that must accompany a first javelin when he visits so great an official, but it was only half a century, reflecting the status of the Procurator. Thus a visit to the Chief Jusice would have required a full century, and one to the Governor, a century from the legion's elite first cohort, because nobody important every does anything alone under Rome, because that is the Roman way.

Fortunately the Procurator—Quintus Veranius Scapula—was most helpful, being greatly affected by the murder of Gershom, whom he had obviously valued as a subordinate and liked as a person. Scapula was actually in mourning: unshaven, with a ceremonial rent in his tunic, and with a streak of ash on his brow. So were his personal attendants, who were just like those that attended Petros: shaven skulls, sharp faces, and well-armed with note book and abacus. Scapula received us in his private office with just his six attendants behind him, facing myself, Morganus and the bodyguards. Wine and cakes were offered and taken, and Scapula, Morganus and I sat, while the rest stood around us. Scapula was thin, middle-aged, and had missing teeth that embarrassed him such that he was reluctant to open his mouth. He was an intelligent and active man—who had obviously gained his appointment by merit—but he was addicted to quotations, which were an irritation.

'As Horace says,' he declared, early on in our meeting, '*Troubles wake talents which sleep in good times.*' He nodded in agreement with himself. 'Thus all good men in the province look to you, Ikaros the Greek, and to you Honoured Morganus, to find out who did this dreadful thing, and bring them into court.' He shook his head in sorrow at the loss of Gershom. 'As Cicero says: *what sweetness is there in life, if you take away friendship?*'

The quotations were an affectation, but his horror at the crime was genuine and he was not alone in his affection for Gershom, as I found when I questioned Gershom's staff. Scapula agreed at once that I should do this, asking only that one of his attendants should be with me throughout, to take notes on the proceedings for his own records. This formality proved unexpectedly useful, because although Gershom's people were helpful, giving us ready access to all their records, I soon detected that something was being held back.

Gershom's office was large, it was on the first floor with shutter-windows opening on the Via Principalis with a fine view of the avenue, and a constant background noise of people, beasts and wheeled vehicles outside the building. Gershom had—*had* had—seven subordinate clerks, all of whom were in deepest mourning, and were headed by an elderly Egyptian named Tadashi. He was very old, quite deaf and short-sighted. But he was highly educated man who spoke many languages, and his mind was sharp.

At first I was daunted by the extent of Gershom's records. Thus Tadashi showed me a into a side room with racks from floor to ceiling holding book-tablets. There was a very great number of them.

'These are from the last three years, and this year's so far,' said Tadashi. 'We keep the rest in the cellars.'

'How far back do the records go?'

'Forty years, Your Worship,' he said, 'back to just after Boudicca's time, when the city got going again.'

Morganus shook his head. 'We're going to need more than Optio Silvius and his lads to go through that lot.'

'Don't worry,' I said, 'I doubt we need go back further than five years.'

'That still leaves a lot,' said Morganus.

'Honoured Sir, Your Worship,' said Tadashi. 'Perhaps I can help?'

'Yes?' I said. 'How?'

Tadashi bowed, and glanced back into the main office. He looked at the other clerks from his department, he looked at the bodyguards, and he particularly looked at Procurator Scapula's shaven-headed attendant, who was standing right beside us with stylus and tablet in hand.

So Tadashi picked up a book tablet and opened it. It had five leaves, wired together, each one about a foot wide by a foot and a half high. The wooden leaves had wax on either side, giving ten wax sheets in all, and the wax was covered with small writing. It was a standard Roman accounts book. It was completely ordinary. But Tadashi held it close to his face, to help his failing eyes, and pointed at one of the pages. I noticed that his index finger was crooked with age, and the joints disfigured with the bony swellings that afflict some old people.

'Look here,' he said, and said something in a language I did not know. He tried another language. I shook my head. '*What of Hebrew?*' he said.

'*Hebrew*?' I said, and replied in the same language. '*I understand Hebrew.*'

'*That is well,*' he said, '*for there are things that may not be spoken here.*' It was difficult for me to follow him, because while I can read Hebrew, I am not used to hearing it spoken, nor speaking it myself. Scapula's shaven-head was even more puzzled.

'What's that?' he said in Latin. 'What are you saying?'

'I am showing his worship a document,' said Tadashi.

'Yes,' said the shaven-head. 'But I'm taking notes, so please speak plainly.'

'May I finish my explanation?' said Tadashi.

The shaven-head frowned, then nodded. *What could be the harm?* he thought. I read it on his face. 'Yes,' he said, 'but after that, speak Latin!'

Tadashi bowed politely and we conversed briefly in Hebrew:

'*Let us meet in another place. There is a wine shop called The Sign of Five Stars.*'

'*I know it! It is close by the new shrine to Isis.*'

'*Blessed be the name of the goddess, and yes, that is the one.*'

'*At what time?*'

'*At noon: the sixth hour.*'

Later, as I marched back to the legionary fortress with Morganus and his escort, he and I discussed languages. It was an interesting discussion, at least to me.

'How many languages do you actually speak?' he said.

'Well, Greek and Latin of course,' I said, 'Macedonian, Hebrew and Aramaic, and I'm trying to get my tongue round Celtic, as you know, and I can read in Egyptian but can't speak it. Those, and a few others.'

'A few others?' he said, and laughed. 'Just a few? And what's Aramaic anyway?'

'It's related to Hebrew. It's a language of the Palestine region.'

'So why do you know Aramaic?'

'I learned it in the time of my old master, Scorteus who was Fortunus' father. I had to translate some religious books from Aramaic into Greek. Scorteus bought them, and eventually gave them to me. I've still got them. They're in your house.'

'What books were they?'

'The books of Matthew, Mordecai and Zoltan, about the life of the rabbi Jesus Bar Joseph.'

'The one we crucified?'

'Yes. Him.'

The boots tramped, we marched on and I attempted to pursue the matter. 'Those books are fascinating,' I said, 'and exceedingly rare. They're probably the only copies in the western Empire.'

'Are they?'

'Oh yes. I became quite expert in the study of them, especially the book of Zoltan which was philosophically the most interesting, because it was full of crossings out, and insertions and had obviously been adapted from the book of Matthew, such that...'

'Do tell me,' said Morganus, 'tell me every word, and don't miss out a single one.'

His sarcasm could have been measured by the mile and weighed by the ton. So the bodyguards sniggered and I dropped the matter, just as I always do when I attempt any discussion with Romans on matters that are not severely practical. It is yet another burden that I bear—and another reason for taking refuge in wine.

Then, just before noon, I went with Morganus and the bodyguards to meet Tadashi at the Sign of the Five Stars. To avoid attracting attention, Morganus and the bodyguards were incognito. They wore cloaks and tunics like any ordinary man, except that the bodyguards wore their army swords slung on baldrics under their cloaks, where they could not be seen. Morganus looked older without his helmet. His face was scarred, and his short-cut hair was white.

The Sign of The Five Stars was exclusive, serving fine wines at high cost. It was exceedingly well furnished, with smartly-dressed staff. It was deep and narrow, with seating in small booths that opened around a central aisle, and it had a beautifully painted ceiling that displayed the gods and beasts of the heavenly constellations, against a dark blue background. It was elegant and pleasing and I knew it well, as a source of some of the best wine in the city. Thus I was more than happy to go there: or rather, to go there again, because I had been before, and the staff knew me and summoned the owner as I entered with Morganus and the bodyguards.

'Your Worship,' said the owner to me. 'Your Honour,' he said to Morganus, who was very visibly a senior Roman even without his armour. 'May I offer you a seat with a good view of the city?' We looked at the booths near the doors, which were wide open, looking straight out into the life of the forum itself. All the booths were full, since it was mid-day and the city was at lunch.

But the owner bowed again, and spoke to Morganus whom he really did recognise, since it was his business to know the great and powerful of the city. 'Any customer would happily move to accommodate the Spear of the Twentieth,' he said, and Morganus looked at me. I nodded slightly towards the deep interior, where there were still booths vacant. Discretion was more important than prestige. So we sat far back, the staff instantly served wine, bread and olives and we ordered food so that our presence should not be overly noticed; except that the bodyguards sat to attention with straight backs, and hands at their sides.

'What pleasure it is to see the legions at drill.' I said, and Morganus scowled at me.

'Sit comfortable, by all the gods,' he said to the bodyguards.

'Yes, Honoured sir!' said all four together.

Tadashi arrived before our food did, and joined us at table. He walked slowly, leaning on a stick, peering hard to try to find us, and gasping with effort. He was heavily wrapped in a thick cloak, and I felt for him, poor fellow. The weather of Britannia is bad enough for a Greek, so imagine what it must be like for an Egyptian! I stood and waved to catch his attention, and he hobbled forward, and nodded as finally he recognised me.

'*Shalom aleichem*!' he said to me in the ancient Hebrew greeting.

'*Aleichem shalom*!' I replied, as waiters pounced with more wine, bread and olives, and Tadashi too ordered food, choosing only a snack. Then he looked around to make sure that nobody was listening. He leaned forward, bowed slightly to Morganus, and spoke to me in Hebrew.

'We have little time, but I can tell you the names: the names of those who most likely ordered the death of Gershom.'

Chapter 13

I looked at Tadashi in growing excitement. I wanted Morganus to hear this for himself.

'Tadashi,' I said, 'you may speak freely. You are among friends.'

Tadashi looked at Morganus. *Even him?* he thought.

'You may speak freely,' I said. So he did—as best he could, because he fought for breath, and whispered harshly as he spoke. Also, although he knew so many languages, Latin was clearly not his best; he spoke it strangely and conversation was made difficult by his deafness. I had to repeat everything several times, but I omit these repetitions since they would be tedious to read.

'I have brought list for you,' he said, 'here is list.' He reached into a pouch on his belt and produced a thin, wooden letter-tablet and gave it to me. It was folded and sealed. 'I have inscribed all names whom Gershom most offended,' he said, 'offended since death of his beloved.' He paused and looked at Morganus. I could see the doubt in his mind.

'Tadashi,' I said, 'I ask in the name of your late master, that you tell me what is in your mind, because I know that you have something important to say.'

He gasped in sudden fear, and his distorted old fingers touched a holy amulet on a chain around his neck, as he sought the protection of his gods. Obviously he knew my reputation. Then he wagged his head from side to side in an odd, oriental gesture of resignation, thinking—I suppose—that he might as well tell me, since I had seen his secret already. So he spoke.

'Gershom changed,' he said, 'He changed at death of beloved wife.' He looked at me questioningly. 'Is it known to you that Jews have only one god?'

'Yes,' I said.

'Is it known to you that the Jewish god is vengeful and punishing god?'

'Yes!' I said.

'So: when the beloved of Gershom died, Gershom made search for reason of death, and believed that her death was punishment from god. Punishment for sins.'

'What sins?' I asked. 'What had he done?'

Tadashi leaned across the table.

'Please understand. Gershom was good servant of Father Rome.'

'Yes?'

'But,' Tadashi made the head-wagging gesture again, 'always with the rich Celt, we make negotiation, make price, and make smooth.'

'What do you mean?' I asked. He nodded.

'I will explain to you,' he said. 'Imagine rich Celt. Imagine he tax collector. Imagine he make deceit. Imagine he make hiding from Father Rome of some millions.'

'Yes?'

'But perhaps we cannot make proof in court. Or perhaps we still want make use of rich Celt, because though he is bad, all others are worse.'

'Yes?'

'So we make agreement: *Gershom* make agreement.' He looked at me, urging me to understand. 'Everyone do this,' he said, 'not just Gershom! All men in revenue do this.'

'Yes?'

'So, we make agreement with rich Celt. He make payment to Father Rome. He make payment of what he stole. But still he keep some... and...'

'And some goes to Gershom?' I said.

'Not just Gershom!' he insisted.

'I understand,' I said.

'By that path,' he said, 'Father Rome get money, no Celt get punished, but Celt is warned not to make theft again, and all is made smooth, and business continues.'

'And Gershom becomes richer and richer. 'He spread hands in a helpless gesture. *What could I do?* he was thinking.

'But this stopped when his wife died?'

'Yes,' he said. 'He believed that god made punishment upon him, and that he must never take money again.'

'And so?'

'And so, he make no more agreement. Instead, he make big, big fine upon some rich Celts who steal Father Rome's money: very big! Very great fines! And other rich Celts—all names in letter I give you—other rich Celts are angry. They think Gershom make betrayal upon them. They are very angry.'

'Did Gershom know this?'

'Of course! And he was afraid. So he make purchase of sword and make learning in the skill of the blade.'

'Even though slaves cannot own swords?' I said, but he brushed that away.

'The law make forbiddance of sword in street. The law make no search inside house. Not for imperial slave.'

'Who taught him this skill of the blade?' asked Morganus. 'Did he go to the imperial gymnasium?'

'Yes,' said Tadashi, 'at baths of Trajan. He make learning because he fear rich Celts send men to kill him… and they did!'

Our food arrived at that point, and conversation ceased. It was good food and good wine but I hardly paid it any attention. I wanted to open the letter to look at the names inside. So we ate almost in silence, then I asked a few more questions after the dishes were cleared, to make sure Tadashi had nothing else to say. Which he did not, except to urge us to find the killers.

'Gershom very good man,' he said, 'good master. Kind man. Good servant to Father Rome.' I must have smiled at that, because he swiftly repeated, 'Good servant,' with emphasis. Perhaps he was right. Perhaps that is how the world runs. How would I know? I am an engineer not a tax official.

'One more question,' I said, before he left. 'There were eight guests at a dinner club I attended with Gershom. That's six apart from myself and Petros.'

'Yes,' said Tadashi, 'The dinner club. I know of that.'

'Could any of these men have wanted to kill him?' I spoke all the names. He paused and thought deeply. He made the head-wagging gesture.

'See my list,' he said, 'but otherwise, no. Gershom was good man. Kind man. Everybody liked Gershom.'

It was plain truth. I saw it in his face but I took one final step.

'What about Petros himself?' I said, treading on the most exquisitely thin ice that the mind could imagine.

'No!' he said, 'Petros was great friend of Gershom. Dear friend indeed.' Again it was truth, and I learned to my surprise that Petros had a friend: or *had* had.

We left shortly after, Tadashi going back to his office, and myself burning to look at the list of names, which I would not do in the street. In any case Morganus had a suggestion.

'We're near the Baths of Trajan,' he said, 'they're only just over there,' he pointed. 'Why don't we go into the gymnasium to see if we can find this sword instructor? The one Gershom used. He might know something.'

So we went to look for him. We went into the baths of Trajan, which were enormous, with pillars outside, marble walls inside, granite floors and huge domed ceilings. There was the full range of hot rooms, cold rooms, sweat rooms and plunge pools. It was too early for the baths to be full, as the city was still at work. But there were men in the gymnasium, which was a typical Roman exercise hall, built on to the side of the bath complex. It was a plain, rectangular brick building, a hundred yards long by fifty yards wide,with an earth floor, high walls, and a row of cubicles down one side where the various teachers and instructors had their offices. These specialists offered instruction in running, wrestling, discus, javelin and various ball games, and of course, sword play. So the whole building echoed with the shouts of those who were at work on their clients, as they yelled and encouraged and cursed.

'Run-run-run… and… *jump!*'

'Give it some effort!'

'Easy, easy, don't just chuck it!'

'Gods of Hades! Not like that!'

The bodyguards grinned. It was like army drill, which was not surprising as many of the instructors were time-expired veterans. The sword-master certainly was. He got up from the bench where he was sitting with his assistants and came towards us, with a fat smile on his face. He stood to attention and raised his right arm in a formal Roman salute.

'Hail Morganus!' he bellowed, his voice bouncing from one end of the hall to the other. 'Hail Leonius Morganus Fortis Victrix!' Morganus smiled, stood to attention and returned the salute.

'Hail Septimus Archontis!' he cried, and Septimus the sword-master looked back over his shoulder to make sure that his assistants had seen that he was recognised by the first javelin of the Twentieth. Archontis was a squat, broad man in his fifties, with very long arms. His skin was leathery and he had the odd little scar under the chin that veteran legionaries have, from twenty-five years of chafing by the leather thongs that keep their helmets on their heads. His speech was coarse, like that of Gallus the centurion of Silesian, because Septimus was also from the back streets of Rome.

'Gods give you good day, Honoured Sir,' he said to Morganus, and gave a deep bow. 'Don't tell me Your Honour's come for lessons in stabbing coons? Not you that's stuck more of the bastards than all the legions put together?' He looked over his shoulder again, to make sure he was basking in Morganus' fame. 'But if that's what you've come for, Your Honour… it's free of charge!'

Everyone smiled, except perhaps Morganus, whose expression did not display limitless joy at this reunion with an old comrade. But he was polite. He exchanged a few words with Septimus about his past service with the Twentieth, then referred him to me.

'This Greek gentleman is Ikaros of Apollonis,' he said. 'He is my comrade and he would like to ask you a few questions.'

Septimus turned to face me. He was a full head shorter, and emotions chased across his face as he looked up at me. He frowned and concentrated. He wondered, as Romans do, if I were free or a slave. And what questions would I ask? And then his mouth fell open as he realised who I was. I was the smart-arsed Greek that looks inside men's heads! The one that follows Morganus around! Then he frowned and pushed his jaw forward to show that he wasn't having *his* mind read by no sodding Greek! Then he looked at Morganus, and knew that he would have to give me respect, and his mouth fell open again.

It was comical. I very nearly laughed.

'I give you good day, Septimus Archontis,' I said.

'And I to you, Ikaros of Apollonis,' he said, and glanced at Morganus to check that this good behaviour had been noticed.

'I have some questions about Gershom Bar Meshulam,' I said.

'You mean that yid what got done?' said Septimus. 'It's all over the town. Everyone's talking about it.'

'Yes, him,' I said, 'We believe he took instruction from you. Sword instruction.'

Septimus considered the question. He swallowed, and wondered what he might have done wrong.

'It was only wooden staves,' said Septimus, 'army practice swords. No steel! I knew he was a slave, and I know they can't have swords. And anyway, it's only wood for all of em!' he pointed to his cubicle. I saw that behind the bench where his assistants sat, there was a rack of wooden swords. 'We never give any of 'em steel. They'd kill one another, the silly bastards. Or kill me!'

'Of course,' I said, 'and that's not what we're interested in.'

'Oh,' said Septimus, much relieved.

'We want to know *why* he took instruction. We think he was afraid of someone, but we don't know who. Did he say anything to you about that?'

He shook his head. He didn't know.

'Did he talk about anything?' I asked, 'Anything at all?'

Septimus nodded.

'Yeah. He said he wanted to fight. Proper fighting, not like some of them.'

'What do you mean?' I asked.

'Well, some of the rich young buggers we get in here, it's just for show. Some of them even bring their tarts in to watch, so they can get their hand up the tart's leg later on, 'cos tarts get excited when they see men fight. It's like watching gladiators.'

'So what did Gershom want?'

'He wanted to fight, really fight. He wanted the works, so I gave it to him. Kick, punch, chuck, bite: anything to get the other bugger off guard and then in with the point, quick-sharp!' I saw Morganus nodding.

'Was he any good?' said Morganus. 'Could he keep a straight blade?'

'Oh yes,' said Septimus, 'he was good. He got himself fit, he practised hard, he listened to what I told him, and he had long reach. And unlike some of the silly little sods, he got the message straight off, that you go in with the point and keep stabbing till the other bugger goes down, 'cos it's just as important to pull out and stab *again*, as it is to stab once! You don't just give him one, you give him two or three, right? And then when the bugger's down, you give him some more, and Gershom got all that without hardly telling.'

Morganus nodded in approval: it was standard army drill.

'Gershom was attacked by at least three men with swords,' I said, 'and they killed him in the end. But do you think he might have wounded one of them in the fight?'

'Yes,' said Septimus, 'he'd have got one of the bastards, or at least he'd have had a sodding good go.' He dug into his memory. 'He was… it's hard to explain… he was sort of fierce, like a barbarian. I didn't have to shout or anything. He gave it all he'd got.'

Septimus nodded. 'He wasn't a bad bugger for a Jew. Always paid up-front.'

Soon after, we left and walked back into the forum.

'How did you like Septimus Archontis?' asked Morganus.

'Not much,' I said, and he nodded.

'A notorious defaulter in his time,' he said. 'Septimus spent more time on fatigues than ever he did soldiering. But he was good with a sword.'

'So was Gershom, it seems.'

'Yes,' said Morganus, 'you wouldn't think it of a pen-pusher in an office.'

'Not normally,' I said, 'but I think Gershom was driven from inside. I think he was morbidly driven. He thought that his god was frowning on him, and I think he may even have *wanted* someone to come after him, so he could pay for his sins in blood. Men do strange things to keep faith with their gods: especially if they're in fear of punishment.'

'Is that why he put such effort into the sword practice?' said Morganus, and I paused as another thought came to me.

'Yes,' I said, 'In fact I'm *sure* he wanted them to come. Just think: first of all, he had no guards in the house when he could easily have had them. He was a very senior man. He could have had a dozen auxiliaries permanently on guard if he'd wanted. His boss, Scapula, would have fixed it, or Petros would have.'

Morganus nodded. 'Yes,' he said, 'But didn't his major domos—Katarix—say that Gershom's wife wouldn't have soldiers in the house?'

'And that he was honouring her memory?' I said. 'Yes, possibly. But it didn't have to be soldiers. He could have had some hefty farm boys on guard with clubs. That'd be a lot better than nothing. And there's more. When those men got into his house, he must have heard some noise from his bedroom, but he didn't come downstairs. I think he waited in the bedroom, so they'd have to come through the door one at a time, which would give him his best chance to use his sword. And if he did that it was deliberate, because he'd thought about it.'

Morganus looked at me with an odd expression on his face.

'How can you know that?' he said.

'I don't *know* it,' I said, 'I'm guessing.' Indeed I was, but Morganus was unsure.

'If you say so,' he said, and I saw the fingers of his right hand move, just a fraction, as if they were making the bull sign.

'I'm not reading the past,' I said. 'I've told you a thousand times that I don't do magic.'

'If you say so,' he said, and changed the subject. 'What now? I suppose you'll want to open Tadashi's letter. So will it be The Sign of Five Stars, which is just over there? Or some other wine shop?'

I chose the Five Stars. We sat deep inside again, because although the shop was no longer full, I wanted nobody around us.

'Well?' said Morganus when I had opened the letter.

'That's interesting,' I said. 'Look, there's a Roman name. Five Celtic names and one Roman. And all of them are contracted tax collectors, who Tadashi thinks might have wanted to kill Gershom. The Roman name is at the bottom of the list, but it's there.'

Morganus looked and shook his head.

'No,' he said, 'can't be. I know that man.' He looked at me. 'And so do you! He was at the governor's levee with the other men from Flavensum, and isn't he a member of Gershom's club? You told me you saw him when you went to that dinner.'

'Yes,' I said, and I read the name aloud. 'Aurelio Tobias Bethsidus.'

'That's right,' said Morganus, 'but you can forget about him! He's a duovir of the city council of the Flavensum veteran's colony. He's Roman all through. Surely he can't be fiddling his tax returns?'

I laughed.

'Do you know any man who *isn't*?' I asked, and he smiled.

'Well let's do the Celts first,' he said. I looked at Tadashi's list.

'He's added a note,' I said, and read it '*I make list in order of probability of guilty.*' I looked at Morganus. 'Well, at least your Roman is at the bottom.'

'So who do we do first?' he said.

'The one at the top,' I said, 'Felemid! And we know him, too. We interviewed him in the case of my late master's murder. He's probably the richest man in Londinium, but I didn't know he was a tax collector.'

'Felemid?' said Morganus, 'that little dark lad, from the Brigantes tribe up north?'

'Yes,' I said, 'him! And this might be political after all, because he's deep into Britannic politics, he's very clever…'

'And he fancies you!' said Morganus with a huge smile. 'He's the one that was always trying to buy you from your old master.'

‘And by the grace of Apollo, my old master would never sell,’ I said.

‘But he does fancy you, doesn’t he?’ said Morganus, and laughed.

‘It is a burden that we Greeks have to bear,’ I said, ‘every man in the Empire assumes that we prefer men to women.’

‘The Spartans certainly do!’ said Morganus.

‘I’m not a Spartan.’

‘And the Athenians! They lock their women in the house so they can watch the boys on the sports field.’

‘I thank Apollo that I’m not Athenian, either.’

But that was the end of our consideration of Felemid’s sexuality, because there came a distant blast of horns and a roar of people cheering. We all looked out into the forum, which was filling with shouting, waving people and an excited man ran into the wine shop. He yelled at the top of his voice.

‘It’s the racing drivers!’ he cried. ‘They’ve just arrived at the piers and they’re coming to the temple of Jupiter. It’s all the big names: Portatius the green, Diocles the white, Juvencus the red…’ He gave other names, all unknown to me, but not to Morganus and the four bodyguards, who leapt to their feet in delight.

‘Let’s go and look!’ said Morganus.

‘Yeah!’ said the bodyguards.

So we went out, and the bodyguards pushed a way through the excited eager crowd, and I must stress that women as much as men seemed enthralled by the prospect of seeing some of Rome’s greatest drivers. The noise was enormous, and the brazen blare of a military band came up the broad avenue of the Via Principalis, as the charioteers and their followers came to pay respect to the gods of Rome at the temple of the divine triad: Jupiter, Juno and Minerva, which rose over the north side of the forum.

Thanks to the bodyguards we had an excellent view, just where the Via Principalis meets the forum, and soon the bodyguards were cheering with all the rest as a strong guard of legionaries, in mirror-polish parade armour marched forward to clear the way, and the band of the Twentieth came behind, blowing their hearts out.

The charioteers—there were a dozen of them—stood up above the crowd in actual racing chariots: light, strong structures, skeletal and open, and boldly decorated with team colours.

For this processional entry into the city, each chariot was drawn by four men of the Twentieth Legion, every one grinning all over his face and waving to the crowd in delight. Roars of cheering rolled up and down the Via Principalis, as every soul in the city who could walk, crawl or be carried, was getting out on the streets and yelling and waving the colours: white, red, green and blue.

'See?' yelled Morganus, as the first chariot went past. 'Juvencus the Red!' It was easy to know the drivers' names because a man went before each chariot holding a large placard with the driver's name in big, bold letters. 'Juvencus!' said Morganus again. 'Over two thousand wins, 150 won in the final dash, and …' There was much more. The bodyguards were shouting the same to each other, as was every other in the crowd who wished his neighbours to understand how very well informed he was on all matters of chariot racing. But I concentrated on the drivers.

They were surprisingly small men, some quite young, others middle aged, but all of them bold and confidant. They stood upright, waving slowly to the crowd with palms turned inward. They bowed to left and right as if recognising prominent citizens, and they wore the full costume of chariot drivers: leather helmet and body armour, and leather guards strapped to their thighs and knees to protect them if they were thrown and dragged.

Then Morganus was yelling into my ear again.

'This is the real thing!' he said. 'We've had the amateur version, even without a proper stadium,' he looked at the vast crowd, 'that's how everyone got the taste. But that was only Celts with home-made rigs and local horses.'

'Have there already been chariot races in Britannia?'I said, and Morganus laughed.

'What world do you live in?' he asked, so I sought further instruction.

'Aren't some of them slaves?' I said, pointing at the drivers.

'Yes!' he said. 'Diocles and Portatius are both slaves.'

'And aren't the others ...'

But the crowd surged, and an enormous wave of cheering rose up, and I was separated from Morganus and the bodyguards as Portatius himself, who was obviously the most famous of all of them, went past.

The crowd yelled itself hysterical, and I puzzled over the fact that some of these drivers were slaves, and all of them were classed as infami, which is a very Roman snob-word for persons who do disgraceful work. Thus torturers, pimps and prostitutes are infami. But so are gladiators, actors and racing drivers, even though they may be world famous, idolised by everyone and monstrously overpaid. This oddity of Roman perception has to do with do with the fact that a Roman citizen is supposed to be dignified, reserved, and devoted to public life. He is not supposed to cavort before the vulgar crowd for their entertainment. So I watched the procession and learned how profoundly Britannia was obsessed with chariot racing and racing drivers. In due course I saw the value of this lesson.

The next day Moranus and I went to see the billionaire, tax-gathering Felemid.

Chapter 14

Felemid was easily found. He lived in Londinium in a huge mansion: a whole city block, staffed with hundreds of slaves. Morganus sent a runner to the mansion when we got back to the fortress, and got a swift reply. It came when we were in Morganus' house, where he was buckling on his war harness after the incognito expedition. As Morgana Callandra brought in the runner, Morganus was still working his arms and shoulders round in circles to settle his armour.

'That's better!' he said, and the bodyguards brought his sword and dirk. The messenger, still panting after his run across the city, bare-legged in a short tunic, saluted Morganus and handed over Felemid's reply. Morganus dismissed him, and waved the document at me.

'Look!' he said, 'No wood or wax. Actual papyrus on a scroll, and bound up with silk cords! It must be nice to be rich.'

'What does he say?' I asked. Morganus read the scroll.

'He'll see us at the first hour after dawn tomorrow.' Morganus smiled. 'He says he'll make special time for us,' he looked at me, 'which means *you*, I shouldn't wonder, seeing as he likes you so much! He says he'll do so even if he has to cut short his salutatio.'

The salutatio was the most important event in the Roman day, so Felemid was indeed trying to oblige us. It was the dawn event whereby needy persons—the clients—stood outside the gates of some mighty person—the patron—waiting to be received so that they could ask for his favours and in return give their support to whatever enterprise he had going forward, which mainly meant voting for his choice at elections and following him in processions, together with whatever else he asked. The salutatio was also the time for an exchange of news, gossip and instructions. Every prominent man in the Roman world held a dawn salutatio, and no business moved without first being agreed at one.

So, at the end of the first daylight hour Morganus, the bodyguards and I marched up to the main gates of Felemid's mansion. The street was already alive with traffic: handcarts, beasts, people, and also clients who were still emerging from the mansion. So there was a rumbling of noise and conversation in the miserable Britannic morning.

Some few of the clients were citizens in togas who were prosperous men in their own right, seeking business connection or political favours. These mostly emerged smiling in the warmth of Felemid's promises, though some were downcast and wondering what they had said wrong. All these citizens were met by their waiting slaves, who bowed and followed their masters home. By contrast, the poorest clients—shabby Celts in native dress—came out with sacks of bread and cheese, which were the dole that rich men give to the hungry, and the poorest of all found their wives and children waiting to thrust thin hands into the sack.

As always, everyone made way for Morganus in his splendid armour and swan-crest helmet, and we entered the mansion where the Major Domos and house slaves bowed repeatedly and led us to the atrium: the usual Roman structure with its open roof, and marble-lined pool below, though I noticed that this one was not reserved to collect drinking water, but swam with exotic fish—all bright red—probably imported at colossal cost from faraway China.

The Major Domos bowed low.

'Honoured Sirs,' he said, 'His-Honour-my-Master rejoices in the joy of your arrival, and begs that you would graciously condescend to follow my humble self, and be conducted into the presence of my Honoured Master.' That, to the best of my recollection, is what he said though it was longer and more elaborate, because that is the way Felemid liked things done. Thus the atrium, as with the rest of the house, was a madness of over-decoration, and of over-elaboration, and the cramming into every corner of every ornament in every material—gold, silver, bronze, ceramic and costly wood—that trade and money could buy. It reminded me strongly of the house of my old master Scorteus, because he too was a Celt and he too loved over-decoration.

'I thank your master for his greeting,' said Morganus, standing aloof of the vulgarity all around. The bodyguards did likewise, though they probably liked it. 'You may now take us directly to your master. Directly now!' he said, because Morganus was displeased that Felemid was not here to greet us in person.

So the Major Domos repeated more flowery words, and bowed some more, and all the other slaves bowed some more, and then we were finally led off through room after elaborate room, all full of slaves, and finally through an ante-chamber, completely tiled, which led to a large pair of cedar wood doors with golden handles, and a house boy at each handle, ready to open the doors.

'Wait!' said Morganus, and stopped. We all stopped. Morganus sniffed.

'Honoured Sirs?' said the Major Domos.

'I can smell steam,' said Morganus. 'Are we going into the bath chamber?'

'Yes, Honoured Sir. My master always takes his morning bath *after* salutatio.'

Morganus looked at me.

'The bath-chamber?' he said.

'So it seems,' I said. Morganus shook his head. Then he shrugged.

'Lead on!' he said, so the doors opened and we marched into the hot, wet, scented air of the largest private bath complex that I had ever seen. Even my old master never had one of this size.

Everything was lined with black granite and all the metal fittings were solid gold. The dome above was glazed for light, and the glass of the glazing was stained in lovely colours. There were white marble statues everywhere, in wall niches and on pedestals and free-standing, life-sized. There were nymphs, satyrs, fish, octopuses and Celtic deities. There was an enormous, deep plunge pool, twenty feet square at least, with steps leading down into the water, and huge golden taps so that the bather could himself mix the water if he chose.

There were four tall, blond, German slave boys, each chosen for beauty of face and standing with a linen towel over his arm. There was also a black granite massage table, laid out with towels and cushion, and a fat masseur standing with his flask of oil in hand.

There was also Felemid himself, emerging from the plunge bath, streaming with water and entirely naked. He was young—less than thirty—and he was a typical example of the Brigantes tribe: small and slender with a prominent, nose, heavy brows, thin lips and a yellowish-white skin. He was small, but he was formidable. He had made a huge fortune very fast, by trading between the Celts and the Romans, and he had done this entirely by his own efforts.

'Honoured Sir,' he said to Morganus, 'and you, Worshipful Sir!' That was to me, with a graceful bow: right hand sweeping down, left hand sweeping back, and a smooth knee bend. Then he spread wide his arms. 'Honoured Sirs, I am at your disposal!'

His speech had improved since the last time I met him, though he still had a strong native accent. I assumed he'd been taking lessons. Meanwhile, he stood before us naked.

I stress that nakedness is neither a special nor an exceptional condition, in the Roman and Greek worlds, and it is common for men and women to go naked in the public baths, though we do separate the sexes. However, there was an element of display in Felemid's nakedness that was unusual. It certainly was not the typical behaviour of a Roman gentleman, but of course he was a Celt, and I remembered that my old master and his family—all of them Celts—had no modesty: not in the bath, nor the dressing room nor even on the chamber pot. None the less, I saw that Morganus and the bodyguards were uneasy and disliked Felemid's behaviour.

So, for once, I spoke first.

'Honoured Felemid,' I said, 'we appreciate your gracious manners in receiving us here, and would beg the gift of conversation.'

'Ummm,' said Morganus, 'yes.'

Felemid looked back at us and an open display of feelings swept over his face: open to me, at least. Thus I record, because it is truth, that he did indeed gaze upon me with desire. I likewise record that although women have always liked me, I do not usually appeal to that proportion of men who, by the will of the gods, seek pleasure from other men. So in this respect Felemid was an oddity, and I knew the reason why, from past experience. Felemid not only preferred men to women, but was one of those persons who enjoys chastisement. He therefore perceived my ability to read minds as an extreme form of that procedure. He felt that it stripped him naked in a mental sense, just as now he stood before us physically naked. In addition I must say, because it too is truth, however uncomfortable, that I had not previously realized how *strong* were Felemid's feelings for me, because it was obvious that these feelings were very considerable. Or perhaps they had grown since our last meeting. Who knows?

So much for his gazing at me. But then he looked at Morganus and the bodyguards, and it was obvious that he would say nothing of importance in their presence, and so he looked back at me with a tiny question in his eyes. I nodded, and he gasped in pleasure at my understanding. As I have said so many times, I most emphatically *do not* work magic, but sometimes it is very hard to persuade people of that truth.

'Honoured Felemid,' I said, 'there are matters of sensitivity to discuss. Might we speak in private?'

'We *will* speak in private,' he said, and gave a slight wave of one hand which caused the German boys and the masseur to bow and back out of our presence, closing the cedar-wood doors behind them.

'And might I further ask, honoured Felemid, on behalf of the valiant and honourable Morganus Felix Victrix, and his men, that they might withdraw to preserve their armour and gear from the deleterious effects of hot steam?'

It was nonsense, but sometimes nonsense works, and in any case Felemid obviously wanted them gone, while Morganus knew my methods very well, and understood that Felemid would not talk in his presence.

'They may go where they please in my house,' said Felemid

'Indeed,' said Morganus. 'We would prefer to wait in the antechamber.' He gave a small bow, then looked at me. 'We will leave you to speak with the honoured Felemid,' he said, 'we will leave you two alone,' he paused, very straight-faced, then added, '...though do call us, if we can give you any assistance.'

So I was soon sitting on a black granite bench, next to the glistening, naked, happily leering Felemid, who radiated such hot physical excitement as to make a stone statue blush. I would have begun my questioning without delay, but he had some of his own first. He leaned close and put a hand on mine.

'So have you changed your mind?' he said.

'About what?' I said.

'About coming to work for me,' he said, 'there would be a most honoured and desirable place for you in my house.'

It was a difficult moment. I knew exactly what he wanted from me, and I was not in the least inclined to give it. But I had to speak carefully, or risk losing any chance of his answering my questions. So I attempted diplomacy.

'Honoured Felemid,' I said, 'I am an imperial slave, exclusively dedicated to the service of the Emperor.'

'Gods save the Emperor!' he said. 'But I have great influence with His Grace the Governor.'

'Gods save His Grace,' I said, and he laughed.

'You are so clever!' he said. 'You are so Greek!' He leaned back and looked into my eyes. 'Perhaps I could speak to His Grace, and ask for a special favour of His Imperial Majesty?'

'You could try,' I said, 'but I don't think Petros would approve.' I was thinking only of my value to Petros as a detective agent, but Felemid misunderstood completely.

'Ahhh!' he said, and shook his head. 'Petros would be jealous? He too has feelings for you?' He nodded to himself. 'It is always that way with Greeks,' he said, and I said nothing. But Felemid moved an inch away from me and sat up straight. 'Perhaps we shall speak again sometime,' he said, 'But *this* time, clever boy, what do you want of me today?'

'I am here to seek information on the death of Gershom Bar Meshulam,' I said.

'Rest his soul,' said Felemid, and raised hands.

'Yes,' I said, 'and I have learned, honoured Felemid that you—among your other interests—are a certified tax collector, receiving taxation from the Brigantes tribe on behalf of Rome.'

'It is true,' he said.

'And your supervisor and inspector was Gershom Bar Meshulam.'

'He was, and I mourn his death. Everyone mourns his death.'

'Yes,' I said, and in that instant I saw that he knew something. He gave not the slightest twitch or tremor of guilt, but there was *something* in the back of his mind. So I moved on.

'I have learned that Gershom became a new man after the death of his wife.'

'Rest her soul,' he said, piously, but I saw the little blink of understanding about Gershom *the new man*.

'Yes,' I said, 'I have learned that after the death of his wife, things were not done as in the past.'

Felemid smiled.

'You understand the old ways,' he said, 'I see that.'

'Yes,' I said, 'and I understand that Gershom found new ways. He was in fear of his god and would take no more bribes to connive at deceit.'

'Bribes?' he said. 'Deceit?' And he pretended shock. 'Such ugly words!'

'Call it what you like,' I said, 'I'm not here to talk about that.'

'Oh good,' he said. 'Oh, so very good. So what *are* you here to talk about?'

'His murder,' I said, 'Gershom's murder. Somebody sent a very expert team of assassins into Gershom's house. They killed him and searched his library. I want to know what they were they looking for, and who sent them.'

'Not me,' he said and raised a hand in self protection. 'Not me, nor anyone I know.'

I believed him. I believed him at once, because I could see written in his face that he was telling the truth. So I considered his words.

'You said *not you*,' I said, '*nor anyone else you know*.'

'Yes.'

'What do you mean by that?'

He nodded, he leaned close and put his hand on mine again. He was so close that his breath was on my cheek.

'I mean Celts,' he said. 'I mean the big traders, the men on the provincial council.'

I nodded. 'Go on.'

'You are magic,' he said, 'look into my head. Look now and see that I am speaking the truth, yes?'

'Yes.'

'So what is it that we want? We big Celts with all the money: we Catuvellauni, we Brigantes, we Belgae. All of us! What do we want now?'

'Tell me,' I said.

'Listen, clever Greek,' he said. 'Your people were trampled by the legions just like ours. Yes?'

'Yes.'

'That's because nobody can beat them in battle. It's hopeless, it can't be done. They are too good. They never give up. Yes?'

'Yes.'

'So! We give up all hope of ever getting rid of the Romans, and instead we want to *become* Romans. *Real* Romans. You understand?'

'Go on,' I said.

'So we become citizens,' he said, 'we spend enormous money on public works to be made citizens. We give presents, we give bribes—yes of course we do that—we do all that to become Roman citizens.' He shook my arm. 'I am a Roman citizen now. Yes? I am not a shitty-leg native. Yes, I am a citizen! My son will be a citizen, and his son after!' He shook my arm hard. 'But still we are not quite right. The Romans call us *wogs in togas*. Do you know that?'

'Yes,' I said. 'I've heard that.'

'They tolerate us because we're useful,' he said, 'but they don't *like* us, and perhaps they would like to get rid of us, and bring in some other traders from Crete, or Corinth… or anywhere!'

I nodded. The Romans would be capable of doing just that, because the Empire was built for Romans and not the conquered races.

'So!' he said, 'We are nearly there. But we are not quite there. And we want to *be* quite there, and be true Romans like them. Do you follow me, clever Greek? If that's what we want and we work for it, I ask you: would any of us send killers into the house of a Roman official? Would we do that, knowing what Rome would do if we were found out? Or if we were even suspected? Or if there was even a tiny whisper in the streets? We would be biting the tail of a wolf!' He shook his head. 'No,' he said, 'It wasn't me, or any Celt.'

He drew breath and leaned back against the wall behind, with a sly expression on his face. 'Oh yes,' he said, 'I *could* have men killed, and maybe, sometimes, perhaps I do. It's not a great expense. A few silver coins.' Then he leaned forward and stabbed a finger at me, hard. 'But, by all the gods, I do not kill big officials in the Roman tax office. It would ruin *everything*. Everything we work for.'

I was impressed.

'Yes,' I said, 'I believe you.' Then he leaned very close and whispered with his lips touching my ear.

'Listen to me, lovely, clever boy,' he said, 'because I like you very much. So you must wait and be patient, because I *will* find a way to have you.' He laughed. 'I will find a way, even if you do not want it! So wait and be patient, and while you are waiting, and you are looking for who killed Gershom...don't look at Celts, look at Romans! There is a wrong thing about some of your Romans. I don't know what. Nobody knows what. But *something* is wrong. So you be a clever Greek and go look at Romans,' he grinned, then kissed the side of my neck with considerable relish.

'Didn't you read all names on that list?' he said 'The list you got from Tadashi?'

Chapter 15

We found a wine shop. It was mid morning and most of them were open. It was nothing special, but it was clean. So we sat down and were served. I took a full cup to clear my mind, and Morganus and the bodyguards sipped sparingly as always and looked at me.

'Well?' said Morganus. 'How did he know about that?'

'Tadashi's list?' I said.

'Yes.'

'He's rich,' I said. 'Felemid is very, very rich.'

'Yes?' said Morganus.

'And he's deep into Britannic politics: provincial council, friend of the Governor, pushing for advancement: everything.'

'So?'

'So he's like all of them,' I said, 'He's like everyone in the Roman world. He's got spies, he listens to his clients at salutatio, his slaves bring him street gossip, and he's probably got paid informers at the best food shops, at the theatre and at the races.'

I reached for the wine flask and re-filled my cup. I offered it to Morganus and he shook his head. 'Isn't that how Petros works? And the Lord Chief Justice? And the Procurator, and everyone else? That's how the great and powerful operate.'

Morganus nodded. That was indeed how the Roman world worked. Everyone knew that. 'So,' I said, 'someone saw Tadashi at The Sign of Five Stars and saw Tadashi give me a list, and that person told Felemid.'

'Who was it?' said Morganus.

'I don't know,' I said, 'maybe the head waiter. That's who'd I'd pay, if I wanted a spy.'

'But how did Felemid know what was in the list?'

'He'll be paying someone in Gershom's office as well,' I said. 'That would make sense, because it was the office that was supervising Felemid's tax-collecting, so he'd want to keep one step ahead of them.' Morganus nodded. 'So my guess is that Tadashi wasn't very careful when he wrote out his list, and someone looked over his shoulder.'

'Yes,' said Morganus. 'Tadashi's deaf and half blind. Anyone could creep up on him.'

'So Felemid knows there's a Roman name on that list,' I said. 'Aurelio Tobias Bethsidus.'

'Bethsidus!' said Morganus. 'Tax collector and treasurer at Flavensum. And he's one of the duovirs.'

'And Felemid says there's something wrong at Flavensum,' I said.

'*Did* he say that?'

'Not *precisely* that, but I'm sure that's what he meant.'

'But there can't be anything wrong,' said Morganus, 'it's a veteran's colony. Every man is a citizen, and loyal to his boot nails! Their fathers were soldiers of Rome and the sun would fall out of the sky before any of them went bad.'

'Oh?' I said. 'So Romans all love one another? And there's never been civil wars between Romans? Or political murders?'

He did not like that. He frowned heavily. But he could not deny the truth behind my sarcasm.

'No,' he said, 'I'm not saying that. What I *am* saying is that Roman politics only goes bad when someone tries to get rid of the Emperor and put someone else on the throne, or tries to do the same thing to a provincial governor.'

I nodded. Morganus was my friend, so it was wise to concede a point even if I did not entirely agree with it. Also, I wanted to hear the rest of what he had to say. 'So,' he said, 'Flavensum is rock-solid loyal to the Emperor and the Governor. I know. I've been there!'

Coming from Morganus, that was a very convincing endorsement of

Flavensum and it almost persuaded me. But Tadashi had put a Roman name on his list for some good reason.

'We still need to talk to Bethsidus,' I said. 'The colony may be loyal but he personally may have gone bad, and may have wanted revenge on Gershom.' I re-filled my cup. 'And I really do think we'd be wasting our time talking to any more of the Celts on Tadashi's list.'

'Did you believe Felemid, then?' said Morganus, 'That no Celt would dare to have a Roman official killed?'

'Yes, I most definitely do,' I said. 'Felemid was telling the truth.'

'So let's talk to Bethsidus,' he said, and I hesitated to speak on because I knew that Morganus would not like my next words.

'And we do need to find out if Flavensum does have… any… any sort of *smell* about it,' I said, and Morganus frowned.

'What sort of smell?' he said.

'Any sort of bad reputation.'

'And how do we find that out?' he said, and I hesitated again, though for very different reasons.

'I shall talk to Allicanda,' I said. Morganus rocked back on his bench and laughed. Even the bodyguards smiled. He grinned at me.

'You'll see her purely in the interests of our investigation?'

'Well …' I began, not knowing how to answer, and he laughed again and the bodyguards strained not to. Then he leaned forward again, and spoke to me as a friend.

'What are you going to do about this woman?' he said. 'You poor, mad fool of a Greek, the thought of her's been sitting on you like an elephant for months! So are you going to buy her, or what? And how, in the name of Hercules, will you even get to see her?'

Taking those questions in order, I was not quite sure what I was going to do about Allicanda, even though the thought of buying her was never out of my mind, and I had researched the matter in some depth, and asked questions of experts. But I had at least worked out a means of getting to see her. The solution was Agidox, Major Domos of the house of Fortunus—my old master's house.

In the days that followed, and by the intercession of Agidox, I was able to exchange messages with Allicanda who, as a senior, was fully literate. Indeed her smooth, curved writing put my engineer's scrawl to deep shame. I still have her letters, even now, and those thin sheets of wood are very precious to me. Thus, by exchange of letters, Allicanda and I agreed to meet one day at noon, in the northern corner of the vegetable market where it runs into Fish Street. This would be busy with people, which was good because it is easy to hide in a crowd and Allicanda frequently visited the south end of Fish Street where the garum merchants had their shops.

I must confess that I turned again to Morgana Callandra, in order that I might look my best, but this time I insisted that I take no escort since the meeting would be in full daylight in a market place where no harm could come to me, and this time Morganus agreed.

'If that's what you want,' he said.

So I met her in the market, which was bursting full of people. For once the Britannic sun shone, and the sky was blue. The crowd was dense, the wooden stalls were in long rows, covered with canvas awnings. They were laden with produce and fronted by vendors who seized the arms of passers-by, bellowing out the virtues of their wares with equal lack of respect for house boy and matriarch alike. The sound was raucous but it was full of life, and I enjoyed it. Or perhaps it was the sunshine and the person I had come to meet. So I listened and smiled.

'Over here, darling! Celery, garlic and cabbage!'

'Two pound o' kale and lettuce, cheapest in town!'

'I got onions! I got leeks! I got radish!'

'Get your lovely olives here! Fresh out of Italia!'

Then I saw Allicanda and a great nervous excitement filled me up, from head to toe. My heart raced and my hands shook. She was lovelier than Venus and more gracious than Athena. The green eyes and red hair were wonderful, and she seemed so small and smooth and full of womanly allure.

I saw her before she saw me, and I saw that she was accompanied by four other slave girls. All of them were well dressed—better so than many free women in the market—and they looked towards Allicanda with respect. She was, of course, a senior and those around her must have been fellow slaves of the house. Indeed, looking closely I remembered some of them.

Then she saw me, and gave a small bow. I returned it and raised a hand in greeting and pushed through the crowd. I am tall man, bigger than most, and kept sight of her through all the bustle. And then I was standing in front of her, in all the noise and clatter of the market. I wondered what to say. But she spoke first. She was worried, even frightened.

'You can't stay!' she said.

'Why?' I asked.

She did not reply but looked away from me. I followed her gaze and saw a man leaning by a wall some twenty paces off. He was leering at Allicanda, and at me. He was a slave by his costume and was a big, handsome, smooth-faced young man, with a German's yellow hair, and excellent white teeth that he was picking with a tiny stick.

I looked at him and hated him on sight. Perhaps I had already looked into Allicanda's mind. Perhaps I really do work magic. Who knows?

'Who's that?' I said.

'Wulfrik,' she said, and shrugged. 'Wulfrik the fair.' I scowled and turned towards him. 'Stop!' she said, laying a small hand on my arm, and I saw that the girls with her were in great fear.

'Why?' I said.

'He's a sneak,' she said, 'he carries tales.' The girls all nodded.

'Why does he do that?' I said.

'Leave it!' she said. 'He's new. He came since your time in the house.'

'So what does he do?'

'He carries tales against the girls… unless they give themselves to him… and he saw me with you at Constantinos' cook-shop on the festival of Esidos.' She raised hands, 'Blessed be the name of Esidos,' she said, and looked at me in great sadness and distress.

I am not a man given to temper or to anger. I have lived too long and seen too much. Also, since I became a slave there has been little opportunity for me to express anger because it is not an emotion that slaves can afford to express. But anger—great anger—fell upon me as

I looked at Allicanda and saw who it was that Wulfrik wanted now. But I was still a philosopher. I was still a stoic. So I ground down anger and tried to smile.

'Leave this to me, *lady*,' I said, using an honorific never given to slave girls. I was trying to reassure her with my smile, though only the gods know what sort of a face I made, because she was not reassured but alarmed. None the less I bowed to her, and turned and pushed through the crowd towards Wulfrik.

He saw me coming and he stood away from the wall, and looked around for escape such that I read instantly that, despite his size, he was not a man to fear in any physical sense. On the other hand, I doubt that my face was radiating flowers and sunshine, so I suppose I might have frightened better men than Wulfrik.

Indeed, I saw that he was about to run, and I acted swiftly for fear that I might lose him. I pulled a coin from my pouch and held it for him to see, and I forced my face into a proper smile.

He hesitated, I nodded, he relaxed and his face showed a crafty greed, and with a few steps I was within touching distance of him.

'Wulfrik?' I said. 'Wulfrik of the house of Fortunus?'

'Yah,' he said, with a Germanic accent.

'That's for you,' I said, giving him the coin. He snatched it, hid it away, grinned and relaxed still more. He leaned against the wall again, and worked his toothpick.

'What's it for?' he said. And then I too relaxed, because I had got him. He was in a corner and could not get out without pushing past me and I did not think he would try that. So I spoke to him. I spoke with the utmost care of which I was capable.

'The coin is for your future,' I said, 'because we are going to discuss your future.'

'Oh?' he said, and frowned, because he did not understand.

'We are going to discuss what might happen to you, in the future.'

'What do you mean?' he said, still puzzled.

'First,' I said, 'do you know who I am?'

'Yah,' he said, 'you are the Greek that follows the Roman centurion.'

'Precisely,' I said, 'so let's talk about the Twentieth Legion and their men.'

'Why?' he said.

'Because they come into Londinium on their off-duty time, for the wine-shops and the whore-houses and the food. They come in almost every night, and they wander through the city.'

'So?'

'Well,' I said, 'sometimes they get into fights with the local men.'

'They do?'

'Yes,' I said—which was a complete lie, because any such fighting was a flogging offence and the men did not dare to start fights. But Wulfrik did not know that.

'And do you know what happens to the men they kill?' I asked.

'*Kill*?' he said.

'Oh yes!' I replied. 'They kill their man and throw him into the Thames. Usually they put him in a sack with stones to sink him, and they throw him from the middle of the bridge where the river is deep.' I leaned close and lowered my voice. 'Sometimes the man's not completely dead when he goes into the sack,' I smiled, 'but he soon drowns once he's in the river.'

I said nothing after that, because I judged him capable of working out the rest by himself. Unfortunately I was wrong. After some time had passed, he was still wondering. So I prompted him.

'My friend Morganus is first javelin of the legion,' I said. 'He will do anything to oblige me, and the men of the legion will do anything to oblige him, especially as one more man in the river makes no difference to them, especially if he's a slave.'

Wulfrik nodded, and his knees began to shake.

'So I offer you this advice, Wulfrik the fair. It would be good for your future if you keep away from Allicanda.' He nodded in great terror. 'And it would be very good,' I said, 'if you do not talk about her, and you do not talk about me.' At this he nodded repeatedly, and I saw that the warning was planted deep. 'And now,' I said, 'you are free to leave.' I leaned close again. 'But do take care as you go round the town. Take very great care, especially at night.'

I turned my back on him and pushed through the crowd to Allicanda. She and her girls gazed at me as if I were Perseus, hero of mythology, who saved lovely Andromeda from the monster. It was an intoxicating moment and at first I did not properly listen to what Allicanda was saying: I only gazed back at her and was happy. But then I realized that her girls were gone and she was explaining how slave politics works in a great mansion.

'You weren't touched by it,' she was saying, 'you were an exotic. You were the house favourite. But the rest of us have to make friends and support one another, because there's always some who go sneaking to the seniors and to the master.' She pointed. 'Look!' she said, and I saw a food shop for lower persons and slaves. It bore the sign of a leaping stag, and the plasterwork, though faded, was supposedly Mediterranean blue. With the sun shining there were stools and chairs outside on the pavement, and Allicanda's girls were already sat there looking at us. 'They are my friends,' she said, 'they will swear that nothing passed between you and I,' she looked at me steadily, 'nothing that was not proper,' she said, and I realized, as never before, that slave gossip could be dangerous as well as fascinating. 'We are safe to sit and talk,' she said, 'Now that you have got rid of Wulfrik.' Then she smiled, most wonderfully. 'What did you say to him?'

'Can we sit first?' I said, so we did, taking care to keep on opposite sides of a table, and later taking care to pay separately for our food and drink. Then I told her what I'd said to Wulfrik, and first she gasped, then she laughed, and the intoxication came over me again, and in that delirious mood, the words flowed from me in great turbulence and without control.

'Allicanda,' I said, 'the Romans pay me well. Ridiculously well. I have nearly a hundred thousand in the legion's bank and the price in the slave markets for an expert chef is only about fifteen thousand. I've checked it, and I know. So: I could buy you, Allicanda. I could buy you from your master.'

I saw her frown.

'It would be a formality!' I said, knowing that she might say no, and that she might reject me. 'I'd do it only if you wanted it! I'd buy you and then instantly make you free. And then, as a free woman, I'd ask you to marry me.'

I must have said that many times over, because she seemed not to understand. But at the third or fourth time she took a deep breath, considering what I had said. And then she shook her head.

'You can't marry me,' she said, 'Not even if I were free. You're an imperial slave and imperials are never freed. Everyone knows that, and everyone knows that a slave can't make a marriage. Not under Roman law.'

'I know,' I said, 'but there's marriage in the temple of Apollo or any other gods that you chose, and you yourself would be free: legally free, under Roman law. You'd be the owner of your house and property.'

'House?' she said. 'Property?'

'Yes!' I said, 'What else should I do with the money the Romans pay me? You could have a shop. You could trade in garum. We'd be together!'

She thought long and hard again, and finally I saw understanding in her face. I did not see unbounded joy, but at least I saw understanding. And then, to my wonderment, and despite all good sense and precautions, she stretched out her hand, and it shook and hesitated, and then she nodded and briefly rested her hand upon mine. It was a small gesture of enormous meaning. If she accepted my offer, she left behind the security of being a senior slave in a great house, where she was fed and clothed and lived in considerable luxury. Set against that was every slave's hope of freedom, and in addition to that freedom, I was offering myself, for what I was worth. So I looked at her closely.

'Yes,' she said. Just that word, but it was enough, and I felt such happiness as I had not felt in many years. We talked and talked, and then she sat back on her stool and looked at me with a serious expression.

'And now why did you *really* want to see me?' she asked, and I was shocked. But then I saw that she was joking. 'Well,' she said, 'what item of gossip is it, that will help your investigations? There is always a question and there is always an investigation.'

I shifted in my seat, in guilt. 'Well?' she said again.

'Well,' I said, 'What does the world say about Flavensum? What do people think of it?'

'Flavensum? It's a veteran's colony. They're all Jews.'

'Are they?' I said.

'Yes,' she said, 'they're Jews. They don't follow the Roman gods.'

'And is that it?'

'What do you mean?'

'Is there anything bad about them? Any sort of *bad smell*? Anything?'

She frowned and I could see that she was searching within her own mind, because she did indeed believe that there *was* something unusual about Flavensum. But she did not know what it was. I saw that even before she spoke, because that is the curse of my gift.

'They're odd,' she said, 'but nobody knows why.'

'What does *odd* mean?' I said. 'Strange? Mad? Deluded? Pitiable?

'I don't know,' she said, 'they're just odd... funny.'

She knew no more about Flavensum, and we returned to talking about the future. It was a happy time in the sunshine, and I left—which soon I did, for fear of staying too long in Allicanda's company—promising to approach Fortunus, her master, with my offer of purchase, and to write to her very soon.

Then I got up from my stool, and walked off, forcing myself not to look back.

On the other side of the market, while congratulating myself on what I had said to Wulfrik, the gods saw my arrogance and punished me with four assassins who came at me from two directions at once, with knives in hand.

Chapter 16

As I have said, there are no officers of police in a Roman city. Nobody patrols the streets to keep order. Neighbours come to each other's aid if they are attacked, and rich men surround themselves with slaves and bodyguards. But a loner like myself has neither neighbours nor slaves, and when he is threatened, the natural tendency of strangers is to keep out of the fight. So the busy crowd parted like the sea before a ram-ship's prow, and I was left alone to face four knives and four men.

I owe my life to two things, the first being an olive vendor's repairs to the awning over his stall. The canvas cover was supported by poles, one of which one had broken and he was replacing it with a fresh one. The replacement was leaning against the side of his stall. It was about seven feet long and over an inch thick. It was hard, old wood and it made a perfect quarter-staff.

I snatched it by instinct, and swung as my instructors had taught me, many years ago. The move was drilled into me. It was liking riding a horse: a skill a man never forgets, and my body was moving before my mind could think. So the staff whizzed sideways, slamming hard into the knee of an attacker, smashing bone and tumbling him onto the stone flags of the market square, with the knife escaping his fist, and the man behind him falling over him. I spun with the staff and faced the other two attackers. *Jab, jab!* A swift, double thrust of the staff, right hand pushing, left guiding and smashing the nose and breaking the jaw of a man who staggered back, while his comrade pressed forward, leaving me swirling on my heel again, in fear of the two behind me, of which one was on his feet again and charging. I aimed at his head in a down-swing, but he raised his arm, blocked it and staggered back, as I whirled round yet again and dropped to one knee, planting butt to ground, staff jutting out, rigidly braced, to catch an opponent such that the entire force of his own momentum concentrated a lethal, rib-crunching thrust into his body.

But there were two men left. One I had not touched, and another who pressed home his attack, even with broken jaw and bloody nose. These two would surely have killed me, because there is only so much that one man can do on his own.

So the second thing that saved me was the sudden arrival of two large men with cloaks wound round their left arms, to serve as shields, and with Roman army swords in their right hands. Their drill was highly effective and the sword-master Septimus Archontis would have approved. They each picked one of my attackers and charged him full tilt, taking any blows on their cloak-wrapped arms and knocking down their victims by brute force. Then: stab-*pull*! Stab-*pull*! And the same again to make entirely sure: stab-*pull*! Stab-*pull*! Then before I could even think, they finished the other two in the same way, because that is how the Roman army deals with its enemies, and my saviours were two of the army's finest. They were two of Morganus' bodyguards.

'The Big Man sent us,' said the elder of the two, as he helped me to my feet, because though he was hardly winded, I was gasping and choking. 'The Big Man said, never mind what *you* said—we was to watch your back.'

'Thank you!' I said. 'Thank you!' What else could I say? *The Big Man* was the army's nickname for Morganus, and he had been so obviously right and I was so obviously wrong. So I stood and looked at the bodies of four young men, laid out—still twitching—on the civilised flagstones of a Roman vegetable market, with a gawping, pointing, chattering crowd pressing in on every side.

I repeat yet again that Romans had no officers of police. Indeed they did not, but they had public officials of every other kind imaginable, with specific roles in the running of a city: civil tribunes, censors, quaestors and others, and at the bottom there were humble wardens who were responsible for streets, or parts of streets. Thus a succession self-important persons pushed through the crowd, attempting to take control, and I was questioned first by two street wardens, then by the block warden of a nearby building, and finally by the most senior man present: the aedile mercatis, the magistrate in charge of the market. He was an actual Roman citizen, formally dressed in his toga and preceded by lictors, six men bearing ceremonial fasces—bundles of sticks with an axe in the middle.

There was much conflict and yelling between the wardens, until the aedile stamped his foot, shouted louder than all the rest, and everybody—bowing to his superior status—fell silent as he adjusted his toga and came close to question me. He was a fat man, his fading hair plastered over his scalp with an oily dressing, and he smelled strongly of perfume. He studied me closely, to establish my status, just as I studied his face to follow his thoughts, because four men were lying dead and *somebody* would have to answer for it.

So he noted my excellent clothes, which proclaimed wealth, and he noted my Greek features, which proclaimed that I was a clever foreigner. He probably concluded—rightly—that I was an imperial slave, but then he showed extreme puzzlement at the fact that two men had fallen in behind me with sheathed swords, and were standing to attention like the soldiers they obviously were. But then the sun arose upon his understanding.

'You are Ikaros of Apollonis,' he said, 'the Greek, who is the comrade of Leonius Morganus Fortis Victrix!'

He gave just the tiniest bow: a mere nod of the head, but a hugely significant, because he was a citizen and I was not. 'And Petros of Athens is your patron!' he added. Then he reflected very carefully on that last statement, and gave a full, formal bow, which was fascinating indeed, because I was used to being recognised as *the Greek that reads men's minds,* but it seemed that street gossip now knew of my close relationship with Petros.

'Honoured Sir,' I said, taking care to bow low and to give proper respect. 'Yes, I am Ikaros of Apollonis, and I am acting under a commission from His Grace the Governor as signed by Petros of Athens.'

'Gods save His Grace!' said the aedile. 'How may I be of assistance?'

His words and his reaction showed how great a power was invested in the name of Petros. But I had to use that power at a time when I was still shaking from the exertion of fighting for my life, and was still leaning on my awning pole for support. Worse still, my head was pounding with ideas, each one shouting for attention.

Fortunately, Apollo must have smiled upon me because I managed moderately well, taking care before all else not to alarm the people because Petros, my great and powerful patron, would not thank me for doing that when he was strained to his limits to make success of the governor's games.

'Honoured sir,' I said to the aedile, and I pointed at the four corpses. 'These men were bandits!' I said that loudly for all to hear. 'They were common criminals, and have been justly punished.' In fact, I had no idea who my attackers were, and was puzzling mightily to guess, but my words satisfied the crowd.

'Ahhhhh!' said the everyone, and heads nodded.

'But we must get them away from here,' I said to the aedile, quietly. 'We must get them to some private place, where I can look at them, and we must send runners to the legionary fortress with a message for the honoured Morganus, and to Petros of Athens informing him of this, and to whichever other officials must be notified in such a case.'

The aedile swallowed, gulped and looked at his six lictors. I could see what he was thinking. The lictors were not any sort of athletes. They were portly, well-fed creatures accustomed to proceeding at a dignified pace. But they would have to do as runners.

'And we mustn't spread alarm,' I added. 'Not with the games coming!'

'Not with the Games coming,' he repeated, 'And the gladiators due tomorrow.'

He understood. All credit to him in that respect. He was extremely helpful, too. He sent his lictors on their way with messages, and added, 'My house is close by. We can take the bodies there. I'll send for my slaves.'

'Thank you, Honoured Sir,' I said, and one of the ideas in my head—a question—shouted so loudly that I could not ignore it. 'Do you know the dead men?' I asked him. 'Does anyone here know them? Can we ask the people?'

'Yes,' he said, and paused, wondering how to address me, slave as I was, and himself a Roman magistrate. He dredged his memory for the correct protocol and finally took refuge in the formal, vocative prefix '*O*'. So... 'Yes, *O* client of Petros of Athens,' he said. Then he bowed again, pleased with his verbal ingenuity, and took over.

After that, everything was all very Roman and very efficient, especially when the aedile's slaves arrived in numbers. Also, the two bodyguards helped. They laid out the four assassins in a row, as the aedile yelled at the crowd, and there was an organised parade past the bodies, so that everyone in the market and its surrounding streets could get a good look at the dead faces. As news spread, the parade grew longer, and it was still going on, with the people arguing, wondering and shaking their heads, when Morganus arrived with a large escort of legionaries that shoved past everyone and formed up around me.

'Are you all right?' Morganus asked. 'No wounds?'

'No,' I said.

'Are you sure?' he said. 'Sometimes you don't even notice till later, and it's only the wet feeling,the blood, that tells you. So have a look!'

'I know,' I said, 'I was...'

'*...a soldier once!*' he said, and smiled. 'I gather you're a good man with the quarter-staff, too.'

'I do my best,' I replied, and then I did look myself over. But there was no blood. There were no wounds. The two bodyguards who had saved me took their places beside the other two, behind Morganus, and I turned to them and thanked them again. This time I thanked them properly, and with much sincerity.

'Blessings be upon you, valiant soldiers of Rome,' I said, and raised hands to them. 'I pronounce blessing in the name of Apollo!'

'Blessings upon you and your house,' they said, in formal response.

'Well done, lads,' said Morganus, in rare praise.

Then we waited until no more people filed past the bodies. The aedile spoke, this time addressing Morganus, rather than myself, which was no more than proper and required no puzzling whatsoever over protocol.

'Honoured Morganus,' he said, 'nobody knows these criminals. Perhaps they are strangers to the city? Wild men from the interior?'

'Thank you for your help, Honoured Aedile,' said Morganus and bowed in return.

After that we did not take the bodies to the aedile's house, but took them to the legionary fortress, and laid them on work benches in one of the arsenal store rooms, among rows of shields and racks of helmets and body armour. There, I made careful examination of all four bodies, and their clothes and knives and everything else that they had about them. Morganus stood by and the bodyguards helped, stripping the bodies and turning them over when I asked. Such an examination was now routine, but grisly as it was, it was profoundly absorbing because the four bodies were a puzzle, with much to tell me if only I could understand…

Fortunately, I was able to complete my work before the stiffness of death came upon the bodies, which it does some few hours after death and may then last for days afterwards, which would have made examination difficult.

Later I did not just wash my hands, but took a bath in Morganus' house, after which I was chastised by Morgana Callandra—with her daughters stood behind her—for conducting a post mortem examination in the clothes she had put out for my meeting with Allicanda.

'Don't you care?' she said. 'Don't you know the cost of a tunic like that? It's pure, best wool from Italia, and you've got blood all over it! And you don't take care when you go out. You don't look around. You're away in your dreams, and wicked men attack you.'

She railed in loud anger but then impulsively threw her arms around me, and she and the daughters sobbed. I was so profoundly touched by this, that my slow mind realised at last that these ladies and Morganus really cared about me. Thus while I might hold other loves in reverent and blessed memory, they must stay in the past where they now belonged. It was an important moment in my life: a great and tremendous moment.

Later, I sat with Morganus in his garden, with a large wine flask and two cups, and the bodyguards seated nearby, with mugs of beer. The two who had saved me were in their armour again, the evening came, the sun sank and Morganus and I talked.

'So how was your meeting with the fish-girl?' he asked me.

'Allicanda,' I said, and I told him everything. Morganus listened and nodded.

'So will you speak to her master, to the boy Fortunus?'

'Oh yes,' I said, 'though I'm not sure how best to do it.'

'Well you know what I'd do,' he said. 'I'd go straight to him and ask to buy the girl!'

'But I'm not you,' I said, and he shook his head.

'Then you must deal with it in your own way,' he said, 'and meanwhile, what did we learn today?'

I pulled my mind away from Allicanda, and thought about other things.

'We learned today, that I am a target in this matter,' I said. 'I'm a target just as Gershom was a target, and we don't know why.'

'What about the men who tried to kill you?' he said.

'They were Celts.' I said. 'Probably strangers to the city, and they were fit, young men, with long hair and moustaches.' I paused, remembering the smooth faces. 'Well,' I said, 'they were *trying* to grow moustaches. They were hardly old enough for that, and they had dirty, worn clothes, and only a few bracelets in copper or iron, so they weren't wealthy. Their hands showed that too: black fingernails and calloused skin. And they stank of sweat and dirt. They'd never washed or bathed in all their lives.' Morganus nodded again. 'And,' I said, 'they had sacred ikons in little bags round their necks.' I paused. 'You said *they* were Regni ikons.'

'Yes,' he said, 'The wheel of Belenus, the disc of Tissiridua and a fresh daisy flower. Those are holy to the Regni. And you only had to look at them to see they were Regni: tall and thin with curly hair.'

'Regni it is then!' I said.

'They were very different from the team that killed Gershom,' he said.

'Yes,' I said, 'Those were Romans, and very likely citizens.'

'And they had army swords, while your Celts …'

'Not *my* Celts, if you please!'

He laughed. 'Have another drink,' he said. So I did.

'*My Celts* had tribal knives.'

'With pattern-welded blades. And that's Regni too. They're good at metalwork of all kinds.'

'But,' I said, thinking of the attack, 'they weren't very good at what they did, not as compared with the team that killed Gershom.'

'What do you mean?'

'I mean that they ran at me, which gave warning, when they should have crept up quietly and stabbed me from behind. And they didn't co-ordinate their attack.'

'Didn't you say they came from two directions?'

'Yes, but that's all they did. What they should have done was to separate completely and attack from four directions, closing in so I couldn't escape. But they didn't. And one of them followed right after another, and got tripped when he fell, which is sloppy work for assassins.'

'You sound upset!' he said. 'If they'd done a good job, you'd be dead.'

'That's not the point,' I told him.

'It would have been, if they'd been more careful,' he said, 'because then *you'd* have got the point!' He shook his head, then took a full drink of wine. 'And you'd have got it anyway if I hadn't sent two of the bulldogs after you.'

'Yes,' I said, 'and thanks for that. I should have taken more care.'

'I know,' he said. 'The trouble is that you get used to having an armed guard all the time. I'd probably had walked into trouble myself.'

'What I'm thinking,' I said, 'is that someone sent four ordinary tribesman after me: four peasants who weren't even proper warriors. Somebody picked out four young lads and sent them to Londinium specifically to kill me.'

I paused and filled my cup from the flask. Morganus was frowning; he was uneasy.

'I know where this is going,' he said, and defiantly made the Mithraic bull sign that wards off evil. 'It's druids, isn't it?'

'Yes,' I said. 'Who else could force plough-boys to do murder?'

'But if they wanted you dead, why didn't they send real trained killers? Why not the cennad angau fanatics? Look what they did to that druid Bradowr. They did a very thorough job on *him*.'

'Of course,' I said, 'but you Romans warned them off the last time they sent cennad angau into Londinium. You said if they did that again, you'd send the army into the tribal kingdoms and burn everything to the ground.'

'Yes,' said Morganus, 'and what a pleasure that would be.'

'There you are then. So they used four peasants.'

'But why should the druids want you dead, anyway?'

'Perhaps because I was responsible for the death of two druids and their escort?'

'No! You weren't the only man involved, and all the captives died—they killed themselves. So how could the other druids know you were even there?'

'Two of the escort ran off, remember? Perhaps they saw me. Or perhaps someone saw me riding round the Stone-Ring'

Morganus shuddered at the mention of theStone-Ring and made the bull sign again, as I thought on. 'Or perhaps we're digging into something that the druids want left alone?' I said.

'What? Gershom's murder?'

'More likely Tribune Celsus's murder,' I said, 'because that was *definitely* caused by the druids. They turned the girl Viola, and made her kill him.'

'So what are we going to do?'

'We've got to carry on digging. We haven't got any proof that the druids were responsible for anything. It's all guesses, and we know that Rome won't touch the druids as long as they stay in the tribal client kingdoms and behave.'

Morganus nodded.

'What we can do, though, is stop saying it's *the druids* that are doing this. We have to ask *which* druids, and I think I know.'

'Go on,' he said, 'tell me!'

'Well,' I said, 'the men that attacked me were Regni, yes?'

'Yes!'

'So, who is the chief druid of the client kingdom of the Regni tribe, and High Druid of all Britannia?'

That made Morganus profoundly uneasy. He sighed and took another drink before saying the name.

'Maligoterix,' he said.

'Maligoterix!' I said. 'And we'll have to question him.'

'Question him? Go into the Regni tribal kingdom? Can we get out alive if we do that? Are we even allowed to go in there?'

'I'll ask Petros,' I said, 'but we've also got to go to Flavensum to see Bethsidus the tax-gatherer, to find out if he had anything to do with the death of Gershom. ' I drank my cup and re-filled it. The evening was becoming warm and comfortable, fortified with good wine. 'Can we have a lightning for the journey?' I said. 'Can we do that tomorrow?'

'Yes,' he said, 'but it can't be tomorrow.'

'Why not?'

'Because of the gladiators. They're coming into the city tomorrow at noon.'

'So what?' He looked at me and shook his head, as if sadly. But he was joking.

'You've got some enormous holes in your enormous mind.'

'What holes?'

'Chariot racing. Gladiators. You don't know anything about them, do you?'

'Perhaps not,' I said and he laughed at the understatement.

'Listen,' he said. 'You've seen how the mob reacts to chariot drivers, haven't you?'

'Yes.'

'Well it's the same with gladiators… only different.'

I frowned. 'What does that mean?'

'It means that a lot of people will turn out to see the gladiators march through the town, but it'll be a different sort of people. It'll be mainly young men, and they get swollen up with male pride, trying to be as tough as the gladiators, and they swagger around in supporters' teams, getting drunk and looking for fights with other supporters' teams, and then they wreck the wine-shops and they piddle in the streets, and they smash everything that's not solid stone. That's what they're like, the gladiator fans. They make trouble.'

His words stirred my memory and I recalled an event that even I had read about.

'Like the riot in Pompeii?' I said. 'The town that was buried by the volcano? Wasn't there a great riot there, about fifty years ago, caused by gladiator fans?'

'Yes!' he said. 'And it wasn't just a riot, it was a battle: a battle between two rival teams of fans. It was so bad that the games were forbidden in Pompeii for ten years afterwards , and we certainly don't want that happening in Londinium! So the Twentieth will be on the streets tomorrow, and I'll be in command under strict orders from the Legate, and I can't get out of it, not even with our investigations going on.'

'We need to go to Flavensum without delay,'I insisted. 'Can't we speak to Petros?'

'Don't even bother,' he said. 'It was Petros who told the legate to put the troops on the street. And, anyway, you might find it interesting. Gladiators *are* interesting. But I'll order up a lightning, ready for us to go to Flavensum. Meanwhile let's enjoy the show tomorrow—providing it doesn't turn into a riot!'

Chapter 17

The gladiators and their considerable retinues had been camped outside Londinium for some days. They had landed at the naval base of Dubris, which was the main Roman port on the Britannic side of the Channel Ocean. From Dubris they had come by the Roman military road, travelling in their separate teams.

Then, outside Londinium they had camped in separate enclosures—likewise team by team—except that the Romans did not call them *teams*, but schools. In each school there were dozens of men, and some women too, ranging from the billionaire owner-managers who were Roman citizens of rank, down to the slaves who cooked, swept and cleaned. And of course there were the gladiators themselves, of whom some were as famous as the chariot drivers who had already processed through Londinium. But now, the full complement of four schools had arrived, and had made ready for their joint and ceremonial entry into Londinium, via the South Gate and up the broad avenue of the Via Principalis, to make sacrifice at the great temple of Jupiter, Juno and Minerva.

It would be another great procession, and Romans adore processions, because it is in their hierarchical, march-in-step, militaristic blood to do so, and now it was not only Romans who loved processions but all the subject races too, because they liked a good, free show.

But the gladiators' procession was very different from the earlier procession of the racing drivers, and I had a most perfect view of this, since I rode beside Morganus among an escort of legionary cavalry, within a marching unit of two centuries of the Twentieth Legion's first cohort. This heavy escort was present in armoured and dominating force, to make it perfectly clear to the gladiator fans that no riot or tumult would be permitted, because the great avenue was filled with a roaring, stamping, yelling crowd which, just as Morganus had warned, was almost exclusively male, almost exclusively young and almost exclusively drunk or getting drunk. So in addition to the two marching centuries, the avenue was lined with legionaries and auxiliaries in a shield-wall turned *away* from the procession, *towards* the mob, and the men were armed not only with real swords, but with the wooden practice swords, which made formidable riot batons. These were used with much force, whenever one of the mob tried to break through the shields, or gave offence by cursing and spitting—it being a favourite insult of gladiator fans, to spit.

'Dirty animals,' said Morganus, as one of the fans got his head cracked with a blow that sounded out over the vast din. 'If they're not careful it won't be wood they'll get but blades, and serve them right!'

But I hardly heard him, because I was fascinated by the gladiator schools in procession. We were in the middle of the parade, but I could clearly see the two schools ahead of us, and by turning in the saddle I could see the two behind.

I could also see something that puzzled me: a marching body of about a dozen men, who all wore knightly togas and were attended by slaves and followers. Every one of them—even the slaves—strutted as if he owned the city, and they were received by the mob with a mixture of huge cheers and howls of derision. I asked Morganus who they were.

'Masters of the games,' he said, 'They're from the imperial college of Marcus Quintus Superbus, in Rome. They're the most famous referees in the Empire.'

'Referees?' I said. 'Do gladiators fight with referees?'

He shook his head in pitiful contempt of my ignorance.

'Just watch the parade,' he said.

So I did. I watched and listened although there was no army band today, since gladiators come with their own music; horns, bugles, flutes and drums, as well as the loud voices of the schools themselves, with team anthems sung to give time to their elaborate processional steps. They came with their own music, because gladiator schools did not march like legionaries. Rather they delivered a stylised advance, with heroic pauses and gestures. Each school had a different style, but each was delivered with excellent choreography and every man smartly in time. It was a piece of theatre. It was entertainment. It was part of the show.

Thus the men of the school right in front of us, the Askodus school, which was one of the most famous, would take a dozen bold steps forward, then stop and turn to the mob with a great shout and right arms sweeping out to one side.

'*HUH!*' they barked, and stamped three times, and their music blared, and the school roared out a loud and holy hymn summoning Charon, the mythical boatman who took dead souls across the river Styx to the underworld.

'Charon make ready, for we are here!
To fight with pride and never fear!
To give the blow and take the steel!
And stand and fight and never kneel!
All rivals be in fear of us!
We are the sons of Askodus!'

It was impressive, I admit it, and so was the sight of them because each team was led by its owner—in formal toga—and by men who displayed sacred images of bulls, lions, wolves and other fierce beasts, raised up on staffs like legionary standards. Then there were images of the gods of the school: Pluto, Mars and Fortuna, then the school's musicians, then the servants who bore the gladiators' arms and armour, all gleaming and decorated with gold and silver. Then came the gladiators themselves, each one preceded by a man bearing a huge placard giving the gladiator's name. The gladiators marched barefoot, bare headed and near-naked, wearing only vestigial loin cloths, to display the most magnificent male physiques I had ever seen. The development of their muscles was phenomenal, and was enhanced by an oil dressing that made them shine. They were bold, magnificent creatures, and the fans roared themselves hysterical as they passed, and chanted their names and thundered their feet on the paving stones in approval.

In this manner the gladiators proceed to the forum, where they were received by His Grace the Governor, at the great temple, and there made sacrifice and offered prayers to the spirit of the Emperor. Then, they were conducted out by the North Gate to the gladiator barrack-blocks—one for each school—built outside the city walls by the ever-busy Twentieth Legion. They were also building a big, wooden amphitheatre for the gladiatorial games, though no work had been done on that today, with the troops on duty in the streets.

Much later, and at last, Morganus and I were dismounting outside the stable block in the fortress, where men were waiting take our horses, and the thousands of legionaries who had lined the streets were tramping back to their dinners, bawling out a cheerful marching-song. They were in merry mood, happy to have kept the city un-wrecked, with no need to draw steel and only a few heads broken by wood: all of which were well-deserved and a good job too, as far as the men of the Twentieth were concerned.

I was pleased to see men waiting to speak to Morganus, because I was anxious to proceed with our investigations. There were three of them, and one was Silvius, the clerk-optio that I had put in charge of re-organising Gershom's library. But he stood behind two men of greater rank. These were a tribune in muscled cuirass and scarlet cloak, and a centurion with sideways crest. Naturally the tribune spoke first, and yet again I saw a young aristocrat who out-ranked Morganus, bow politely in deference to him.

'I give you good day, O Spear of the Legions!' said the tribune, in exquisite and formal Latin.

'I give you good day, Honoured Sir,!' replied Morganus and returned the bow.

'O Sword of Empire,' said the tribune, 'I come from His Noble Honour the Legate, who would be grateful for your presence in the Principia at your earliest convenience,'

'I'll go at once,' said Morganus. 'But can I first deal with these men who are waiting?'

'Of course, O Fist of Rome. I will carry your word to His Noble Honour and await you in the Principia, O Champion of the Host.' And with that, he saluted and marched off.

'Spear of the Legions? Fist of Rome?' I said to Morganus. 'How long can he keep *that* going? Do they teach it to them as boys, when they learn their times tables?'

Morganus frowned.

'Why do you say things like that?' he said. 'The lad was only being polite.' He turned and spoke to the centurion.

'Good day!' said Morganus.

'Good day, Honoured Sir!' said the centurion. 'We've got a lighting ready for you to go to Flavensum. We can hitch up the team whenever you want, and you'll be ready to go. Ready at instant notice, Honoured Sir.'

'Good,' said Morganus. The centurion saluted and stood back and Optio Silvius stepped forward. He saluted Morganus, but spoke to me.

'I give you good day, Ikaros of Apollonis,' he said.

'And I to you,' I said 'So, it's Gershom's library, isn't it? I see you've not found the special book.'

I read that in his expression. For me that was as easy as telling a black stone from a white. It is nothing clever, but people think that it is.

'Yes,' he said, un-nerved by my wretched gift, and his words rushed out. 'We looked and looked. We put them in order, best order we could, but we couldn't find anything that you'd kill for. Not that or even anything nasty. Nor even dirty books that you might want to hide. Just history and geography, and news, and certainly nothing political.'

I nodded and tried to make amends

'Well done, Optio Silvius,' I said, 'I'm sure nobody could have done better.'

'Thank you, Your Worship,' he said.

'Where are the books now?'

'In the offices of records and finance,' he said, 'where we work.'

'Good! We'll go there and I'll have a look at the books.' I smiled. 'And your list!'

'What list?' said Morganus. 'The optio's got a list,' I said, 'a catalogue of the library: Gershom's library ...'

My words faded away as I saw the look on Morganus' face. It was the same as the look on Silvius' face, and I realised that I had been too clever by half. My mind had unconsciously reasoned that if Silvius had come to me without being asked, then he must have completed the task I had set him: he must have catalogued Gershom's library. Also, Silvius had a satchel slung over his shoulder on a strap. So what must be in that satchel? Even a child could guess. But the world is full of wonders, and men take the lazy, easy path of believing these wonders to be magical. It is another reason why I cannot sleep at night and take refuge in wine.

'You *have* got a catalogue of the library, haven't you?' I said, at last.

'Yes, Your Worship,' he said. 'How did you know?'

'I guessed,' I said. Further explanation would have been tiresome. Meanwhile Morganus looked at me almost nervously, which made me sad, but at least he did not make the bull sign. Then he shook his head, and stood straight, because duty called.

'I'll have to go to the Legate,' he said. 'That won't wait. But I'll see you later at my house.'

'Yes,' I said, and he went off with the bodyguards, and I followed Silvius to a big office in another building where his team of clerks stood to attention beside the books of Gershom's library. These were now drawn up like a legion, laid out on tables in rows and numbered for reference.

Also, Silvius took out his catalogue, which was indeed in his satchel, and put it on one of the tables. It was a beautiful piece of work, in elegant calligraphy on sheets of fine vellum. It was vellum, because Silvius was clearly seeking to impress, and never mind the cost. So he spread out the sheets so we could all see them, then stood back and bowed politely to me.

'So,' I said, 'what have we got?'

He pointed at one of the sheets and explained.

'First, Your Worship, here's a list of books in Hebrew and other languages that we don't know. I've numbered them for reference, but I can't read them. Not me or any of us.' The clerks behind us all shook their heads.

'Don't worry. I'll do that,' I said, and everyone nodded.

'Thank you, Your Worship,' said Silvius, and turned back to the catalogue. 'And then, for the rest of the books, we've divided them up by subject matter. That's history, geography, engineering, great events, wars, rebellions, disasters and some other smaller categories.' He looked at me. 'That's what he liked, Gershom, facts, dates and letters. There are lots of letters, mostly by famous men, but not personal letters. They're all reports of things that happened. For instance there's a copy of Pliny the Younger's letter about the volcano eruption that buried Pompeii.' I nodded in considerable approval, and Silvius relaxed. He even smiled . 'We divided up the books like that,' he said, 'and then cross-referenced them by authors and by some other factors,' he pointed to another sheet, 'it's all there, Your Worship. We've done our best.'

'Well done indeed!' I said, but Silvius gave a small gesture of failure: shrugging with hands and shoulders.

'But we didn't find the killer book,' he said.

'Killer book,' I said. 'Is that what you're calling it?'

'Yes, Your Worship. The killer book. That's what we call it, the men and myself, and we haven't found anything that might be it. I'm sorry Your Worship.'

'Never mind,' I said, 'I think we'll need help from some other source to find that book.'

'May I respectfully ask what source that might be, Your Worship?'

'I don't know,' I said. 'But I'll start with the books that we *have* got.' I looked at the neat rows. 'Where are the books you couldn't read?' I asked, and Silvius pointed.

'Over there, Your Worship,' he said.

There were not many of them: a few dozen, perhaps. They were mostly in Hebrew, with a few in Aramaic. I read a few pages of one, then gave it to Silvius.

'This is a report of the siege of Jerusalem thirty years ago, ' I said, 'It's by the Jewish historian, Josephus Bar-Matthias. Put it with *Great Events*.'

'Yes, Your Worship!' said Silvius and passed it to one of his men to put in place, while another noted content and author. So we worked through the pile, and unfortunately I found some of the books enticingly fascinating. There was an engineer's notes on the techniques used to build a tunnel to carry fresh water into Jerusalem in King Solomon's time, a thousand years ago. It gave practical and mathematical detail and I longed to study it. But I knew that I had no time.

So I worked fast, and I had just finished the last book when Silvius and his men all stood to attention, as Morganus came in with his bodyguards. He looked straight at me.

'It's the Legate,' he said, 'His Noble Honour really wants to speak to you, not me.'

'Ah,' I said, 'but protocol dictates that he sent for you, as my keeper.' Morganus frowned heavily. I could see what he was thinking.

'Why do you say these things?'

'I'll come at once,' I said.

'How gracious of you!' he said.

'We wouldn't want to keep His Noble Honour,' I said.

And we did not. We proceeded at quick march time, through the various gates, sentry posts, password checks, corridors and two broad staircases into the inner heart of the legionary fortress: the Legate's offices in the Principia.

The office was large, plain and military, furnished with massive chairs and tables and cabinets for documents, and it had windows looking out over the fortress, all glazed with fine, clear glass. His Noble Honour the Legate Africanus—dressed in plain civilian clothes—sat with his staff of tribunes and clerks behind him, and to my great surprise, Petros sat next to Africanus, with his six shaven-heads behind him. One look at their faces told me that something bad had happened.

We stamped, bowed and saluted and were received into the company of the two most powerful men in Britannia. Africanus spoke first, being a free man and a nobleman.

'Out!' he said, and the tribunes, clerks, shaven-heads and Morganus' bodyguards all bowed and left the room, closing the door behind them.

'Sit!' said Africanus. So we sat on the opposite side of the big table, and Morganus took off his helmet and set it down in front of him. As our chairs scraped, Petros closed some book-tablets that were spread out on the table, as if to make them neat; or perhaps to hide their content? But Africanus saw my expression. 'Don't bother, Petros of Athens,' he said. 'The Greek has already seen them.'

Africanus was entirely correct.

'It's the druids,' I said, 'it's Maligoterix. It's a threat to the entire province. You've had news. What have you heard?'

Once again I was too clever by half.

Morganus gasped at my words as if in the presence of the uncanny, and even Petros—for all his Athenian intellect—was so confounded at my instant unlocking of secrets that he shook his head in disbelief. But Morganus always did believe I worked magic, while Petros held the more sophisticated opinion that however I did it, I certainly looked inside men's heads. Only the legate was unmoved, being a hardened old veteran and steeped in Roman self-discipline. He had lived an exceptionally long life and had seen many more things that shocked, than a Greek slave who could read men's thoughts. To him I was no more wonderful than a juggler or a sleight-of-hand conjurer. He none the less regarded my skills as useful, and he nodded slowly at my words, thereby confirming that my deductions were accurate.

So yet again, I must point out how easy it was for me to make these deductions.

The fact that Petros and Africanus sat side-by-side, proclaimed that something very serious was happening, and the fact that Africanus' military staff were present, and grim-faced, proclaimed that it was a military threat. Since that threat could only come from the tribes, the rest followed because only the druids could rouse the tribes, and the books Petros had just closed, concerned the client kingdom of the Regni tribe which was dominated by Maligoterix, High Druid of all Britannia.

In addition—and from a purely personal viewpoint—who else but Maligoterix could have taken four young farmers of his own Regni tribe, and turned them into killers and sent them after me? Having personally faced their daggers, this question resonated so loudly inside my own head, that I had little need to look inside the heads of others, even if I had that power—which I do not!

However, if a Greek may be allowed a little vanity, perhaps I take pride in the fact that I make such deductions intuitively and at a speed that amazes others. But the amazement of others was as nothing compared with my own amazement at the complexity of relations between the Romans and the druids, as revealed by what Africanus and Petros said next.

Chapter 18

'Well done!' said Africanus, addressing Morganus. 'Your Greek has once again displayed the talent which persuaded us to conscript him into service.' He waved a hand gracefully towards Morganus. 'I commend you, First Javelin,' he said, 'for bringing this talent to our attention.' Only then did he actually look at me. 'So, Ikaros of Apollonis,' he said, 'is there any need for further briefing? Or have you already read and learned everything in my mind?' He spoke with patronising condescension, as if asking a child, *have you had enough to eat?*

He irritated me. I knew very well that his attitude towards slaves was perfectly normal in a Roman nobleman, but still he irritated. So I retaliated.

'I read only those thoughts that are in the front of your mind,Noble Sir,' I said, 'I can't read anything buried in the back of it.'

'Huh!' he said. 'Guard your tongue, Greek!' But he said no more, and I *think* he believed my nonsense. He turned to Petros. 'Tell them!' he said. 'Tell them everything.'

Petros bowed in his chair, then spoke.

'There have been developments in the client kingdoms,' he said. 'I have already warned you that the druids fight among themselves.'

'Yes,' I said,

'Yes,' said Morganus.

'Well,' said Petros, 'the latest fighting has ended with complete victory for Maligoterix.'

'How can you know that?' I said.

'Don't ask!' said Petros, 'and don't look into my mind, because I have taken you at your word, and banished these thoughts to the *back* of my mind.' He continued. 'We further believe that the cause of this particular dispute was a plan for a general rising of the tribes against Rome. Other druids were reluctant to face the Roman army, but they've all been persuaded or killed.' He sat back in his chair and looked at me, awaiting a response.

I was puzzled.

'So you fear a rebellion,' I said, 'but isn't this normal in Britannia?' I turned to Africanus. 'Isn't that the reason, Noble Sir why you command three legions plus auxiliaries? If the tribes give battle, surely you'll defeat them yet again?'

I saw the slightest hesitation in his face, and that was a surprise indeed. 'We can defeat any major tribe if it rises alone,' Africanus said, 'and we can defeat several. But if they all rise together… in that case we might have to summon help from Rome.'

I understood at last.

'And that would be a disaster, ' I said, at the time of the governor's games?'

'Yes,' he said,. 'with the province supposedly pacified. And there's more. Tell them, Petros.'

'With all respect, Noble Sir,' said Petros, 'we should first hear from Ikaros and Morganus.'

Africanus nodded. Petros bowed. 'Ikaros,' he said 'We need full details of your investigations so far. Tell us what you know of the murders of Celsus and Gershom.'

'I have kept you fully informed,' I said, 'I send regular reports to your office.'

'Yes,' he said, 'we have the facts but we need your judgement, your insight.'

'Indeed we do!' said Africanus, speaking with surprising emphasis. He was actually paying me a compliment. So I told them what I knew. 'Celsus was murdered by his slave girl Viola, who had been turned by the druids,' I said. 'We don't know which druids, but possibly Maligoterix himself. I believed that the motive was to insult the Empire, but from what you have just told me, it might have been to display power, so as to impress the other druids and the tribes.' I paused to check that they were following. They were. 'But in either case, this is nothing new. Druidic hatred of Rome is the normal condition of Britannia. But the murder of Gershom is something new, something different. The killers were Roman citizens who acted like soldiers. They wanted Gershom dead because he knew something that was written in a book in his library. They killed him for that, then searched for the book, and failed to find it, and then tried to destroy the library.'

Africanus interrupted. 'Get to the point, Greek, what were they looking for and why?'

'I am coming to that, Noble Sir,' I said. 'We must ask, what could be in a book to justify murder?'

'Get on with it!' said Africanus, 'what was in the book? What did it mean to the killers?'

'It meant either profit, envy, jealousy, revenge, religion or guilt,' I said.

'Which one bears on this case?' he said.

'Well,' I said, 'Nothing was stolen. No rage was displayed. No gods were invoked. The killers behaved with callous efficiency. They had no other purpose than killing Gershom, then finding or destroying a book. So it's guilt!'

'What guilt?' said Africanus.

'What makes a man guilty?' I said, 'Crime against the law, or faith, or some offence against family and friends, perhaps? Or it could be political.'

'Ah!' said Africanus. 'That's what I feared!'

'This is only speculation,' I said.

'Then *speculate*!' said Africanus.

'If it's political,' I said, 'it might be fear of the discovery of past actions like an indiscreet letter to a seditious person or faction.'

'Which faction?' said Africanus.

'I don't know,' I said, 'and it might not be politics at all. It might be religion. Gershom comes from Palestine, and that's a volcano of religions. It spews out new ones every day. It's chaos.'

'Bah,' said Africanus, 'don't speak tome of religion. Who *kills* for religion?'

'The druids,' I said.

'The fighting between the druids wasn't religious,' said Petros, 'it was political. Maligoterix was eliminating his rivals.'

'Yes!' said Africanus.

'That's not what I meant,' I said, 'I meant human sacrifice, and I meant the two druids and their men who killed themselves after I saw them captured. They did that to save themselves from damnation. They believed that a clean death, and passage to paradise, was better than eternal torment. That's what faith can do to a man's mind!'

'No! No! No!' said Africanus, thumping the table. 'It *can't* be religion. When was the Empire ever threatened by religion? We let the natives get on with their gods, and we get on with ours.'

'We *don't* let the druids get on with their gods,' I said, and he stared me hard in the face.

'We are not talking now about druids,' he said, 'we are talking about Roman citizens with swords, who very efficiently murdered a Roman tax official. And that, my clever, mind-reading Greek, is a *political* act!'

He looked at each of us in turn. 'Does anyone disagree with that?' Nobody disagreed, not even me, because I could see no flaw in the statement. Whatever other motives might have driven the killers of Gershom—even assuming there were other motives—the act was political, because the Empire would perceive it as political—and it therefore *was* political.

'Good!' said Africanus. 'Enough discussion. This is what we shall do.' He turned to Petros. 'You will continue with your usual energy, to organise the governor's games.' Petros nodded. 'I will alert the legions to be ready at instant notice to take the field, in case of rebellion.' he turned to Morganus. 'While you, First Javelin, will deal with the political threat by taking your Greek into Flavensum, to seek out *anything* political that might be festering there.' Africanus was then so generous as to look at me. 'It's where you would have gone next in any case, is it not? To Flavensum?'

'Yes, Noble Sir,' I said, but Morganus interrupted.

'That's true,' he said, 'But Honoured and Noble Africanus, I have to say that I know Flavensum well, and I can't believe there's anything wrong there.'

Africanus smiled.

'I respect your opinion in all things, First Javelin, especially regarding loyalty to the Empire. But this Greek,' he pointed to me, 'is cunning and devious like all his kind. He is therefore more able than an honest Roman, to recognise treachery when he sees it. So you will go to Flavensum.'

'Yes, Noble Sir,,' said Morganus.

'Yes, Noble Sir,' I said, and then added, 'but I have a question.' Africanus frowned.

'Which is?'

'On what pretext do we go to Flavensum? We can't simply arrive and say that we wish to question all the city's officials. What do we tell them?'

To my surprise he laughed. 'You are clever,' he said, 'invent something! I leave the details to you, but in my experience the best lies are those which are closest to the truth.' And then a further layer of secrecy revealed itself as Africanus got up and we all stood with him, in respect. 'Now I have heard enough,' he said, and gestured towards the door, and I realised that, as the lowest creature present, it was my duty to usher him from the room. So I stepped forward, opened the door and bowed.

Is it any wonder that I drink?

Africanus went out and found his staff and officials sat waiting for him in the corridor outside the meeting room. They sprang to their feet, saluted, and greeted him.

'Ave Africanus!' they cried, in formal Latin. I closed the door and sat down again with Petros and Morganus, as a considerable degree more of stamping and yelling came from outside the door. It was Africanus going about his military preparations, but we paid no attention. We had other things to consider.

'What did he mean,' I asked Petros, 'that he had *heard enough*?'

'My dear Ikaros,' he said, 'have you not noticed that we have just put the army on a war footing, while carrying on with the biggest expense in the province's history—the governor's games—as if everything were normal? And all that without involving anyone else?'

'What do you mean?' I said.

'I mean,' he said, 'that decisions at that level should involve *all* the great officers of the province: the Lord Chief Justice, the Fiscal Procurator, , the senators of the Londinium Council and Provincial council. All those and their senior men, not to mention His Grace the Governor.'

'Gods save His Grace!' said Morganus.

'Indeed,' said Petros, with little sincerity.

'Indeed,' I said, with less. 'But none of those honoured persons are here.'

'No,' said Petros, '*because there are things they don't want to know*.'

'About the druids?' I asked.

'About the druids,' he said, and looked at Morganus, 'and I'm now going to tell you some things that even a First Javelin might not want to know. So I offer you, Honoured Morganus, the chance to leave now and allow any crime to rest upon the shoulders of mere slaves.' Morganus just laughed, and jabbed a thumb towards me.

'If he can bear it, so can I!' he said.

'So,' said Petros, 'we have decided that the most pressing danger is the political threat from Flavensum.'

'Rubbish!' said Morganus. 'I didn't want to argue with Africanus, but that's rubbish. Flavensum is as loyal as I am!'

'Regardless, you will go there,' said Petros.

'Can we move on?' I said. 'What is it that the Legate doesn't want to hear?'

Petros closed his eyes. He paused. He drew breath.

'What I am about to tell you,' he said, 'is treasonable and most profoundly secret.'

I gasped, as I guessed what he was going to say.

'Gods of Hades!' I said, 'You don't just get information *from* the druids: you talk to them! You exchange messages. You are actively in contact with them. *That's* why you saved that creature you've got hidden in the hospital!'

Perhaps I am more gifted than I imagine. How would I know if I were? If I really were magic, then would I even recognise the magic?

In any case, and however I reached these conclusions, they seemed obvious to me, but Petros shuddered. He stretched palms towards me, with fingers splayed out as if in defence.

'Get out of my head!' he cried. 'At least let me form the words!' So I shut up and sat back. 'Yes,' he said, 'I do exchange—or rather exchanged—messages with the druids of all the client kingdoms. You would not believe how often they call upon me, and the army, in their struggles, except that now I speak only to Maligoterix. The rest are silent, and I can only assume they have been silenced, or killed by Maligoterix.'

'How do you do it?' I asked, 'exchange messages? Do you ...'

But Petros shouted at me. 'GET OUT OF MY HEAD!' he cried, and looked away. 'You already know too much.'

'Leave him alone,' said Morganus, to me, 'you aren't helping. In the name of Mithras, let him think without you digging his head open!'

'I'm sorry,' I said.

'Yes, yes,' said Petros, 'just let me be still.' So we sat silent a while. Then Petros continued.

'The threat from Maligoterix is severe, but it is something that we understand. It is a military threat to be met with military force. But this political matter—Gershom's murder—which concerns Flavensum...'

'It *can't* be Flavensum!' said Morganus.

'So you say,' said Petros. 'But there *is* a political threat, and we don't know where it might come from other than Flavensum, because Flavensum is the only city in Britannia that's full of Roman citizens, and it's only citizens that can take part in Roman politics! So you will go there first, you will complete your enquires at utmost speed, and then I will arrange for you to meet Maligoterix, to interrogate him on whatever it is that the druids are doing.'

'You can do that?' I said.

'Yes I can,' he said, 'and do not ask how, because I shall now recite the hymn to Holy Athena, to block out all other thoughts.' He closed his eyes and muttered to himself in Greek.

'All right! All right!' I said, 'I won't look. I promise!' He opened his eyes and ceased declaiming.

'Good!' he said, and looked at one of the windows. 'The light is fading,' he said, 'You will go to Flavensum tomorrow, at dawn.' He stood up from the table. 'And now I ask a favour of you, Ikaros of Apollonis. I ask that you leave my presence, to allow me free thought of the duties that I have to perform, this day before I sleep! I ask as one Greek to another: just go away. Go now! Get out!'

So we returned to Morganus' house, and made ready for the journey to Flavensum the next day. But I had something else to do, besides packing, and I needed Morgana Callandra's help. Naturally, I first asked Morganus if I might speak to her on such a matter, and he laughed.

'Are you sure you don't need a pull at the wine flask,' he said, 'to gather courage?' I ignored that.

'May I speak to The-Lady-your-Wife? In her kitchen?' I said.

'In you go,' he said, 'but mind she doesn't put you in the stew pot.' I ignored that, too, and went to the kitchen where Morgana Callandra always sat with her girls in the evening at lamp time, politely leaving the reception rooms for myself and her husband.

I liked the kitchen. It smelt of spices and food and bread. It was warm and comfortable and provided with every convenience known to the arts of Roman—or even Greek—cuisine. And it was neat, and clean and polished, with copper pots hanging in rows, and even a run of lead-lined sinks with an actual pump for water so that nobody had to bring buckets in from the well—an unheard of sophistication in the kitchens of my own city. So I was forced to concede that Rome *was* more advanced than Apollonis in a matter of technology. I was also forced to concede that Morgana Callandra was my superior in a matter of intellect.

I was sat with her on a stool by a large, scrubbed-clean table, where she had generously served small cakes and little cups of wine. She and her girls had similar stools, except that the girls withdrew to the other side of the room and affected not to hear what their mother and I were saying. They listened anyway, but I did not mind. I was used to them. I was fond of them.

'I need your advice, Honoured Lady,' I said.

'Oh,' she said, 'how could that be? And yourself a Greek engineer?' The girls giggled.

'I have to write to Fortunus, son of my late master,' I said.

'Ah!' she said. 'You want to buy the girl Allicanda .'

'You know?' I said.

'Do you think my husband doesn't talk to me?'

'I see,' I said, 'but there is something that troubles me.'

'What is it?'

'The trouble is, that I profoundly believe that truth is…'

'Invincible!' she said.

'Oh. You know that too?'

'Yes, and so does my husband. You tell him that all the time.' The girls giggled again.

'I see. But the fact is… that I know… that when buying an item… that is to say, when bargaining for an item… there are different rules than plain truth, and I am unsure…'

She leaned forward.

'Are we to spend all night on this?' she said. 'Listen to me Ikaros the Greek, this is what you must do. You write to Fortunus telling him that you are setting up a household, and that you need slaves, but you are always careful when you buy anything, so you are approaching him because you already know the slaves of his house, because you were one of them. So you give him a list of those you want, and tell him that you haven't got much money and will have to take out loans to buy them, so you can't buy at all if they're too expensive. Then you put Allicanda down near the bottom of the list. Not actually *at* the bottom because that will draw attention to her. You do that, and you start your bargaining from there.'

'But I don't *want* a household of slaves,' I said, 'I want only Allicanda, and I've got plenty of money! Do I have to tell lies to get her?'

'Blessed be the gods,' she said, 'because understanding has fallen upon you!' The girls laughed.

So I wrote a letter exactly as she had suggested, and it was sent to the house of Fortunus at dawn the next day. It caused me pain to put down lies in writing, and I recalled with new understanding, the old Apollonite saying '*don't send a philosopher to buy a horse*'.

Also at dawn, we set out for Flavensum: myself, Morganus, the bodyguards and the lightning's driver.

It was a swift journey to a strange place.

Chapter 19

The lightning was fast and brutal: a lightweight, four-wheel carriage drawn by four highly-bred horses from the imperial mail service, with iron-shod hooves for work on paved roads. Each carriage bore three rows of seats behind the driver, and could be covered with a canvas hood on iron hoops, against the ever-present Britannic rain. But the hood was usually folded away, as it slowed the carriage and the entire purpose of the carriage was speed. It was speed at the expense of everything else, including comfort, because the combination of iron hooves and iron-tyred wheels on a Roman road deafened everyone aboard, while the constant wind in the face and the dust and grit thrown up by the horses stung the eyes and inflamed the nose, and the leather-cushioned seats—while soft at the outset—soon felt like stone slabs.

But a lightning moved at an average speed of twelve miles per hour including stops, which meant full gallop when under way. By this means a lightning could run the eighty-mile distance from Londinium to Flavensum in less than seven hours, while a wagon or marching troops would need four days for the same journey. Such speed could be maintained only with post-stations every ten miles or so, where exhausted horses could be changed for a fresh team, but that was all part of the imperial mail service, because Romans may be dull but they are exceedingly thorough, and once they get hold of a good idea they never let go of it.

So, having left the Londinium fortress at dawn, we could confidently expect to arrive in Flavensum in the early afternoon, and while speeding along the Great West Road, Morganus and I managed a conversation, despite the creaking, swaying motion, the constant road noise, and the driver yelling at the horses and laying on with his whip.

'What are we going to tell them at Flavensum?' said Morganus. 'Have you thought up something clever?' I did not answer at first. 'Ikaros?' he said.

'We'll have to take a risk,' I said. 'I'm going to tell them that it's all about druids.'

For once, Morganus did not flinch at the word. I took that as a good sign. 'We'll tell them that you and I are on the Governor's orders, with a commission from him—and we do actually have a commission to show them.'

'The one we got from Petros?'

'Yes. I've brought it with me. So we'll tell them that his grace has information that druids are active in the countryside, and you and I are being sent to all the main cities of south Britannia to ask civic officials what they know, and that it's all profoundly secret, and that you've been sent because you are so very senior.' He smiled and shook his head. 'Well, you are!' I said. 'And I'm your assistant because I'm a clever Greek.'

'Yes,' he said, 'That might work. I do wonder about all this nervousness in talking about them: druids. I know what they can do, and I admit that it scares me to the bones sometimes.'

'You?' I said.

'Yes, me! But all this pretending that nobody knows they're still active , and that nobody must even talk to them… I wonder if Petros is the only one who breaks that law.'

'That's what I think,' I said, 'but the main thing is that it's an excuse to talk to the leading men of Flavensum, without letting them know that we're really interested in Roman politics.'

So that was agreed between us and we made good time, even with a stop for a mid-day meal at the last post-station before Flavensum. They served fresh bread, with olives, garum, apples, cheese and rabbit pie, together with a flask of modest white wine for me, and some pints of beer for those who prefer that thin and diuretic beverage. Afterwards,

I was amazed at Morganus' tolerance in allowing the carriage to be stopped no less than three times for the bodyguards and driver to empty their bladders at the roadside. But my gift of intuition told me that a sufficiency of drink was part of the tradition of lightning travel, and Morganus himself had to get down twice, so I suppose that persuaded him to be indulgent.

Finally, we did indeed arrive at Flavensum in the early hours of the afternoon, and I have to declare that my first impressions of the city were totally in accord with what Morganus had already said, because it would be impossible to imagine a more Roman city, built in the Roman way.

To begin with, Flavensum was heavily fortified, with a stone cladding laid on to the outward face of what had originally been an earth and timber wall. There were three complete lines of V-bottom ditches in front of the wall, and the ditches were heavily planted with sharp stakes. The wall was topped with a continuous fighting platform, with crenulations to give protection to the defenders, and there were complex works on either side of the main gates, to give further defence in case of attack. In addition, the roadway which crossed the three lines of ditches before the gates, narrowed steadily as it approached the gates such that any attempt to rush the gates would result in men being shoved off to either side by their own comrades, to fall on to the sharpened stakes below, and of course the roadway ended twenty feet before the gates and was spanned by a drawbridge.

'See?' said Morganus, as our lightning slowed to merge into the busy traffic of people, beasts and wagons going in and out of the town. 'It's a proper fortress. It was built just after Boudicca's rebellion, when Camulodenum and Londinium were massacred. So themen of Flavensum weren't having any of *that*!'

But Flavensum was more than a fortress. With only 6,000 inhabitants it was far smaller than the giant Londinium, but it was a market town, a regional capital, a centre of manufacture and an example to all Britannia. The city gates were crammed with people shouting and laughing and arguing, while pigs grunted, sheep bleated and geese honked. There were craftsmen, housewives, slaves, farmers, drovers and children all round as we rumbled across the wooden drawbridge, where we were stopped by four armed men and an officer. They were smartly dressed and armed, and wore mail shirts like auxiliaries, but had the hemi-cylindrical shields of legionaries. The shields bore the insignia of the city and a loyal dedication to the Emperor, but no legionary markings. They were some sort of city guard.

I supposed that we were stopped because we were strangers, and perhaps we were, but then I saw the awe-struck expressions on the faces of these soldiers, on sight of a helmet with a swan-feather crest: the insignia of a first javelin. At once, the officer yelled and another twenty men poured out of a nearby guard-room, and they doubled on the spot, forming up in two lines facing Morganus.

'Attennnnn-*shun*!' yelled the officer. The soldiers stood still and our driver took his cue.

'Give honour! Give honour! Give honour!' he cried, 'To Leonius Morganus Fortis Victrix, Father of the Twentieth and Hero of Rome! Gods save the Emperor!'

'Gods save the Emperor!' cried every living thing around us. Not just the guardsmen, but the civilians too, and possibly even the pigs, sheep and geese. I had seen exactly the same on other occasions, because Morganus was famous throughout the army and his sudden arrival always caused delight among the military. So there was respect and bowing from the guard officer.

'I greet you in the name of the people and senate of Flavensum!' said the officer.'You bring honour within our walls, and I have sent runners to warn our city's duovirs and decurions of your arrival. Meanwhile it would be my duty and privilege to lead you to the forum, where you will be properly received!'

Morganus smiled and nodded, and the officer formed up his men around the lightning, and we were escorted along the city's Via Principalis towards the forum.

I saw Morganus looking at me as we drove through the town. 'See,' he was thinking, 'didn't I tell you?' And he was right. Flavensum *was* the grid-pattern model on which a Roman town should be built. It even had an aqueduct, stretching in from the countryside. Very properly—but at great expense—the aqueduct stopped outside the walls, to avoid giving an enemy a bridge into the city, and the water was conducted under the fortifications in pipes. There were even pressure towers at the street junctions, to regulate the flow of water through the domestic mains. It was very, very impressive, and the whole town was neat, and square in the Roman way, and clean and swept and proud.

The only slight oddity was the fact that—as I had seen at the governor's levee—some of the citizens of the town, especially the men, did not look Roman. They looked like Jews or Syrians. But they acted like Romans and spoke only Latin.

The Via Principalis, as always, led directly to the forum and the two principal buildings of the city: which *should* have been the basilica and the temple of Jupiter, Juno and Minerva: the Capitoline Triad. The basilica was there all right, as town hall, tax office and law courts in one, but instead of the temple of the Triad, there was a huge synagogue and an enormous temple devoted to the imperial cult: to the divine spirit of the Emperor. I looked at the elaborate structure of this building—the tallest structure in the city—with its rows of pillars and sculpture-laden pediment. It was very impressive and Morganus was delighted with it. He nudged me and pointed to it. Again, I guessed his thoughts.

'What did I tell you? What could possibly be wrong here?'

He was even more delighted with the formal reception that we received. The elite of the city was waiting for us in hastily-draped togas. Some even had slaves around them, still hauling and poking to get the long, heavy garment into its elaborate folds. There were some dozens of these citizens, formed up in rows, by order of precedence, outside the gates of the Basilica. They were led by two men that I recognised as the duovirs of the Flavensum senate, whom I had seen at the Governor's levee. Standing together and in a block, they must have been the biggest group of toga-clad Roman civilians I had ever seen in Britannia. More relevant to the day's business, one of them was the man I had met at Gershom's club meeting. He was the man who, before all others, I had come to interrogate. He was Aurelio Tobias Bethsidus. The other was Annonias Neronis Solis, of whom I knew nothing, except that he—like Bethsidus—was a man in his fifties, well-fed, well-dressed and prosperous, with the self-satisfied manner of a man who is used to being surrounded by inferiors. If first appearances are significant—which sometimes they are and sometimes not—I would have judged Bethsidus to be a practical man of commerce, and Solis to be a thinker, perhaps a philosopher like myself.

As ever, and as usual, and as I should have expected—and yet still it annoyed—every one of these citizens ignored me and stared straight at Morganus. They stared at him in welcome, and respect. Then as Morganus and I, and the bodyguards got down from the lightning, the two duovirs stepped forward and raised their right arms in salute.

'Ave Caesar!' they cried in salute of Emperor Trajan.

'Ave Caesar!' cried all the rest.

'Ave Morganus!' cried Bethsidus and Solis.

'Ave Morganus!' cried the rest. It was something of a performance. As nicely done as if choreographed. They did not quite stamp feet and come to attention, but they gave the impression that they had done just that. Then Bethsidus bowed and spoke to Morganus.

'I greet you, Honoured First Javelin of the Twentieth,' he said, 'I am Bethsidus, Duovir of the city, together with the Honoured Duovir Solis.' Solis bowed.

'I greet you, Honoured Duovir Bethsidus!' said Morganus. 'I greet you, Honoured Duovir Solis!' and he bowed to each.

'Be welcome in our city, Honoured Sir,' said Bethsidus, 'and I regret the poor nature of our greeting, but we were not warned of your coming. Perhaps a messenger was sent, yet did not arrive?' Morganus nodded in understanding and spoke quietly.

'Honoured duovir,' he said, 'I am here with my companion, Ikaros of Apollonis,' he glanced at me.

'Ikaros!' said Bethsidus, and looked at me. 'We met before the tragic death of Gershom.' He turned to Solis. 'Honoured Solis,' he said, 'this is the Greek engineer who reads the thoughts of men. I have described him to you.' Solis nodded to Bethsidus, and the two bowed to each other with contrived smiles that spoke of an antagonism between them.

They were carefully polite but I saw that these two men disliked each other heartily. Then Solis was about to speak, but Morganus interrupted.

'Bethsidus! Solis!' he said. 'Forgive my lack of ceremony but it is vital that I speak to you privately. I am here on business of great importance, that must be treated with great discretion.' With that, he stood back, and said no more.

The result was eyebrows raised on all sides, and much puffing and blowing, and whispers spreading among the ranks of togas. But Bethsidus and Solis rose to the occasion, so Morganus and I and the bodyguards, were taken into the Basilica, and an office found, and chairs and a table, and slaves sent for the inevitable wine and cakes. Then with even more puffing and blowing and exasperation and explanation, the door was closed on those few very senior citizens who had clung to our footsteps, hoping to be included in the private discussions. Perhaps it soothed their pride that the bodyguards also waited outside.

Finally, Morganus sat, took off his helmet, placed in on the table in front of him, and spoke.

'We have little time, Honoured Sirs,' he said, 'so it would be best if my comrade Ikaros explains our purpose here. He is a now an imperial slave, but in his own city he was a cavalry officer and a senator.'

Solis looked puzzled, but Bethsidus smiled. He smiled at me.

'I know you by reputation, Ikaros of Apollonis,' he said, 'and I was impressed by your conversation in Gershom's house. So please proceed.'

So I did. I told them the invented story about druids, and about Morganus and myself touring the cities of southern Britannia. Perhaps it is still further vanity on my part, but I judged that the story was believed, and I continued.

'We will need to speak to the leaders of Flavensum,' I said, 'to the decurions of your city council, and to the leading men in the crafts and trades, and anyone else whom you advise. We will need to speak to them personally and privately,' I paused in my play-acting about druids and did my best to display sympathy and understanding, 'because no Roman citizen wants to admit in public, that he knows anything about such matters, and so it's best...'

I spoke on. I said the same thing several times over because I was reading signals in their expressions all the while. Thus Bethsidus and Solis kept glancing at each other, measuring each other's reactions to my words, and frowning. The two men seriously disliked each other. It was obvious and it was exciting. *There was something here.* There was something going on. But what was it? Could it actually be something to do with the druids? I pursued that.

'Honoured sirs,' I said, 'you are the elected leaders of this community, so there can be no need of secrecy in this room.' I swept my hand in a gesture to include us all. It was a piece of pure nonsense, because I certainly did not trust either of them, and I doubt that they trusted each other., but it was part of my act. 'So may I start at once and ask if either of Your Honoured selves knows anything of druidic activity? Either in or near to Flavensum?'

I watched them closely. I studied each face.

'No,' said Bethsidus.

'No,' said Solis.

Each spoke easily and comfortably and was hiding nothing. I could see it. So my fantasy had not become reality. I took a step further.

'The druids are infinitely cunning,' I said, 'could they work in some other way than religion? Could they attempt to affect civic life… even politics?' Again I was talking nonsense, because what I was saying was only a route to uttering the word *politics* so that I could see their reactions when I said it, and by all the gods they jumped: not in any physical sense, but the twitch of their faces and the blink of their eyes told me that something important and political was in their minds. It was indeed exciting, and I wondered if I had found the source of some dangerous political event so easily and swiftly as this.

After that I had to step carefully. I could hardly, then and there, ask what was their part in the murder of Gershom Bar Meshulam. I had to step back. I had to be subtle. So we talked in generalities, we drew up a list of prominent persons whom Morganus and I would meet—in private—and left it to Bethsidus and Solis to arrange the meetings.

Then we all sat back with business completed, and we smiled politely at one another, and Bethsidus offered hospitality.

'Honoured Morganus and Worshipful Ikaros,' he said, 'my house is at your disposal, with food and clothes for you and your men, for the duration of your time in Flavensum.'

'We are grateful, Honoured Bethsidus,' said Morganus, 'we gladly accept your offer.'

'Also,' said Bethsidus, 'I know that it would be the pleasure of the The-Lady-my-Wife to entertain you as guests at a formal dinner this very evening.'

'Ah,' said Morganus, 'you are most gracious, Honoured Sir, but my companions and I have had a day's hard pounding of our backsides on the road,' everyone smiled, 'and what we'd really like is a bath and an informal meal, if that is possible?'

He nodded at me, and I knew that what he really wanted was to avoid a formal dinner with reclining couches because a slave could not attend one, and my exclusion would embarrass Morganus. He was a good friend.

'Of course, Honoured Morganus,' said Bethsidus, 'and of course, Ikaros of Apollonis is most cordially invited to my table.' So everyone—except perhaps myself—nodded in approval of protocol observed, since no slave may even sit down to eat with a citizen without permission.

After that, Solis and the other togas dispersed, the lightning and horses were taken to the imperial mail stables and the driver accommodated there, while the bodyguards, Morganus and I were given rooms in Bethsidus' large house, which—as might be expected—was laid out on the classic Roman plan, with atrium complete with pool and open roof, surrounded by rooms and with a colonnaded garden to the rear. It seemed very typically Roman, but when we entered the atrium, to be greeted by Bethsidus' wife, his family and slaves, there was much bowing and formality—all of it aimed at Morganus—and I looked around and saw something, at last, that was *not* Roman to the marrow of its bones.

I saw something very strange indeed.

Chapter 20

There was no shrine to the household gods—the lares as the Romans call them—and this was amazing, because every Roman house in the Empire had its shrine in the atrium, dedicated to the lares. The shrine was called the lararium and it was often in the form of a model house with little statues of whichever gods favoured the family. It was always prominent, and always raised up on a pillar to a convenient height so that the paterfamilias or the matriarch could honour the shrine with little gifts or sacrifices, and it was the place before which—every morning—the household met for prayers.

Every Roman household had its lararium. Even households that were just one room in a slum tenement would have a little niche in the wall with sacred images. By contrast, Morganus' house had a large and splendid lararium, even though he was a follower of Mithras. But that was common sense, because the great gods are good for great matters, while the affairs of a family are best guarded by the small gods whom they love, and who love them in return.

Yet despite all this, there was no lararium in the house of Bethsidus. It was an enormous absence. It was like meeting a man with no face.

Instead of a lararium and exactly where a lararium might be, there was a pillar set against a wall, and on top of the pillar there was mounted a six-pointed golden star, and a stone slab inscribed with writing in Aramaic. I was so surprised that I read it aloud in that language:

'Thou shalt love the Lord thy Master with all thy heart, and with all thy soul and with all thy mind.'

Morganus frowned. 'What did you say?' But his puzzlement was as nothing compared with the look on Bethsidus' face, and on the faces of his wife and family. They were staggered and shocked.

'You read our language?' said Bethsidus.

'Oh yes,' I said, 'I learned it to study some religious books.' I pointed to the stone slab. 'That's from the book of Zoltan, isn't it? Chapter thirty?'

Bethsidus gaped and turned to his wife. She gaped back.

'What does it mean?' said Morganus, so I told him in plain Latin.

'Well,' he said, 'there you are then,' and he smiled at Bethsidus. 'Didn't I tell you that this is the most loyal city in Britannia?' he pointed at the slab, 'Obviously *the Master*, means the Emperor, because look there!' and Morganus pointed to something else. A pair of wired-together bronze plates was mounted on the wall, above the tablet and star. The plates were a citizenship diploma like those I had seen Morganus give the men of the First Squadron Third Pannonians. Morganus looked at Bethsidus.

'Is that your father's?' he asked.

'Yes,' said Bethsidus. 'Earned after twenty-five years' service. You will find one of those in every atrium of this city. God bless the Emperor!'

'Gods bless the Emperor!' said Morganus. But I was gripped with a passion of inquiry. I was fascinated by the Aramaic writing. I looked again at the stone.

'There's a very similar phrase in the book of Matthew,' I said, 'In the twenty-second chapter. But it differs. Matthew says: Thou shalt love the Lord thy *God* with all thy heart, and with all thy soul and with all thy might.'

'We do not follow Matthew,' said Bethsidus. 'We follow the book of the holy apostle Zoltan.' He turned to his family and slaves. 'Blessed be the word of Zoltan!' he said.

'Blessed be the word of Zoltan!' they repeated. I listened to their words, and putting this with what Allicanda had said of Flavensum, I began to understand.

'You're Jews, aren't you?' I said, 'but followers of the rabbi Jesus Bar Joseph.'

'We are all Jews in Flavensum,' he said, 'and you are speaking of the Messiah!'

'He that was crucified?' I said.

'And who rose from the dead!' said Bethsidus.

'So you're resurrectionist Jews,' I said.

'Yes!' said Bethsidus with fierce emphasis.

'And you follow Zoltan not Matthew, even though the book of Zoltan is…'

'Ikaros?' said Morganus, and his hand gripped my arm quite hard. I turned and saw him staring at me with eyes like spear points. 'Perhaps we could talk about this later?' he said. 'My arse is crying out for a soak in hot water. Can we go to the baths? *Now*?'

'Oh,' I said, 'yes. Yes, of course.' So we did. It was the word *arse* that persuaded me. Morganus seldom used so coarse a word. It meant that he was emphatic in his insistence. So I said no more and we went to the baths, which was normal Roman practice before any sort of dinner party. Bethsidus did not come with us, pleading the urgent need to begin making appointments for us with the citizens on our list, but he directed us to a good bath house, close by.

'Give my name,' he said, 'and they will honour you, and ensure that your clothes and gear are well guarded while you bathe.'

We were honoured indeed. We were taken to a clean and excellent hot plunge, and all other bathers asked to leave us in privacy, which they most graciously did. Morganus stayed silent until we were sitting in the pool, under a tiled, domed ceiling, with steam swirling over the water, and the pleasant, echoing sound of a bath house. The bodyguards discretely took the other end of the pool.

'By all the gods,' said Morganus, free to speak at last. 'Can't you stop being a blasted philosopher all the blasted time? You and your blasted books and languages! Can't you see when you should shut your blasted mouth and hold your blasted tongue?'

'Oh,' I said, because—from Morganus—that was serious swearing.

'Oh?' he said, 'Is that all? Just *Oh*? How do you think I'd like it if you started to question me about the Lord Mithras?' He raised his fist in the bull sign, and the bodyguards instantly copied him. 'So they're some sort of Jews, right?' he said. 'And they haven't got a lararium, right? But they're loyal Romans! Didn't you see that diploma up in a place of honour?'

'Yes,' I said, 'I saw that. And the town's so Roman it's barely true.'

'There you are then!' he said, 'So just leave their religion alone. There are secrets of faith that worshippers don't talk about,' he shifted and turned to face me. He was red with heat, and moisture trickled down his sparse hair and on to his nose and the scars on his cheeks. He looked round to check that nobody was listening: an instinctive movement because there was nobody present than ourselves. His expression was intense, and his voice lowered to a whisper, 'I keep the vows of my faith, don't I? And I don't talk about the Lord Mithras, even to you!'

'No,' I said, 'you don't.' It was true. The worship of Mithras was what Romans called a *mystery* cult, practised in secret, because Romans were like that. They had their public gods, like Jupiter, Juno and Minerva, who were celebrated in great temples and were state institutions. But they also had cults like those of Isis, Baal and Mithras himself, involving private worship with secrets known only to initiates, and as long as the initiates were loyal to the Empire, nobody minded.

'I understand,' I said.

'Right!' he said, 'So think on that, and don't talk religion with these people. No more damned Oramaic, or whatever it is.'

'*A*ramaic,' I said.

'Bah!'

'But there's something I *do* have to talk about,' I said, 'and I told him what I had seen in the eyes of Bethsidus and Solis. He nodded at that.

'So they don't like one another and they're covering up something political,' he said, 'is that it?'

'I think so,' I nodded.

'So the Legate might be right? Perhaps there *is* something political going on?' He frowned and shook his head. 'No,' he said. 'I can't believe it.'

Later, we dined at the house of Bethsidus, where I was not surprised that pork was served and cheese after that, since the prophet Zoltan preached abandonment of the ancient Jewish food laws, along with circumcision and the need for men to cover their heads. What with that, and the celebration of Jesus Bar Joseph as Messiah, to my mind they were hardly Jews at all. But I followed Morganus's advice and avoided all such matters, and in any case another topic dominated the conversation.

We went to dine in a large, south-facing room, all painted in cheerful Mediterranean landscapes and with a view of the gardens through opened, folding doors. The evening was warm, and a good light came in over the flowers and shrubs, with no need for lamps. By courtesy of Bethsidus, we all wore comfortable dining robes and slippers, Bethsidus' wife, the lady Lyrillias, wore her best jewellery, slaves were in close attendance, and Morganus and I sat down with her, Bethsidus, and two of his sons: they were lads in their teens, and already full citizens. They said little, but when they did speak they were somewhat unmannerly towards their parents, and I saw none of the odd, embarrassed respect for myself which I usually receive from young Romans. But Bethsidus and his wife were most gracious.

'Be welcome to the house of my lord husband,' said Lyrillias, as we sat down to table, and the slaves settled our chairs behind us. She was a woman in her late fifties, distinctly older that her husband, and distinctly heavy in flesh. I guessed that theirs was a marriage between prestige in the man and wealth in the woman. I also guessed—in fact it was obvious l that some great sorrow was troubling the lady, as indeed it was. 'I apologise for the absence of my eldest son,' she added, 'but he cannot be here as he lies in the care of the surgeons.'

'We pray to our gods in his name,' said Morganus, courteously.

'We look to the grace of God,' said Bethsidus.

'Honoured lady,' I said, 'may I ask what has happened to your son?'

Sadly she did not reply, because she could not. She did her best to suppress emotion, as a Roman matriarch should, but the grief was too strong. She only sighed and looked down. So Bethsidus spoke for her, though he too was now burdened with emotion. I supposed that he had controlled this while on public duty, but in his own home and at ease, he could do so no more.

'Our young men go their own way, these days,' said Bethsidus. 'Thus my eldest son, Alexander, was with others seeking to pen a bull when it turned on him and gored him,' Bethsidus placed a finger to the left of his umbilicus, 'the horn penetrated here,' he said. He gathered strength to add the next words. 'It's a bad wound,' he said, 'very bad.'

'Such wounds need great care in treatment,' I said, 'they must be fully explored, and kept free to drain, and the bandages made damp in wine before application: damp, but not wet.'

Bethsidus looked at me in surprise. 'Are you a surgeon?' he asked, and looked at his wife. 'He's Greek,' he said, 'and Greeks are famous surgeons. They're the best!'

'If you are a surgeon, will you look at my son?' she asked.

'Honoured Sir,' I said, 'Honoured Lady, I'm not a surgeon, I'm an engineer. I studied medicine for three years, but then gave it up.'

'Yes, but you're a Greek,' said Bethsidus, 'and Greeks are clever!'

'In God's name, will you look at my son?'said the lady. I looked around the table. There was hope in everyone's eyes. Even Morganus was nodding in encouragement: but he believes that I work magic. So I wished I had said nothing, but I could not call back my words.

'I would be honoured to look at your son's wound,' I said, 'and offer any advice that I may.'

'God bless you!' said the lady.

After that there was awkwardness, because while every person present—other than myself—wanted me instantly to visit the wounded son, Roman protocol dictated that we should proceed with the meal. The lady Lyrillias was even beckoning to her slaves to begin service. But I was not Roman and I could not bear it.

'Honoured Lady, Honoured Sir,,' I said. 'This is a case where practicality should overcome good manners. So I most humbly ask that I be taken at once to your son, so that I can do what I can, even though it may not be very much.'

Everyone stood at once, and a huge guilt fell on me, at the hope in the eyes of Bethsidus and his family, because at best I was only half a surgeon. But what could I do? I could not deny them my help, and the medical school of Apollonis was the finest in the world, so perhaps it may have taught me something useful… So Bethsidus and his wife led me and Morganus, and a procession of slaves and family, to a bedroom in the house—quite close by—which had been furnished as a sick-room, and where Alexander, son of Bethsidus and Lyrillias, was laid on his bed. There was a slave in attendance and also a young man, well dressed, who sat on a stool beside the bed, with a box of instruments beside him. He was obviously a surgeon, and had neat, clean hands with well-trimmed nails.

The surgeon and slave stood as we entered, and I looked at Alexander and feared the worst. He was a large, bearded man in his early twenties, unconscious and yellow-grey in the face. His cheeks were sunken and his nose was sharp. He was resting on pillows and was covered by a sheet and blanket. Everything was clean, there was no smell of a rotting wound, there was no nonsense of incense, chanting or quackery, and—looking at the surgeon—I already guessed that there was nothing more that I could do.

Bethsidus spoke to me.

'Ikaros of Apollonis,' he said, 'I present Festinus Julius Marcos, the leading surgeon of our community, and trained to army standards.' Then he addressed Marcos. 'Ikaros is Greek, and studied medicine at the school of Apollonis. He has come to offer advice.'

I looked at Marcos, and saw conflicting emotions. He was annoyed to see a rival who might challenge his decisions, but pleased that a clever Greek might save his patient, and there was some other emotion at work besides, and I saw that like the teenage sons, the surgeon looked at Bethsidus with less than proper respect, and all three of these young men had the truculent look that a boy gives his father when the boy thinks he knows more than the old man.

But having come this far, I thought it best to proceed.

'May I see your patient's wound, honoured Marcos?' I said, and he hesitated an instant.

'Of course,' he replied, then leaned over the bed and carefully drew back the covers to reveal a neat set of bandaging over Alexander's abdomen. The dressings were damp with wine, but not wet, and were expertly applied.

'This is well done,' I said to Marcos, 'I could do no better. But could I see the actual wound?' He hesitated again and a different emotion showed on his face. Was it fear? Reluctance? I could not tell. As I constantly protest, I have no magic powers. So sometimes I cannot read an emotion, and this was one of those occasions. But his words made sense.

'I really don't want to disturb the dressings,' he said, 'they were changed only recently, and each change causes bleeding, and a lot of pain to the patient.' I nodded, and stood back and addressed Bethsidus and Lyrillias.

'Honoured Lady, Honoured Sir, there is nothing I can add to the excellent treatment that this honoured practitioner is already applying.' I bowed to Marcos, who bowed in return. And that was all. We had a miserable dinner, then went our beds, and the next day Morganus and I began to work through the list of men whom we had to interview.

We were given the same office in the Basilica where Morganus and I had first spoken to Bethsidus and Solis, and a succession of decurions, guildsmen and other prominent citizens were brought in to see us. It was tedious, repetitive work, very tiring and it took us five days to interview each man, all of whom were mature men in middle life, which was hardly surprising since these were the city's foremost men. They were uniformly willing to speak; they ranged from the thin and active to the fat and lazy, and with one odd exception they had nothing to hide about anything.

I give here, as one example, a passage of speech with decurion Lassis Cranius Oprom, whom we interviewed early on the first day. Having gone through the pretence of asking about druids—of which of course he knew absolutely nothing—I attempted to find out why Bethsidus and Solis disliked one another. It was the best route I could think of to approach anything political.

'How are things in the city generally?' I asked.

'They are well,' he said, 'and we are happy to be contributing to the governor's games.'

'Gods save His Grace,' said Morganus.

'God save His Grace,' said Oprom.

'I met Bethsidus and Solis at a governor's levee in Londinium,' I said.

'Yes,' he said, 'they were there to pledge money.'

'And do they get on well?' I asked, 'Bethsidus and Solis?'

'Of course!' he said. 'Any disputes in our community are settled by voting.'

'*Was* there a dispute?' I asked.

'Certainly not about the governor's games,' he said, and chattered on about the way the city's young men—the rising generation, he called them—were drafted into running the games. 'You'll hardly find a citizen left in Flavensum that's under twenty-five,' he said, 'because all our young men are in Londinium! They are so passionate in all things, and sometimes prone to go their own way, but they are gripped with enthusiasm for the games.'

He smiled and smiled, but—and this was the odd exception to their open manner—he, and every other man we questioned, was evasive on the matter of the dispute between Bethsidus and Solis. I got closest to a straight answer with the chairman of the college of butchers on day three. He was a squat, dark man, full of Celtic Silure blood, presumably from a Celtic mother.

'Was there ever any dispute between Bethsidus and Solis?' I asked him, having worked the conversation to this subject.

There was a slight pause before he answered. He considered his words carefully and for the first time I had the impression that a door was closing within his mind. Finally he spoke, affecting a dismissive manner.

'It was synagogue business,' he said. 'Synagogue business, that's all.'

'Some matter of religion?' I asked, but Morganus leaned forward.

'It was nothing to do with the Governor or the province,' he said, 'right?'

'Nothing like that,' said the butcher.

'Nothing political?' I asked, looking closely at him.

'No. Nothing political.'

I could see that he was telling the truth, so I said no more. I would have pursued the matter of religion, but I knew Morganus would have stopped me.

As for Gershom, the leading men of Flavensum knew only that he was dead. They had nothing to hide and they expressed about as much sympathy as any man does when he hears that a tax official has been murdered.

'I hope he's in heaven,' said one of them, and smiled, 'though I doubt it!'

Apart from that we learned nothing, other than some details of the founding of the city, because one of those whom we interviewed proved to be an enthusiastic historian, and I made the mistake of a polite compliment on the prosperity of Flavensum as he sat down, whereupon he instantly turned the subject, so that he could give his favourite lecture.

'Well of course,' he said, with a smug little smile, 'we have indeed prospered greatly, since the city was founded, which was in Nero's time, and which is why the full name is Colonia *Neronis* Flavensum, when 360 of our ancestors came to Britannia on five ships after the rebellion at Lixus, which, as you know, is the capital of the North African province of Mauretania. They were discharged veterans of the Fourth Flavensi Regiment, and were welcomed after the Boudiccan wars because the province needed citizens who were trained soldiers.'

'How interesting, I said, 'but can I ask…?'

'Yes, yes,' he said, 'well of course, our ancestors were welcomed by the then governor, Gaius Seutonius Paulinus, who granted land to found our city…'

He was extremely boring, but the dinner on the second night was worse. It was far worse, because it was the turn of Solis the duovir to entertain the honoured guests. He too offered a dinner, with chairs not couches, but otherwise it was heavily elaborate, and I supposed that Solis was attempting to surpass anything delivered by his rival.

The house of Solis was another Mediterranean villa transplanted into Britannia, and there was another south-facing dining room, elaborately painted, and a long and complex procession of dishes served by slaves in uniform tunics. But there were differences. To begin with, no women were present. No explanation was given for this, and we were received by Solis himself, and four young sons, every one of whom treated Solis with grovelling respect.

'Yes, Honoured-Sir-my-Father, No, Honoured-Sir-my-father. After you, Honoured-Sir-my-Father.'

Before we dined, we stood round the table with arms raised while Solis declaimed a very long prayer to the god of the Jews, and to his son the messiah, and to the spirit of holiness, and to the virgin mother of the son. Then just as I was thankful that the prayer was finished, and the torture by boredom ended, Solis bowed briefly to one of his sons, who bowed profoundly in return, and Solis turned to me and Morganus.

'We shall now hear a recitation from the holy book of Zoltan,' he said 'which is passed by memory down the generations.' He stared at us, and some response was appropriate.

'Very nice,' said Morganus, displaying formidable stoicism.

'Indeed,' I said, attempting to do the same.

'Proceed!' said Solis, and the boy treated us—in fluent Aramaic—to the Rabbi Jesus' sermon on the mount as reported in the book of Zoltan.

'*Blessed be the strong!*' he cried. '*For they shall prevail!*'

'*They shall prevail!*' cried all present other than myself and Morganus.

'*Blessed be those who are prepared! For they shall be ready with swords!*'

'*They shall be ready with swords!*'

'*Blessed be those who shed blood in just cause! For they shall be the kingdom of God!*'

'*They shall be the kingdom of God!*'

There was much more, all of it incomprehensible to Morganus. But when I explained later he was delighted with the sentiments expressed, which he thought were admirably Roman.

'It's why we needed these men in Britannia, after the Boudicca disaster!' he said, and when I pointed out that Matthew's version of the sermon said: 'blessed are the meek', and 'blessed are those who are persecuted', he simply laughed.

During the actual dinner, Solis fastened upon me as a leech does to a bather's leg. He recognised me as a philosopher and kept asking me questions, so that he could correct my answers, and he constantly smiled with the self-satisfaction of a man who knows better than everyone else.

'In your city of Apollonis,' he asked, 'were there any Jews?'

'Yes,' I said, 'they were strong in the professions, especially engineering and medicine.'

'Ah,' he said, 'a profound mistake! Things mechanical adorn only this life, while faith brings life eternal.'

'Life eternal!' said his sons, repeating his last words as they did throughout his non-stop question-and-answer discourse, which should have been dull but was not, because Solis was very convincing: even inspirational. He was a broad-framed man, short and strong, with a large head, dark eyes under thick brows, and he had such a gift of animation in his speech that he was entertaining. I found him fascinating—if strange—and even Morganus was following his words and smiling.

After that, by the grace of Apollo, the leading decurions took it in turns to offer us dinner each night, until we left Flavensum and suffered the return journey. I stress that I left convinced that nobody in that city was responsible for the murder of Gershom, and as for the dispute between Bethsidus and Solis, I allowed myself to be persuaded that it was a religious dispute with no political consequences. Later experience demonstrated that I should have thought further in all these matters, and I stand forward in admitting guilt that I did not. But all such thoughts were driven from my mind on our return to Londinium, where much had happened in our absence.

Chapter 21

There were letters waiting for us at Morganus' house in the fortress. Two for me and one for him: an elaborate scroll bearing the insignia of Government House. Morgana Callandra gave me my letters as we came in through the door on our return from Flavensum, and was then busy giving formal greeting to Morganus with her girls behind her, and Morganus was looking at his letter as I looked at mine.

One was a plain wooden-sheet letter addressed to me in Allicanda's handwriting. I broke the seal and opened it, fumbling several times before I could do so. Perhaps I was tired from the journey, perhaps my emotions were stirred. The letter was two days old and very short.

'From Allicanda to Ikaros,

We must meet. I can say no more.

May the gods be with you and around you.'

The second letter was a scroll of Egyptian paper, sealed with the emblem of the house of Fortunus and written in the bold handwriting of a scribe.

'From Fabius Gentilius Fortunus to Ikaros of Apollonis, slave of His Imperial Majesty.

I am in receipt of your honoured and recent letter inquiring as to the possibility of your purchasing slaves of my estate. I would be most pleased to open discussions in this respect. Therefore and herewith, to expedite any possible sale or sales, I give a list of the prices which present market values dictate.

I looked at the list. The slaves I had named at random were now classified by skills, type and price. There were such entries as:

Baroc the Gaul
Expert planter and husbandman.
GARDEN BOY: 3,500 sesterses.
Sistrania the Artebate
Clean and diligent lady's maid.
HOUSE GIRL: 2,500 sesterses.

But I hardly looked at these, because at the top of the list I saw:

Allicanda the Hibernian
Exquisite mistress of cuisine
EXOTIC: 2,000,000 sesterses.

I must have groaned aloud, because Morgana Callandra and Morganus turned to look at me. I think everybody did.

'What is it?' said Morganus. I showed him the letters. His wife looked up at him, saw the dismay on his face, then turned to me.

'It's Allicanda, isn't it?'

'Show her,' I said, 'show her the letters.'

Morganus passed them to her. She read them, and sighed.

'I'm sorry, Ikaros,' she said.

'Why?' I said.

'I told you what to write to him, didn't I? To Fortunus?' I smiled, or did my best to smile.

'It's not your fault,' I said, 'somebody's told him I want Allicanda. It's not really surprising. His senior slaves all saw me with her in Constantinos' cook-shop, and all the rest have known me and her for years. I did warn off one of them—a little toad called Wulfrik—but someone must have told Fortunus. And I suppose Fortunus thinks all the money of the Empire is behind me, because I'm an imperial slave.'

Morganus gave me back the letters, and his expression told me that he was about to say something that I would not like. He hesitated and showed me a letter he had just opened.

'It's addressed to me,' he said, 'from Petros. But really it's for you. There's big trouble. A gladiator was killed yesterday. One of the most famous ones: Tadaaki the German. Another gladiator deliberately killed him in a practice bout, and that's never happened before. They've got the man who did it, but this is unheard of. It just never happens. Gladiators don't behave like that. It could ruin the games because it's a shame and a disgrace, and it can't wait.'

There are times when a man's head is so full that he can admit no further thoughts, and my head was now full of the realisation that I had not known how important Allicanda was to me. I had lost my own family in the siege of Apollonis, my beloved wife and our dear children, and it took me ten years to recover from that, even though for much of that time I lived the easy life of an exotic in the house of Scorteus, father of Fortunus. After that I was made an imperial slave under the authority of Morganus, whose family had graciously accepted me. I had become so content that the longing for Allicanda had grown within me without my being aware of it. But now I *was* aware of it, and wanted to dwell upon it. I wanted to dwell, even, on the impossible price that Fortunus was asking for Allicanda. But Morganus was thrusting the letter at me.

So I did my best to be a stoic. I read the letter, which was signed by Petros of Athens for His Grace the Governor, and by Africanus as acting head of the army of Britannia. The last sentence was forcefully explicit. *'You will cease all other investigations and deliver an instant and accurate report establishing the reason for the murder of Tadaaki the German, and you will then visit the racing teams and drama companies to uncover and prevent any similar conspiracies that might affect the governor's games.'*

'Who was Tadaaki the German?' I asked, and saw Morganus and the bodyguards shake their heads in amazement.

'Don't you know *anything* about gladiators?' said Morganus.

'No,' I said.

'Tadaaki is—*was*—the star of stars. He was the biggest name brought over for the Games. Every man in the Empire knows his name. He was a murmillo.'

'What's a murmillo?' I said, and everyone gaped at my ignorance.

'Gods of Rome!' said Morganus. 'Jupiter, Juno and Minerva!'

'I'm sorry,' I said, as emotions boiled within me, 'but I take no interest in your Roman sports, and it escapes my understanding that every man in the Empire knows the name of a butcher in a slaughterhouse.'

'He's not a butcher, he's a gladiator!'

'What's the difference? And what are your gods-forsaken games but butchery and murder?'

Morganus paused. He looked around at the shocked faces of his family and the bodyguards.

'You're shouting,' he said.

'I am not!'

As I have said, my head was full of Allicanda. I was not acting as a stoic should. Morganus took my arm and led me out into the garden. He sat me on a bench and went back into the house. He came out with a wine flask and a cup.

'Go on,' he said. 'Drink up.' So I did. 'Now then,' he said, 'you are without doubt the most brilliantly clever man I have ever met, and you work magic too.'

'I don't!' I said.

'You do,' he insisted, 'but you can be amazingly ignorant. Have you really, truly never heard of Tadaaki the German?'

'No,' I said.

'Then we'll have to start by me explaining that gladiatorial combat is a martial art, conducted according to rules, and fought under the supervision of referees.'

'But they get killed,' I said. 'Isn't that the whole point of it?'

'You've got a lot to learn,' he said. 'We can talk as we go to the new arena. We'll have to go there at once. I'll show you the arena, and explain it, and I'll tell you about gladiator owners, trainers and referees. I'll do that before we meet anyone or you'll say something like *I've never heard of Tadaaki* and they'll think you are a crap-head idiot.'

The new arena—the gladiatorial arena—was close to the legionary fortress, to the north of Londinium. It was far smaller that the chariot racing stadium, timber built and of the classic oval form that Romans build all over the Empire. Six rows of seats looked down on a central, sand-covered space about sixty yards by forty, where combats would be held. The sanded area was twenty feet below the lowest seats, and walled in so that nothing could get out, and get at the spectators. There was room for about five thousand of them, and a continuous line of upright poles ran round the top of the arena, enabling canvas covers to be rigged in the unlikely event that the Britannic sun shone too fiercely.

The structure was typically Roman: neat and sensible, with multiple exits and stairs to get spectators in and out with ease. It was not quite finished and legionaries were at work with saws, hammers and nails, installing seats. The centurion in charge took me, Morganus and the bodyguards to the sponsor's box—the place of honour—on one of the long sides of the arena, that gave the best view of everything. Even I knew that the sponsor who paid for these games was the Governor, who would preside over the gladiatorial combats.

There were legionaries working in the sponsor's box too: carpenters, and a team of sign-painters who were working on a big wooden, notice board at the back of the box. They were covering the notice board with bold writing in big letters. All these men stood to attention as we arrived, but Morganus told them to carry on, and he gave a lecture for my benefit, raising his voice over the noise and voices of men at work.

'First of all,' he said, 'you mentioned butchery, didn't you?'

'Yes,' I said.

'Well that gets done in the morning, when the criminals are executed. They're brought in down there,' he said, and pointed to the gates at either end of the sanded area,

'What criminals?' I said.

'The worst kind!' he said. 'The scum, the noxii: child killers, rapists, arsonists and such. And *they* do get butchered, believe me! The sponsor of the games buys them from the law courts, so they can be executed as a public spectacle. They get torn by the beasts: dogs, wolves, bears, lions even.'

'What about the gladiators?' I said.

'They come on after mid-day. There's a big parade, they march round the arena, then they fight in pairs. And they fight under rules.'

'What rules?'

'These,' he said, and turned to the work of the sign painters behind us. 'These are the rules of Marcus Superbus Quintus, who was a famous patron of the games, a hundred years ago. It's the college of Quintus that's providing the referees for these games, and these rules are the most respected in the Empire,' he pointed to the notice board, 'and there's one of those at every entrance to the arena, so everyone knows that the rules of Quintus are in force.'

I looked at the rules and was so impressed with their detail that I have attached a transcript to the end of this book as an appendix. It is a document worthy of study, proving that gladiatorial combat was indeed a martial art, and the surprising fact that it was only on rare occasions that gladiators were killed in the arena.

While I was reading, there was a bustling of men climbing the stairway that led to the sponsor's box. Boots clumped on wooden stairs, and voices echoed off the planked walls. The sign-painters, carpenters, and bodyguards stood aside as a three men entered the box. Each one was a Roman citizen, and two wore tunics with the narrow purple stripe of the knightly class. These were rich and senior persons who came with a retinue of slaves in their wake, but they were worried and angry. The two knights were smooth men with cultured accents, but the third was grim and scarred, with one ear missing. He reminded me of Septimus the sword master in Trajan's baths.

One of the knights stood forward and spoke to Morganus.

'Are you the first javelin of the Twentieth Legion?

'Yes,' said Morganus.

'Good!' said the other. 'I am Askodus, owner of the school of Askodus. I bring with me the Honoured and Knightly Commius Principal Referee of the college of Quintus. I also bring my chief trainer of gladiators, the Honoured Civilis.'

'May the grace of the gods be upon you, Honoured and Knightly sirs,' said Morganus.

'So,' said Askodus, 'why you are here? Why did you not immediately present yourself to me?'

'Indeed!' said the principal referee.

'Yeah!' said the chief trainer.

I felt the floor of the Sponsor's box tremble slightly as the four bodyguards stamped forward to stand behind Morganus. They stood grim-faced, with hands on swords. Morganus also took a step forward. He never so much as raised his voice, but stood looking down at Askodus, Commius and Civilis.

'When you speak to me, you speak to the Twentieth Legion,' he said. 'And when you speak to the legion, you speak to the Empire and the Emperor.'

'Gods bless Him!' cried the bodyguards.

'Gods bless Him,' said the three men, quietly, and they fell back, and glanced at each other with expressions that I found most revealing. Then Askodus drew himself up in such dignity as he could muster.

'May the grace of Jupiter be upon the Twentieth Legion and all its men,' said Askodus. He spoke with little sincerity and much resentment. 'I regret any impoliteness, but I have lost a gladiator, valued at over three million.'

'I'm not here to talk about money,' said Morganus, 'I'm here to find out how a man was killed.' He looked at me. 'This is my comrade, Ikaros of Apollonis, who is in the service of His Imperial Majesty, and who will explain how we shall go on.' He let them think on that, then added, 'My comrade has the power to read men's thoughts. So be warned and beware.'

I nodded and took advantage both of Morganus's words, and of what I had just seen in these men's faces. I spoke first to Askodus.

'*You*, are wondering who to approach in Rome to get back your three million and you are trying to blame others for the death of Tadaaki.' I turned to Commius. '*You*, are in fear for your reputation, and likewise hope to shift guilt.' I turned to Civilis, 'While *you*, simply wish to avoid being blamed.'

The babble of protest that followed proved that I had hit the mark. The three men talked over one another, and stabbed fingers, and shook their heads at everything. I don't really read minds, but I certainly make good guesses. Morganus nodded to me in approval. Then he raised a hand for silence.

'Silence!' he said. 'My comrade has more to say.'

'Thank you, HonouredSir,' I said, and spoke to Askodus. 'I must immediately see where Tadaaki was killed. I must speak to everyone who knows anything about it. I must see his body, and I must speak to the man who killed him. I assume you have the killer under guard?'

'Of course!' said Askodus. 'He is Valdox the Regni! I curse his name and the day I bought him. We've got him locked up, but you'll get nothing out of him. He's strange.'

'Strange?' said Commius, seizing upon the word. 'Then why did you buy him?'

'Because my chief trainer advised me,' said Askodus.

'Yeah,' said Civilis, 'but you saw him and you said…'

'I said that I accept your recommendation!' said Askodus, interrupting.

'So the fault is within your school,' said Commius, 'and not with my referees.'

They argued a lot more. Morganus would have stopped them, but I let them go on because what they said was revealing. For instance, I learned that it was common for masters to get rid of aggressive slaves by selling them to gladiator schools.

'They're outside our gates every day,' said Civilis. 'You can't get rid of 'em! There was even a line of 'em waiting outside our camp at Dubris, the morning after we arrived: masters with their nasty bastards.'

'Yes,' said Askodus, 'but Valdox was willing. He knelt at his master's feed and asked for blessing.'

'And he was the fittest man I've ever seen,' said Civilis, 'he could run and jump and fight and everything. I thought we'd got a marvel there.'

When they finished arguing, I had them take us to the place where Tadaaki had been killed, and that was also revealing. We went in procession: myself, Morganus, the bodyguards, Askodus, Commius and Civilis and their slaves. We went to their school's barracks, outside the arena. There were several of these barracks buildings, one for each school, timber-built by the army with accommodation for the gladiators and staff, and even a bath house. Each one was surrounded with a palisade, and had a small practice arena, sanded and fenced.

As we passed through the gates, we were saluted by auxiliaries, defending the school on Petros's orders, and the first thing I saw was a pair of gladiators in training. It was most instructive. There were two athletic young men, in armour and helmets, stabbing and feinting with wooden swords, while two referees kept control. One—the senior referee—stood back: circling, watching and shouting orders, while the other—the junior—kept close to the gladiators, holding a long white rod which he could use to catch their attention without coming within reach of their weapons. Both referees wore tunics with knightly stripes.

'Break!' cried the senior referee as the gladiators jammed together, and the junior referee rapped each man sharply on his helmet. Instantly, the two gladiators stepped back, and stood still, panting and gasping and sweating.

'And ... *engage!*' cried the senior referee. The gladiators saluted each other with their wooden swords and fought on, and I turned to Morganus for guidance.

'What are they?' I said, whispering to hide my ignorance. 'Which type?'

'The one with the big shield is a murmillo,' he said, 'Tadaaki was a murmillo, as you know. The other one's a thraex.'

I nodded and looked at the equipment of each man. Both wore elaborate bronze helmets which entirely covered their faces, and had high ridges on the crown and wide neck-guards at the back. Both wore padded linen protections bound round the sword arm and leading shoulder. Both wore further padding, with steel greaves on top, to protect their legs. Both were barefoot and both wore white loin-cloths fringed with gold. Likewise, both carried shields, though the murmillo had a hemi-cylindrical Roman army shield, grasped by its handle with the left hand, while the thraex had a small, round shield strapped to the left forearm.

However, their weapons—accurately made in wood and painted to resemble the real thing—were entirely different. The murmillo had a gladius, while the thraex had a curved, sickle-shaped weapon with which he attempt to hook his opponent round the side of the shield, aiming mainly at the middle of the back.

All this was interesting, but what shouted aloud at me was the fact that, unlike soldiers, gladiators fought with chest and belly unprotected. Thus a gladiator did indeed have his helmet and shield like a soldier, but a Roman soldier wears body armour to guard against a thrust to the heart, or a slash that spills intestines, while leaving his limbs uncovered to allow greater agility, since a wound to the limbs is rarely fatal. But in bizarre contrast, a gladiator's limbs were heavily protected while his torso was naked, inviting a wound from any blade that touched it! At first, this perversity of gear was beyond my understanding. But then I realised that it enhanced the excitement of the spectacle, since the audience would be gripped in anticipation of the cunning stroke that slips past the defences and slices into vulnerable flesh.

I said so to Morganus, who agreed but then surprised me with a further thought.

'No breastplates? No mail?' he said. 'Oh yes, it's for the thrill of it. But there's more.' He looked at me. 'You know gladiators are all *infami* don't you? Disgraced persons?'

'Yes,' I said.

'Well, fighting without body armour is a form of redemption. Everyone admires them for it, because it shows true Roman spirit. It shows manly courage, and it shows contempt for death and wounds. It's the spirit that built the Empire!'

'Oh,' I said, fascinated by these concepts as I stared at the two gladiators in their training.

Then I realised that everyone was looking to me to begin the investigation, and so I began, and never in my entire career as a detective agent did I discover the motive of a killing with so little effort.

It was all blatantly obvious.

Chapter 22

A crowd had gathered. Some dozens of men were now standing by the practice arena, including the murmillo and thraex who had completed their sparring, and who stood in the ring of sand with the referees beside them. Other gladiators had come out of the barracks building to take their turn at practice. They muttered and whispered to each other, and to the slaves who held their gear including the heavy helmets, which were put on only immediately before bouts. I refrain from describing their various styles of dress and gear, so fascinating to aficionados yet so boring to me. Thus there were secutors, samnites, provocators and others, with shields and weapons of every imaginable kind. The only one that I immediately noticed was a splendidly handsome young man, wearing just a tiny loin cloth and a padded sleeve, whose slaves held a fisherman's net and trident.

Morganus saw me looking, and whispered.

'That's a retiarius,' he said, 'that's only one who doesn't wear a helmet. Always a pretty boy and one for the ladies.'

But it was time to begin.

'So!' I said to Askodus, Commius and Civilis. 'We know that Tadaaki was killed in practice. Did it happen here?'

Askodus and Commius looked at one another, reluctant to speak.

'You tell him,' said Askodus to Civilis, 'you're the chief trainer. You were here.'

'So were you!' said Civilis, forcibly, 'and so were all the referees, including Commius.' And the three began to argue.

'I'll hear from all of you,' I said, 'but you first!' I pointed at Civilis the trainer. Then, with a victim found, the rest fell silent and stood back. Civilis rubbed his hands on his tunic, nervously. He sniffed, took a breath and spoke. His voice was coarse, his vocabulary sparse, but he gave the facts.

'It was here. They were both of 'em in the ring. There was Tadaaki the German and Valdox the soddin' boy wonder!' There was a growl of anger from the surrounding gladiators at Valdox's name. 'Yeah!' said Civilis. 'Him, the little sod!' He shook his head and continued. 'Commius was senior ref, and him there,' he pointed to one of the other referees, 'he had the white rod. But everyone else was there too,' he spread an arm to include Askodus the school's owner, and all the rest. 'It wasn't just me! They was all there to see the boy wonder with iron in his fist for the first time!'

'What does that mean?' I asked.

'Well,' he said, 'him—the boy wonder—was so soddin' good, and he learned so fast and he moved so quick, that we shoved him up the scale fast, and give him a sword.'

'A real sword?' I said.

'Yeah,' he replied, 'you train the buggers up, which normally takes months, and you give 'em only wood. Then, when they're ready, you train 'em with iron so they get the feel of it, 'cos you don't want the first time they hold iron, to be when they go out in front of a crowd.'

'So they both had real weapons? Tadaaki and Valdox?'

'Yes,' said Civilis.

'Yes,' said all the gladiators, nodding agreement on this technical matter.

'Were they sharp?'

'Yes. They have to be. You have to train the buggers to keep calm, and follow the rules even with sharp iron.'

I looked around.

'Is that usual?' I asked.

'Yes!' said everyone.

'So what happened?'

Civilis sniffed, he cleared his throat. He hawked and spat into the sand.

'Well,' he said, 'we put the little sod—Valdox—to spar with Tadaaki, 'cos the little sod was so good. So fast, so quick, and such a good boy who did what we said, and we thought we'd got a world-beater, one who'd be famous and make millions.'

'Yes!' said Askodus, shaking his head in sorrow.

'Yes!' said Commius.

'So you set him to spar with your best man,' I said, 'Tadaaki as murmillo, Valdox as thraex, and both with sharp steel.'

'Yes!' said Civilis. 'It's what we do when they're ready. They have to make standard moves, and they mustn't make contact or draw blood. That's the rules of the house!' He looked at Askodus and Commius. 'That's house rules, isn't it? It wasn't just my idea!' Askodus and Commius said nothing, but both nodded.

'Go on,' I said. 'What happened?'

'Well,' said Civilis, 'soon as they was on the sand, Valdox, the little sod, he went forward *before* the command to salute and engage!' He glared at me to ensure that I understood how disgraceful this was, and all the gladiators roared in anger. 'I'm saying *before the soddin' command!*' he repeated, and the gladiators roared again. 'I'm saying the little bastard went straight in with his blade and sliced Tadaaki across the back, which was foul, rotten, dirty play!'

There was a deep groan from all the gladiators. I looked at them and noted their horror at this breaking of rules. 'Yeah!' said Civilis. 'And the little sod really meant it, and it came out of nowhere, 'cos the little bastard had always been a good boy, and…'

'Then what happened?' I said.

'Well,' said Civilis, 'Tadaaki slammed the little sod with his shield and then stood back, all right and proper, and raised the finger, according to rules.'

'Yes,' said all the gladiators, nodding to each other.

Fortunately, Morganus had explained what was meant by 'raising the finger', or rather raising a hand with the index finger extended. It was the sign by which a gladiator appealed to the referees if he had sustained a serious wound. It was then the senior referee's duty to present both men to the sponsor of the games for judgement when, usually, if the contest had been well fought, the wounded man was declared loser, the other winner, and both marched off to applause.

'So what happened when Tadaaki raised his finger?' I asked, and there was such a growl of anger from the gladiators that Civilis had to shout to be heard.

'What happened? What happened? I'll tell you what soddin' happened! What happened was Tadaaki fell back, and honourably lowered arms, and with the blood runnin' all down his back, and he looked to the ref,' the growls grew louder, 'but the little bastard, the little sod, he waited till Tadaaki was looking away then jumped in with his hook sword and shoved it in Tadaaki's throat! We pulled him off, the little sod, but there was nothing we could do for Tadaaki. He died on the spot.' Civilis pointed to the middle of the practice arena. 'He died right there!'

'What did you do with Valdox?' I asked.

'What did I do?' yelled Civilis, 'What did I *do*? I wanted to kill the little bastard!'

'Yes!' roared the gladiators.

'I said,' yelled Civilis, 'I said, I said, gimme a sword! Gimme a knife! Gimme anything! I'd have done him there and then,' he turned in rage upon Askodus, 'But this one,' he said, shouting into Askodus' face, 'this one, he said, he said: *No! He's lost his temper that's all, and it's an accident?'* Askodus blushed. He could not meet Civilis' eye. It was obvious that even with Tadaaki dead, he'd been thinking of the future cash value of Valdox.

'What did Valdox do then?' I said. 'Did he attack anyone else?'

'No! No, he didn't,' said Civilis, 'once we got hold of him he just dropped his blade and went all quiet, and started saying things in some soddin' language or other. So we gave him a soddin' good kicking until *he*,' he glared at Askodus, '*he* stopped us, and told us to lock up the little sod.' Civilis shook his head, 'I never saw such a thing,' he said, 'not in all my years.'

I think that even then I realised what was going on, but I asked another question.

'Are you sure that's how it happened?' I said, and looked around. 'Is everyone sure? Couldn't the young man—Valdox—just have been too quick for Tadaaki? Better than him as a gladiator?'

Civilis sneered. 'Naaah!' he said, It takes years to be a gladiator. You can't be one straight off, just because you're young and fit, and nasty with it. A lot of silly little sods think that. And they're wrong! They're wrong 'cos they don't have the range of strokes to get through a gladiator's guard. You have to be trained, 'cos it's a skill and a soddin' art. So even if a new boy fights a veteran who's old, the boy gets tired first because he can't get through, and he just jumps around wasting himself while the veteran stays calm.'

'Yes!' said everyone.

I looked at Morganus and I could see what he was thinking.

'*No. It can't be. Not again... can it?*

I looked around. I looked at all the faces full of emotion and anger and dismay. I looked at Civilis, Askodus and Commius. My judgement was that Civilis had given a true and accurate account of what had happened and that questioning of others would be pointless.

'Askodus?' I said, loudly over the muttering and growling, 'I need to see Tadaaki and Valdox. I need to see them now!'

I saw Tadaaki first because he was the nearer. They had him laid on a bench in the barracks surgeon's room, since all gladiator schools have surgeons and the best available medical equipment. There was not room for all, so Morganus and I and the bodyguards stood over the dead gladiator, next to the surgeon and Askodus, and I looked down at the yellowing body of one of the biggest men I had ever seen.

He had been stripped, washed, and laid out under a sheet with lamps burning on stands at the four corners of the bench. At his feet another stand bore a bowl of bread, salt and herbs, and several small figurines. It was obvious that these arrangements were sacred to Tadaaki's beliefs, so we all raised hands.

'With honour and respect for the spirit of the departed,' I said, loudly, 'and with respect for his gods!' I said that before I removed the sheet, because you can never be too careful with the gods.

So I looked at the dead man, and saw that Tadaaki was—or had been—the German that Romans imagine in their fantasies. He was about twenty-five years old, and huge and blond and hairy and formidable. He was broad in the chest, narrow in the waist and long in the arms and legs. He was a magnificent creature and the sculptors would have loved him. They'd have used him as their model for Hercules. But now he was dead, with his throat torn open in a wound that showed the bones of his spine.

To my surprise, Askodus was overcome with emotion. He kissed his fingertips and placed them on Tadaaki's brow.

'What a man,' he said, 'what a performer! Nobody could do challenge and defiance like him.'

'What's that?' I asked.

'Challenge and defiance before the fight,' he said, 'to work up the crowd. They don't just go out and fight, you know. Not the good ones. They do a performance first, before they put the helmets on. They look at each other and growl and stamp, and the horns blow and the crowd roars, and they stand nose-to-nose defying one another, and they turn their backs on each other and dare the other one to try anything.' He kissed fingers again and touched the dead gladiator. 'Nobody could do that like Tadaaki!'

'I see,' I said, 'And he was a good fighter, too?'

'Huh!' said Askodus. 'Thirty fights, thirty wins. He was never even cut, and never raised the finger.' Askodus gulped. 'Oh!' he said in tearful sorrow, remembering how Tadaaki had indeed raised the finger, just once, and then died. Then, just as I was thinking I had misjudged him, he looked to me for sympathy and added, 'Three million! Just think of it. Maybe even more if I sold him in Rome.'

With such overwhelming evidence of the cause of death, and since Tadaaki's body had stiffened, I conducted no examination other than getting the bodyguards to turn him over to see the long slash that his killer—his murderer—had inflicted before the lethal stabbing. Then I replaced the sheet, raised hands again, bowed to the corpse and asked to be taken to Valdox the Regni.

Again we went in procession, with a growing attendance of gladiators and their followers, and again there was room for only myself, Morganus, the bodyguards and Askodus, in the place where Valdox was imprisoned. It was a small room at the back of the barracks block.

'This is the punishment cell,' said Askodus. 'Sometimes they get drunk, or answer back. Especially the new ones. So they get a night in here with no blankets.'

There was a heavy door with a heavy lock, and a barred grill at head height so that the occupant of the cell could be seen. 'You needn't worry,' said Askodus, 'I doubt he's dangerous any more. He just sits there. He won't move, even if you slap his face. And he won't eat or drink.'

I stepped forward and looked inside the cell. Valdox the Regni, a young, dark-haired man, was crouched on the floor with his arms round his knees, steadily muttering to himself. I stood back and beckoned Morganus to come and look. He did so. He took a very careful look.

'Hmm,' he said and turned to me, 'are you reading my thoughts, Greek?'

'Yes,' I said, 'and you can hear what he's saying, can't you? It's a prayer, isn't it?'

'Yes,' he said.

'What,' said Askodus, 'what are you talking about?'

'Have you got the key?' I said, 'I need to go inside.' Askodus dithered, and looked at the figure inside the cell. 'He's harmless, isn't he?' I said.

'Well,' said Askodus, 'I suppose he is,' and he looked at the four bodyguards. 'I suppose so,' and he produced a key and turned the lock, 'but be careful,' he said, and stood back as Morganus and I and the bodyguards crammed into the cell.

There, Valdox ignored us and kept up his chant, and Morganus raised an arm to stop me as I moved forward.

'Are you sure about this?' he said.

'No,' I said, 'but we have to find out,' and I spoke to the bodyguards. 'Get him up. I need to look at him.' So Valdox was hauled to his feet and stood with head bowed, and one big Roman on either side of him, holding his arms. He was small by comparison, but his muscles were extraordinarily developed. He looked like a dancer or a tumbler. If

Tadaaki had been a bull, then Valdox was a panther. I looked at Askodus, who stood outside the cell.

'Does he understand Latin?' I asked.

'Not really,' said Askodus, 'just a few words. But we have men in the school who speak Gaulish, and he understands that.'

I looked at Morganus. 'You'll have to translate,' I said. Morganus nodded. I moved close to Valdox.

'Valdox!' I said, sharply. He ignored me. I put a hand under his chin and raised his head so that he was looking at me, or rather looking *through* me, into nowhere. 'Valdox!' I repeated, as he carried on chanting. 'I know what you are.' I said that and Morganus turned it into Britannic, 'I know what you are and who sent you.' Again Morganus translated. Again Valdox ignored us. 'You're a cennad angau,' I said, 'sent by Maligoterix.'

Instantly, before Morganus had even translated, the chanting stopped, Valdox looked me in the eye, and his muscles went from slack to hard. Then Morganus added something else in Britannic and Valdox gasped in horror. He gasped in fear. He thought a moment… and then he went mad, in movements so fast that nothing could stop him.

He wrenched free of the body guards. He leapt at Morganus. He snatched Morganus' dirk and reversed it. He put the sharp point to the centre of his chest, grunted with supreme effort and drove the blade straight into his own heart.

He fell to the earth floor of the cell before any of us could even react. But even before Valdox had stopped twitching, Askodus was inside the cell.

'Well who's going to pay me for *that*?' he said, glaring at me. 'I gave good money for him! I gave six thousand and I'd have got back more than that if I just sold him to the games, to be thrown to the beasts!'

I suppose I was enraged. Morganus told me later that I spoke with much anger.

'Gods of Olympus!' I said, 'this man's just killed himself. Killed himself in front of you. Is that all you've got to say?'

'It's all right for *you*,' said Askodus, '*you're* not out of pocket!'

I ignored that contemptible remark and challenged Askodus on fundamental matters.

'Have you heard of the druids?' I asked him, and he flinched. The vile reputation of the Britannic druids had spread round the Empire. 'And do you know the penalty for trafficking with druids?'

'What, me?' he said. 'Me? Traffic with druids? Nonsense!'

'It's death,' I said, 'It's death without option for lesser penalty and irrespective of whether it was done knowingly or in ignorance. Any trafficking with druids carries death by imperial decree!'

'So what?' he said, 'I've never even met a druid.'

'No?' I said. 'You bought Valdox at Dubris, didn't you?'

'I… I…' said Askodus.

'And when you bought Valdox, how did he behave?'

'What do you mean?'

'You said he knelt at his master's feet and asked for blessing. You said that, didn't you?'

'Yes. So what?'

'What was he like, this master? An elderly man with attendants who treated him with great respect?'

He gasped.

'Yes,' he said, 'How did you know?'

'Because he was a druid. You bought Valdox from a druid and that's a capital offence under Roman Law!'

Askodus went a sickly colour. Sweat appeared on his brow. 'How can you know he was a druid?' he said.

'Just believe me that I know,' I said, 'and that I act for His Grace the Governor of this province, and for the commander of the legions of this province. So, what do you think your chances would be of escaping a capital charge in any law court of this province?'

Askodus crumpled. He looked around. He lowered his voice.

'Wait,' he said, 'let's not be hasty. Why should things go so far? I respect your intellect, Ikaros of Apollonis, as I respect the rank of your comrade Morganus, and I wonder if perhaps we could avoid troubling the courts?' He attempted a smile. 'I am an exceedingly rich man,' he said, 'and you would find me exceedingly grateful.'

'Be silent,' I said, 'I don't want to hear any more from you because

I'm going to tell you something in confidence. I'm going to tell you a secret, which is, that the governor of this province is about to become one of the most powerful men in the Empire. So it would be very good to be his friend, and very bad , and very dangerous , to be his enemy. Do you follow?'

'Yes.'

'Then take note that anyone who makes the governor's games flourish will be his friend, and anyone who spoils the games will be his enemy. Do you understand?'

'Yes,' came a weak, little, frightened voice.

'Then find some way to explain the deaths of Tadaaki and Valdox: something you can tell the world. Then go ahead and make the games a success with the gladiators you've got left. You've still got plenty of them, haven't you?'

'Yes.'

'Good. So bury the bodies. Accept the loss. Get on with the games and don't buy any more slaves from old men with long beards.'

We left after that. There was nothing more to do, except talk to Morganus as we marched back to the legionary fortress.

'Well done,' he said, 'Petros'll like that.'

'Like what?' I said.

'The way you made Askodus keep quiet and get on with the games.'

'It wasn't that hard. It was obvious.'

'Was it all true about the druids and the law courts? No punishment than death and you're guilty if even you don' t know it's druids?'

'I haven't the slightest idea,' I said, and he laughed.

'How soon did you guess that Valdox was a cennad angau?' he asked.

'When Civilis was talking about his fighting skills, and certainly when Askodus said that he wanted a blessing from the man who sold him.'

'Me too,' said Morganus, 'and he was chanting a death poem in that cell. Something the druids taught him. He was getting ready to die, rather than tell anything about who sent him and why. He'd have starved himself to death.'

'Yes,' I said. 'So what did you say to him? After I said he was a cennad angau sent by Maligoterix? You said something else in Britannic.'

'Oh,' said Morganus, 'perhaps I shouldn't have said that.'

'Said what?'

'I said that you can read minds and would know what he was thinking.'

'Ah!' I said, 'so he killed himself instantly, to protect Maligoterix.'

'Gods of Hades,' said Morganus, 'is that the sort of power that they have over men? To make them kill themselves for a cause, for a religion? What if they're wrong, and the poor devils just end up across the Styx like all the rest of us?'

'I don't know,' I said, 'but we already know that men will kill themselves for religion.'

'So it *is* druids that are behind all this,' he said. 'Maligoterix planted Valdox in Askodus' school to kill one of his best men, and turn him against the games. It's all down to the druids. It's another one like that girl Viola, only this time they used a proper killer.'

'Yes,' I said, believing that to be the case. Then after we'd gone a bit further I said something else. 'Morganus,' I said.

'Yes?'

'We've dealt with this haven't we? The murder of Tadaaki? And I think we'll have no more trouble from Askodus.'

'So?'

'Well, the death of Tadaaki was the urgent matter, and Petros and Africanus only *suspect* there may be trouble with the actors and racing drivers, and so…'

'And so you want to go and see Allicanda.'

'Yes. Do you mind?'

'Holy Mithras, of course not! The way you put a fright up Askodus was a piece of genius! I don't know where you find the words. Not even your Socrates could have done better, nor Cicero nor any of those old lawyers. So the games will go on, and that's what counts, and if you want to go and see your garum girl tonight. then I'll send a runner to fix the time and place, and I'll even pay for your drinks.'

So that is what we did.

Chapter 23

We met at the sign of the leaping stag, the food shop near the northern corner of the vegetable market. It was where we had met previously, and within sight of the spot where I was ambushed by the four Regni farmers. But it was dusk and everything was different. The market was closed, the stalls were gone, and the people on the streets were looking for pleasure. So the whores and sailors were about, and the farm boys had come for a beer and a fight. It was not a good time for young female slaves to be out alone.

But Agidox, the major domos of the house of Fortunus, remembered the favour he owed me and had sent out Allicanda, escorted by four of the big Africans who were the master's litter bearers. They sat by themselves, close enough to defend Allicanda but not so close as to intrude. Also, Allicanda had brought four friends, slaves of the house, who would swear that nothing improper had occurred between her and me. They were all of them already seated when I arrived and chose an empty table where Allicanda joined me, because only by such manoeuvres, with three groups at three tables, could a female slave meet a man without offending decency.

'You're tired,' she said as she sat down, 'What have you been doing?'

'Working,' I said, and the emotions surged within me, because she looked so small, and smooth, and lovely that I wanted to do everything for her. I wanted to seize her and hold her, and make her mine for ever.

'What are we going to do?' she said. 'Do you know what price he's asking for me?'

'Yes,' I said, 'Fortunus wrote to me. He wants two million. He's ranked you as an exotic.'

Then slaves of the Leaping Stag appeared, having spotted my expensive clothes and marked me as a desirable customer. They grovelled and bowed, and I ordered wine, bread and olives. 'Oh!' I said to Allicanda. 'Would you like something better? A proper meal?' She just smiled.

'Here?' she said, and I recalled the nature of her profession and the refinement of her tastes. So I smiled, too. But when the bread and olives arrived, I found that I was not hungry after all, though I poured the wine and drank it, bad as it was.

'What are we going to do?' she said, again.

'I don't know,' I admitted, 'I haven't got that much money,' and I sighed and searched for something cheerful to say. 'Well at least he's ranked you as an exotic. I suppose that's all over the town by now?' She smiled, weakly.

'Yes,' she said, 'everyone knows, and they know my price too. I'm second only to Agidox himself now.'

I thought of the old saying *every slave knows his price*, which is literal truth because slaves in a household *are* ranked by their price, and they are just as much obsessed with rank as everyone else in the Roman world. Fortunately, I had the sense not to speak these thoughts aloud. My relationship with Allicanda had been scarred by careless words, and I feared I might say something wrong.

'And he can't go back on my ranking and price now,' she said, 'because nobody would ever believe his asking price again.' She hesitated, and lowered her eyes, and reached her hand towards me. 'But he might come down a little,' she said, 'as if he were bargaining.'

I answered the unasked question.

'I'm sorry,' I said, 'I've got nearly ninety-five thousand. I checked with the legion's bank. That's all I've got.'

'And he'd never settle for less than one and half million,' she said.

'Wouldn't he?'

'No.'

We were silent a while, because I did not know what to say. Then:

'Do you know who told him?' I asked. 'Who told Fortunus that it's you that I want, and not any of the others on my list?'

'I think so,' she said, 'I had a few enemies in the house. Although now I'm an exotic they're crawling round to be friendly. I think it was one of them.'

'Was it Wulfrik?' I asked. She smiled.

'No. He's still afraid of you. It was a woman. I once slapped her for being cheeky and she's never forgotten it.'

'Oh?' I said, 'You did that, did you?'

'Yes I did! She showed no respect.'

'Well she will now,' I said.

'Yes,' she said, 'Everyone thinks an exotic is the master's favourite, so they fawn all over you.' She reached out her hand towards me again. 'At least I can thank you for that. I've never been so secure in the house.'

Which was as far as our discussion went. We found no answers and we dared not stay long. So I left with my head full of uncomfortable thoughts. I could see no way around a price of two million, or even one-and-a-half, and I thought of the consequences of Allicanda becoming an exotic. Her new status removed a slave's greatest fears: being sold to a bad master, or turned out in old age to starve, because only another millionaire could afford her, and he would have a luxurious house, with a fine place in it for Allicanda. Also, unlike a beautiful exotic, who lost value every year, Allicanda would keep her high price even in old age, because she would still be an *exquisite mistress of cuisine*. All of this was good, and I was pleased for her. No wonder she felt she had never been so secure.

But then my mood plunged. Had I tipped the scales too far? Even if I really did work magic—which I do not—and I could conjure up two million in cash, would Allicanda now want to give up her luxurious, privileged life to live with a Greek slave who could not legally marry her? Would she accept being the slave of a slave? I did not even know if I had the legal power to set her free!

Later, it was another sleepless night. Much wine was drunk and in the morning I had a headache.

Morganus looked at me over the breakfast table.

'Was it that bad?' he said. 'With Allicanda?

'It was,' I said, and told him.

'Brace up, Greek,' he said. 'Worse things happen. You're both still alive, so who knows what will come to pass? And you'll like what we're doing this morning.'

'What's that?'

'We're out riding. We're going to the race track. We're supposed to be checking the works again, but we're really looking for any trouble from them... from the druids.'

He actually managed to say it without flinching. Familiarity breeds contempt, as the poet says.

'Come on Greek,' he said, 'give a smile, you know you like horses.'

I do like horses. I adore horses. My father sat me on a pony before I could walk. So a ride in the sunshine lifted my despair and blew away most of the headache. We rode with an escort behind us, Morganus and the bodyguards bumping and rolling, and myself and the escorting troopers—Hispanic auxiliaries this time—riding easy and smooth, being bred up to the saddle. I know that I boast, but how else can I convey the joy of being on horseback?

I pause only to remark that since we—which is to say, Morganus—was escorted by auxiliaries instead of legionary cavalry, there had to be twice the number of them to give equal respect. Thus no less than forty horsemen followed us in plumes and mail, and bright-painted shields, in columns of four and led by their officer: a procession which offers yet another insight into the Roman mind.

Britannia is at least green, which is kind to the eye, and Londinium is surrounded by lakes and hills. So when the rain stops the countryside is pleasing, and the ground good for cavalry. It was a brisk, fine ride out to the racing stadium, and I was amazed at how far the works had progressed since last we saw it. As before, we halted while the cavalry officer and his bugler rode ahead to ensure that Morganus would be properly received, and we waited on rising ground which gave a fine view of the almost-complete stadium.

'It's huge,' I said to Morganus.

'You should the Circus Maximus in Rome,' he said. 'You can't imagine the size of it.'

'And look at that!' I said. 'That's new.' We both looked at a vast encampment of tents and huts and people to the north of the stadium. It was an enormous, settled mass of humanity, together with unmoving wagons with shafts tipped up, animals grazing, the smoke of countless fires, and a great business of folk going to and fro: men, women and children.

'The tribes have turned out for the games,' said Morganus. 'You can see their emblems on poles by the biggest tents: there's the wheel of Belenus for the Regni, the green oak for the Artrebati, the black rock for the Silures. And more. Lots more.'

He looked at me in deep concern. 'There must be more people here than the entire population of Londinium!'

'And more joining,' I said, pointing to a narrow column of horses and people coming from the north, towards the encampment.'

'Is this good or bad?' said Morganus.

'I don't know,' I said, 'but if you remember, Petros told us that he wants to *teach the heathen savages to love Roman civilisation.*' I waved hand at the enormous encampment of native Celts. 'Perhaps he's doing it,' I said. 'Why else would they be here, all around the racing stadium? Perhaps they're here for the show.'

'Is that what you think?' he said. 'Couldn't it be dangerous to let so many of them be here? Right next to Londinium?'

'How should I know?' I said. 'But Africanus can't be too worried, or he'd have already turned the army on them.'

Morganus did not agree.

'Perhaps it's already too late for that,' he said. We discussed the matter without conclusions, and then the troop leader was back with a mounted legionary officer from the stadium. He was Terentius, senior tribune of the Twentieth whom we had met on our previous visit. There was the usual process of formal greetings of Morganus, which had to be endured. After that we rode to the stadium, pausing at the request of

Terentius, who wanted to show off the starting boxes, now completed in all their technical complexity. So we rode up and down the line of them, and I must admit I found it fascinating.

'Here's where they start, Honoured Ssir,' said Terentius to Morganus as we trotted into the open end of the stadium. always referred to as the lower end. 'As you can see, there are starting boxes, each with just enough room for a four-horse racing chariot and driver.'

'Ahhh!' said everyone, and grinned in delight.

'There are twelve boxes, built in a curved line,' said Terentius, 'because the line of boxes is much wider than the race track, so the boxes have to be staggered, or some would be nearer the track than others, giving unfair advantage.'

'Ahhh!' said everyone.

'So as they come out of the boxes, there is a dash, diagonally across the bottom end of the stadium to the track starting line, and it's fierce competition because there isn't room on the track for twelve chariots to run abreast. So some get ahead, some get left behind and some smash into each other, even before they're actually on the track.'

'Ahhh!' said everyone again.

'So before the race,' said Terentius, 'Each chariot and driver goes into the box here,' and we wheeled and rode down the side of boxes that faced *away* from the track. 'They go in here,' he said, pointing to the rear gates, which were all open. 'Then we shut them in, with the track-side gates still lowered, so they can't get out.'

At this stage, we stopped and dismounted, and Terentius approached a group of young men, about ten of them, all bearded and well dressed, who stood looking at us, attended by slaves at one end of the starting boxes. Their leader seemed to be a slim, well-groomed man with a thick black beard, short hair, and neat folds in his garments. He was accompanied by another man who loomed over him in large, soft-bodied clumsiness, pale of face and vacant of expression. They all stared at Morganus and myself with intense interest, and whispered to one another. Looking at their features, and knowing the part the young men of Flavensum were playing in the games, I had already guessed who, or rather what, they were.

'Honoured Sir,' said Terentius to Morganus, 'it is my pleasure to present, some of the much valued men of Flavensum, who—as full Roman citizens—give not only dignity but true Roman lustre to the building of our stadium and to the proceedings of our races.'

He declaimed these mouth-filling words with such grace, that he almost convinced me that he meant them. But recalling Petros's insistence of the *political* necessity for Roman citizens to run the games, I guessed that Terentius regarded the Flavensum men as surplus to requirements, as welcome as a thistle in the rectum. None the less, he introduced them with formal politeness.

'I present first, the men who will discharge two of the most high and important of roles within the stadium.' He turned to the two leading men. 'I present his Honour Neronis Solis Propius, the race starter, and his Honour Toma Taddeo Grantius, the deputy race starter.' Meanwhile I recognised familiar features in Propius and spoke to him.

'Are you, Honoured Sir, related to Annonias Neronis Solis, Duovir of the city of Flavensum?' I asked.

'I am his son!' he declared, stretching to full height with jutting chin and proud eyes. All the rest of them likewise reacted to the name of Solis as if someone exceedingly special had been named. It was very interesting. I nodded and spoke

'The honoured Morganus and I had the pleasure, recently, to dine with the duovir Solis, at his house in Flavensum,' I said, 'and I am pleased to report that he is in excellent health.'

'I rejoice to hear it!' said Propius.

'We rejoice!' said all the rest, receiving this news with joy. They were just about managing not to shout *God save the Solis*. Then all of them looked at me with such an expression of superiority on their faces, that I began to share Terentius' opinion of the young men of Flavensum. After that, Propius fell silent, obviously wanting no further conversation. So there was an awkward silence until Terentius intervened.

'Propius,' he said, 'might I ask that you demonstrate the mysteries of the starting boxes? Such matters are indeed within your responsibilities and capabilities, are they not?'

Again the sarcasm went undetected, and Propius and Grantius took Morganus and me into one of the starting boxes. It was planked on either side, but open to the sky, and two of Propius' slaves closed the rear gate behind us and stood waiting for further orders.

'As you can see,' said Propius, 'We are now shut in, just as a racing driver and chariot would be.'

'Yes,' said, Morganus and I.

'The rear door stays closed,' said Propius, ' but see here on the *track* side,' he pointed to a light wooden grid, fixed in vertical slots, 'this barrier is designed to shoot upwards. At the top there is a ring-bolt with a rope, and if you look there,' he pointed again, 'the rope runs over a pulley, and is attached to a lead weight which is constantly trying to pull up the grid.'

'Yes,' we said.

'But the grid stays down, until the sponsor gives the signal to start.'

'Yes,' we said.

'Then … *up*!' cried Propius, and the grid shot up in its slots, leaving the box open. We all smiled. 'Now come and see the mechanism,' he said, and he and Grantius took us to one end of the line of boxes, and up a flight of stairs to a platform which gave a clear view down into the starting boxes. 'This is the starter's platform,' said Propius. 'My platform! And when I see the sponsor's signal, I pull this.' He showed us piece of steel mechanism fixed to a post, at waist height.

'Huh,' said Morganus, 'it's a catapult trigger.'

'Yes, Honoured Ssir, and the trigger holds a line which is attached to other lines running to each box. Those lines stop the pulley ropes going down, and the grids going up. So when the Starter pulls the trigger…'

'It lets go the line, the grids fly up and the race starts!' Morganus was positively beaming by now. 'I've seen races,' he said, 'and seen the grids go up, but never seen how it's done.'

'It is a great wonder,' said Grantius, the first words he had uttered, and looking at his somewhat simple face, I saw that—to him—a catapult trigger and a run of cables was almost beyond understanding.

After that we climbed down the stairs and would have re-joined Terentius. But first we had a brief conversation at the foot of the stairs, and that conversation was very revealing. Morganus and I thanked Propius for showing us the starting boxes. Then, to fill another silence left by the un-responsive Propius, I mentioned the young man with the severe wound, whom I had examined at Flavensum. At the time I thought that I mentioned this by chance, but I think perhaps, that I had pondered on the matter without being aware of it.

'I assume you know Alexander, son of the duovir Bethsidus?' I said.

'Yes,' said Propius, just that one word, but I studied his face and my gift told me that I had touched on something significant: something that disturbed Propius, and caused his self-assurance to wobble. It was exciting. I suppose a hound feels the same when it detects a scent.

'I have some skills as a surgeon,' I said, 'but I regret that I was unable to help poor Alexander.'

'Ah,' said Propius: just that and no more.

'And you know how he was wounded?' I said.

'Yes.'

'Where did it happen?' I asked. This time Propius said nothing, and this time I let the silence go on, because sometimes a silence produces more answers than any number of questions. In due time my patience was rewarded, because Grantius broke the silence.

'It happened here,' he said, 'outside Londinium.'

Propius glared. Grantius flinched and I switched attention to him, because the strength of a chain is that of the weakest link.

'How did it happen?' I asked. Grantius gulped and looked at Propius.

'It was a bull,' said Propius, 'we have our own cattle here. It was a bull.'

'Oh,' I said to Grantius, 'so how was he injured?'

'He was trampled,' said Grantius.

'No!' said Propius. 'He was gored. Impaled on a horn.'

'Oh yes,' said Grantius, 'of course. That's what it was. It was a horn.'

It was a moment of delight. Everything came in a rush. It was like removing a blindfold and seeing flowers.

Propius and Grantius were lying.

Alexander had not been gored by a bull.
He had not been trampled by a bull.
He had been wounded in quite another way.
At last I was at beginning to understand.

Chapter 24

Morganus knew me very well.

'What is it?' he whispered, as we walked away from Propius and Grantius towards Terentius and his staff, with the bodyguards behind us. 'You saw something, didn't you?'

'Not now,' I said, 'Too many ears.'

It was very hard. My mind was whirling, and I truly wanted to discuss the matter with Morganus, but I could not. We had to be somewhere quiet and private for that. So with anguish and suppressed feelings on my part, we proceeded with our fake inspection.

Thus we mounted up again and rode round the race track in procession, accompanied by Terentius and our troop of Hispanics, so that we could see how the works were going. The spina was fully complete, with its shrines and statues and paint, and the huge dolphins that would mark the completion of laps were finished in white paint and being gilded over with gold leaf even as we rode past. Likewise the seating was complete, and the main job still remaining—in fact, coming to completion before our eyes—was that of preparing the track surface by putting down layers of stones and gravel of decreasing size with sand on top, and then compacting the layers with enormous stone rollers pulled by teams of legionaries. It was all very Roman, with hundreds of men working in disciplined silence, apart from the *heave-ho* of the hauling teams. So there was not the slightest doubt that the stadium would be ready on time.

Next, we asked for a meeting of all senior persons involved in building and running the stadium: everyone at or above the rank of centurion, and that was a waste of time because when Morganus gave warning of the vital need to protect the racing drivers from harm, Terentius had each centurion list his duties and arrangements, and these became boringly thorough as each man spoke:

'... we keep three centuries ready in battle kit in case of serious attack.'

'... every driver is personally accompanied by a watch of four men.'

'... and a troop of horse when they drive.'

'... that's day and night.'

'... yes, Your Honour, even in the latrines.'

But afterwards we saw something that was far from boring.

Terentius took us for a mid-day meal at the tribunes' mess in the legionary encampment, and after another stodgy dinner on outdoor tables, with no sunshine and native beer, he said:

'If you'd be interested, honoured and worshipful sirs, we have practice races planned for this afternoon.'

'Oh,' said Morganus, 'who's running?' And he tilted his mug of beer to finish it. Terentius gave a little smile. The other tribunes smiled. The men clearing away our food smiled.

'Oh, it's just a practice,' he said, as if it were nothing. 'Just two chariots on the first run, if you've got time to see them... it's Juvencus for the greens and Diocles for the blues.

Morganus choked. He spluttered and sprayed beer in all directions, and everyone laughed, including him, thereby informing even an ignorant Greek that Juvencus and Diocles were two of the Empire's greatest sporting heroes: renowned, famous, god-like and adored.

'Why didn't you say?' said Morganus, dripping beer from his chin. But then he looked at me and wondered what to do. It was a most rare and unusual occasion, the only time I ever him dithering.

'Have we got time?' he asked, and everyone looked at me: six tribunes, assorted legionaries, and most especially the renowned and revered first javelin of the Twentieth Legion. I considered the matter and spoke in serious tone.

'I think we should devote time to this spectacle,' I said. 'It will be informative and may cast light upon our investigations.' Then I smiled , to show that while a philosopher is appallingly ignorant of sport, he can still try to make a joke. Everyone was kind enough to laugh, and so we saw the practice race.

We saw it, and so did every man in the legionary camp who was not physically chained to other duties. There were at least a thousand men present, though that number barely filled the first rows of seats, and they grinned and chattered, and made bets.

These men cheered enormously when the first two drivers walked out from a door at the top end of the track, and marched to the bottom and the starting boxes, followed by their horses and chariots, which were led by slaves. They came past the sponsor's enclosure, where I was sitting with Morganus, the bodyguards, Terentius and his senior officers. All gave formal salute to the sponsor's enclosure, since this was a full dress rehearsal, and I looked at these two famous drivers.

Juvencus was thin, grey, middle-aged and scarred down one side of his face from a drag-wound. Diocles was far younger: a dark-skinned African with a great head of woolly hair. He wore bright gold earrings, and wrist-bands in his team colour.

The two were different in features but similar in expression: serious, intelligent, withdrawn and reserved. They had the authentic air of experts about to perform a complex and difficult task, and paid attention to an entourage of advisers who poured words into their ears, while ignoring the slaves who carried their helmets and limb-guards, and masseurs who pummelled their arms and necks even as they walked. It was like watching bees that buzzed and swarmed around each other in purposeful movement.

But all bowed low before the sponsor—or rather Terentius, on this occasion—and stood in respectful silence until he waved them on. Soon the drivers and chariots were in their starting boxes, Propius of Flavensum was ready with his trigger on his platform, and Terentius—taking the role of sponsor—stood forward, at the edge of the sponsor's enclosure. He looked towards the starting boxes and waved a large white cloth.

Instantly, a corps of buglers in the row of seats in front of us stood and blew a fanfare. Terentius waved the cloth a second time. Another fanfare, and the off-duty legionaries began to bellow and yell. Another wave of the cloth, a final and mighty blast of bugles, and Terentius dropped the cloth, Propius pulled his trigger, the starting gates went up and two chariots shot out like bolts from a ballista, and dashed for the starting line, as a thousand men together with Morganus, Terentius, the tribunes and the bodyguards leapt to their feet and yelled. Even I was moved to stand, because such was the excitement of the moment.

The noise alone was thrilling, the roar of wheels the pounding of hooves and a huge growl from the crowd. The two chariots came up the track, and past the sponsor's enclosure at full speed: leather-clad riders cracking whips, reins bound around their waists and leaning so far forwards that it was a miracle they did not fall over. The chariots were so light and open that they barely existed: just a pair of big, ultra-light, exquisitely-specialised wheels, spokes blurred into invisibility, bright paint, gilding, a minute platform for the driver, a central shaft jutting forward, light as a wand, and four magnificent, high-bred horses to each chariot, with flowing manes and tails and each one matched for identical looks. The horses alone must have cost a fortune, and only the gods knew the value of driver, chariot and horses in total.

'Hi-Hi-Hi-Hi-Hi!' yelled Juvencus, to encourage his horses—and all his supporters echoed him.

'Hi-Hi-Hi-Hi!'

'Yo-ho! Yo-ho! Yo-ho! cried Diocles, and *his* supporters joined in.

'Yo-ho! Yo-ho! Yo-ho!'

They were gone in a blur and a cloud of dust, but followed close behind by two troops of legionary cavalry: two troops of ten, twenty men in all who'd dashed out from either side of the starting boxes, with their riders whooping their battle-cries as if charging home on the enemy. They leaned forward in the saddle and urged on their mounts to utmost exertion. As they shot past I noticed that one troop had long green streamers trailing from their helmets, and the other had blue.

'See!' cried Morganus, 'even the horseman have turned out proper,' and everyone yelled approval and I—poor Greek that I was—realised that the troopers were supposedly guarding the drivers, though enjoying every wonderful instant of being on the same race track as Juvencus and Diocles, and wearing their team colours in pride, and doing their utmost to catch the chariots, which they could not, because a four-horse racing chariot was faster than a man on horseback.

Then the chariots and the horsemen were round the bend at the upper end of the stadium, and galloping down the far side of the spina, though still visible from the sponsor's box, going thunder-and-lightning for the finish line and the first lap, and the first golden dolphin dipping as they went past, then another sliding, whirling, pounding turn at the bottom end of the track and up the near side for the second lap.

It was wonderful. I freely admit it. As a spectacle, even with just two chariots it was superb, and it was not only Romans who cheered and stamped as the two chariots and escorts came past us for the second time, and so to the full seven laps and not a dull instant from start to finish. Juvencus won by a clear lead, but—or so I was told—by racing standards, neither driver was exerting himself to the full, but going gently!

There were several more practice races after that and we watched them all, so the sun was sinking as Morganus and I, the bodyguards and our escort, left the stadium to return to the fortress. Once we were on the road, side by side, we could finally talk.

'Well,' said Morganus, 'I see you've become a supporter.'

'Yes,' I said, 'I think I have.'

'Which team? green, red, blue or white?'

'All of them!'

He smiled and shook his head.

'No,' he said, 'that won't do. You have to pick one. You can't say you like them all, or you'll offend everyone.'

'Is that how it works?'

'Oh yes!'

Then we rode in companionable silence for a while, because we were both enjoying the moment. It was a peaceful moment after the thrill of the chariots, and a pleasant moment in the green Britannic countryside, and the slow dusk. But then we had to go back to work. Morganus led the way, being Roman.

'So what was it that you saw in that young man's head?' he said, 'That Flavensum boy?'

'Propius,' I said, 'him and his fat friend Grantius. Did you notice how full of themselves they were?'

'Yes,' said Morganus, 'Terentius said the same thing to me, over lunch.'

'Did he?' I said.

'Yes. He said they're all like that. All the Flavensum men. They think they're better than everyone else and they don't mix. They don't even have a drink with anyone but each other. That's why he doesn't like them.' Then he leaned across from his saddle towards mine and spoke softly. 'So what did you see inside his big, fat head?'

'I saw lies,' I said. 'Lies about Alexander. Do you remember Alexander? Solis's son who was supposed to have been gored by a bull?'

'*Supposed*? Only supposed?'

'Yes,' I said, 'Propius and Grantius were lying. I don't think Alexander was anywhere near a bull. I think he was stabbed with a sword. I think we've found out who murdered Gershom and wanted something from his library.'

'*What?*'

'Yes,' I said. 'Think about it. Gershom was murdered by Roman citizens.'

'We don't know they were citizens,' he said, 'not for sure.'

'I know. But let me talk. Let me develop the idea.'

'Go on.'

'Gershom's major domos thought his master's killers were citizens, and nobody is a bigger snob than a major domos, or can judge status like a major domos!' Morganus nodded. 'So: if they were citizens, and they didn't come from Londinium, and I don't think they did because Gershom had no enemies in Londinium—none that would kill him—then they had to come from somewhere, and that must be Flavensum, because nowhere else in Britannia is full of Roman citizens.' Morganus sighed.

'It can't be,' he said, but I continued.

'And remember when I asked to see Alexander's wound?'

'Yes,' he said, 'That young surgeon wouldn't let you see it.'

'No! He said it would disturb the dressings, and I couldn't quite read his face at the time, but now I think he was lying because it was a sword wound, not anything inflicted by an animal, and he didn't *want* me to see it.'

'So who stabbed him?' said Morganus, 'Gershom?'

'Yes,' I said, 'I think Alexander was one of the team that killed Gershom and then searched the library for whatever it was that they wanted.'

'Well,' said Morganus, 'I give salute to Gershom's sword arm! At least he went down fighting, and you can't do more than that.' After that very Roman sentiment, he said nothing for a while. Then: 'So what did they want in that book they never found?'

'I don't know,' I said, 'but it's the next thing we must find out, so we're going straight back to the fortress, to find Optio Silvius, and turn him out of bed if necessary, and have another look at Gershom's books.'

'Aren't we supposed to see the actors?' he said. 'To make sure nobody's trying to kill them? That's Legate's orders. And Petros's.'

'I know,' I said, 'but I think we can ignore that. To start with, where do actors stand as compared with gladiators or racing drivers?'

Morganus smiled. 'Some of the clowns and comics are good,' he said.

'And what about the serious ones? Those who do Greek tragedy?'

'How would I know?' he said, 'I've never seen a Greek tragedy and I don't know anybody who has.'

'That's what I thought,' I said. 'So we'll take the risk, and leave the actors for the moment, because I think I can see a lamp in the darkness.

Fortunately we did not have to turn Silvius out of his bed, but we did need lamps—real lamps—because it was dark inside the office where Silvius had laid out Gershom's books. A small group of us stood by the tables: myself, Morganus, the bodyguards, Silvius and two of his men. It was late but not yet bed-time, though the office was all shadows except where the lamps glowed.

'It's all here, Your Worship,' said Silvius, offering me his catalogue, 'so just ask and we'll give you the books.'

'Thank you,' I said, 'but I would prefer to trust your knowledge of all this,' I gestured towards the dim piles of scrolls and tablets, 'because you wrote the catalogue, and know it better than anyone: you and your men!'

Silvius and his men all bowed. 'Thank you, Your Worship,' he said.

'Do you remember that I said that to find the killer book, we would need guidance from some other source?'

'Yes, Your Worship,' he said.

'Well, I think I've found it,' I said. 'So! I want anything to do with the Fourth Auxiliary Regiment of Flavensi, and the founding of the veterans' colony of Flavensum. Also anything about a rebellion at Lixus, which is…'

I paused, because it was late and I was growing tired.

'It's the capital of the province of Mauretania, Your Worship,' said Silvius. ' It's in North Africa, Your Worship. South west of the Pillars of Hercules. It's a sea port on the Great Ocean of Atlantis. There was a rebellion there, years ago. The town was burned.'

He was a good man. So were his team. They were swift and efficient and soon Morganus and I were walking back to his house with the bodyguards carrying several books. Later, and well past bed-time, fascination gave me strength so I was reading the books by myself in Morganus' living room, with lamps all round me, and a flask of wine for company. It was a long night, but I slept eventually for a few hours, and after a bath in the morning I was ready to talk to Morganus. I was very, very pleased with myself.

The morning was bright and cheerful. The sun rose, Morgana Callandra and her girls served breakfast then politely left us. All but one of Gershom's books were on a separate table out of the way of the food. Just one was on the table in front of me, and the bodyguards sat at the other end of the room. They ate breakfast in silence, in their armour as always, helmets beside them on the table.

'You look happy,' said Morganus as he sat down opposite me, and reached for bread and cheese.

'Prepare yourself for a surprise,' I said, 'one you might not like.'

'Oh?' he said.

'Look at this,' I said, 'pushing the one book towards him. 'It's in

Latin. It's a letter from Pliny the Elder: that's Gaius Plinius Secundus, and it's to someone he addresses simply as *My dear friend.* The letter was in Pliny's papers when he died, and was never sent, because nobody knew who the friend was.'

'Gaius Plinius was killed at Pompeii, wasn't he?' said Morganus.

'Yes,' I said. 'He was in command of the Roman fleet, and took a warship into the smoke to try to evacuate people from the town.'

'And was never heard of again,' said Morganus, 'but at least he tried.'

'Quite,' I said, 'and the letter got bundled up with other papers, and was sold on, and on, and eventually bought by Gershom.'

'So?' said Morganus.

'Just listen to this,' I said, and read from Pliny's letter. '*You ask what happened during the shameful revolt at Lixus in the year of Apronianus and Capito…*'

'When was that?' said Morganus. 'I can never work out years without a written list.'

'The year of Apronianus and Capito was over forty years ago, just two years before Boudicca's rebellion in Britannia.'

'Ah, yes,' he said, 'I remember *that* all right!' I continued reading: 'He goes on '*…It was then that the Fourth Auxiliary Regiment of Flavensi, in the eighteenth year of their service, commandeered a fleet of ships and left Lixus together with their women and riches.*' I stopped reading and stared at Morganus. 'Do you realise what this means?'

'Gods of Rome,' he said, 'Give me that!' He snatched the book. I pointed to the line. He read it aloud.

'*In the eighteenth year of their service,*' he looked at me with horror in his face. 'Jupiter, Juno and Minerva! If this is true, they weren't time-expired veterans. They were only in their eighteenth year, with seven more to go before they got their discharge.'

'So they *weren't* citizens,' I said. 'None of them. Not them, nor their sons and grandsons. So nobody in Flavensum is a Roman citizen. It's all an enormous lie.'

Chapter 25

We went to Petros at once. Morganus sent a runner with the eagle-tipped staff bearing a message saying that we had profoundly important news. Petros sent a swift reply directing us to meet him in the ante-chamber of the Senate House of the Britannic provincial council, just west of the forum.

'That's odd,' said Morganus. 'What's he doing there? That place is empty most of the year.'

I nodded. The Britannic provincial council was a ceremonial organisation, of senior Celtic tribesmen from all over Britannia, who had been made citizens in reward for loyalty to Rome. The council met only for a few weeks each year, giving some limited opportunity for the tribes to express grievances to the Roman government. But it was mainly seen as a device whereby the Roman government kept watch on tribal politics.

Yet, as Morganus and I marched up to the Senate House with the usual escort of legionaries, the building was heaving with life. The steps and gateway were jammed with servants and slaves, while the ante-chamber was packed with more senior men, who gasped and chattered and whispered in animation as they listened to the debate going on inside the chamber itself, from which a steady roar of voices could be heard.

As we approached, the legionaries guarding the building saluted Morganus.

'Inside!' cried Morganus. 'Get me inside!'

'Yes, Honoured Sir!' cried the guard centurion, and together with our escort, his men forced a way through the press, with shields bumping aside citizens, freedmen and slaves alike.

'Make way! Make way!' they yelled, but they were drowned by a booming voice from inside the debating chamber.

'You ask why?' cried the voice. 'You have the weakness of mind to ask *why*?' And there was an angry roar from those in the chamber, instantly echoed by all those outside.

'Make way! Make way!' yelled the legionaries, and '*Geddoutovit*!' and despite loud protests and angry faces from the crowed: *thump-bump-bump* and Morganus and I and the bodyguards were pressed up against Petros and his six shaven-heads, with bodies jostling all round us, and the legionaries were pushing back out of the crowd to get out of the building, and ourselves left standing right next to the open doors that led into the debating chamber. Petros looked grey with worry and sick with exhaustion. I would have greeted him, but he waved me to silence and pointed into the chamber.

'Shhh!' he said, 'Shhh!'

The chamber was huge and high. There was an altar inside the entrance with a winged statue of Victoria, goddess of triumph, and at the far side there rose three great steps, each ten feet deep and a foot high, that curved in successive semi-circles, bearing rows of seats carved from single blocks of black marble: one for each senator of the provincial council. But it was not Celtic provincial senators that filled the chamber, because the assembled dignitaries were pure-blooded Romans. It was citizens, knights and nobles, who at that moment were paying close attention to His Grace the Governor, in his broad-striped toga and crown of gilded oak leaves, because Marcus Ostorious Cerealis Teutonius was up on his feet, delivering classic Roman oratory, just as he had been taught as a boy, just as *all* Roman aristocrats are taught as boys.

He was a handsome man with a handsome voice, and he was doing well.

'As the noble Cicero said,' he declared, '*the safety of the people is the highest law*!' A murmur of approval greeted the quotation, and Teutonius continued. 'To this law, shall I be true!' he said. 'And therefore, when we gaze upon the great numbers of tribesmen now assembled outside our city, I have only this to say...'

I would have listened to him, but Petros seized my arm and whispered in my ear. All the rest of our conversation was like that: close up, urgent and secretive, with Morganus listening in.

'Sorry to bring you here,' he said.

'Why here?' I said.

'Best place. Biggest debating chamber in the city.' But Teutonius' voice rose again and Petros turned to watch and listen, with intense concentration.

'Noble and Honoured Sirs,' said Teutonius, 'here are my reasons for calm satisfaction…'

'Calm satisfaction…' repeated Petros's lips, as he stared at Teutonius.

'First and principally…' said Teutonius.

'First and principally…' repeated Petros's lips.

'…is the sublime nature of the spectacle to which…'

'Spectacle to which…' said Petros. Then he nodded in satisfaction and turned to me. 'He'll manage now,' he said.

'He'll manage what?' I said.

'He'll manage to deliver the rest of the speech that I taught him.'

'Will he?

'Yes. He's well trained. Trained by me over many years.'

'What's he saying?'

'He's saying that the mass of tribesmen outside our city is no threat.'

'Do you believe that?'

'I have to believe it! The games must succeed. We've gone too far to retract.'

I would have pressed him on that, but Teutonius' voice rose again.

'These simple natives, in their naïve simplicity, are awestruck at the racing of chariots!' he cried. 'It is the noblest of spectacles! The finest! The most sublime…' he paused, 'and the most *Roman*!' which won a huge roar of applause from the assembly.

'Who are those men?' I said, pointing into the chamber.

'They are everyone,' said Petros. 'Governor's staff, army staff, city council, chief justice, procurator, trade guilds, Celt billionaires: everyone! It's an extemporised meeting. We couldn't keep things quiet any longer. Not with the army ready for war.'

'Ah,' I said, 'and is everyone afraid of the encampment around the racing stadium?'

'They're in mortal dread! Most have already sent their families across to Gaul, to be safe.'

'Are *you* in mortal dread?' I asked.

'I can't afford to be,' he said, 'I have to believe that the tribes are here to see the games, I have to believe …' But again there was applause from the chamber, because Teutonius was sitting down, and men were drumming their feet on the ground in approval. Then the assembly Chairmen spoke in a deep voice.

'I call His Noble Grace the Lord Chief Justice!' he said, and the Chief Justice arose and stepped forward, arranging his toga into pleasing folds as he came, then taking up the stance of a public speaker, right arm outstretched, left arm to his breast.

'Wait!' said Petros, to me, 'I have to listen to this.'

'Your Grace! My Lords! My Knightly and Honoured sirs!' began the Chief Justice, and Petros listened in fearful anticipation. 'In supporting His Grace the Governor…' he said, and Petros nearly fainted in relief.

'Supporting!' he said. 'Thank the gods. If he's with us, the rest will follow.' He sighed and turned his attention to me again, and both of us tried to ignore the debating and cheering and noise.

'Now,' he said, 'What's this profoundly important news that you have to tell me?'

So I told him everything, and he seemed to age before my eyes. His once-black hair was white at the temples, and there was white in his beard, near the corners of his mouth. When I revealed that the men of Flavensum were not citizens, he actually leaned forward and sank his head into his hands, in grief and horror. But then he rubbed his brow with his fingers, and stood straight and forced himself to face facts.

'First,' he said, 'and with special emphasis on Flavensum, you will keep these matters entirely secret. Do you understand?'

'Yes,' I said.

'Now,' he said, 'I will summarise our predicament, and you will respond with *yes* or *no* when I pause, and you will not look into my mind. Just *yes* or *no*.' So he paused.

'Yes,' I said.

'Now, I will remind you that making a success of the governor's games is more important than anything else.'

'Yes,' I said.

'Good,' he said, 'because if the games succeed, then His Grace will become governor of Italia and be the second most powerful man in the Empire. But if the games fail, then His Grace's enemies in Rome will come swarming out from under the stones where currently they hide, and they will rend and tear his reputation, and even his body if they can get hold of it, and that will be the end of everything. Do you understand?'

'HA! HA! HA! HA!' came a great peal and bellow of laughter from the debating chamber at some joke by the lord chief justice.

'HA! HA! HA! HA!' cried everyone else, and I continued my conversation with Petros.

'Yes,' I said.

'So,' said, Petros, 'You say that the druids—probably Maligoterix himself—caused the killings of the tribune Celsus and the gladiator Tadaaki, and the attempt on your own life. And you say that in all cases the killers were under magical…' he saw my expression and corrected himself '…under *hypnotic* control, and the motive was either to disrupt the games, or through pure Celtic spite, or a mixture of both.'

'Yes,' I said.

'And you say that the taxation officer Gershom was killed by men of Flavensum, in the attempt to keep secret the fact that they are not Roman citizens?'

'OOOOOOOH!' gasped the crowd around us and there was a great swirl of emotion, and then drumming of feet in approval at some point that neither Petros nor I heard.

'Get on with it!' said Petros. 'Was that why he was killed?'

'Yes,' I said.

'And you say that there are further mysteries at Flavensum: some religious dispute between the two leading men, duovir Solis and duovir Bethsidus, and a dissonance between the generations, such that the older men, and the young men behave differently: the older men being open and friendly, while the young men are superior and cold?'

'Yes,' I said.

'And meanwhile it seems that most of the Celtic population of Britannia is encamped around the racing stadium, in numbers too great to count.'

'Yes,' I said.

'And now my oh-so-clever, mind-reading Apollonite,' he said, 'in your profound wisdom, can you bring together these separate facts into one common stream, and thereby enable me to make success of the games? And can you particularly avoid discovering anything else that is wrong, or bad, or dangerous?'

He sighed, he took a breath. He forced himself to be calm. 'Go on,' he said, 'Speak! Give me your opinion.'

I thought for a while, then spoke.

'The efforts of the druids and of the men of Flavensum may be connected,' I said.

'Why?' said Petros.

'Because the attempt on my life by the druids, came only after I had started to investigate the death of Gershom, which—we suppose—has nothing to do with druids. But perhaps it does, and someone, perhaps Maligoterix, did not want me to look into that matter.'

'Why?'

'I don't know,' I said, 'and can I ask a question?'

'Ask. Just get on with it!' But the assembly Chairman spoke again.

'I call upon His Knightly Grace, the Fiscal Procurator!' he said, and Quintus Veranius Scapula, the Fiscal Procurator came to the centre of the chamber, with his bad teeth and his self-consciousness, and did his best to look like a nobleman.

'Your Grace! Noble and Honoured Sirs…' he said in a thin voice.

'No need to listen,' said Petros. 'He's on our side. He's been bought.' And he ignored Scapula after that.

'Whose idea was it that the men of Flavensum should support the games?' I said. 'Did you approach them, or did they come to you.'

'They came to me,' said Petros, 'they were rich and ready to spend money. They came with ready gold.'

'And Gershom?' I said. 'You knew him well. If that letter from Pliny was in his library, why didn't Gershom know that the men of Flavensum aren't citizens?'

Petros nodded. He knew the answer.

'Probably because he never read it,' he said. 'Gershom was a collector. He liked to have complete sets of things. You'll find most of Pliny's letters in his library, but that doesn't mean that he ever read any of them.'

'So who *did* read it?' I said. 'How did the men of Flavensum find out about that letter?'

'I have no idea,' he said, 'You're the mind reader. You find out!'

'I'll do my best,' I said, 'but I'm going to need your help.'

'BOOOOOOO!' roared the assembly. 'BOOOOOOO!', but they were laughing, not angry. Despite his talents as an administrator, His Kinghtly Grace the Fiscal Procurator had neither eloquence nor manly bearing, and had just forgotten his words and then dropped his notes, while trying to find them again.

'Ho! Ho! Ho!' cried his audience, and Petros waved aside the interruption.

'Get on with it,' he said to me.

'First,' I said, there are some things we need to know about Flavensum.' I turned to Morganus. 'We've got to ask in Flavensum about religion,' I said. 'We need to know why Solis and Bethsidus quarrelled.' Morganus looked glum. He spread hands in an apologetic gesture.

'I'm sorry, Greek,' he said, 'I should have let you ask. I was wrong to stop you. It's just that some things are more than private: they're sacred.'

'I know, old friend,' I said, 'and so is friendship.' He smiled and I turned back to Petros. 'And we need to know why the young men of Flavensum are so proud, and why they don't give respect to any of their fathers except Solis!'

'I agree,' said Petros, 'but what's the help that you need from me? I have the feeling that it will be something difficult and unpleasant.'

'I need to meet Maligoterix,' I said, 'I want to see him before I talk to anyone from Flavensum again. I want a different viewpoint: one that cuts across what I already know. You, honoured Petros, have said previously that you can arrange a meeting with Maligoterix.'

Petros nodded.

'So I need to see him,' I said. 'We must find out what the druids are trying to do to the governor's games, whether there is any connection with Gershom's murder and Flavensum.'

'Hurrah! Hurrah!' cried the assembly, in sarcastic applause, and they whistled and stamped and cheered as the Fiscal Procurator left the floor, blushing red with embarrassment, and the Chairman spoke again.

'I call next, His Knightly Honour Secundus Albinus Terentius,' he said, 'scion of the clan Albinus and senior tribune of the Twentieth Legion.' There was much applause, since the clan Albinus was powerful in Rome.

'He's sound,' said Petros, looking at Terentius. 'He's one of us!' Petros stepped forward, to be just inside the debating chamber, so that the great and powerful should see him give applause to a valued ally. Then he turned to me.

'Do you think Maligoterix will tell you?' he said. 'Will he even talk to you?'

'I don't know,' I said, 'but I have to try.'

Later, we left the Senate House and walked back to the fortress. Later still, it proved difficult to arrange my meeting with Maligoterix. I assume that intermediaries were involved: perhaps traitors made use of? Officials bribed? I do not know. I merely guess. Thus, ten days passed before the meeting and in the meantime, I investigated some matters which—at the time—I thought were of lesser importance. I also found time to see Allicanda. But I spoke to Morganus first, on our way back to the fortress.

'It seems we have nothing to do at the moment,' I said.

'Aren't we supposed to see the actors?' he replied. 'We put that aside, didn't we.'

'Of course,' I said, 'but I don't think they're anywhere near so important to the games as the gladiators and racing drivers.'

'So?' he said.

'Well,' I replied, 'in that case... I wondered... I wondered that... if we have some spare time ...'

He smiled.

'Oh, by Hercules,' he said, 'if you want to see your fish girl then go and see her! Rome won't fall if you stop work for a few hours. How are things between her and you, anyway? What's the latest news?'

I told him. 'Hmm,' he said. 'One-and-a-half million is a lot. But you're the governor's golden boy, and Petros likes you.'

'Does he? It didn't look like it, in the Senate House.'

'Never mind that. He's just tired, that's all. So let's march forward with standards raised, and imagine the future. Let's imagine that the games go on, and that you've solved all these problems: druids, Flavensum, Lixus rebellion, everything. Then, in that case, you'll have saved the Empire a vast sum of money.' He looked at me in puzzlement. 'What's bigger than a million?'

'A billion,' I said, 'a thousand million.'

'There!' he said. 'It takes a Greek to know that. So if you've saved billions, then I shouldn't be surprised if Petros would fix it for you, with your fish girl.'

'Would he?'

'Yes! He'd have a little word in the ear of young Fortunus and knock the price right down. One favour for another. These rich Celts are always after something. Look at your friend Felemid whom we met in his bath. He just wants us Romans to like him. He'd give anything for that.'

'Oh,' I said.

So I met Allicanda that afternoon, with arrangements as before, except that we chose a different cook shop. It would have been dangerous to meet too many times in the same place. She chose The Silver Fish, off the Via Secundus. It was quiet and clean and respectable. Allicanda came with four friends as before, who sat at a separate table, but there were no Africans because it was daylight and the streets were safe: safe for them but not for me, because if Maligoterix sent more killers, there might not be a quarterstaff handy and I might not see the knives coming. So two of the bodyguards followed me, in civilian clothes, with swords under their cloaks. They sat by themselves, where the Africans might have sat, had they been there.

But at least I could sit down with Allicanda, and by the grace of the gods it was a happy meeting. I told her what Morganus had said, and she was delighted, and her joy was glorious to behold. It lit her face with smiles and I thought she had never been more fresh and beautiful. So we talked and talked. At first we spoke of each other, but then—even though I tried to avoid slave gossip in case she thought I wanted her only for that—the conversation turned to the topic that was consuming the entire city. The governor's games.

'Have you come across these young men of Flavensum,' she said, 'with their black beards? The men who are running the games?'

Instantly, I was stabbed with conflicting emotions, because I really did want to know what *she* knew, but I knew I must keep secret about what *I* knew. Thus I felt that if I encouraged her to speak I would be dishonest, and would be taking advantage of her. But then I told myself that it was in our shared interest for me to make use of her knowledge, in order to succeed in my inquiries and to win Petros's gratitude and thereby free her from Fortunus. Then, finally, I recognised that I was simply fascinated by inquiry itself and wanted to know more.

But I am not the only person who looks at another's face and reads signs. 'What's wrong?' she asked. 'You've gone sad again. What's in your clever mind, and why does it always make you sad?'

Given my dishonesty, her kindness was unbearable—and then it got worse.

'I know what it is,' she said. 'You want me to tell you what they're saying in the streets. You want to know and it makes you feel guilty.' I bowed my head. I was ashamed. 'But I forgive you,' she said, 'because you can't help it. So what do you want to know?'

I looked at her and felt my spirits lift.

'Ah!' she said, 'That's better. You're smiling. So what do you want to know?'

'What are people saying about the young men of Flavensum?'

'They're saying that there's a lot of them, and they're funny… they're odd.'

'In what way?'

'They're stuffed fat with pride and they look down on everyone, but they're out every night in the cook shops getting drunk, and they're so often in the brothels that the usual customers are complaining they can't get in!'

'Really?' I said.

'Oh yes,' she said, 'and all the girls are worn out because the Flavensum boys are behaving as if there's no tomorrow and they'll never get a woman again.'

'Anything else?' I said.

'Yes,' she said, 'despite all the drinking and whoring they're very, very religious. You know they're Jews, don't you?'

'Yes,' I said, 'it was you that told me.'

'Well, they're Jews and they have meetings in a big house they've hired off the Via Principalis to be their synagogue. It's funny really,' she said, 'The house used to a cook shop, called The Old Bridge.'

'I know it,' I said, 'cheap wine, full of drunks and next to a dangerous bridge.'

'And now it's a synagogue,' she said. and we smiled. 'And one of the important men of their city comes to join them,' she went on. 'He's also taken a house in Londinium. His name is…' she pondered, 'Solik, Solus…'

'Solis?' I said.

'Yes. That's it.'

That was all she knew of the young men of Flavensum, but she knew something powerfully interesting about the great encampment of Celts.

'All the tribes are there,' she said, 'men, women, children and cattle. Nobody knows how many of them and mostly they don't come into the city.'

'Don't they?' I said.

'No. The tribes don't like Londinium or any of the Roman cities, and they mostly despise the Celts who live in those cities. They think they're weak. They think they've given up.'

'But do *some* of them come in?' I asked. 'Come into the city?'

'Yes,' she said, 'the tribal leaders come in. They come in with their attendants…'

I interrupted. 'Attendants?' I said. 'Do you mean warriors?'

'No!' she said. 'Nobody gets in through the gates bearing arms.' She frowned. 'You should know that. Nobody's closer to the Romans than you are.'

'I know,' I said, 'what I mean is, are they aggressive? Do they look hostile?'

'No,' she said, 'they just wander round and look at the big buildings, and try not to be impressed. But you can see that they *are* impressed. Big Roman buildings make them feel nervous, because they can't build anything like that.'

'And do they talk to people in the city?'

'Oh yes. There are people in Londinium from all the tribes. There's always someone who speaks their tribal languages.'

'And what do they say?'

'They ask for wine and beer. And meat pies! They like meat pies.'

'What about the races? Do they talk about that?'

'Yes. They talk about that all the time. Celts believe chariots are holy because of their wheels. Ordinary cart wheels—solid wheels—are nothing special. But the lightweight, spoked wheel is magical. It is the icon of the god Belenus,' she raised hands, 'blessed be the name of Belenus!'

'Blessed be his name!' I said, and likewise raised hands.

'So they're fascinated by chariots,' she said, 'and they've all heard about the races, and some of them have even seen them.' She looked at me and smiled. 'You look puzzled,' she said, 'you do know that there have been chariot races in Britannia already, don't you?'

'Yes,' I said, 'I do know.'

'But you don't care,' she said, and I laughed.

'Is there anything else?' I said, 'anything else that the Celts talk about?'

'Yes.'

'Well?'

'They're waiting for something. They don't say what it is, but they're waiting for *something*.'

I immediately thought of the Roman practices of divination and of augury. Despite being so desperately disciplined, Romans placed great value on signs and omens: the flight of birds, the gathering of clouds, the shape of a beast's liver. It was superstition, but it was powerful superstition.

'So all those tribesmen, in countless numbers outside the city walls,' I said, 'and camped round the racing stadium, they're waiting for something, and they don't know what?'

'No,' she said, 'that's not what I said. I said that *I* don't know what they're waiting for, and the people of Londinium don't know what they're waiting for , but I think the tribes know.'

I thought about that, and it worried me, and I was absolutely right to be worried. But at least I parted in happiness from Allicanda, and she from me, because at least we had cause to hope.

Chapter 26

The next day Morganus and I did our duty as ordered, and visited the Londinium theatre to check that everything necessary had been done to protect the artistes so expensively imported from Rome to perform for the people of Britannia. Before we inspected the theatre, I would have said: 'imported from Rome to perform for the people of Britannia… whether they liked it or not.'

I would have said that because in my city, Apollonis, we were committed to the physical sciences: engineering, medicine, geometry, astronomy, chemistry and the like. Thus unlike the supposedly glorious city of Athens, we were not committed to the decorative arts: sculpture, literature, painting, poetry and—of course—drama. We did have a theatre, but that was used mainly to celebrate festivals to our patron god Apollo, and only occasionally used for drama, and that was only when cities such as Athens or Corinth sent colleges of dramatic actors who graciously condescended to visit us in order to bring culture to the savages. But these artistes typically performed to empty benches and left vowing never to return.

In short, there was no flourishing of Greek drama in Apollonis, and knowing the philistine nature of Romans I assumed it would be the same in Londinium. But I soon discovered how wrong I was.

In Londinium it was far easier to reach the theatre than either the gladiator schools or the racing stadium, because the theatre was right in the centre of the city, behind the baths of Trajan. In fact it had been built at the same time as the baths, and in the same Britannic stone.

It was typical of theatres in most cities, so a bird looking down on it would see a great, D-shaped structure, open to the skies, with banks of seats curling around the stage, each ring of seats rising above the one in front, and with a complex of highly-decorated stonework rising to the rear of the stage, with pillars, doors, shrines and niches. The theatre was small by Greek standards, with room for only a thousand people, and the wooden stage had only a single trapdoor, and nothing like the complex machinery for special effects that was common in Rome and other great cities.

Since the theatre was complete, with no works in progress by the army or anyone else, Morganus and I told the plain truth, that we were coming to inspect the arrangements for protecting the artistes, and a runner was sent in advance to warn the tribune in charge. This meant the usual formalities, with Morganus attended by myself, the bodyguards, and a century of regulars; and we were met in the square outside the theatre main entrance, by the tribune and a guard of honour found from his men—all auxiliaries—with trumpets, cheers, marking time, salutes and greetings. Everyone's metal work was polished like gems, and curious city-folk stopped in the street with shopping in hand, to point out the military to one another.

Then, Morganus and I and the bodyguards were solemnly taken inside, marched up a flight of stairs, and received in a foyer that was lined, draped and decorated in marble, onyx, granite and statuary, with huge representations of the Greek drama masks on the walls all around us. It was all very lavish, but even more lavish was the line of artistes drawn up to be presented to us—or perhaps it was us who were being presented to them, because the tribune, Cerialis Quintus Grabius, was plainly stage-struck, while the artistes were fully dressed in costume, ready for a rehearsal. They stood in splendour, with the posture and manner of Greek gods. Which is to say, the posture and bearing that professional actors *thought* was that of Greek gods, and of goddesses too, because half of the artistes were women: exceedingly fine women, with layered cosmetics, bold eyes and exaggerated figures, though I suspect the latter owed more to padding than to nature.

Despite such artifice, and the gaudy nature of costumes designed to be seen from a distance and not close up, , the experience of being in the presence of these actors and actresses was exceedingly pleasing and I realised that this was due to the charisma that good actors are reputed to possess, and which indeed they did.. Though I should also point out, that behind the artists a prosaic line of auxiliaries stood in full battle kit, just as others had stood at all the entrances to the theatre, and still more were clustered here and there about the building, such that it was instantly obvious that Tribune Grabius was doing everything possible to protect the artistes. Meanwhile, Grabius was speaking.

Honoured Sir,,' he said to Morganus, ignoring me as was entirely proper and yet deeply annoying. 'It is my duty and privilege,' he said, introducing the first actor, 'to present the celebrated thespian Artos Brantius Calldis!'

He spoke the name with such reverence that I realised Calldis—like the gladiators and racing drivers I had already met—was one of the great ones of his profession, and the fact that I had never heard of him was due to my own ignorance. But as the poet says, *an Apollonite would rather go to the tooth-puller than the theatre.*

Calldis bowed to Morganus, then took a heroic stance, and spoke in so rich and melodious a voice that he made Latin sound like Athenian Greek.

'Valiant and warlike sir!' he declared, staring straight into Morganus' eyes and putting on the most amazing expression of respect and admiration, 'I salute you, great soldier of Rome! I salute you as the very exemplar of the martial splendour that has made our city the mistress of the world!' He bowed again, to polite applause from the other artistes, and a spontaneous drumming of feet from the auxiliaries, who really did admire Morganus. Meanwhile Morganus himself—who was always uncomfortable with praise—was visibly embarrassed, and began to blush, and yet I could see that he was also pleased, and so he smiled. I suppose that he too felt the charisma of these actors.

'I give you good day, Honoured Sir,' said Morganus, 'and I greatly look forward to the entertainment that you will present to the city,' which was handsomely said by a man who disliked the theatre even more than I did.

But then Calldis spoiled things by pointing out the underlying religious significance of drama.

'Valiant Sir,' he said, 'we seek to entertain, and yet to honour the immortal gods with catharsis and example, whereby deep and spiritual thoughts may be implanted in the minds of our audience, as shall cause...'

I refrain from recording the rest, except to say that Morganus' smile grew strained. Eventually, we came to the happy moment when we had been introduced to all the artistes, and they marched off to their rehearsal, followed by their guard of auxiliaries. Then Grabius took us to a reception room for the usual wine and cakes, and Morganus was about to go through the ritual of questioning him about defensive arrangements when we were interrupted. Someone knocked on the door.

'Enter!' said Grabius, and an auxiliary optio attempted to come in and salute, but someone came right in with him, and pushed past. Morganus' bodyguards instantly leapt forward and stood between ourselves and any danger, drawing blades even though the intruder looked harmless. He was a fat, untidy man in middle age, with sparse hair under a small skull-cap, and the heavy cloak and leg-warmers that mark out a recent arrival to cold Britannia. He was of eastern Mediterranean appearance, frowning and angry, and seemed unconcerned that he was facing four swords.

'Beg pardon of Your Honours,' he said, 'but needs must, with works to be done, and nobody to do them, and I'm deep in shit, and I need help, and I need it now!'

'Stand easy, lads,' said Morganus, and the bodyguards sheathed blades and stood back.

'Nablus!' said Tribune Galbius. 'Not now. I can't speak now.'

'Not now? Not *now*?' said Nablus. 'Not now, he says? And he wants a big show for the people? And he wants something new? And where am I supposed to find a man who knows how the machinery works? Can he tell me that?'

Nablus stood with hands on hips, panting with effort and trying to catch his breath. The auxiliary optio stood nervously beside him, waiting for orders and shuffling his feet.

'Oh get out!' said Galbius to the optio, who went out and shut the door.

Galbius stood. We all stood. 'This is Nablus Bar Amman,' said Galbius. 'He is an impresario of theatre. He is manager and principal shareholder of the college of holy dramatics of the temple of Dionysius, brought out from Rome. And,' Galbius grudging added, 'he is a very senior person among the artistes. He is, in effect, their employer.'

'That's me,' said Nablus, 'the big, big impresario of theatre,' and he remembered his manners and bowed. 'I give you good day, Your Honours.' But then he waved his hands and grew angry again. 'I need help, I need help, I need help! I got machinery but I got no engineer. My first one fell out of a boat and drowned his idiot self in the idiot ocean. And he was the good one, 'cos my other one don't really know how anything works, and what am I supposed to do?'

'Nablus,' said Galbius, 'not now!' But Nablus frowned. He looked at Morganus.

'What about the army?' he said. 'They got engineers. Can I get an engineer out of the army?' Morganus instinctively looked at me. 'Ah!' said Nablus. 'We got a Greek here. But a Greek that don't talk!' He stepped forward and peered at me as if I were something strange. 'Are you an engineer, you Greek?'

'Yes,' I said.

'Ah!' said Nablus and beamed in delight, and had the impudence to leap forward, clasp my head with both hands and kiss me on the brow. 'So! You come with me you-Greek-that-don't-talk,' he said, 'because I have some big, big problems for you!'

I pulled free and frowned. But Morganus was smiling, and so were Galbius and the bodyguards too, because Nablus had a certain charm.

'What's going on?' I said, 'What are we talking about?'

'Stage machinery,' said Nablus. 'You'll love it, you Greek. So what's your name?'

'Ikaros,' I said, 'Ikaros of Apollonis.'

'Ikaros of wherever,' said Nablus, 'you come with me.'

'First tell me what's going on,' I said.

'No time,' said Nablus, but Galbius explained.

'The college of Dionysius is famous for its stage machinery,' he said.

'Yes,' said Nablus, 'so let's go, Ikaros-of-wherever.'

'And Nablus is particularly famous in this respect.'

'True, true. So *very* true!' said Nablus, and paused in his urgency to make a show of modesty, lifting his hands as if protesting, and grinning at us. He made even me smile.

'So,' said Galbius, 'we were promised a spectacular special effect, at the climax of Euripides' *The Bacchante*, which is...'

'A famous play,' I said, which it was. Even I had heard of it. It was famous in my city for being hideously, appallingly, unbearably dull.

'But you get no special effect if the machinery don't work, so come on you Greek and make it work!'

I freely admit that this talk of machinery had intrigued me. So I looked at Morganus.

'Are we done here?' I asked. So Morganus looked at Galbius. Galbius looked at Morganus, and they both nodded, while the bodyguards looked like boys promised a birthday treat, and I realised that they too—all of them—were intrigued because while Romans are not addicted to Greek drama, they most certainly are addicted to stage machinery and special effects.

So off we went, following Nablus down passageways and stairs, and down and out into the open air and on to the big stage that ran from side to side of the theatre. We stood in the cold, fresh air, birds did in fact circle overhead, and the sound of city streets came faintly to our ears. But Nablus did not stop to listen.

'There!' he said, 'See the disaster, and see the villain!'

The villain was an unfortunate young engineer—he could not have been more than eighteen years old and was smooth-faced as a baby—who was wearing a leather apron, and kneeling with a couple of slaves to help him, while trying to untangle a thin, tough hauling line that had jammed into a pulley attached to what looked like the outline of a huge cylinder over twenty feet wide and ten feet high: just two circles of bent wood, like the rims of a giant wheels, joined by vertical poles.

'There he sits,' said Nablus, 'on his Roman bum, with his Roman fingers that don't know nothing and can't make nothing work!'

Other slaves stood idly by, and almost the entire stage was full of mechanism, and a whole series of similar cylinder-frames, though of varied size. In addition there was a great stack of canvas rectangles painted to look like masonry, like heavy blocks cemented with mortar. The painting was excellent and the effect most convincing, such that I instantly guessed the purpose of all this gear—which presumably had been brought out from Rome. I guessed its purpose and I guessed and what was needed to make it work. I could do this without the slightest effort, because we of Apollonis had collapsible watch-towers of similar design on our city walls, and I knew them well.

So I could have solved Nablus' problem at once. But sometimes there needs to be a fanfare before the performance. Thus, I was there with many people looking on: Morganus, Galbius, the bodyguards and various slaves and auxiliaries, not to mention the young engineer. And so:

'Honoured Nablus,' I said, 'can you tell me what effect you hope to achieve with this machinery?' Everyone looked at Nablus.

'*What effect*, he asks, this Greek?' he said. 'I tell you what effect.' He walked to the stage trapdoor. 'It comes up here. It comes up from below. It is the bottom of a stone tower. Then the tower grows, and grows and grows, till it is high over all, and then a man appears on top, in a golden robe, with golden wings and we fly him in the air. He goes up, and up and away!'

'I see,' I said, and everyone looked at me, 'so I suppose these canvas sheets,' I pointed at one of them, 'are fixed around the frames,' I pointed at one of them, 'to make a complete cylinder?'

'Yes!' said Nablus, 'but we know that. That's not the problem, you Greek.'

'So, you will have a number of cylinders that will all fit inside one another. First the biggest, then the next, and so on to the smallest?

'Yes,' said Nablus.

'Yes,' said the young engineer.

'Go on,' said Nablus.

'And the cylinders are strong but light, and each one has pulleys—the top and bottom—and hauling lines are fed through the pulleys, and when men haul on the lines, the cylinders rise up, one inside the other, to make what looks like a big stone tower. The tower grows before the eyes of the audience and everyone is amazed.'

'Yes!' said everyone. Even the bodyguards were nodding, in wonder if not in understanding.

'But the problem is,' I said, 'that nobody here knows exactly how to run the hauling line through the pulleys.'

'Yes!' said Nablus.

So I showed them, which was not clever or inventive, because I already knew the answer. In principle, starting from the biggest cylinder, the line is run from below the cylinder, to the top of the cylinder, then over a pulley at the top, to the bottom edge of the next smallest cylinder. Thus when the line is pulled from below, the smaller cylinder is pulled up. In practice, matters are more complex, because there must be at least three hauling lines to each cylinder, for a balanced pull, and of course the pull must be transmitted again and again to each cylinder. Also there must be guide rails and wheels to make sure each cylinder moved smoothly against its neighbour, and finally the three hauling lines must be fed through pulleys below stage, and then bound together so that a team of men—unseen by the audience—can throw their weight on the lines to provide power.

It took some hours before everything worked, but finally the tower rose, with twenty auxiliaries down below on the hauling lines, and cheers all round, and the young engineer appearing on top, standing in for an actor, and waving his hands in triumph.

'That's it! *That's it*!' said Nablus, and threw his arms around me in delight. 'My lovely, my clever, my Greek!' he said, 'Your mother would be proud!' He pointed at the young engineer up on top of the tower. 'So we pull that villain up there, and when there's not a villain but an actor up there, the actor spreads his wings…'

'And you haul him off with a thin line attached to a harness under his costume,' I said, 'using a crane that's hidden up there,' I pointed to the top of the stone works behind the stage, 'and you fly him round the stage to tremendous applause.'

'Yes! Yes!' he said, 'The god from the machine: deus ex machina. All the people love it!' He laughed. 'You are some big, big Greek, Ikaros-of-whatever. Let's eat! Let's drink! My throat calls out for wine!'

So we all went to a big room in the theatre that was set aside as an eating place for the artistes and their various attendants. It was brightly decorated with wall paintings of scenes from famous plays, and the floor was entirely covered with an elaborate mosaic depicting all the entertainments: the races, the gladiators, the theatre and some grisly images of noxii being thrown to the beasts. Before we sat down, there was some discussion of hierarchy and who might sit where at which tables, because some were reserved for leading artistes and other seniors, while some were for lower persons and—of course, no slave was allowed in whatsoever, other than those which cooked, served and bowed. Nablus saw Galbius looking at me in puzzlement, as we entered, through doors held open by slaves.

'Ah… er…' said Galbius who knew who I was, and what I was.

'Oh?' said Nablus, looking at me and pointing to Morganus. 'Are you his boy? I didn't see *that* coming. You don't look like a slave.'

'My comrade is in His Imperial Majesty's service,' said Morganus, sternly.

'Gods save His Majesty!' said the bodyguards and Galbius.

'From his hair to his toenails,' said Nablus.

'My comrade sits with me,' said Morganus, 'he sits wherever I sit, and whenever I sit.'

Galbius looked relieved at such clear instruction. His problem of protocol disappeared, and he gave me a tiny, polite bow.

'Then be welcome,' he said, and sought for a title. 'Be welcome Worshipful Sir,' he said, and Morganus nodded in approval. So we sat at the highest table, with the bodyguards standing nearby until Morganus told them to sit, and Galbius pointed to a table appropriate to their rank. We were served good food and good wine, and I saw that Nablus' enthusiasm for wine was even greater than mine. Indeed he soon filled himself up, and beamed and smiled and sat next to me, and told stories about the theatre that made us all laugh, and he explained how his production of Greek tragedies differed from all others.

'We play for laughs,' he said.

'Even the famous Calldis?' I asked. 'Does he play for laughs?'

'Huh!' said Nablus, 'He does when *I* tell him! Actors, actors, actors: they're up their own bums. But they do what I say, or they're out. So we make jokes, we build towers, we make men fly, and the people laugh and they come back.'

He kept winking at me and smiling, and I got the impression he had something to say, because he kept looking sideways at the Romans: Morganus and Galbius. So I followed up this possibility.

'Honoured sir,' I said to Morganus, when we had finished eating. 'If perhaps you wish to discuss the safety of the artistes with the honoured Galbius, I would be happy to continue my studies of theatre machinery with the honoured Nablus.'

Morganus understood at once, because it was a commonplace of our investigations that some people would not speak freely in the presence of so senior a Roman officer.

'Of course,' said Morganus, 'the honoured Galbius and I will tour the theatre and I will meet you later.'

So I was left in the big dining room with Nablus. It was nearly empty now, with nobody near enough to hear what he was saying. He poured more wine, we drank, and he poured still more.

'I like you, Ikaros-of-whatever,' he said.

'Apollonis,' I said.

'Whatever,' he said, and I smiled. I liked him in return.

'It's good to have a friend,' he said. 'It's not easy for a Jew under the Romans.'

'So you're a Jew?' I said, and he leaned back in exaggerated amazement.

'Are you saying *I* can see a Greek's nose, but *you* can't see a Jew's?' We laughed. 'Have some more,' he said, and tipped the wine flask.

'So why is it hard?' I asked.

'Why do you think? They smashed us. They burned the Jerusalem temple.' He looked at me. 'If you're from Apollonis, you know what that's like.'

I did know. Apollonis fell to the Romans after a long siege. They burned the city, and all who survived were made slaves, including me.

'At least you're free,' I said.

'At least *you* are at peace with your god,' he said.

'What do you mean?' I asked, and he blinked at me dozily. He had taken a lot of drink.

'It's easy for you,' he said, 'you have many gods, and none of them care if you say a prayer to another one.' I nodded. That was true. What did Apollo care if I called on Athene or even Isis, once in a while?

'But it's not like that for us,' he said. 'Listen, Ikaros-of-whatever, there are not many gods, nor a few gods, nor just one or two. There is only one God, and He is a jealous God, and we are damned to Hell if we displease him.'

I thought about that. I thought of the druids and their fear of damnation. I wondered how many other faiths went in such fear?

'I see,' I said, 'but why is this so very bad under the Romans?'

'Because of the Emperor's birthday,' he said. 'Do you know that day, Ikaros-of-whatever? Do you know what we have to do, on that day?'

'Yes,' I said, 'we offer prayers to the divine spirit of the Emperor. It's a formality.'

'Not to us!' said Nablus. 'We can *never* do that. Never, never, never. If we pray to any other god than God, we are damned.'

I frowned.

'But I've seen Jews offer prayers on the Emperor's birthday,' I said.

'And did you listen to what they said?' he asked.

'Yes,' I said.

'So how good is your Hebrew?'

'Not bad.'

'But not native. Not fluent.'

'No.'

'So next time, listen carefully.' And he switched to Hebrew. '*Because we do not offer prayers* to *the Emperor, but* for *him.*'

It was an illuminating moment. The prayer to the Emperor's spirit was a declaration of loyalty to the Empire, and an outright refusal to offer that prayer was treason under Roman law, and punishable by death.

'Do the Romans know this?' I asked. 'Do they know what you say?'

'Ikaros! My lovely, my clever, my Greek… do you think we even ask?'

'No,' I said.

'No,' he said, 'we just leave things as they are. And they just use us because we're clever. And we get on. But if ever they should find out and turn nasty…' He shrugged and poured more wine. 'You want some?'

'No,' I said.

'Or,' he said, 'we could pray *to* and end up in Hell. And that's why it's hard to be a Jew under Rome.'

Chapter 27

On the way back to the fortress after leaving the theatre, I had an idea. As we tramped down the Via Principalis: Morganus and I, the bodyguards and our escort, I was thinking over what Nablus had said about the difficulty of being a Jew under Rome, and my mind shifted to the Jews of Flavensum—if indeed their strange faith *was* Judaism.

'Morganus?' I said.

'Yes?'

'We're coming to a junction that runs across the Little Fosse, one of the Thames' tributaries.'

'Are we?'

'Yes,' I said, 'it's the next on the left. There is—or there used to be—a cook shop there. One that sold cheap wine.'

He laughed.

'Well you'd know, wouldn't you?'

I ignored that.

'Half way down the street,' I said, 'there's an old wooden bridge that crosses the Little Fosse, and it was famously rotten and the drunks used to fall through it into the river.'

'Oh?' he said. 'Did you know anyone, personally, who did that?'

'Never mind,' I said, 'the cook-shop was just by the bridge, and was always known as The Old Bridge, even though it had some other name that nobody ever used.'

'Do go on,' he said, 'I suppose you know every cook shop in Londinium that sells wine, so why don't you just tell me all their names?'

I smiled. 'Not today,' I said, 'because the young men of Flavensum, those excellent citizens with the big black beards, they've bought The Old Bridge and turned it into a synagogue.'

'A synagogue?' he said. 'That's a temple, isn't it? A Jewish temple?'

'Yes,' I said. 'And I think I'd like to take a look at it, and speak to the people who live in the street.'

'What?' he said, 'Now?' And he jabbed his thumb at the steel-clad regulars crunching along behind us with their army boots, helmet crests, and scarlet shields. 'Not with them behind us?'

'No,' I said, 'I'll come back later, by myself.'

He nodded, and we marched past the street at that moment. 'That's it,' I said, 'everyone calls it Bridge Street.'

We looked as we passed. It was a perfectly ordinary Londinium street, neither rich nor poor, elegant nor squalid. The buildings, two or three stories high, stood shoulder to shoulder, with washing hanging on lines running across the street. There were shops, children playing in the street, people gossiping—and we could just see where the flagstones turned into the timbers of the bridge where the street crossed the Little Fosse.

'All right,' said Morganus, 'you can come back later when you're not surrounded by the army. But you'll have two of the bulldogs behind you, in civvies,' he tapped me on the shoulder, ''cos I've got to look after you,' he said, 'I'm under serious orders!'

'From the legate?' I said.

'No,' he said, 'higher up than that! Orders from The-Lady-my-Wife.'

So I came back later, just before dusk, wearing a plain cloak and trying not to be conspicuous, an effort which was spoiled by the hulking figures of two of Morganus' bodyguards who followed behind me, likewise wrapped in cloaks. As bodyguards, they had been chosen for muscle not brain, and were simple Romans, trying hard to do their duty, even this strange duty, out of armour. So they made every effort not to march in step, and frowned with the exertion of not looking like soldiers. It was comical to see them at it, and the people in the streets spotted them for what they were in an instant. City folk have an instinct for smelling out officials, and they nudged one another as we passed.

As we turned off the Via Principalis into Bridge Street, we were favoured by fortune because the synagogue was in session. Even as we entered the street I could faintly hear the sound of chanting and declaiming coming from the direction of the bridge, or rather, from the direction of what was now a synagogue and had once been a cook shop. And there were people standing in clumps before their doorways and shop fronts, muttering to each other and pointing.

I moved slowly down the street, politely excusing myself and trying not to jostle anyone.

'Beg pardon, Honoured Sir!' I said, 'Beg pardon Lady!'

I did so because under Rome, it is a flogging offence for a slave—*any* slave—deliberately to bump into a citizen, and I wanted to be discreet in any case. But my efforts were again spoiled by the two bodyguards, who moved through the people like lumbering bulls, until I had a quiet word with them. They nodded.

'Yes, Your Worship. No shoving, Your Worship. Right you are, Your Worship.' and they stood to attention.

'No salute!' I said, *just* before the right arms were thrown out.

'No salute, Your Worship.'

Fortunately, the chanting and yelling was rising ever louder from within the closed doors and shuttered windows of the synagogue, so the street people were not really interested in an odd Greek and his two big friends. The people around us were indignant, grumbling and affronted. I stood silent a while, then shuffled carefully forwards in the fading light to listen to what some of them were saying.

There was a baker standing outside his shop, with two slaves behind him who nodded at everything he said, and a couple of fat matriarchs in stolas, and a lamp-lighter with his ladder trying to get the lights burning over the baker's shop. Other neighbours were standing around listening, as were three hand-cart men, who had stopped, with piles of building stone in their carts, ready for delivery somewhere even at this time of day.

'It's a disgrace,' said the baker.

'It is,' said one of the matriarchs, 'something ought to be done.'

'Where's the block warden?' said the baker. 'That's what I want to know!'

'Paid off,' said the matriarch, 'that lot in there,' she pointed to the synagogue, 'have got money coming out of their ear-holes! They paid for the Old Bridge in cash. Actual gold coin!'

'You just wait,' said the lamp-lighter, from up on his ladder, 'you wait till they're done and they all come bursting out, singing and yelling.'

'It's a disgrace!' said the baker again and there was much more of the same from other groups as I moved quietly down the street. I tried smiling and nodding to attempt conversation, but these sharp-minded city-folk took one look at the bodyguards and turned away from me. Then finally I found someone who *was* prepared to talk to a stranger. He even approached me.

'Who are you then?' said an old man, who smelt like a latrine. 'You're a Greek, aren't you?' He leaned forward and grabbed at my cloak, breathing halitosis and stale wine. 'Athens? Corinth? Thebes?'

'Apollonis,' I said.

'Ahhh!' he said, and switched to good Greek with the accent and vocabulary of a learned man.

'May the gods ease the sorrow that falls upon an Apollonite,' he said, 'that princely city of engineers, crushed under the heel of Rome.'

'May the gods bless you in your sympathy,' I said, trying not to recoil at the stench of him.

'I sympathise, because I know the pain of hard times,' he said.

'May the gods lift your pain,' I said. 'What was your city?'

'Athens,' he said. 'Glorious Athens. I was a sculptor, then a slave who was valued at one hundred thousand! And now this,' he raised his hands to show how crippled they were with an old man's arthritis. 'I cannot lift a pen now, let alone chisel and mallet. And thus I was turned out homeless by my master,' he clutched at me again, 'so what charity might an Apollonite give to a fellow Greek, so cruelly abandoned to starvation?'

I looked down at him and did not quite believe his story. He was well fed, and dressed in clothes that would have been decent except for his incontinence. Also, while Roman law strictly forbade the casting out of old slaves, with severe penalties for anyone who did so, every beggar on the city streets claimed to be a slave thrown out by a cruel master. Furthermore, the old man had a very strong grip on my cloak for someone who was unable to lift a pen. But at least he was ready to talk. So I gave him a coin, which went straight into his mouth to test for brass. He smiled as he tasted gold.

'You are a scholar, a philanthropist and a nobleman,' he said, and having got his coin he would have made off to the nearest wine shop. But I conquered distaste and took hold of him.

'What happens in there?' I said, looking at the synagogue.

'The rites of Flavensum,' he said. 'The rites of the new Jews who celebrate the rabbi Jesus Bar Joseph as messiah.' In fact he did not use the Hebrew word messiah, instead he described the rabbi Jesus with the Greek word Christos, meaning *the anointed one*, the first time I heard that word used in this context. But the old man was tugging at my cloak again. 'The young men of Flavensum meet here every day,' he said and grinned at me, 'those exalted young men from whose anal apertures the sun shines each day in his glory—or at least, we must suppose this to be the case, given the adulation heaped upon them by Rome. They meet here at the close of day to receive the wisdom of their priest, the duovir Solis of Flavensum, and he and they together achieve orgasms of spiritual consummation, as you shall see for yourself within the time of an eye-blink.'

He was a true prophet. Either that, or he was used to the noises coming from the building, or it might have been simply the volume, because now I could clearly hear what was being said insider, or rather what was being sung at the utmost volume of men's voices. It was the Sermon on the Mount, as given in Aramaic by the book of Zoltan, except that it was set to music and roared out with manic enthusiasm.

'Blessed be the strong! For they shall prevail!
Blessed be those who are prepared!
For they shall be ready with swords!
Blessed be those who shed blood in just cause!

For they shall be the kingdom of God!'

Then all was confusion and riotous clamour, because the doors of the old cook-shop, the typical sliding, folding doors of a Roman eating place, were slid apart and a great body of young men, all bearded, burst out onto the street, singing and chanting and raising hands over their heads, or gripping hands and dancing in furious circles, and bumping into the street people, and knocking over the flower pots and hand carts, and staggering and yelling, with heads thrown back and eyes staring. Such behaviour was strange to see in Romans, who normally worship their gods in formal dignity. By contrast, these men were in a state of ecstasy.

'You were correct in your description!' I said to the old man, but he had slipped away with his coin, and the two bodyguards were standing in front of me with heavy fists, systematically knocking down any of the religious ones who might otherwise have staggered into us. But the others seemed not to mind. I doubt that they even noticed, because soon there was a swirl in the movement of bodies and the young, beaded men were crowded up against the entrance to the old cook shop as Duovir Solis emerged.

I was close enough to see him clearly, and he looked like a man just pulled from the sea. He was so drenched in sweat that his clothes hung soaking wet, his hair was slimy on his brow, and his nose and chin dripped steadily. I supposed him to be in this condition because of the abandoned passion of his preaching, and even now his mind was intoxicated beyond reason: this much was obvious from his staring eyes and stumbling gait.

So the young men cheered and sang and yelled, and hoisted Solis up on to their shoulders, and they carried him off, yelling a chant in Aramaic:

'*The day shall come! The day shall come! The day shall come!*'

'Let them pass,' I said to the bodyguards.

'Yes, Your Worship!'

So we pressed back against a house, as Solis came by, raised up and slowly recovering from his trance, while the bodyguards and I were jammed against other people who presumably lived in the street.

'Every night they're at it,' said one.

'It's a disgrace,' said another.

Then Solis saw me looking at him, and his eyes focussed, and rational thought returned, and he laughed as if in contempt of me. Then he waved and shouted.

'*The day is coming!*' he cried in Aramaic. '*And what will a clever Greek do then?*'

Chapter 28

When I told all this to Morganus over dinner that night, at first he refused to be as worried as I had been.

'What's wrong with saying *The day shall come*?' he asked. 'That probably means the games. They're busy planning the games, aren't they?'

'Are they?' I said. 'We can't carry on thinking that the men of Flavensum are so loyal that everything must be all right. Not anymore. Not when we know that they're not real citizens and some of them killed Bethsidus, to keep that fact quiet.'

'Only some of them,' he said, 'and maybe the rest don't *know* they're not citizens? Maybe it's a secret that the fathers keep from the sons?'

'Perhaps, but they looked like religious maniacs to me. You didn't see them.'

'And you haven't seen the ceremonies in other mystery cults,' he said, 'maybe they're all like that?'

'Are you like that when you worship Mithras?'

'I don't talk about the Lord Mithras.'

'Yes, but do you chant and yell and roll your eyes?'

'No, we don't. We act like Romans.'

'There you are then,' I said, and we talked some more but reached no conclusions during the days it took Petros to complete his secret dealings with Maligoterix, such that the druid leader—for whatever reasons of his own—agreed to meet me.

By this time all arrangements for the governor's games were so advanced that only a days would pass before the grand opening ceremony.

This would be held in the racing stadium, which was now fully complete and by far the biggest place where crowds could gather. Even so, it was expected that the stadium would not be big enough to contain the vast numbers of tribesmen and families that had now gathered in the Celtic encampment, together with the people of Londinium themselves, who quite reasonably thought they should have priority of seating. This caused yet another burden to fall upon Petros, and upon his shaven-head attendants, and upon the young men of Flavensum, too—wherever their loyalties lay—in organising tickets and passes, all of which had to be free of charge and must be distributed among tribesmen and townsmen alike, without provoking actual riots.

Morganus and I saw this process in action, as we climbed aboard the legionary lightning that would take us most of the way to our meeting with Maligoterix. Under orders from Petros and the Legate Africanus, the lightning would take us to the military camp at Sadunum, far to the west of Londinium, where we would receive final—and deeply secret—guidance to the meeting place.

The lightning was ready and waiting at the fortress stables, which happened to be near the south gate, where a heavy, wooden log hut had been built to distribute tickets for the grand opening ceremony. The hut was just inside the fortifications, where it was protected by the earthworks and could not be not be over-run by the mob. Dawn had just come, but people had been waiting in the darkness. There were thousands of them, and the noise they made was appalling, because not only adults were present but children too, and infants in arms that squalled and bellowed. In the deep press, illiterate tribal Celts jostled educated townsmen, while among the tribes Silure argued with Atrebate, and Regni with Catuvellauni, because they did not properly understood one another's accent, and there were ancient rivalries between the tribes. So fists were waved and hair was torn, and fights broke out and everyone shouted at once.

But the flow of bodies was under control because the great, untidy column could get into the fortress only by crossing the drawbridge over the ditches surrounding the massive embankments. Also, the living stream was penned in by the locked shields of legionaries and auxiliaries, formed up in walls, on either side of the column. Then, once inside the fortress, the shields surrounded the ticketing booth to make sure that only manageable numbers fell upon the booth—with eager and grasping hands—at any one time.

Inside the booth, behind a protective counter, still more legionaries were handing out wooden pass-tickets as fast as they could, and the happy, beaming, yelling ticket-holders were coming away, waving their tickets in the air, and were funnelled between two more lines of shields, towards another gate, so that the outgoing stream should not jam into the incoming stream. As always with Romans, the process was efficient. Even a Greek must admit that.

We had just got up into the lightning, and were about to move off, when one of our four horses, the offside leader, gave a snort of fear, and rose up on his hind legs in terror at the noise, and throwing off the grip of the legionary holding his head. The other horses whinnied in fright, and tugged at their handlers too, and I could not help but leap down and catch the leader's head, and stroke him, and talk to him and soothe him until he was calm.

It was a happy moment because I dearly love horses, and I think they like me too. At least I hope so.

Once the horse was settled, I put my brow to his and said a final word to him, and he made gentle sounds, and I got back into the lighting and was surprised to see Morganus and the bodyguards looking at me with respect.

'You could've been killed doing that!' said Morganus. 'These beasts have got iron shoes!'

'Yeah!' said the bodyguards, but I shook my head because in all my life I could never see a horse in pain without stepping forward. I was bred up to the care of horses and it is in my blood. To me, the care of horses is like breathing. It is something that I must do.

'And the animal listened to you,' said Morganus, 'he listened, and then he spoke back. It's like your mind-reading: it's magic.'

'Yeah!' said the bodyguards.

'It's not magic,' I said, 'it's...' but I said no more, because someone ran forward shouting and waving. He arrived out of breath and hanging on to the side of the lighting. It was Optio Silvius, and he had his leather satchel hanging round his neck.

'Honoured Sir! Worshipful Sir!' he said, with chest heaving and sweat on his brow.

'Take your time, optio,' said Morganus, 'and make your report.'

'I thought I'd miss you, Honoured Sirs,' he said, 'we've been at this for days, the lads and me.'

'Doing what?' I said.

'We had an idea,' he said, and looked at me, 'well, Your Worship, you had a quick look at the books and papers that we couldn't read, right? The Hebrew and Aramaic?'

'Yes,' I said.

'And you said roughly what was in them, but you didn't read them all through?'

'Yes,' I said. 'I had a brief look. That was all.'

'And you told us to look for a number of things,' he said, 'and one of them was anything to do with Lixus?'

'Yes,' I said.

'Well, we know a leather merchant that sells skins to the army for tents. We know him very well because our normal work involves buying stores for the legion. And he's a Jew, and a good lad, and we got him to write down the letters of the Hebrew alphabet.' He paused to fumble in his satchel and pulled out a wax tablet. 'Here they are, Your Worship ,' he said, and I looked at the familiar, cursive letters.

'Yes,' I said. 'And so?'

'Well, we worked out how you'd write some of the things we were looking for, in Hebrew. So, since Hebrew doesn't have a letter for X, we guessed Lixus would be like LIKSUS in Latin, which is the Hebrew letters lamed, kaf and then samech twice, which actually would be like LKSS in Latin, because they don't write down vowels and you have to guess them from the context.' He paused and smiled, and took a deep breath. 'And so we found this,' he pulled a scroll from his satchel and gave it to me. 'You said this was letter to Pliny the elder, about the lions of North Africa, and it is, and it's in Hebrew, but half way down the word Lixus appears several times.' He looked at me in triumph, 'Perhaps it's about the Lixus rebellion? It's the only thing about Lixus that's famous. Nobody's heard of it otherwise.'

'Did you check this with the leather dealer?' I asked.

'No, Your Worship, because all this is supposed to be secret.'

'Well done Optio Silvius!' said Morganus, and he turned to me. 'Well?' he said. 'What does it say?'

Everyone looked at me as I read the letter, trying to clear my mind of the noise and clamour of the mob yelling for their tickets. Soon I looked up again.

'Optio Silvius is right,' I said. 'He's a highly intelligent man who has shown great initiative and he's a credit to the legion.' Silvius stamped to attention and threw out his right arm in salute. He stood like a real, fighting soldier, not just a clerk, but he was grinning enormously.

'Gods bless you, Worshipful Sir!' he said, 'And you, Honoured Sir!'

'Accepted!' said Morganus. 'And now I think we should be gone, before this mess,' he pointed to the surging mass of humanity, 'before this gets any worse.' And he looked at me. 'You can tell me on the way what's in that letter.'

So the driver took the reins, and we moved off with the current of bodies flowing away from the ticket booth and out of the western gate, leaving the fortress and civilisation behind as the driver found the Great West Road, for an eight-hour journey of ninety-six miles, from Londinium, via the fortified settlements of Pontes, Calleva Atrebatum and finally, Sadunum.

Once on the main road, it was the usual, buttock-pounding, dust-stinging gallop, with breaks at the imperial way-stations to change horses and get food. Travelling by lightning is never comfortable, and the Britannic countryside is dismal. It is empty, wild and green and damp, with not a bridge or a tower, or even so much as a brick, to be seen for miles but only wilderness and desolation. At least we had plenty of time to talk.

'Go on then,' said Morganus, once we were under way. 'What's in the letter?'

I looked down at the scroll.

'It is indeed a letter about the lions of North Africa, but the writer has added something about Lixus.' I looked at Morganus. 'Optio Silvius is a really good man. He deserves promotion.'

'I agree,' said Morganus. 'He'll be Centurion Silvius when we get back!'

'Good,' I said, and looked at the letter. 'It's from an educated man, someone who knew Hebrew, and who signs himself Iacosheth the Scholar.'

'Another Jew?' he said.

'No,' 'I said, 'Iacosheth isn't a Jewish name, and Assyrians and Canaanites sometimes write in Hebrew, because they know Hebrew, and it's more widely understood than their own languages.'

'Is it?'

'Yes.'

'So could Pliny read Hebrew?'

'I don't know, but he could always get it translated.'

'So what's in the letter?'

'I think Iacosheth knew Pliny well,' I said, 'and was used to sending him information on plants, animals and geography, which are subjects Pliny liked. So the letter is about lions, mostly, but here,' I pointed to a place in the letter where the ink colour changed, 'I think he left the letter a while, and then started again, because he had something far more serious to write about. I think the letter was written on a ship sailing out of the port of Lixus.'

'Go on, read it!' said Morganus. So I did, starting at the place where the ink colour changed, and giving my best effort at translation.

> *'The terrible events of recent days have reached dreadful conclusions. The blame will fall on the Fourth Regiment of Flavensi Auxiliaries, but how else could they have acted? The city was given over to riot by Rabbi Jesus Jews, whose faith was being suppressed because they would not pray to the Emperor's divine spirit. The Fourth Flavensi were ordered to put them to the*

sword, but refused because they too are Rabbi Jesus Jews, and so the governor threatened to send to Rome for troops to enforce decimation on the Flavensi.'

I looked up, 'Decimation?' I said,. 'That's killing one in ten of them isn't it?'

'Yes,' said Morganus, 'it's the ultimate military disgrace. The unit has to draw lots, and one in ten are killed by their own comrades. It's a dreadful thing: shocking! But go on, what happened next?'

So I read on:

'Then the governor was killed with all his staff, while trying to reason with the mob, and the mob set on fire the basilica, the temple of The Holy Triad, the tax office and Government House with all its records. Thus the Flavensi were left defending the city treasury, and fearing decimation. In this predicament they took counsel with one another, and carrying their women with them, and much gold from the treasury, they fled the city in ships containing rich cargo, including spices, corn, blank bronze diplomas and silks of China. The mariners were pressed into service, and I myself saw these ships go by, passing my own outbound vessel, while the city burned behind us. All the world will blame the Flavensi, but I know them well and they are not fanatics but loyal soldiers made desperate by circumstances and seeking to reconcile faith with patriotism.

I am old and have not long to live, but never have I seen such times as these.

With this I bid you farewell,

Iacosheth the Scholar.'

I stopped reading and rolled up the scroll.

'What about that?' I said, and Morganus thought as the lighting rumbled and roared and the hoof-beats pounded and the wind stung our eyes, and we hung on to the swaying, bouncing vehicle.

'Well I can see where they got their citizenship diplomas,' he said, 'they must have stolen them out of one of the ships and filled their own names in, with the unit details and everything! And once they'd got their diplomas, they could go anywhere as free men. They could escape—really escape—if they could get away with it.'

I looked at Morganus. 'Could they?' But he just shook his head in horror.

'That's a sacrilege,' he said. 'It's appalling, it's against all the gods. Faking citizenship diplomas is against everything that holds the Empire together!'

'Could they get away with it?' I repeated. 'Didn't you say that details have to be sent back to Rome and inscribed on… on… where was it?'

Morganus shook his head in sorrow and faced a truth that he most heartily detested.

'Yes,' he said, 'they *could* probably get away with it, because all the names and unit details go on master plates,' he said, 'fixed to the wall outside the temple of the deified Augustus in Rome. I've seen them, and there's rows of them. But nobody ever checks, because nobody would ever try to fake citizenship. It's unthinkable. Nobody would do it! '

'But someone did,' I said, 'and besides that all the Lixus city records were destroyed, which—if anyone ever wondered—would explain why no details were sent to Rome. And the governor of Lixus presumably never wrote to Rome about decimation, because he got killed.'

'And the governor of Britannia,' said Morganus, 'thought he was blessed by the gods when a full regiment of trained Roman soldiers arrived looking for settlement, just after the Boudicca rebellion. So he wouldn't have looked too hard, even if he had doubted that they were citizens.' Morganus thought further and came up with an ever deeper realisation. 'Come to that,' he said, 'I doubt that they'd have looked too hard even in Rome. Not when a province like Britannia was at risk, and they had the chance of planting a veteran's colony right where it was needed.'

I nodded in agreement. 'They were rich, too,' I said, 'since they'd looted the Lixus treasury.' I frowned. 'I know they're prosperous at Flavensum, but I wonder if some of the money they're spending on the governor's games originally came from Lixus? Because if it did, then it's stolen money. It's tainted money.'

'Hmm,' said Morganus. 'Petros won't like that and neither will His Grace the Governor.'

'So we'd better keep that thought a secret too,' I said, and Morganus frowned.

'I don't like all this secrecy,' he said, 'all these plots and secrets. It's not *army*, it's not *Roman*.'

'Huh!' I said. 'Tell that to the ghost of Caligula!'

He just looked at me and shook his head. I could see what he was thinking:

'Why do you have to say these things?' But the bodyguards sniggered. I heard them.

After that the journey was uncomfortable and boring, with the boredom accentuated by the fact that Roman roads are so uncompromisingly straight, and routinely cleared of trees and brushwood for a hundred paces on either side, to prevent ambush. So there is not even the relief from tedium that comes from driving round some hill, swamp or forest, with the expectation of a new prospect opening up before the traveller's eyes. It is just one, long gallop down a ruler-straight road. Even the ten-mile way-stations were boring, because they were all the same, laid out on an identical pattern of stables, canteen, latrines, baths and accommodation. They were all the same because they were army built, and the Roman army builds by the rule book. But they were efficient, right down to the taking off and putting on of teams of horses, and the speed with which food and drink was consumed, and we were climbing up for another dash down the road.

But I hesitate to complain, because we achieved the astonishing feat of going in eight hours a distance equal to several days' march for the infantry.

Sadunum, when we reached it, was a miserable place in the great western plain which unlike most of Britannia, is not covered in forest but is sparse, rocky land open to sight for mile after mile. It was supposedly a market town, clustered along the Great West Road in miserable thatched houses, many of them Celtic round-houses, with fields behind them, marked out with dry stone walls. In addition there were a few Romanised buildings that were taverns, shops and brothels, because the town could not have existed at all except for the presence of the military camp placed there to secure the region. The camp was a fully-fortified, permanent structure, with walls, gates and artillery, and it was manned by the Fourth Cohort of the Second Legion, a force of just nearly 600 legionaries, accompanied by a regiment of auxiliary cavalry and five hundred horses. There were more men in the fort than in the town, and the town was merely a place where the soldiers spent their leisure time and money.

So our wheels rumbled over the drawbridge and we came to a halt before the open gates, with the thickness of the walls on either side of us, and a fighting platform over our heads, which linked the wall walkways on either side, giving the defenders the easy opportunity to drop stone shot and javelins on the heads of attackers. There we stopped as the gate guard of six men came forward, behind their shields, in slippery wet, glistening armour in the slippery wet Britannic drizzle, and they looked up at us with the damp dripping off their centurion's horse-hair crest. The centurion spoke first.

'I give you good day, Honoured Sir,,' he said and saluted.

'I give you good day, centurion,' said Morganus.

'Have I the honour to address the valiant Morganus, Spear of the Twentieth?' said the centurion, in an acutely-abbreviated address to an officer of such rank.

'I am First Javelin of the Twentieth,' said Morganus.

'We were warned to expect you, Honoured Sir,' said the centurion, 'and may all the gods forgive us for not turning out the cohort in welcome, but we've got to take you straight to the Tribune, who has special orders for Your Honour.' He looked up at us with an expression that puzzled me at first. But then I realized that it was a mixture of sorrow and grief, over the nature of those special orders and what they would mean for the honoured Morganus. Perhaps the centurion even sorrowed over myself?

But I doubt it. He never even looked at me.

Chapter 29

The Tribune's office was a miserable place. Not that it was shabby or cramped, because it was stone-built, roofed with heavy timbers and neat and tight and dry. But the grey drizzle dripped outside the half-open, unglazed windows and a grey wind rattled the shutters, and the grey Britannic sky peered in at us in all its Celtic gloom. At least that's how it seemed to me, though perhaps my mind was dwelling on our purpose in being here.

But the Tribune was bright enough: Marcus Aurelius Alba of the Second Legion. He was a rare example of a Roman aristocrat—he was a knight. who had found that he liked the legions so much that he made them his career. He was a large, cheerful man in his forties; tall, thick built and with heavy hands. He was well past the age when his contemporaries had all gone back to Rome and into business or politics, and was obviously happy in his work. He was a serious soldier, and was working with his orderly clerks on cohort business when Morganus and I and the bodyguards were shown in. As we entered he leapt to his feet, pushed away his pen and documents, stepped out from his desk towards Morganus, and came to attention. He clicked his heels.

'Leonius Morganus Fortis Victrix!' he said, and bowed. 'I give you good day, and offer every service that my command can deliver!'

He said it with feeling, but he said it with a smile because while he admired Morganus as much as any spotty young officer straight off the Dubris ferry, he was a mature man who kept his dignity and did not suffer a fit of the vapours at meeting one of the army's heroes. I liked him at once. I liked him a lot, especially as he immediately turned to me and held out his hand. 'Ikaros of Apollonis,' he said, 'the engineer and reader of minds! I rejoice to meet you, since any comrade of his honour,' he bowed again to Morganus, 'is welcome in my cohort and in my house.'

So we shook hands, made polite talk, and there was much bustling and clearing of desks, and bringing in of chairs and little tables for the usual cakes and wine, and Alba's senior officers were summoned to join us, and the shutters closed when the wind blew in the rain. So Morganus and I sat opposite Tribune Alba, while centurions marched into the room and lined up, marking time—knees up, knees down—beside the bodyguards and clerks. Just as they stamped to attention, I helped myself to the wine which, by the gracious forethought of Alba, was served in large cups and was blessedly warm. Indeed his first words as we sat down showed his kind consideration.

'Honoured Sir,' he said to Morganus, 'I shall be as brief as I can because I don't doubt that your bones are aching for a bath after your journey.'

'Indeed they are,' said Morganus. 'It must be my age!'

'Oh no!' said everyone, and laughed politely.

But then Alba got to work. He reached out a hand to a clerk, who stepped smartly forward and put a scroll into his hands, without even being told which one. Alba gave Morganus the scroll and sat back.

'Those are sealed orders for Your Honour,' he explained, then he looked at me, 'and forYour Worship too. But I know what's in them because in this fort,' he waved a hand to encompass everything around him, 'my men are specially trained, and there are too many involved in what we do, for me to keep secrets. And anyway, I don't like secrets because we work better as a team if we all know what we're doing.'

'Quite right too!' said Morganus, emphatically. 'I won't have secrets kept from anyone under my command!' He and Alba beamed at one another. 'So,' said Morganus, 'let's get on with it. How do we arrange this meeting with...' he hesitated like a horse facing a jump, 'Maligoterix?'

Everyone blinked at the name, and nailed boots shifted uneasily, as if a large and hideous spider had suddenly appeared. But Alba looked steadily at Morganus

'Well spoken, Your Honour,' he said, 'and boldly spoken.'

'So what do we do?' said Morganus.

'First I must introduce you to someone you already know,' said Alba, 'a specialist even among specialists!' He beckoned to one of the centurions, who stood forward and took off his helmet, then saluted. He grinned at Morganus and me, and we smiled because neither of us had recognised him in armour and helmet. He was Centurion Gallus, commander of Troop Four, Regiment Three of the Silesian Slingers, immaculate in gleaming steel, shiny brass and transverse plume. But he was still barefoot, still a follower of Paragh the slinger.

'Huh,' said Morganus, 'nice turnout, centurion. Last time we saw you, you looked like a bundle of rags!'

Everyone laughed and Gallus nodded.

'It'll be a bundle of rags again tomorrow, Honoured Sir, gods willing!'

'Oh?' said Morganus.

'Yes,' said Alba, 'because this is what we do here.' He leaned forward, and despite his dislike of secrets, he unconsciously lowered his voice. 'We're the unit that keeps watch on the Stone-Ring.'

'The Ti Carregmawr?' said Morganus.

'Yes!' said Alba, 'the Ti Carregmawr. We're here to prevent the tribes from using it as a religious rallying point. As long as we are here in force, they can't hold ceremonies in the stones. We send in scouts to keep watch, and we send them at varied times so the Celts don't know when they're coming, though they know we're watching. We don't occupy the circle, or try to knock it down. It's a sort of agreement. We think—in fact we know—that if we flattened the circle or took it, then every tribe in Britannia would rise in rebellion. Do you understand, Honoured Sir? It's deeply sacred to them.'

'Yes,' said Morganus,' I understand.

'So,' said Alba, 'we're here for that, and for something more, because we act for Petros of Athens. We are the last line in the chain whereby...' and he paused, just as Morganus had paused before admitting a dangerous truth, 'we are the last line in the chain whereby Petros communicates with the druids, and we pass messages to and fro. My men meet the druids' men in the Stone-Ring. And that's what we do.'

Alba paused, to see how this outright admission of death-sentence treason would be received by Morganus. Morganus looked at me, and I nodded, and he looked back at Alba.

'Well that's also well spoken, Marcus Aurelius Alba,' he said, 'and boldly spoken too, though my comrade and I had worked out for ourselves that something like this was going on and we're not really surprised. So let's raise our standards and march forward!' He smiled, 'Go on, Tribune: tell me how we come face-to-face with Maligoterix.'

There was a huge sigh of relief in the room. The centurions nodded to one another, and stood easier, and Alba shook hands with Morganus.

'Thank you for that, Honoured Sir,' he said, and then he became serious. 'But *you* don't come face-to-face with him. Not you Your Honour. You don't, but Ikaros of Apollonis *does*. Maligoterix has asked for him, and only him, and won't meet anyone else.'

Everyone looked at me. It was an uncanny moment.

It was uncanny, but not as uncanny as the moment—the next day, late in the afternoon—when I was to go forward on my own, leaving Morganus and the bodyguards, and Centurion Gallus and his slingers, and a squadron of auxiliary cavalry, to walk towards past the Stone-Ring, Ti Carregmawr, across the western plain with the sun low in the sky. I comforted myself that at least there was clear sight to the horizon all around, so I should be able to see danger coming. At least, that is what I thought before Gallus spoke.

He stood beside me in his ragged tunic and turban, bare-armed and barefoot again, seeming impervious to the cold wind, though at least the drizzle had ceased. He wore a sword this time, slung on an army baldric, while his barbarian Silesians stood around us on either side. They formed no ranks as legionaries do, but each one took ground of his choice, each one with sling in hand, and a pouch of shot—murderous lead this time—and each with an army dirk at his belt. But they wore no swords, because those got in the way of a slinger's movements.

They made a strange contrast to Morganus and the bodyguards, in their gleaming armour, and boots and helmets. The Silesians did not look Roman at all, but their animal senses and silent movement gave comfort to men in fear of an ambush. Indeed they looked more animal that the horses of the cavalry squadron. A troop of horse is never quite still, and those behind us shuffled and nudged, and spoke to each other in whispers and snorts, and a troop of horse will take fright and give warning if wolves or lions are about. But they don't scan the horizon with such purpose as the Silesian slingers, and they don't sniff the wind to catch scent and listen to every mouse that crept.

But Gallus was talking.

'You have to be careful, see?' he said, and pointed. 'You see that little mound over there? The one what looks small?'

'Yes,' I said.

'Yes,' said Morganus.

'Well it ain't small, see?' said Gallus. 'It's big. It's big enough for men to hide behind. It's bigger than it looks, see? 'Cos it's further away than it looks. And it's all like that, see? The ground goes up and down all round, and it's never quite flat, though it looks like it's flat, but it ain't, see?

'I see,' I said.

'And this is a far as we go on horses, because *them* buggers they're over there somewhere, on their way here, see?'

'You mean the druids?'

'Yeah. And it's Maligoterix himself this time. The biggest bugger of all! Coming here.'

'We hope so,' I said.

'Oh he'll be here,' said Gallus. 'You can't make the sods do anything they don't want to do, but if they do want something, then they come after it and you can't soddin' stop them!'

'And what do they want this time?' I said.

'Ah!' said Gallus, 'Ah! Well… well… that would be… that would be… *you*, Your Worship. He wants you. Maligoterix wants you… I mean he wants to speak to you.'

'I don't like this,' said Morganus, 'I'm going with you.'

'Us too!' said the bodyguards.

'Quite right lads!' said Morganus. 'We go together!'

'Ah!' said Gallus, 'I mean, I mean, you *can't,* most Honoured and Respected Sir.'

'What?' said Morganus, 'What did you say to me?'

Gallus bowed low. His Silesians copied him. They all bowed to Morganus.

'It's in the sealed orders, most Honoured and Respected Sir,' said Gallus, 'it's orders signed by the Legate and the Governor,' and he quoted, '*you will strictly and scrupulously obey the advice of the officer commanding the troops on the spot and take that advice as imperial command.'* Gallus had trouble pronouncing the word *scrupulously*, but he got through his recitation and stood to attention. His men copied his example and they too stood to attention and everyone looked at Morganus.

'Jupiter, Juno and Minerva!' he said.

'You can't go, Honoured Sir,' said Gallus, ''cos if the sods see you coming, they'll run. There won't be no meeting at all, see?'

I nodded. It was obvious sense.

'Thanks for the offer,' I said to Morganus, 'but it's got to be just me. Centurion Gallus is right.'

'Huh!' said Morganus, and turned to Gallus. 'Can we trust him? Can we trust Maligoterix?'

'This is a sacred truce,' said Gallus. 'They've sworn by their gods, and we've sworn by ours. There's to be no arms carried forward and no…' he stopped speaking, stared into the distance and pointed. 'There they are,' he said, 'that's them! They've come.'

We looked where he pointed and saw horses on the skyline, several dozen of them. They were coming slowly forward. 'Well that's all right, then,' said Gallus, 'at least the sods have turned up, and they've come as agreed from the north, and we've come from the south, so nobody's got the sun in his eyes as it's going down, and we're all equally lit, with the big stones on *our* left, and *their* right.'

He spoke on and on, because he was nervous, and he repeated a warning he'd already given me hours ago, back at the fort, thus he looked at the sinking sun and frowned. 'It has to be near sunset, see Your Worship? ''cos that's sacred to the buggers. But *we* won't have that 'cos it gets dark quick and you can't see the buggers! So we meet late in the day to keep *them* a bit happy, and to give *us* a bit of light. And we make sure to get out and away before it's proper dark!' He looked at me. 'So you'll do that, Your Worship, won't you? You'll get out quick before it's dark? Like we said?'

I said yes. I said yes with more emphasis than ever in all my life before, because—by all the gods of Olympus—my determination to get out and away before dark was bigger than the mountain of Olympus itself.

'What do we do now?' I asked.

'We go forward,' said Gallus. 'They've seen us, and we've seen them.'

'Then?' I said.

'The terms of agreement are, that as soon as the riders see one another, which is now, the riders stop. Then the agent of meeting…'

'Agent of meeting?'

'Yeah,' he said, 'agent of meeting. That's what we call the poor sod who goes forward,' he corrected himself instantly, 'I mean, I mean the *volunteer*, 'cos he's always a volunteer.'

'Including me?' I said.

'Ah… yes… well… I mean…'

'Never mind,' I said. 'I hereby volunteer.'

'Very kind of you, Your Honour. Spoken like an officer and a gentleman.'

'Go on,' I said, 'then what?'

'Well. The agent of meeting, which is you, Your Worship - goes forward with men on foot behind him, which is me and my lads, and on *their* side one of theirs comes forward with warriors behind *him*, see?'

'Yes.'

'And we come with you until we are two bow-shots apart from the other buggers, and then *we* stop and *you* go forward alone, and we're bound by sacred oath not to come with you, and their lot are bound just the same, and they can't come forward with their man either, see?'

'I see,' I said. 'Then shall we go?'

So we did. Gallus, Morganus, the bodyguards and I went forward over the thin grass, the uneven rocks and the undulating ground. The Silesian slingers came with us, though you could not hear them at all, and hardly saw them in their tribal costume against a green background, as they spread out with each man following his own path. Gallus gave some more advice as we went.

'Pick your ground if you can, Your Worship,' he said. 'You'll see the other bugger coming: Maligoterix, that is.' He paused and looked at me. 'You know him, don't you? You've met him.'

'Yes,' I said.

'Yes,' said Morganus. 'We've had that pleasure.'

'So you'd recognise him?' said Gallus.

'Yes,' I said.

'Good,' said Gallus, ''cos if it's anyone else, then you come back quick, 'cos that means they've broke faith, see?'

'Yes,' I said.

'Right,' said Gallus, 'so you pick your ground. You pick somewhere as flat as possible, where no bugger can be laying in wait, see?'

'Why?' I said. 'Don't you trust them? What about the sacred oaths?'

'Well… well, that's all very fine, oaths and gods, but you can never trust the buggers really, because they soddin' well hate us, and they'll soddin' well never forgive us for being here, see?'

'Oh,' I said, and we walked forward until, coming over a mound, we saw a company of Celts coming towards us on foot. They were several hundred paces off, but it was easy to see the warriors with their long shields and elaborate Celtic helmets. It was equally easy to see a man with long white hair and a white robe, who led them.

'That's him!' said Morganus. 'Maligoterix.'

'Is it?' said Gallus. 'I've never met him. Is he the one in white?'

'Yes,' I said, 'he has no colour in his hair or eyes. He looks old, but he isn't. He's strong and fit.'

As we spoke, the distant figure of Maligoterix raised an arm and the Celtic warriors stood fast. Gallus likewise raised his arm, and our company halted.

'This is it then, Your Worshhip,' said Gallus. 'We stop here.' And he looked at me and did his best to smile. 'It's down to you now, Your Worship, and I'm saying—for me and my lads—that we know what *that* bugger can do,' he pointed at Maligoterix, 'so we all think that you are a very brave man indeed.'

'Thank you,' I said, because I supposed that he was paying me a compliment. But if so, I wished that he had chosen better words.

I would have gone forward at once because it is best not to dither in such matters, but Morganus stopped me.

'I've got two things for you before you go,' he said, and unbuckled his dirk—sheath and all—from his harness and gave it to me. 'Shove this under your tunic,' he said, 'it's got an edge like a razor and a point like a needle.'

'Honoured sir!' said Gallus. 'We've sworn not to go forward with arms!'

'*You* may have,' said Morganus, 'but I haven't, and neither has the Greek gentleman.'

'Oh,' said Gallus, 'I suppose that's all right, then.'

'What's the second thing?' I said to Morganus.

'It's this,' he said, and took my hand. 'It's something to tell Maligoterix,' and he looked at me, grim-faced. 'You tell that druid bastard in the name of the Lord Mithras, that if you don't come back fit and well, then I personally will lead the Twentieth Legion—horse, foot and artillery—into the client kingdom of the Regni, and slaughter every living thing there, including him. You tell him that.'

'What about the Legate?' I said, 'And Rome? What would they say if you did that?'

'Huh!' he said. 'What would The-Lady-my-Wife say if I *didn't*?'

I tried to laugh. Perhaps I did. Then I went forward alone.

Chapter 30

I left my comrades and walked across the plain. It was windy and the ground was rough. It is strange what snatches attention when man is under stress, thus a criminal being sentenced in court might notice a fly on the wall behind the judge. So I stopped to examine a rock that been cracked by the weather to reveal—half buried in its stony substance—a thing, an object, a something, that looked like a great snail, two feet across. I had seen such things before. Perhaps they are creatures turned into stone by the gods? So I wondered if this one had ever lived. But then, being otherwise occupied, I put this puzzle alongside steam-powered machines in that part of my mind where I lodge matters which, alas, I will never pursue.

So I walked on and saw Maligoterix a hundred paces off, coming towards me and going up and down with the terrain, sometimes disappearing into a hollow then rising again, while far away the small figures of his warriors stood with standards raised above them. I stepped out, wondering what I was doing here. Why was I risking death or torture? So I looked at Maligoterix, who nodded in recognition even so far off, and I assembled the questions that I needed to ask.

What was the nature of the fighting between the druids that Maligoterix had won? Why had Maligoterix ordered the killing of Celsus, Tadaaki and myself? Why did the duovirs of Flavensum, Bethsidus and Solis, hate one another? What was their argument on 'synagogue business'? And why precisely was Gershom killed? Was it just to destroy Pliny's letter revealing that the men of Flavensum were not citizens?

So I was here to get answers, because Maligoterix was the best qualified person in all Britannia to speak for the druids, and I hoped that his vast spy network, with its Celtic informers and messenger pigeons, might also have told him what was going on in Flavensum. After all, there were slaves in Flavensum: Celtic slaves, every one of whom would know someone, who knew someone, who spoke to the druids.

Which left two more, closely related, questions. Why did I have any hope that Maligoterix would tell me anything at all? And why did he want to see me? In fact, I was sure that I already knew the answer to both questions, and the answer was the reason why I was so very afraid as we finally came face-to-face. And it was literally that, since different cultures have different ideas of the proper distance at which to hold conversation, and while Greeks and Romans keep a dignified distance, Celts do not. Among the Celts, one man stands so close to another as to smell his breath, feel the warmth of his body and almost touch noses. It was uncomfortable for me, and Maligoterix knew it. But I could not back off. That would mean defeat before ever a word was spoken.

Then concentration drove away fear.

Maligoterix was about thirty-five years old: vigorous, fit, and as tall as me. He had white hair, white skin and the pink eyes of the albino. He wore a long robe, bound with rope at the waist and dirty at the hem where it had trailed in the grass, and his face was profound with intelligence. He was a formidable man, confident, arrogant and dominating. He was master of many languages and many mysteries, and he was at least as clever as me.

He was also a dedicated fanatic, bred up to defy Rome and to exalt the power of the druidic faith. He was a man with whom Rome could never, never, *never* negotiate, because he was a religious mystic exalted by the promise of paradise and ruled by the dread of damnation. He was also a man who killed his enemies hideously: by skinning, roasting, or drawing out the bowels. He was an aggressive user of violence who instinctively began our conversation with an insult.

'Ikaros of Apollonis,' he said, in Athenian Greek, 'that dog on a Roman string, who pretends to be an engineer, a surgeon, and a reader of minds.'

So I did my best in reply.

'Maligoterix,' I said, 'who could not hypnotise a dog on a string.' That was true. During our last meeting, he had tried his hypnosis on me, and failed.

'Huh!' he said, and frowned, because Celts do not hide emotion as Romans do. He was annoyed. I had scored a hit. But that sent our conversation skidding off into a direction that I had not planned, and neither had he, because we began to compete in knowledge.

At first this was merely trivial, but in the end I think that it was the reason why he told me so much. Also, and in my vanity I believed that he feared my investigations and that he certainly feared Greek learning. He was therefore anxious to prove that he knew greater things than I did.

'What do you know?' he said, 'with your machines and your science?'

'I know that the earth is a sphere,' I said, 'and I can calculate its diameter precisely.'

'That does not impress,' he said, 'we know that. The earth is centre of the universe and its servant the sun goes around it.'

'No,' I said, 'the astronomers of my city have proved that the sun is fixed and the earth moves around it.'

'Blasphemy!' he said. 'Blasphemy and nonsense!'

'No,' I said. 'Look into my eyes, druid, because you know that I read minds.'

'So do I,' he said.

'So much the better, ' I said, because I could see that he was telling the truth. This remarkable man, with his many talents, had the same gift that I had. That was shocking, but useful. I could use that against him. 'So,' I said, 'You can look a man in the eyes and tell if he speaks truth or lies.'

The pink eyes blinked. He nodded so slightly that only I could have seen it. 'Then look me in the eyes,' I said, 'and see that *I* am telling the truth. The earth goes round the sun! It is fact. It is truth.'

The pink eyes blinked again. The pale lips worked. His tongue swept across them. He was impressed, but swiftly recovered.

'What does that matter,' he said, 'when I know that the wife of Morganus thinks you are her son? She cuts your hair, her daughters clean your boots and she weeps in fear if you are harmed,' he touched my brow with a finger, 'I read all that in your mind,' he said.

Thus I too was impressed. I was impressed and uneasy at his knowledge of such intimate matters. Had he read that from my mind? Judging by the crafty look on his face, I thought not. So I responded accordingly.

'You picked that out of slave gossip,' I said, 'one of the girls told some legionary who told someone in the town, and your spies heard it.'

He laughed.

'Is that what you think? Do you think we need slave gossip?' He pointed to the great stones of Ti Carregmawr. 'We, whose ancestors raised those sacred stones by the unaided power of the spirit?'

'But they didn't' I said. 'You should read *The History of the Pretanic Isles* by Pythaes of Massalia. He visited Britannia four hundred years ago, and states clearly that the stone circle was already here. But he makes no mention of druids. There *were* no druids in those days, so whoever built that circle, it was certainly not you druids!'

That hit like a forty-pound shot from the siege artillery. He obviously knew that what I had said was true, and a great druidic lie was thereby exposed, causing Maligoterix to lose his temper. So he stamped and ranted, and in his ranting he struck back hard. He stabbed into my soul.

'What are you?' he said, 'Ikaros of the broken city, the city the Romans took? Ikaros who did not fall in the battle? Ikaros who was shamefully made a slave?' He jabbed a finger into my chest. 'I know why you did not die! And I know why, and how, your wife and children died!'

I will not say more, because some things are too painful to write down. But Maligoterix gave every detail concerning the fall of Apollonis and death of my family. He gave such precise and accurate detail as to make me fear that he really *was* looking into my mind. Either that, or he was looking into the past by druidic magic and Morganus was right in that respect, after all.

Thus I was wounded indeed. I was badly wounded. But I thought of Morganus, who would never give up or surrender, because that is what Romans are like. I thought of him, and his -wife, and I fought back in their name.

'And I know why you want me here,' I said. 'I discovered that by Greek intellect. So you can safely tell me the few things I have not already found out for myself. So what are you druids doing to one another and the governor's games? Why did you have men killed? What do you know of Flavensum?'

He laughed at that. He actually laughed.

'Clever little Greek!' he said. 'Yes, I can tell you. Why not? It was part of the pleasure of bringing you here, that I could spit in your face,' which he did, then and there, and the spittle ran down my nose such that in anger I slid my hand into my tunic for Morganus' dirk.

'Ah!' he said, feeling my movement, 'so you came armed? You broke faith?' He spread his arms wide. 'So strike, little Greek! Strike if you will. I will not stop you.'

That was the power of the man. He made no attempt to grapple, no attempt at self-defence. He stood totally vulnerable and totally confident in his belief that I was so anxious to hear what he would say, that I would do him no harm. Perhaps he really did read my mind. How should I know? How should *anyone* know? Sometimes I despair of reason. But I let go of the dirk hilt, and stood still.

'Good!' he said. 'Now listen to me, little Greek, because you are a festering splinter under my thumbnail. You are an ache in my head and a pain in my liver. You are troublesome in your investigations. You never cease digging and searching, and you have interfered with my plans.'

I took that as a great compliment. My vanity was not vanity after all.

'Hence the four farmers of my tribe that I sent after you,' he continued, 'and as for Celsus, he was killed to insult your Roman games. He was killed by a woman we had long since turned, in preparation for some future need,' he smiled, 'just as we have turned others, and are always turning more, awaiting the right moment to use them in our struggle against Rome.'

'And Tadaaki?' I said.

'That was more interesting,' he smiled, 'has your Greek cunning told you that we are in contact with the men of Flavensum?' I must have shown surprise. 'Ah!' he said, 'I see you did not know that!' He shook his head. 'Such failing in your Greek intellect,' and he laughed. 'We know everything that goes on in Flavensum, including the synagogue dispute about damnation and the rivalry between Bethsidus and Solis. And so we approached Solis. We put ideas into his head. Ideas about the governor's games.'

'You knew about the games?'

'Oh yes. We knew long before anyone else.'

'And so?'

'We came to agreement with Solis,' he said. 'Each side would show the other its determination. Each side would make blood sacrifice.'

'Go on,' I said, and Maligoterix shrugged.

'Thus Solis killed Gershom. He sent young men to do the work.'

'Including the son of Bethsidus?' I said.

'Especially the son of Bethsidus, because he holds his own father in contempt and sought atonement.'

'And why did Solis kill Gershom?' I said.

'Because of you, little Greek. Solis knew that Gershom had a certain letter because Bethsidus found the letter in Gershom's library and warned the elite of Flavensum that it was there.'

'You mean Pliny's letter that confirms the Flavensum men are not Roman citizens?'

'Yes,' he said, 'but the elite of Flavensum believed Gershom would never read it.' He smiled. 'Gershom read very few of his books. Did you know that?'

'Yes,' I said, 'or at least I guessed it.

'How clever of you! But then you came along and were shown Gershom's library, and *you* might well have read the letter, and therefore Solis judged it necessary to remove the letter and kill Gershom, and send a signal to me in blood, putting Solis' signature to our bargain.'

'What about Tadaaki?'

'That was my return signal to Solis. My signal in blood. My signal that the bargain was made, and that I would speak to the tribes.'

'About what?'

He sneered. 'About what? Do you not know?'

'No.'

'Then why do you think that I have waged war within the tribal kingdoms? Why do you think that I have removed all voices other than my own?'

'Gods of Olympus,' I said, 'you want to raise the tribes. All of them!'

'Whatever else should I do? he said. 'Whatever else in the name of my faith, my people and my blood? And whatever else should I do with those druids—supposed brothers within the faith—who spoke against me, in fear of the Roman army?'

'Is that why the tribes are massed outside Londinium?' I said, and he nodded and stepped back a little.

'Wait,' he said, 'be patient an instant, because I have to untie this,' and his fingers worked on the knot that fastened the rope holding his robe in place.'

'What are you doing?' I said, and reached for the dirk.

'That will not help you,' he said, and threw aside the rope and pulled off his robe, and held it draped in his arms. He wore a short tunic under the robe: a tunic that left his legs free.

'The tribes are awaiting a signal,' he said. 'The signal to rise. The signal will be given as the chariot races begin. Then the tribes shall rise…' he hesitated and frowned: tiny gestures, but I saw them, 'as they must!'

But as he spoke, I saw doubt in his eyes.

'You are unsure!' I said.

'I am not!'

'Yes you are. You are not sure the tribes will rise.'

'Only because false and treacherous druids have spoken against me.'

'All of whom are now dead?'

'All that I could reach!' he said, then he struggled with painful thoughts. 'Bah!' he said, why should I not tell you all? Yes! The matter is finely poised. Some druids still speak against outright rebellion, as do some tribal leaders because they fear the Roman army. There are still great arguments within the tribes. But if the tribes see the signal, they will rise.'

'And if they do *not* see the signal?'

He said nothing, so I answered for him,.'Then they will not rise,' I said. He shrugged. 'Why are you are telling me this?' I said, though I already knew the answer.

'Because you will soon be dead.'

'You dare not kill me,' I said, 'because if you kill me…'

'Then Morganus will take vengeance on my tribe?' he said. 'That is a very obvious threat. Do you think that I did not guess that before I met you? I know Morganus and I know Romans. But no matter, because Rome and Morganus will soon be too busy to take revenge on anyone.'

Then he bowed to me in mockery, waved the white robe over his head, dropped it, turned his back on me without another word and ran off, back the way he had come, at great speed.

I stared at his running figure. The shadows were long. Darkness was coming and I could see the small figures of the Celtic warriors, now waving arms and jumping up and down with excitement as Maligoterix sped towards them, over rock and grass and mound. Then ghosts appeared out of the landscape around me: ghosts, monsters and demons; at least that is what they seemed in that moment, and I was frozen with fear.

Four white figures rose out of hiding, some distant, some near: young men, entirely naked, slim, muscular, lithe and shaven of hair. They glistened with grease, and were painted with streaks and whorls that contorted their features into primordial horror. They were cennad angau assassins in full war paint, each with a dagger bound to his right hand so that it could not be dropped or lost. I knew, from past experience, that each one would grapple with his victim, stabbing repeatedly until the victim was not only dead but butchered, and neither the victim nor anyone else would be able to grasp the assassin, nor pull him off, because his body was slippery with grease.

I also knew that the assassins would fight until death, and expected to die, with the promise of entry into paradise.

Thus the four rose, and silently ran towards me. They moved with such skill that Maligoterix's thudding feet still sounded in my ears while

I heard nothing of the cennad angau. So I took up the knife-fighting position, taught by the drill masters of my city. I turned sideways to the threat, crouched knees, extended my left hand in defence, and drew back my right hand, with dirk held low and ready to strike. But even as I moved, I knew that I could not defeat even one of these hand-bred, hand-trained monsters, let alone four of them. Not when they spent every hour of their lives in exercise and training and could have won laurel wreaths on the athletics field.

In the seconds before they were on me, I sorrowed over my coming death, thinking instantly of my long-dead wife and children, and of Morgana Callandra and her girls, and of Morganus, and of Allicanda. Thus at least I was glad I had enjoyed a life beyond the fall of Apollonis.

Then I tensed muscles as the nearest assassin rushed at me with frightful speed, and I reached out my left hand in futile attempt to ward off the knife... and gasped at the sound of a smack like a hammer blow and the sight of the bald head bursting open, and the cennad angau falling at my feet with the bound-on dagger just touching the toe of my left boot. His limbs twitched and the dagger scraped leather, before I stood back in horror. Then *whizz, whirr, whoosh*! Things flew through the air and two more of the cennad angau were down, one dead even before he fell, with a hole in the centre of his face, and another on his knees, bent forward, clutching at blood that spouted in jerks from the middle of his chest, over the sternum.

That left one still running. He was the one that had started from the greatest distance and he would surely have reached me and killed me, except that three figures in rag-hung tunics and turbans—Silesian slingers—ran past me as silent as the cennad angau and fought him hand to hand, falling and rolling and stabbing in a mad jumble of limbs. I ran forward with my dirk to give what help I could and—for what it is worth—I delivered some strokes. But the battle was already over. The tribal monster was near death, and his dagger hand weak and failing. I stamped on it none the less, and tried to pull the slingers clear of their victim, as other Silesians ran up and helped me.

'Gallus! Gallus!' they cried. 'Honoured Sir!' and wrung their hands and moaned then laid out two of their comrades who were dying, together with Centurion Gallus who had led the attack and was now bleeding from a great wound in his throat. Someone cut off a rag from his tunic and bound it over the wound and the rest, in their fury, stabbed daggers repeatedly into the already dead body of the cennad angau. Others held Gallus cradled in their arms, and gathered around him, chanting in their language.

I knelt beside Gallus, and he saw me.

'Didn't my lads do well?' he said. 'Didn't they, Your Worship?'

'Yes,' I said, 'and I thank you and bless you in the name of Apollo!'

'It wipes out the stain of them letting them other buggers kill one another, doesn't it, Your Worship?'

'Yes indeed,' I said.

'Did you see how good they are with lead shot? Archers couldn't have done that! Arrows don't stop you like a lead shot. Arrows just go through you.'

'Yes,' I said, 'I saw.'

'We crept up, see? 'Cos you can never trust the bastards, and we were right to creep up, weren't we, Your Worship? Never mind sacred oaths and that.'

'You were right,' I said, 'you saved my life.'

'It was the lead shot, see,' he said, 'you can't beat lead shot!' and he closed his eyes and died, and all his men wept and tore their garments in grief.

Chapter 31

The lightning swayed and lurched. Dust and grit hit our faces, thrown up by iron-shod hooves. The padded seats became hard, the driver cracked his whip and yelled at the horses.

'Goooo—on! Gooooo—on!'

The vehicle shot eastwards along the Great West Road, making dangerous speed even for a lightning. We hung on, Morganus, the bodyguards and I, as the ever-green Britannic countryside shot past the ever-boring, ever-straight Roman road, because the need for a swift journey was obvious.

'We should be all right,' said Morganus, shouting over the rumble of the wheels and the pounding of hooves. 'The games start today at dawn, with ceremonies and sacrifice in the forum and…'

'The temple of Jupiter, Juno and Minerva,' I said, finishing the sentence for him. 'You've said that ten times already.'

'Yes, and it's still true,' he said, 'and the chariot races don't start till noon…'

'And we'll be in Londinium well before that,' I said.

'Because we started before dawn,' he said.

'In the dark!' I said, and I may have said it with some irritation.

'What's the matter with you?' he asked. 'You hardly sleep anyway, so you shouldn't mind getting up in the dark, and you should be pleased you're still alive!'

'I am,' I said, 'of course I am, but I wish our cavalry had caught Maligoterix!'

'No chance of that,' he said, 'they were taking a risk going after the Celts at all. It was nearly dark when he ran off, and the Celts had horses waiting, and were off at the gallop, and it was too dangerous to pursue.' He frowned and shook his head. 'But we can't go on like this. We've got to go into these tribal client kingdoms and deal with the druids.'

'Yes,' I said, 'if we can stop an all-out tribal rebellion first!'

'Yes,' he said, 'So what's this signal they're waiting for? The signal to come out in rebellion?'

'You've asked me *that* ten times already, too.'

'Yes, but what is it? What can it be?'

'I don't know. I still don't know, but it's going to happen at the start of the chariot races, and we've already talked about what we're going to do about it.'

'Yes, but...'

We talked it over and over. Otherwise it was a typical lightning journey: fast, boring and uncomfortable. Then mid-morning, well before noon, we drove into the legionary fortress outside Londinium and stopped at the West Gate, where an optio and a small watch guard saluted us. Our horses stood trembling and sweating as we looked down the long streets of the fortress. It was empty, with only bird song and the wind to be heard.

'Everyone's gone to the races, Honoured Sir,' said the optio, 'even the clerks and engineers. Everyone! Defaulters an' all. Everyone that can carry a shield.' His men nodded, looking up at us in our vehicle. Then the optio remembered his duty.

'Where's the letter?' he said. 'The letter for His Honour?'

'Here, Sir,' said one of the men, and took a wax tablet book from his pouch.

'Give it to His Honour,' said the optio, and looked at Morganus. 'It's from his Noble Honour the Legate, Honoured Sir. It's for you.'

Morganus broke the seal, opened the book and read the letter. Then he gave it to me. It was brief:

In haste from Africanus to Morganus

If, by the grace of the gods, you come before the starting of the games, go at once to the racing stadium bringing your Greek. I have urgent need of him concerning what he may have learned in his meeting with M. The tribes have turned out in numbers beyond counting and the province is in peril. I have sent the Twentieth Legion to the stadium and summoned the Second and Eighth to come to our aid at forced march. But I fear they cannot arrive in time. The stadium guards will admit you directly to the governor's box where I will take station with Petros. May Jupiter Juno and Minerva bring you soon.

I read it, and looked at Morganus.

'We'd better go to the stadium,' I said. But Morganus was staring at the empty fortress with its un-manned ramparts.

'Where are the families,' he said to the optio, 'the officers' wives and children?'

'All gone into the city, Honoured Sir. The Governor's Guard are stood fast in Government House, to hold it at all costs, and the women and kids are in there. All of them, Honoured Sir. Your family too, Honoured Sir,' he paused, then added something that he clearly did not believe. 'They'll be safe in there.'

Morganus sighed, and turned to duty.

'We'll go to the stadium,' he said, and rapped our driver on the shoulder with his vine staff. 'Now!' he said.

'Gods of Rome!' said Morganus as we approached the racing stadium. The great Celtic encampment had vastly grown. It was city of tents, a kingdom of tents, an empire of tents that entirely surrounded the huge stadium, while facing the legionary shield walls guarding the stadium entrances, there was a colossal, tremendous crowd of Celtic women. There were no men among them, and the women stood well back from the shields, not seeking to advance or press against them, but stood swaying and singing and waving their hands in the air, while some few of them rent their clothes and shrieked and uttered curses.

The united sound of them, thousands upon thousands of voices, rose up like a great hymn to the Celtic gods, in an uncanny moan that was full of menace and power.

'What are they doing?' I said, turning to Morganus. 'Is this something religious?'

'Yes,' he said, 'I saw this years ago when I was a lad and the Celtic women advanced on us, out in front of their armies, at Anglesey. The tribal women were defying us and calling on their gods just like this,' he pointed to the vast crowd, 'and our men thought they were witches and they were so frightened they wouldn't go forward.' He shook his head. 'Not until the centurions kicked our backsides!'

'But they're not hostile,' I said, looking at the vast horde of women, 'they're not trying to get into the stadium. They're just standing there.'

'Huh!' said Morganus. 'That's worse! That means their men are already inside. The men are inside and the women are content to be out here, calling on their gods.' He leaned forwards. 'Go on!' he said to the driver, 'Take us round all this. We'll go in at the lower end, by the starting boxes.'

The lightning moved off, but we found the lower end of the stadium was also under siege by Celtic women, all heaving and moaning like the rest, though the lower end was now closed by a palisade with a gate, and a full cohort of the Twentieth was drawn up in front of it. Their tribune saw the lightning coming, and shouted orders such that a column of legionaries streamed out, pushing the women out of their way, before opening up to form a clear path for our lightning, then neatly closing up behind us, and reforming in front of the rest of the cohort. There they marked time, dressing their line for straightness, because that—before all else—is what Romans do.

So we climbed down, surrounded by lines of shields, and not even cramped or hustled. But we had to shout over the noise. The Tribune greeted Morganus with the usual bow. He was Terentius, senior tribune of the Twentieth, who had supervised the building of the stadium.

'Honoured Sir!' said Terentius.

'Honoured and Noble Sir!' said Morganus, and pointed to the women, now yelling and screaming out beyond the shields.

'I see that you have visitors,' said Morganus, and Terentius smiled.

'Yes,' he said. 'it must be ladies' day.' It was another display of doing what Romans do: Roman officers, that is. They were both being very cool, very calm and setting a good example to the men. I must admit that we Greeks would have shown more emotion. I certainly would. But they did not.

'What do you think about all this?' said Morganus, as if asking about the weather.

'I think I'd rather be in Rome,' said Terentius, 'visiting the baths.' They both laughed. 'And now, Honoured Sir, I am under orders to take you to His Grace the Governor, and His Noble Honour theLegate.'

'Proceed!' said Morganus and Roman efficiency took over as we went at the double, past the starting boxes, where a considerable body of young, bearded men was gathered. 'Ah,' said Morganus to Terentius. 'Can we have a word as we go?'

'Of course,' said Terentius and the two spoke steadily and urgently as we made our way along corridors and up staircases on the way to the governor's box, passing many sentries who saluted and stamped and let us through.

'Yes,' said Terentius, in response to what Morganus said, and Oh?' and 'indeed,' and 'could I suggest . . .' and more. It was an intense conversation.

Then Terentius was off on his duties, and men of the Governor's Guard, in their antique bronze breastplates, were standing aside to let Morganus, me and the bodyguards into the governor's box, which gave a truly magnificent view of the stadium and everything in it. Though the first impact on coming out of a dark corridor and into the light was the enormous sound of a vast crowd, which rolled into our faces and battered our ears. There was so much sound that nobody in the box noticed our arrival, and we looked over the heads of the great men of the province: Teutonius the Governor, Africanus the commander of the legions, together with the Lord Chief Justice, the Fiscal Procurator, and others, all in their togas and wearing laurel wreaths. Among them, to my enormous relief, I saw Solis and Bethsidus, the two Duovirs of Flavensum.

I had hoped that Solis and Bethsidus would be here, and believed that by virtue of their rank they *must* be here in the governor's box. But hoping and believing is one thing, and actual fact is another.

So Morganus, Terentius, the bodyguards and I looked out over the laurel-draped heads, mostly grey, mostly balding, and we gaped at the awesome sight of the vast stadium, with its sanded track, lavishly-decorated spina complete with giant golden dolphins, and the truly stupendous sight of the greatest number of men that had ever been brought together in one place, in the savage island of Britannia. I stress that it was only men. They heaved and swayed, and songs rose up, and other songs rose to rival them. Men fought for the best seats and argued and yelled, while others swilled beer out of pots. More disturbingly, some white-robed figures stood up over the rest, chanting and preaching.

'Druids!' said Morganus. 'And look there, and there! Tribal chieftains with their standards! Look how the warriors are grouped round them.'

I looked, and saw that the huge crowd was divided into vast, ragged circles, presumably of different tribes, which seethed and clustered round small groups of men who waved tribal banners and symbols raised up on poles. They were there in numbers beyond belief, and I looked at the small number of Roman troops present in the aisles of the stadium, huddled back-to-back behind their shields, and outnumbered beyond hope. Morganus shook his head.

'If this goes bad, we're done for,' he said, 'It'll be hand-to-hand from the first instant, and no chance to manoeuvre. We won't even be able to throw javelins.'

'Ah,' said a voice at my elbow, 'I see you are enjoying the show.' It was Petros. He had been standing to one side of the entrance to the box and now gave a little bow to Morganus and me.. He pointed to the crowd. 'I'm sure you will have noticed,' he said, 'that only Celts are present, because the good people of Londinium took fright,' he smiled, 'they're all locked in their houses—those who haven't gone to the coast seeking passage to Gaul.'

'Oh,' I said.

'And have you noticed which Celts are *not* among us today?'

'No.'

'The kings of the client kingdoms. All seven were invited,' he pointed to empty seats behind the front row of great men, 'but they all gave excellent excuses, and promised to attend the *second* day of the games.'

'So they're waiting to see what happens?' I said.

'Like the good politicians they are,' he replied, and he beckoned to the officer of the guard in his ostrich-feather, red-plumed helmet, then pointed to the legate, Africanus. The officer nodded, interpreted Petros's gestures and went to fetch Africanus to join us. Petros smiled. 'Now who'd have thought a guards officer had the intelligence to do that?' he smiled, 'they're not picked for brains, just breeding and good looks.' He smiled and I realised that he too was being cool and calm in the face of danger.

Then Africanus joined us.

'Morganus!' he said. 'And Ikaros!' So at least he knew my name. 'What did you get out of … out of… that druid?'

'Maligoterix?' I said, and Africanus shook his head, still pretending that no Roman could deal with a druid.

'So give me your report,' he said, and Petros nodded, neither of them making any suggestion that anyone else should join us, even with the elite of the province just a few feet away. But I do not meddle in Roman politics. So I told them everything of my meeting with Maligoterix, and a summary of my investigations so far, noticing how both Africanus and Petros winced at the fact that the men of Flavensum were not Roman citizens. But Africanus instantly grasped the most important fact I had won from Maligoterix.

'So he's in doubt?' he said. 'This great and tremendous wizard has doubts? Everything didn't go his way?'

'No it didn't, Noble Sir,' I said, 'he won the actual fighting against the other druids. He killed or terrified his opponents into silence. But he didn't win their minds. He didn't persuade them. So everything depends on what happens here today.' Africans nodded. Petros nodded. So I told them what Morganus and I had agreed to do next.

Petros looked at Africanus, and would have spoken, except that a huge cheering arose from the audience, and the governor and great men all stood, and the guard officer came towards us with a bright smile.

'Honoured and Noble Sirs!' he said. 'The parade is beginning! The drivers and chariots are coming in, with the band and all their followers!' Horns and bugles sounded as he spoke, and the Governor waved benignly to the crowd.

'Yes, yes,' said Africanus, 'we'll come later.' The officer bowed, but did not move. 'Go away!' said Africanus sharply. The officer's poor little face fell, and he bowed and fell back. Then Africanus looked at me.

'What you propose is deadly dangerous,' he said, 'It's dangerous and it could go wrong.'

'Yes, Noble Sir,' I said, 'but what else can we do? By the time we knew the tribes were in Londinium in force, it was already too late to turn the army on them, and it's a hundred times too late to attack them now!'

He nodded reluctantly, and we argued some more until finally he turned to Petros. 'What do you think?' he said. 'You're Greek. You're as clever as him,' he pointed to me, 'and I know you're loyal to His Grace and the Empire.'

Petros tried to speak, but again there came such a thunder of cheering and such a brazen blare of music, that we could not hear. We turned and saw the procession moving past the governor's box, garlanded in flowers, draped in team colours, and the drivers standing in their chariots waving to the great mob, who cheered and waved in return, in a vast explosion of delight.

'Huh,' said Africanus, 'they like that! Perhaps some of them really are here for the games.' He turned again to Petros. 'What do you think?'

'I think that Ikaros of Apollonis and the Honoured Morganus are right,' Petros said. 'We have no option other than to let them do what they want.' Africanus frowned and thought, then nodded. He was a veteran soldier and accustomed to swift decisions.

'Do it!' he said to Morganus, because even in that moment he did not speak directly to me. 'Do what you judge to be best.'

'Thank you, Your Noble Honour,' I said, and Africanus took up the hem of his toga, adjusted his laurel wreath, gave a brief bow to Petros and Morganus, then walked off and sat beside the Governor, saying something—doubtless coolly and calmly—to excuse his absence.

'You'd better be right,' said Petros, 'because I've given you my backing and Africanus won't forget that.'

'So what?' I said. 'Your master is more powerful than him.'

'Only if the games succeed,' said Petros.

'If they fail now,' I said, 'you won't have to worry about Africanus. You'll have to worry about *them*,' and I pointed to the vast crowd, roaring and shouting and waving at the charioteers.

'Yes,' he said, 'so I hope you're right, because everything depends on you.' And he bowed and went to his own seat, which was beside the front row where the Governor sat, yet apart and lower, reflecting his legal status as a slave: even though Petros ran the entire province.

After that, Morganus and I had nothing to do but watch Solis, because indeed we had to do that. So we sat in the empty seats of the client kings, taking advantage of the fact that this put us right in front of Solis and Bethsidus. We nodded politely to them as we sat down, and I noted their reactions. Bethsidus was merely polite, but Solis went through spring, summer, autumn and winter in his emotions as he saw me, blinking and gaping and muttering to himself, then finally giving a great laugh.

'It's the Greek!' he said. 'The Greek who asks questions!' Then mirth shut down like a trapdoor, and his eyes rolled and his face went pale. 'And now, in God's name he shall have answers!' he said, and he raised a hand to shut out the sight of me, and ignored me thereafter to star at the parade.

So we all watched as the chariots rolled to the lower end of the stadium, and we saw the religious sacrifices on the altars of the spina, noting how the people hooted and jeered at the Roman gods and the Roman troops who were standing in the aisles of the stadium.

'Lord Mithras save us!' said Morganus, as the jeering rose louder. 'Some of them have got swords. Look!'

I did look. Yes indeed. The gleam of long blades showed here and there in the stadium. 'They're getting confident, and they're getting nasty,' he said.

But something like silence came over the crowd as the charioteers, twelve of them in their chariots, were led into the starting gates by the bearded young men of Flavensum. There were dozens and dozens of these. Then the starter on his platform—Propius of Flavensum, assisted by the idiot Grantius—waved a flag, and high up on a tower over the spina, a professional announcer with a voice like rolling thunder attempted to praise the Emperor, honour the Governor, give worship to the gods and pronounce the games open, though nobody heard him. A civilised audience would have fallen silent to listen to the announcement. But not Celts, who hated the Emperor, the Governor and the gods of Rome.

There was a sort of silence after that, because everyone realized that the race must be about to start. Then, after an enormous fanfare from trumpeters lined up just below the governor's box, there was a real and total silence such as sometimes comes over an audience, when someone begins it and everyone else falls silent in the enchantment of the moment. The Governor of Britannia, Marcus Ostorious Cerealis Teutonius, stood forward in that silence. He advanced to the balustrade at the front of the governor's box. He looked down the race track to the starter's tower and raised a hand with a large white cloth. The trumpets sounded again, and he let fall the cloth, and the audience roared and stared at the starting gates…

And nothing happened. No gates opened. No chariots emerged. Rome's greatest known spectacle was failing before our eyes.

The Governor frowned in anger. He waved at the starter's tower. Still nothing happened. The great crowd stirred and growled. The growling grew louder and louder as still the starting gates stayed shut. So the druids stood up shouting and spouting at the warriors all around them and it was obvious what they were saying, baying, yelling and screaming.

Maligoterix was right.

The sign had been given!

Rebellion must begin.

Britannia will drown in Roman blood.

Chapter 32

The Guards officer showed some initiative, entirely useless though it was. He found another white cloth and gave it to the Governor, and he yelled down at the trumpeters to blow another fanfare. So the trumpets sounded, the mob in the stadium took note and left off beating of breasts in battle fury. Instead they looked at the Governor as he stood forward with a second white cloth.

'Again!' cried the guard officer to the trumpeters. Another fanfare sounded, the Governor looked to the starting gates and raised his hand with the cloth, while an uncounted number of heads swivelled to look at the starting boxes. 'Again!' cried the officer: another fanfare, His Grace dropped the second cloth…

And nothing happened. The starting gates remained resolutely closed.

This time there was fury in the audience, and fighting broke out as Celts battered Roman shields, and the druids screamed encouragement to their men while the Roman troops hid behind shields as Celts pressed in from either side. The mob was alive in fury, a monster summoned from hell.

'What's happening at the gates?' said Morganus, standing up and staring. 'It's going to be too late. What are they doing?'

Now the Roman troops were retreating up the aisles, under command of centurions, who were trying to get out of a hopeless position, entirely surrounded by enemies. The only thing that prevented a massacre there and then, was the centurions' wise decision to give no order to draw swords, which would have provoked an ocean of blood and butchery. But Morganus thought we were done for, none the less. So he embraced me.

'Lord Mithras be with you, brother,' he said and turned to the bodyguards, 'and you too, my bulldogs!'

'Lord Mithras be with you, Honoured Sir!' they cried.

'Right,' said Morganus, 'let's fight for the Empire when the moment comes, and may all our wounds be in the front!'

'In the front, Honoured Sir!'

And then everything changed.

The starting gates suddenly opened and a dozen racing chariots, driven by the finest drivers in the world, burst out and dashed for the starting line in a thunder of hooves, a rumble of wheels and a blaze of team colours. The effect, even upon me, was magical. I had seen practice racing of a few chariots, but never the tremendous spectacle of a full dozen chariots driven full-tilt by drivers who leaned forward so far over the horses that they were almost horizontal, and who cracked whips and called out to animals exquisitely bred for the track, with such beauty in their flowing manes and tails as pierced my heart and caused my soul to rise. What joy it was to see such beasts in their glory, stretched out at full pace!

If that was the effect on *me*, how wonderfully greater it must have been upon barbarian Celts, who had never, ever, seen anything like Roman chariot racing in all their tribal, round-house, mud-spattered, colourless lives. For these savage folk, living under leaking thatch and ignorant of baths, books and wine, the colour and drama of chariot racing was so much beyond their dreams that they could help but give it attention. They could not resist the spectacle, and they did not resist, and they turned to look, and the vicious roaring of the crowd fell silent.

Yet the matter was still undecided. The druids ranted and shouted, some even fought with one another, and there were hysterical, shrieking arguments among the druids and the tribal leaders. I saw these things and may the gods forgive my pride that, as a Greek and a philosopher, I was able to tear my eyes from the racing to look into the crowd to study its behaviour. Thus the rebellion did not die in an eye-blink: not when countless thousands of men were worked up into battle fury, and not when their priests and leaders were fighting among themselves.

But as the chariots tore round the track, and the dolphins dipped, and especially when a spectacular smash occurred at the upper end turn and wheels splintered and chariots went over, and two drivers were dragged half way down the straight before cutting themselves free of the reins. Thus the entire stadium rose to its feet unable even to think of anything else.

So the fighting in the stadium stopped, and the Celts lowered their weapons and gaped in awe at the chariots. Even the druids turned to stare, as did the Roman troops, who dared to lower their shields, and look for their favourite drivers and favourite teams. Thus the great rebellion died inch by inch, moment by moment, and the adoration of the races was begun.

But the fighting was not entirely over. Not all of it and not quite, because Solis leapt to his feet and groaned like a man under torture.

'No!' he cried, 'No! No! No!' His face was white, he shook with deranged passion. He wailed and wept and fumbled in his toga, found a dagger, and staggered forward, trapping his feet in the trails of his own robe, and he pushed past Bethsidus—who shrank back as if Solis were a leper—and lunged at Teutonius, governor of Britannia.

The attack was so clumsy that even the Governor's Guard stopped it. The Guard officer and one of his men got between Solis and the Governor, and the guardsman used his shield to knock Solis down. But Solis still had his dagger and stabbed at the guardsman's leg.

'Oh! Oh! Oh!' said the guardsman, as the blood leapt from his calf, and he fell back, dropping his old-fashioned, broad-bladed spear, which the officer grabbed and used to jab down at Solis' head, with the butt end, which smashed Solis' teeth, penetrated his mouth and throat, and caused him to shriek like a pig in a slaughter house, with the officer leaning on the spear shaft in futile attempt to finish the job.

Morganus sneered in disgust.

'Take over!' he said to the bodyguards.

'Yes, Honoured Sir!' they said, and shoved the officer out of the way, while one of them took the antique spear, neatly reversed it, and sent Solis to his ancestors with a single thrust to the neck.

'Good!' said Morganus. 'That saves trial and execution for treason. Now get him out of here. Put him in the corridor behind us.'

'Yes, Honoured Sir!' said the bodyguards.

'And him, too,' said Morganus, pointing at the guardsman, still hopping about and yelping.

'Yes, Honoured Sir!' and the governor's box was cleared of corpses and the wounded at great speed, while everyone else was left wondering whether to gape at Solis' body and the blood-dripping guardsman, or the eye-drawing wonders of the racing chariots. But the chariots soon won, what with their innate fascination and the ear-pounding roars of Celtic tribesmen united in their delight at the show put on by the Romans.

Then Petros came and spoke to me and Morganus, shouting over the crowd noise.

'What happened?' he said. 'Who stopped the gates opening?'

'The Flavensum men,' I said.

'Did your men get them working?'

'Yes. Terentius's men.'

'Why did it take so long?'

'Our men were told not to move until the Flavensum men moved.'

'Dangerous! Your men might have been too late… they nearly were!'

'We had to be sure. Had to know who our enemies are. Stop this happening again.'

'Can you do that, without scandal and with nothing to damage the games or prevent his grace becoming governor of Italia?'

'I think so,' I said.

'Make it so! Do that and I'll be grateful!'

He bowed. I bowed. Then he went back to his low seat and watched the races. Everyone watched the races except me and Morganus: we two and Bethsidus, who looked around not knowing what to do or to say.

'What now, Greek?' asked Morganus.

'Can we leave two of your bulldogs here,' I said, 'so Bethsidus can't run?'

'Yes,' he said.

'Then let's you and I go and talk to Terentius. Let's find out what happened at the starting gates.'

* * *

We found Terentius behind the starting boxes, with troops guarding a miserable-looking clump of young men with beards. Other young men with beards were laid out in a neat row, neatly dead, Propius the Starter among them. Still others were being bandaged by the First Cohort's field medics. The race was nearly over, and the golden dolphins all dipped but one, but the roaring of the crowd was at deafening level. We had to shout to be heard.

'What happened?' I yelled.

'The race starter,' said Terentius, 'he wouldn't pull the trigger.'

'And?'

'They were going to kill the drivers…'

'*Kill* them?'

'Yes! And tie them to their chariots, and send them out dragging the drivers. That was the sign to the tribes! Not just the gates staying shut. It was the drivers dead and dragged behind their chariots.'

'How do you know that?'

'They were yelling it to one another. We heard them.'

'And?'

'I sent in my men. I had them hidden until then.'

I looked at the prisoners and the row of dead.

'Did they fight? Were they armed?'

'Yes, they had swords.'

'But they weren't all killed in the fight?'

He shook his head. 'No. Some came on like maniacs. Others didn't. They just gave up.'

I looked all round. The palisade hid the lower end of the stadium from anyone outside, and the starting gates blocked any view from the stadium, at least any view of the area where there had been fighting.

'Did anyone see what happened here?' I shouted.

'Only me and my men. And them.' He pointed to the prisoners.

'Thank you,' I said. 'His Grace will be pleased.'

'And I am His Grace's man!' he said. Then he turned to Morganus. 'What do I do with the prisoners?'

'Take them to the fortress and lock them up,' said Morganus, 'Bethsidus too.'

'The Flavensum duovir?' Terentius looked surprised.

'Yes,' said Morganus, 'Him. He's in the governor's box. Take him with the others.'

'Keep him away from them!' I added, and Terentius nodded and gave orders to move the prisoners, while Morganus and I and two bodyguards stood back and watched. A great tiredness fell upon me.

'What now, Greek?' asked Morganus.

'I want a bath,' I said, 'and I want to think. Can we go back to the fortress?'

'Don't you want to see the races?'

'No! I just want a bath.'

'There won't be anyone there. The bath house won't be fired up.'

'I don't care. I just want to be quiet.'

So we went home. We went to Morganus' house, which of course was cold, empty and silent. But silence was enough. I went to the bath house and washed in cold water. Then I slept for many hours. Usually I do not sleep much, even in good times, but for many days I had hardly slept at all so I was exhausted in mind and body, and I slept for a day and a night.

When finally I woke up, Morgana Callandra and the girls were back, the bath house was steaming with hot water and there was a breakfast on the table waiting for me. Morganus was also waiting. So were the bodyguards.

'So you're with us again?' he said.

'Yes,' I said..

'Have your breakfast, then we'll talk,' he said. 'Petros has been sending messages, asking what we're going to do with Bethsidus and the rest. He's looking to you to sort that out.'

I nodded. 'Breakfast first,' I said, 'Then Bethsidus. Where is he?'

'In the Principia. We've got him nice and tight in a room with barred windows and a heavy door.'

'Good!' I said, and reached for the hot, spiced wine.

'Are the games going well?' I said.

'Very well. Especially the races. The Celts are loving them.'

'Good.'

So I finished my breakfast, planned what I would say to Bethsidus, and then we went to see him.

As we entered the principia, Morganus spoke.

'Do you want me with you?' he said. 'You often do better on your own.' He was very understanding.

'Thanks,' I said, 'but this time stay with me. I need a Roman beside me and I don't know anyone more Roman than you!' He smiled.

So we went up the stairs to a second-story room, where Bethsidus was indeed nice and tight. He had been made comfortable with food and drink, and a trestle bed, even a commode. But terror struck him as Morganus and I came in, with the bodyguards waiting outside. He thought we were a death-squad.

'I am a Roman citizen!' he said. 'I may not be punished without trial, nor …'

'Sit down,' I said. 'You're not a citizen. Your father's diploma is fake.'

He gasped and sank into his chair.

'Listen to me,' I said, 'because your city faces destruction. Africanus wants to send in the army to kill everyone there.'

I looked at Morganus, who stood armed and armoured under his swan-feather crest. He was the embodiment of Roman power.

'That's how Rome punishes a rebellious city, isn't it First Javelin?'

'It is!' he said.

'Now then,' I said, to Bethsidus, 'this whole business is all about damnation and redemption, isn't it?'

'What?' said Bethsidus.

'You had an argument with Solis in your synagogue.'

'How did you know?'

'Because I read minds,' I said. He shuddered and I continued. 'Your city has a huge temple to the imperial cult, doesn't it?'

'Yes,' he said.

'Although you are Jews?'

'Yes! It shows our loyalty to the Empire, although we worship God in our synagogue.'

'Very nice,' I said, 'very tidy, because you—Bethsidus—believe that when you pray *for* the Emperor, in that temple, on his birthday, then that's all right because your god allows it.' He nodded. 'But Solis thought differently. He believed praying *for* the Emperor was as bad as praying *to* the Emperor, and you'll all go to hell for it. He said that didn't he?'

'Yes,' he said, confirming my guess, because it *was* only a guess, based on what Nablus the impresario had said about the dilemma of Jews under Rome.

'So there was a dispute, and the synagogue voted on the matter, and you won,' I said, 'but you and Solis hated one another ever after, and Solis didn't accept the vote, did he?'

'No,' he said, 'he went his own way and took our young men with him.'

'And then,' I said, 'together with Maligoterix, Solis found a way to please your god, and win redemption for Solis' followers.'

'Did he?' he said.

'Yes,' I said, 'The plan was to ruin the games, raise the tribes in rebellion and destroy the Roman province of Britannia. They were going to offer that sacrifice to your god, together with their own lives, in exchange for paradise in the next life.'

He sighed. 'Yes,' he said, 'Solis would believe that.'

'So,' I said, 'What about your city, Flavensum? Do you want it destroyed?'

'No!' he said.

'Then everything depends on you.'

'Does it?'

'Yes! Go back to that city and preach, especially to the young men who followed Solis. Tell them they did wrong. Tell them they must never do such a thing again. Tell them to be loyal Romans.'

'But they're all prisoners,' he said.

'Who might be made free,' I said, and looked at Morganus, 'Is that possible, First Javelin?' and I gave a tiny nod.

'Yes,' he said, and I turned back to Bethsidus.

'Yes!' I said, 'because the most fanatical of them have already been killed, and those who gave themselves up, might be ready to listen to you.'

'But what do I tell them?' asked Bethsidus.

'That's up to you,' I said, 'but I'll give you two ideas. First, tell them that your god, Christos or whatever you call him, is angry with what they did, and has punished them. Second, you haven't got an *actual book* of Zoltan, have you?' I said.

'No,' he said, 'We hold the text in memory and pass it to the young.'

'Well I *have* got a copy,' I said.

'You have?' he said, with round eyes.

'Yes, in Aramaic, and I'm going to give it to you, and you're going to read it so that you can see that it's really the book of Matthew that someone, called Zoltan, scribbled all over and passed off as his own. Your bloodthirsty Zoltan is as fake as your father's diploma!'

Later, Morganus and I and the bodyguards walked back to his house.

'Will he do it?' he said. 'Can he do it?'

'We'll have to wait and see,' I said, 'but it's in everyone's interest to let him try. Africanus won't send the army into Flavensum, you know that! I just made that up.' He nodded. and I continued. 'And neither Africanus nor Petros wants to know about the Flavensum men not being citizens or trying to kill the chariot drivers. That's bad news they want buried, because they don't want a veteran's colony disgraced. Not when everything's supposed to be wonderful in the province of Britannia . They want everything nice and peaceful and the games to go well, because they're both the governor's men, like the tribune, Terentius.'

'Yes,' he said, 'and they'll all do well when His Grace becomes Governor of Italia.'

'Very well indeed!' I said.

'And so should you,' he said. 'Petros owes you a big favour. But what about Flavensum? Does nobody get punished?'

'A lot of families have lost their sons,' I said, 'including Bethsidus, probably, and that's bad enough. You should know. You have children... I had children.'

'Yes,' he said. 'So what now, Greek? Do you want to see the games?

We've got no duties, and there's racing today at noon. Or the gladiators? Or the theatre?'

'Well, perhaps we'll go to the races,' I said, and I smiled. 'Then later I shall find a way to see Allicanda, because if Petros owes me a favour, I am optimistic in that regard.'

So we spent the day at the races and hugely enjoyed it. We relaxed in the satisfaction of a major task completed and tribal revolt prevented. Thus Morganus, the bodyguards and I were proud of ourselves, and some great and mighty quantities of wine, beer and food were consumed by us at the racing stadium. We were happy in each other's company, and I defy even the gods to say that we were not rightly happy, justifiably happy.

But that happiness was was transient, because when we returned to Morganus' house in the early evening, it was the will of the gods that our happiness was ended. At least mine was. It most certainly was.

Chapter 33

Morgana Callandra received us as we entered Morganus' house. Her girls were behind her. All bowed, and Morgana Callandra smiled at me.

'Look!' she said, 'you have letters. Three of them,' and she handed them to me. One was a cheap wooden strip letter, addressed to me in Allicanda's handwriting. The other two were elaborate papyrus scrolls, bound in silken cords with dangling seals, and boldly written by scribes.

'Ah!' said Morganus and smiled happily. 'There's one from Petros. I think you should read that first. Go on. You'll like it!' So I did.

From Petros of Athens, Secretary to His Grace the Governor of Britannia, to Ikaros of Apollonis, imperial servant of His Majesty the Emperor Trajan:

Greeting and may the blessings of the gods be upon you!

Whereas you, Ikaros of Apollonis, have performed services of inestimable importance to the province of Britannia, and whereas your comrade the Honourable Leonius Morganus Fortis Victrix has communicated the fact that you wish to buy a certain slave, it is my pleasure, and that of His Grace the Governor, that a sum of two million sesterces be advanced to your credit with immediate effect. It is my hope and that of His Grace, that you will be happy in your purchase and thereafter ready to serve the Empire whenever the Empire might need you.

Most cordially given and sealed at Government House, Londinium.

I showed the letter to Morganus and we laughed together. It was happy moment and joy enwrapped me like a warm cloak. Then I opened Allicanda's letter, and at first I was mystified, and then ashamed, and then pierced to the deep of my heart.

To Ikaros from Allicanda

You may know already what has happened. But a slave has no power, so I can only offer my feelings for you. Thus I know that you are enfolded in your work, and that although you care for me, you come to me only in pursuit of your work, and that there are long days when you never think of me at all. But I forgive you because you are kind, and you would cherish and protect me if you could. You are a good man who has been much troubled in life and who is burdened with sadness and worry, and therefore I give you as my parting gift, the fact that I love you.

This letter I did not share with Morganus. It was too moving and personal. Instead I opened the final letter and did so in dread, because the gods had caused me to be afraid of what it might say, and the gods are all-knowing and wise.

From Gentius Civilis Felemidus, known to his intimates as Felemid, to Ikaros the Apollonite, slave of His Imperial Majesty.

I am pleased to tell you that the slave Allicanda the Hibernian—exotic mistress of cuisine—may now be yours. This is so because I have bought her from her previous owner without even bargaining over price. I did so having learned of your interest in a woman even though you are a Greek. Thus I shall keep her safe and will never sell her at any price. So come to me, Ikaros, and let us discuss the means whereby you may have access to Allicanda. I am sure that you can guess what I shall ask in return, and I rejoice that I have found a way for you and I to be together.

My memories of the next moments are unclear. I think I may have dropped the letters. I know for sure that Morgana Callandra eventually held them and read them, and then she wept and put her arms around me.

'Never mind,' she said, 'You'll think of something, and if *you* don't, then Morganus will!' She called him by his name. I definitely remember that. She did not call him, My-Lord-Husband. She called him Morganus and she would never have done that in the presence of slaves or strangers. So at least I truly had a family again, and only the gods knew what might happen next.

Epilogue

Six months after the events described in this book, The Lady Viola went through a trial carefully arranged by Petros of Athens. The jury, carefully chosen by Petros of Athens, found her free of blame in the murder of the tribune, Celsus. Petros then explained to the family of Celsus that since the Lady Viola was innocent and had no money, the vengeance of the family would best be pursued by suing the slave dealer from whom she had been purchased. This they did and the case ran for years to the great benefit of the lawyers.

After her acquittal, the Lady Viola was sequestered as provincial property by Petros and later gifted into the care of The Women's Sisterhood of the Numen of the Imperial Spirit of the Deified Emperor Nerva. This tremendous and thundering name was that of a club of rich wives who sought social advancement by acts of charity, and therefore funded a small hospital where persons of disturbed mind could be locked away for their own good, and for the good of others.

In due time, having pronounced the Lady Viola to be cured, and having noted her luminous beauty, the sisterhood sold the Lady Viola for an enormous price to Adnos Madron, a Lusitanian merchant then visiting Londinium. He took her to his home city of Felicitas Iulia, where he lived happily for some months until the morning when he was found murdered in his bed by a single stab to the throat: another crime for which no person was ever punished.

My awning-pole enjoyed a happier fate. I still had it on my return to the legionary fortress after it had saved me from the assassins. I therefore sent it back to the stall holder with a gold piece in gratitude. Since the events of that day had become famous—at least in the vegetable market—the stall holder ever afterwards hung the pole over his stall, with a sign reading THE STAFF OF APOLLO, and declared that he heard me call on the name of my god when I swung the pole in self defence. I do not remember doing so, but the drill masters of my city taught that shouting puts strength into a blow, so perhaps I did without knowing.

The stall holder's business prospered greatly thereafter.

No mention was made, ever again, of the fact that the men of Flavensum had tried to raise rebellion and that they were not legally Roman citizens. Nor was any attempt made to determine which of them had always known that they were not citizens. Thus Solis and Bethsidus had certainly known, but it was in nobody's interest to look further.

Meanwhile the city of Flavensum remained peaceful because Bethsidus preached a new faith based on the Book of Matthew, and his teachings were followed by the young men of the city. The gods rewarded Bethsidus for this good behaviour by sparing the life of his son Alexander, whose wound closed and healed. Bethsidus sent me tedious reports of his preaching, which reports astounded Morganus since Bethsidus—following Matthew—now held such bizarre beliefs as that the meek shall inherit the Earth, and that a man should love his enemies.

Morganus was more pleased with Alexander's account, confessed to Bethsidus and passed onto me, of the attack on Gershom. According to Alexander, Gershom fought so skilfully that he killed one of his attackers outright, severely wounded Alexander and drew blood from two more. In the end, he fell only when outnumbered and tired. He died like a man.

Maligoterix, HighDruid of all Britannia, also remained peaceful because he took refuge in the client kingdom of the Regni tribe which would never give him up, and all those who were His Grace the Governor's men—including Petros and Africanus—knew that sending the army into a client kingdom to seize Maligoterix would spoil the record of His Grace's term of office, and damage His Grace's chances of becoming Governor of Italia. Thus no action was taken against Maligoterix, and his role in the near-rebellion was kept secret. In response, the High Druid interpreted this as contemptible weakness. He sneered at Rome and made completely new plans for the future.

As for myself, I tried to meet sorrow as a stoic should, and I hoped for better days.

Appendix:

The Marcus Quintus Superbus Rules of Gladiatorial Combat

The Promise of Mq Superbus

That gladiatorial combat shall be an exhibition of skill at arms, displaying courage, martial ardour and contempt for danger, such that each bout shall be a stand-up, open fight between gladiators who are fit for combat and matched according to the traditions of the arena, employing sharpened weapons, true armour and no unfair advantage given to either combatant.

Discussion of the Promise

Gladiatorial combat is presented to the public as a true and genuine exhibition of the martial arts, such that each combatant is given maximum time and opportunity to display his skill at arms.

For the avoidance of doubt, it is stressed that gladiatorial combat is deliberately made different from battlefield combat, or self defence, or any other combat in which combatants seek to defeat each other by any means and with the greatest possible speed.

To this end, gladiatorial combat shall take place according to rules of engagement enforced by a referee, whose decision in all such matters shall be final. The rules are intended to prolong the combat, forbidding any actions that would lead to its sudden or premature termination, and allowing breaks in the combat at discretion of the referee, to enable exhausted combatants to recover their strength before fighting on.

The Rules of Engagement

I Gladiators shall instantly obey the orders of the Referee in all matters.

II Gladiators shall bear themselves with manly dignity and shall treat opponents with respect, uttering no insult, curse or complaint.

III Gladiators shall not advance upon the opponent, nor strike any blow against the opponent until the referee has given the signal to salute the opponent and to engage.

IV Within the rules of engagement and subject to the orders of the referee, gladiators shall display courageous martial ardour and determined intent to defeat the opponent by skill at arms.

V Gladiators shall not flee from the opponent.

VI Gladiators shall not charge with the shield to knock down the opponent.

VII Gladiators shall not trip, nor attempt to trip, the opponent.

VIII Excepting only the casting of the retiarius' net, gladiators shall not throw at the opponent any weapon, or item of equipment, or the sand of the area, or any other object, liquid or substance whatsoever.

IX Gladiators shall not grapple or hold the opponent, nor fall to the ground nor by any other means attempt to avoid an open, stand-up fight.

X When ordered by the referee to break and stand clear, gladiators shall do so at once, and shall not advance upon the opponent, nor strike any blow, until the referee gives the signal to salute the opponent and to re-engage.

XI Gladiators shall display disdain for wounds and shall not seek easy or premature end to the combat simply because blood has been shed.

XII Gladiators truly vanquished in arms shall signal acceptance of defeat by raising the first finger of either hand.

XIII Gladiators shall instantly stand back from an opponent who signals acceptance of defeat and shall await the referee's orders.

XIV Gladiators doomed to receive the final stroke shall display manly courage and shall receive the stroke with dignity.

XV Gladiators ordered to deliver the final stroke shall do so with swift dignity and without any utterance of triumph nor any attempt to delay the despatch of the vanquished.

Duties of the Referee

All such duties shall be exclusively the responsibility and prerogative of the referee, such that none other—with particular reference to spectators, and with particular reference to duties VI, XI and XIII below—shall attempt to assume the duties of the referee on pain of being excluded from the games.

I To give written receipt of combatants from their masters, certifying that the combatants offered to the arena truly are those whose names as combatants were announced to the public by the sponsor of the games.

II To examine combatants before bouts, ensuring all are fit for combat, suffering no hidden or disguised wounds or sickness.

III To examine the arms and equipment of combatants before bouts, ensuring that weapons are sharpened and of true steel, and that armour and equipment are not weakened nor perverted nor liable to easy penetration.

IV To examine combatants before bouts to ensure that no combatant is equipped with any deceitful device intended falsely to simulate wounds or injury.

V To lead forth the combatants, and to present them to the sponsor, and to ensure that combatants stand apart from each other and give respectful salute to the sponsor.

VI To give the signal to salute the opponent and to engage.

VII To ensure that combatants are not overcome with exhaustion, and to give the order for combat to cease if necessary, giving combatants pause to recover themselves, including with drink or other sustenance and then to give the order for the combatants to salute first the sponsor, and then the opponent, and then to re-engage.

VIII To ensure a stand-up, open combat, ordering the combatants to break and stand apart if either or both is holding the opponent to prevent further combat, or if either or both is laid upon the ground and is not attempting to stand.

IX To examine wounds suffered by combatants who have signalled acceptance of defeat, ensuring that these are true and serious wounds and not simulated.

X To stop the combat, proclaiming a drawn bout and to offer the combatants to the sponsor as equal victors if both combatants have given their best to the combat yet neither is able to overcome the other, being equal in skill at arms, courage and martial ardour.

XI To stop the combat and give formal warning to any combatant or combatants displaying contempt for the rules of engagement or the referee and then to give the signal to salute the opponent and to re-engage.

XII After two formal warnings have been given, to disqualify any combatant or combatants continuing to display contempt for the rules of engagement or the referee, and to present such disqualified combatant or combatants to the sponsor for judgement as if vanquished in combat but without right to appeal for mercy.

XIII To offer the appeal of an honourably vanquished combatant to the sponsor, advising the sponsor as to the martial ardour, skill at arms, and courage displayed during the bout by the vanquished combatant.

XIV When the sponsor's judgement is mercy to the vanquished, to order the combatants to stand apart, to ensure that they give salute first to the sponsor and then to each other, and then to call forth those whose duty it is to tend the wounded.

XV When the sponsor's judgement is death to the vanquished, to order the victor to salute the vanquished and the sponsor, and then to deliver the final stroke.

XVI To ensure that the final stroke is truly given, and then to call forth those whose duty it is to remove the dead.

XVII In all cases to lead combatants out of the arena, surrendering them to their masters, taking written certification from the masters that those returned, whether living or dead, are those who entered the arena to fight.

fighting [illegible] vanquished to continue the combat without right to appeal for mercy.

XIII To offer the appeal of a [illegible] honourably vanquished combatant to the sponsor, [illegible] the sponsor [illegible] to the merciful [illegible] [illegible] and [illegible] the vanquished combatant.

XIV When the sponsor's judgement is merciful to the vanquished, to order the combatants to stand apart, to ensure that they give salute to the sponsor, and then to each other, and then recall the officials who shall attend the wounded.

XV When the sponsor's judgement is death for the vanquished, to order the victor to salute the vanquished and the sponsor and then to deliver the fatal stroke.

XVI To ensure that the fatal stroke is duly given, and then to call forth those whose duty it is to remove the dead.

XVII In all cases to lead combatants out of the arena, surrendering them to their masters, taking written confirmation from the masters that those combatants whether living or dead are those which entered the arena to fight.

Afterword

The Ikaros Books

The book you have just read is the second in my series about Ikaros. I hope that you might be sufficiently interested in him to wonder how he became a detective, how he met Morganus, what happened to him in the house of Scorteus (father of Fortunus) and especially, what precisely happened to his wife and family in the siege of Apollonis.

All this and more can be found in *Death in Londinium*, the first book in the series. I hope you might read it and enjoy it, because it concerns a truly appalling piece of Roman law which you will certainly find interesting.

Why the Romans Had No Police Force

I have stated repeatedly that the Romans had no police force, and have been asked to justify this statement. In about 100 AD, when my books are set, in Rome itself there were three organisations who might have been a police force: the Praetorian Guard, the Urban Cohorts and the Vigiles. But the Praetorians were a legion of elite solders, who defended Rome and had the last word in civil, military and political matters. They certainly did not patrol the city with a cheery wave, nor chase thieves, nor help old ladies across the street.

The Urban Cohorts (four of them, with about 500 men to the cohort) were closer to being policemen, though of the heavy-handed kind. Their job was riot control, and perhaps their mothers loved them, but nobody else did, and you wouldn't want to be on the street when they were.

Finally the Vigiles (seven cohorts) patrolled at night and might well have arrested drunks if they fell over them. But the Vigiles were really the Roman fire brigade. Their job was to find and put out fires, and that is what they mainly did.

What Rome did *not* have was a body of men whose primary duty was to prevent crime if they could, and investigate it if they could not: seeking evidence, pursuing criminals and then handing them over to a state prosecution service to be charged in court. In fact, nobody could take that last step, because the Romans had no state prosecution service either.

All this suited the Romans because of the way their society worked. Thus a Roman Paterfamilias (head of the family) lived all his life in his city, where he knew his neighbours and they knew him, and everyone knew everyone's business thanks to gossiping slaves who knew absolutely everything that went on in the house. Then, within that house, the paterfamilias had absolute power to deal with any crime. He could beat, fine, imprison or even kill any member of his household.

How, then, did this affect some of the crimes that we fear most, starting with the worst fear of all, abuse of our children by paedophiles?

In a Roman city, if someone's son had a sexual interest in children, then everyone knew because there was no privacy in a Roman house. I repeat that there was no privacy because the slaves would see everything and then gossip. So the son's oddity would be common knowledge, and his paterfamilias would warn him to behave or else, and if paterfamilias himself was odd, then all his neighbours would know and he would never be allowed near their children.

How about burglary in the night, when most people would be asleep? In Roman law, men armed with military weapons could be seen as a rebels against the state (very dangerous: see below). So the burglar might have just a knife, which could be met by the house-folk with kitchen knives. But more important, a Roman family could be very large. Even a small household might be two parents, several children (some full-grown) plus several slaves, while a large household would contain dozens of slaves. Thus, burglary meant breaking into an armed and hostile community, and I doubt that any Roman criminal would even attempt anything so stupid.

Street crime? Muggers, pick-pockets and such? Romans relied on their neighbours against these, since it was in everybody's interest to defend one another. Also, paterfamilias would always be attended by one or more slaves, who were legally compelled to defend him.

So, most petty crime was dealt with by paterfamilias himself, or with the neighbours, as a private matter in which the state did not intervene. Big crime: legal, financial, commercial or political, was different. That was indeed a matter for the state, via the law courts. But Paterfamilias was expected to bring charges, produce evidence, summon witnesses, and even drag the accused to court.

Also dragged into court were the criminals Rome detested most: the noxii (scum) including rapists, kidnappers of children for ransom, and rebels against the state. They were damnatio ad bestias (condemned to the beasts) providing light entertainment in the arena before the gladiators came on.

That was the Roman defence against crime, and it worked for hundreds of years. It wasn't perfect, but neither is London's Met or the NYPD.

Gladiators Fought by the Rules

As above, I like to present aspects of Roman life that are poorly understood. Another is the fact that Roman gladiators fought according to rules, with referees to control the bouts. Gladiators were like modern boxers: highly-trained, much valued and could be extremely famous. They were definitely not killed as a matter of routine at the end of a bout.

If you want to know more, the following academic paper discusses the nearest thing we have to direct contact with gladiators: the inscriptions left on their graves. See: Carter M J: Gladiatorial Combat: The Rules of Engagement, *Classical Journal* 102, (2006/7), 97–113.

As for the rules themselves, none survive, which is a great shame, so I have filled this void by inventing some. You have seen these already as the Rules of Marcus Quintus Superbus.

Football Fans

In chapters 16 and 17 I have given gladiator fans all the vices of the worst of British football fans. But this is not my invention because the riot in Pompeii that Ikaros mentions in Chapter 16, really happened in 59 AD following gladiatorial games in the city's amphitheatre. The riot was actually a fight between rival supporters from Pompeii and the town of Nuceria, and it was reported in detail by the Roman historian Tacitus, in his *Annales*, XIV, XVII.

The fighting was particularly vicious, with swords used and men killed. Thus magistrates were sent from Rome to investigate, and Pompeii's amphitheatre was closed for ten years in punishment of all concerned.

Centurions Were Not Sergeant Majors

I would like to correct a mistake that I made when young. It was once my opinion that the centurions of a Roman legion were the equivalent of modern non-commissioned officers: corporals, sergeants and sergeant-majors, while the legion was run by the equivalent of modern commissioned officers: the military tribunes, who were equivalent to colonels, and a legate who was equivalent to a general.

This is absolute rot, and my Latin teacher, Mr Parker of the Central Foundation Boys' School, who also taught Roman History should have put me right, and probably did except that I was not paying attention. In my own defence I state that the tribunes and legate were aristocrats like the officers of the British army in past days, while the centurions rose from the ranks, as non-commissioned officers still do.

But the truth is that a Roman legion was run by the centurions who followed a lifetime career, with promotion from the least senior to the most senior century of the legion. There being sixty centuries, there were sixty centurions to the legion, of whom the most senior was called the first javelin, who—like Morganus—was a soldier of enormous experience and seniority.

The sole purpose of the tribunes and the legate, all of whom were mainly politicians, was to command the legion as directed by the Roman state. They were merely the drivers of a military Rolls Royce, which was designed, engineered, built, serviced and maintained by the centurions. In addition, it was the centurions who led the men forward in the face of the enemy. My Latin is not good enough for an idiomatic translation of '*fix bayonets and follow me!*' But it was the centurions who said that, not the tribunes or the legate.

Roman Colonia: Taking Liberties with History

There were several different kinds of city in Roman Britain, ranging from the tribal capitals that were forced on the unwilling natives in the attempt to civilise them, to Londinium which developed naturally, based on trade. These cities had bewilderingly different rights and status, but the most prestigious were the coloniae: veterans' colonies established on land given to retired legionaries as reward for their twenty-five years of service.

In Britannia, there were four coloniae: Camulodenum (Colchester), Eboracum (York), Glevum (Gloucester) and Lindum (Lincoln) and they were beloved of the Empire, since every man of the founding generation was a full Roman citizen, a trained soldier and unshakably loyal. For obvious reasons these cities were planted in newly-conquered territory to secure the conquest.

Please note that I have taken dire liberties with history because in the book you have just read, which is set in c. 100 AD. I pretend that there are only two flourishing veterans' colonies in Britannia: Flavensum, and the brand new (still un-named) colony founded by the men of the Third Regiment Pannonian Horse, who became Roman citizens in Chapter 3. This is only my pretence in the interest of telling a good story.

Manner and Mode of Roman Speech

Please note that phrases such as 'Honoured Sir', 'Honoured and Kinghtly Sir' and 'The-Lady-my-Wife' are entirely my invention, because neither I nor anyone else knows how spoken Latin worked in Britannia, in the first century AD. All we have now is fossilised, medieval, church Latin, plus the works of Roman scholars like the Plinys (there were two of them, Pliny the Elder and his nephew Pliny the Younger) and these gentlemen did not write down spoken Latin but formal, literary Latin for other gentlemen to read. So I have filled this void too, by making up phrases like 'Honoured Sir', to stress the fact that Roman culture was hierarchical, obsessed with rank, and entirely innocent of any concept that men and women were equal.

Likewise I have used the middleweight English swear words, 'sod' and 'bugger', to put vulgar speech into the mouths of vulgar characters. With the exception of a Pompeii graffiti artist who used 'fellator' as a swear word (look it up, because it's a good one) I have no idea how Romans swore. So the s-word and the b-word will do very nicely: that and a few *bastards*.

Beyond that, the Romans had no words for 'yes' and 'no'. The nearest is the Latin expression ita vero meaning 'thus indeed'. Normally Romans answered in the affirmative or negative in such a manner as:

Question: 'Do you want a drink?

Answer: 'I'd like a drink!'

Question: 'Shall we go?'

Answer: 'Let's not go.'

Question: 'Does this make sense?'

Answer: 'It does.'

But if I filled a book with these circumlocutions (lovely Roman word though that is) then readers used to 'yes' or 'no' would find the text very odd indeed. So 'yes' it is, and 'no' it isn't, throughout the book despite whatever the Romans really said, or the Greeks too because they didn't have words for 'yes' and 'no' either, and neither does Chinese, Japanese, Welsh and probably other languages too. So which language really is the strange one?

How Deadly Was Lead Sling Shot?

In Chapter 30 Ikaros is saved by the Silesian slingers whose lead shot doesn't just knock down the cennad angau assassins but actually penetrates their bodies. This sounds surprising, since this lead shot was projected by human muscle power and not gunpowder. But we know that sling shot could penetrate, because the Roman writer Aulus Cornelius Celsus (c. 55 BC–50 AD) described surgical techniques for *removing* sling shot from human bodies in section 7.5.4 of his book *De Medicina.* Also, for an actual demonstration of what sling shot can do, see the following YouTube item, in which some beer-loving young Americans demonstrate the effect of lead sling shot on ballistic gelatine: *https://www.youtube.com/watch?v=IHP-aoQUhlY*

CPSIA information can be obtained
at www.ICGtesting.com
Printed in the USA
BVHW082302251122
652780BV00007B/1284

9 781839 015151